The Winter Garden

Nicola Cornick

ONE PLACE. MANY STORIES

HQ
An imprint of HarperCollins*Publishers* Ltd
1 London Bridge Street
London SE1 9GF

www.harpercollins.co.uk

HarperCollins*Publishers*
1st Floor, Watermarque Building, Ringsend Road
Dublin 4, Ireland

This edition 2022

1

First published in Great Britain by
HQ, an imprint of HarperCollins*Publishers* Ltd 2022

Copyright © Nicola Cornick 2022

Nicola Cornick asserts the moral right to be
identified as the author of this work.
A catalogue record for this book is
available from the British Library.

ISBN: 978-0-00-827855-7

This book is set in 12/15.5 pt. Bembo by Type-it AS, Norway

Printed and Bound in the UK using 100% Renewable Electricity at
CPI Group (UK) Ltd, Croydon, CR0 4YY

In memory of Ashurst Sky Angus MacLeod

Catherine

Knightstone Manor, Winter 1598

They awoke that morning to snow. The garden was cloaked in it. It fell in huge flakes the size of rose petals from a sky as soft and white as down. Catherine, who had mourned the loss of the summer shapes and colours, who had disliked the bare bones of the garden in winter, was enchanted. Here was her creation transformed into something magical and new.

The children were desperate to play outside. The nurses wrapped them in winter flannels and thick woollens; it was astonishing that they could move, let alone run. Robert went with them as they shrieked and tumbled in the snow of the labyrinth, their excited cries echoing in the crisp winter air.

Everywhere she walked, the garden beckoned her on. The clipped hedges of the knot garden were stiff with tiny spikes of frost bristling on each twig. The pebbles of the path glittered with ice. The lake was lost beneath a covering of snow like a flat, blank mirror. The summerhouse – a winter house now – had icicles hanging from the eaves.

She wandered along the bank, wondering whether when the snow had cleared there might still be ice for skating. The boys would love that. She was sure there was an old pair of wooden skates in a chest somewhere. Robert would know; the house had been his grandmother's before him.

She had to be careful climbing the path back to the terrace. The ground was slippery, iced fronds of fern hanging over the stream where the water ran between banks piled with snow. It sounded like music in her ears but then everything was bewitching to her this morning. From the top of the spiral mound she could see for miles across the vale. The snow had cleared away now and the sky was the palest blue of a bird's egg.

She scrambled down the hillside to join her family in the labyrinth. The hem of her gown was soaking now and her feet felt wet and cold but happiness bubbled up inside her, banishing the discomfort. This was how she had imagined it, only far, far better; her garden a place where joy and laughter dwelled.

Robert threw a snowball at her and it melted down the neck of her cloak. She pretended to be angry but all she wanted to do was kiss him, to whirl around in his arms. So she did, and their sons ran alongside; or William did – Robbie was still barely able to stand. The nurses laughed and everyone's faces were rosy, and when they could no longer feel their fingers or toes they went inside to sit before the fire and drink spiced ale to warm up.

Later, when she finally realised that the key was missing from the chain about her neck, she knew she would never find it again. She had explored every corner of the garden earlier that morning. She had no idea which snowdrift might hold it.

They searched; of course they did. They retraced her steps, she and Robert and the servants, digging, huffing and puffing until the snow was trampled and the garden no longer looked enchanted. There was no sign of it.

'I will have a new key made,' Robert promised, as they lay beneath the tester together that night, burrowed in and warm in each other's arms. 'Or buy you a new box for your treasures. Do not fear, my love. Perhaps we shall find it anyway, when the spring comes.'

But the melting of the snow did not reveal the key and although Robert had gone to London and promised a new box for her as a gift, it would have meant breaking open the old one, splintering the highly polished wood she loved, so she was glad when he forgot.

Eventually as the summer came she decided she must put aside any sentimentality and break into the box so she could see the pictures again. She missed them and already the boys had grown and changed almost out of all recognition. But the summer brought with it nothing but trouble and soon the key was forgotten beneath matters much weightier than snow, and it was to be more than three hundred years before it was found again.

CHAPTER I

Lucy

The Present, late July

The house looked exactly as she remembered it.

Immediately ahead of her was a low wall of chalk and sarsen stone, overgrown with a tangle of white and gold honeysuckle, pink wild rose and white star jasmine. Tall pink hollyhocks bent confidingly close towards one another, almost blocking the little wooden gate. Beyond that, a path of irregular flagstones cut across a wide lawn – almost a meadow because the grass was so long and dotted with wildflowers – up to the pale-green-painted door, which nestled beneath a flat porch. The windows were irregular too, two of them set on each side of the entrance, their Georgian casements reflecting a gleam of lamplight within.

Gunpowder Cottage. The pale cream of the chalk stone walls, burnished honey gold in the late, low sun, gave the house a timeless, ethereal appearance, as though it had been settled in the landscape for ever. Lucy could almost hear the centuries whispering to her.

It was a beautiful place, but she'd rather be almost any-where else in the world right now.

'It's the perfect place for you to have a break,' her sister Cleo had said warmly, when she had rung to tell Lucy that she had arranged it all. 'I've spoken to Aunt Verity and cleared it with the lettings agency. They're not taking bookings at the moment because there's some major work being done in the gardens. Aunty Verity did mention she might be heading back from Australia in a few weeks, but for now the place is all yours.'

Lucy hadn't replied because there were tears crowding her throat, tears of combined guilt, gratitude and frustration. When she failed to speak, Cleo had continued breezily: 'You don't need to worry about a thing, Luce. All you have to do is rest.'

'Right,' Lucy had said. Then, thinking this sounded ungrateful, 'Thank you, Cleo. You're a star.'

'I know you're not used to taking it easy,' Cleo said, a hint of reproach in her voice, 'but this time you really are going to have to stop, Lucy.'

'Yeah,' Lucy said. Admitting the truth was hard, even to Cleo, *especially* to Cleo, perhaps, since normally Lucy was the organiser and her little sister was swept along in her wake. She could hear the subtext in Cleo's words, the echoes of friends and family:

'Poor Lucy, she's such a workaholic, so driven… No life outside of her music… What will she do now?'

It was a good question. Lucy didn't know the answer. Not yet. She hadn't even really accepted the reality of it yet, how a month of pneumonia and the complications that had followed it had ended her musical career so brutally. Her entire life plan had been derailed by a jumped-up flu virus.

'New talent Lucy Brown lights up the Barbican concert hall,' one review had said, a week after she had been hospitalised. *'The new Benedetti!'* another raved. *'Full of promise. We can't wait to hear more from the London Gala Orchestra's new star…'*

But there would be no more violin solos and the critics would forget her soon enough because there was always someone else coming up through the ranks. Meanwhile she had to get over it and get on with her life.

Lucy set her hand to the latch of the gate. The now-familiar twinge of pain shot up her arm, and she gritted her teeth against it. The illness had left her with a legacy of fatigue, aching joints and muscles, breathlessness, a whole shopping list of problems that were unfamiliar and exhausting. To start with she had tried to return to rehearsals but the excruciating pain had changed music from being a sublime pleasure to a painful trial. In the end she'd been forced to admit defeat and had cried with fury and frustration.

Her consultant had been matter of fact: 'Post-viral fatigue,' he had said briskly. 'We see a lot of it after the flu, or viral pneumonia like yours…' he'd shrugged, 'it's similar to long COVID, that tail of symptoms that carry on after the initial infection has gone. I'll prescribe you some steroid treatment, but you need to rest.'

Whilst she was still feeling bewildered and scared he had glanced towards the door as though hoping or expecting an interruption, and Lucy had realised that it wasn't that he had not cared, simply that this was all new and frightening to her but for him it was a daily occurrence and he needed to move on to the next patient.

Lucy dropped the latch, the ache faded and the gate swung open smoothly and silently. She had been expecting the squeak of rusty hinges to match the neglected garden. Then she reminded herself that the cottage was usually let for holidays and longer periods; of course it would be kept in good working order even if the grass needed a cut.

Her wheeled suitcase bumped and stuck fast on the rough path and she pushed the handle down with an impatient snap. Ancient charm and uneven flagstones were all very well but the case was heavy and she was very tired. She'd declined Cleo's offer to give her lift from London for no reason other than pure pride. She'd wanted to do something for herself, to prove that she was still capable. It was annoying that she now felt exhausted. The train journey from Paddington to Swindon had seemed interminable. From the station she had taken a taxi to Knightstone, watching the golden twilight start to edge in over the Berkshire Downs to the south as the car had eased out of the Swindon traffic and taken the twisting route through the Ridgeway villages. Down in the Vale of the White Horse, the ripening corn had glowed in a perfect sunset. Beside the road, the ancient hedgerows faded into dusk, the gnarled old trees bent eastward with the prevailing westerly wind.

It was almost fifteen years since she had been in this part of England, the forgotten corner of Wiltshire, Oxfordshire and Berkshire that nestled between the Downs and the vale. As the taxi turned off the road to Wantage and headed downhill on the tiny lane overhung with arching beeches, she acknowledged how beautiful it was and how little she wanted to be there. Instead of this quiet she ached for the buzz of a concert hall packed with people and anticipation, the gleam of chandeliers on the rich old wood of the violin as it came to life beneath her hands...

She picked up the suitcase to heave it over the final few flagstones. The muscles in her arm cramped and the case bumped heavily against her leg for the remaining few steps to the door. She ducked into the cover of the porch and was immediately struck by an unexpected memory of childhood summers spent at Gunpowder Cottage. Perhaps it was the poignant scent of the jasmine, heavy on the evening air, that transported her. She felt helpless, an unfamiliar sensation, as though the past had reached out completely unexpectedly and snared her. In a flash she remembered that the spot where the grass grew less thickly at the base of the ancient apple tree was where she had sat reading in the summer evenings, her back pressed against the warm, rough bark. The lichened staddle stone by the wall, which as a child she had thought was a giant mushroom, cast an elongated shadow across the grass. She remembered that it had once supported the old granary at the back of the cottage, keeping the corn off the ground and safe from the rats. It was one of the many stories that her aunt Verity had told her about Gunpowder Cottage. Verity's tales of queens, knights and dragons had enchanted her on every visit and she had been caught up in the magic of it all.

'I want adventure!'

It was almost as though she could hear her own voice, high and excited, carried to her by the winds of time. What an eager, happy child she had been. And Verity had been a role model – a woman whose entire life seemed one big adventure, who, after a long army service commitment, had set up her own highly-successful explosives and demolitions business. Even now that she was semi-retired, Verity was still much in demand for her expertise, hence her current trip to Australia where she was consulting on a mining operation in New South Wales.

Lucy took a deep, bracing breath. She had promised herself that she wouldn't give in to self-pity. She had achieved her own adventure in her own way and it had been brilliant, even if that journey had now been cut short. Like Verity she would move on to something new. Except that it felt too soon; she didn't want to think about that now, about the blankness of the future. But she did know that she wasn't going to stay here too long. She'd find a fresh purpose. She didn't want to become one of Cleo's lost causes, like a rescue kitten in need of rehoming or a dead cactus that her sister would insist was only wilting. This was a strictly temporary stay.

A cool breath of breeze from the Downs tiptoed along her spine. In contrast to the now-chilly garden, the lamplit room inside the cottage looked warm and inviting. It had been thoughtful of Verity to arrange for someone to leave some lights on to welcome her. Evidently someone was keeping an eye on the cottage whilst it was empty.

Lucy dug in her bag, her fingers closing around the front door key. It should have been a big iron antique to fit the appearance of the cottage but Verity wasn't old-fashioned when it came to security. There were two keys, a mortice and a latch. Lucy took them out with a jingle of metal.

The door opened before she could insert either key into a lock. Light spilled across the step, mingling with the dusk of the garden. A black Labrador rushed past Lucy and cocked his leg against the apple tree. Lucy dropped the keys with a clatter on the step. The dog turned his head at the sound and stared at her, his eyes shadowed and dark in the night garden. He wasn't young; white hairs were beginning to show around his muzzle, but he was very handsome all the same.

The dog gave a little yelp of excitement to see her and dashed back across the garden, wagging his tail madly, beating it against Lucy's leg in an orgy of delight.

'Hello,' she said weakly, crouching down to pat him whilst he stared at her again with his big, soulful brown eyes. 'You're very friendly, but what are you doing here?'

The dog pressed closer to her, his big body warm and reassuring. He smelled of a familiar dog smell which gave her a pang of longing. It was years since she had had any sort of pet – her lifestyle hadn't allowed for it – but when she and Cleo had been children there had been a succession of dogs of many shapes and sizes. Their parents currently owned a Welsh terrier called Tal, short for Taliesin. This dog, she saw from the tag glinting in the faint light, was named Geoffrey.

A shadow fell across them. Geoffrey looked up, panting, his whole body wagging now. A man stood framed in the doorway, a dishevelled tawny-haired giant wearing nothing more than a bath towel about the waist. His hair was wet and droplets clung to his broad shoulders. His narrowed hazel gaze scanned Lucy with incredulity before moving to the bag and violin case at her side. He frowned ferociously.

'Who are you?' he said.

It was not the warmest of welcomes and it was not what Lucy needed right now. She kept her gaze firmly fixed on his face despite an instinct to look lower.

'Lucy Brown.' She considered extending a hand to shake and decided against it. Who knew what would happen to that towel if he took it? 'My aunt Verity owns Gunpowder Cottage and has leased it to me for a few weeks – *this cottage*,' she added in case he was particularly dense, or didn't know the name of the house he was squatting in. 'So perhaps I should be asking who *you* are?'

Surprisingly, his expression lightened at that. In fact, he almost smiled. It was disarming. 'My name's Finn Macintyre,' he said. The faint Scottish burr Lucy had detected when he first spoke was more pronounced now. 'I'm the gardener. I'm also at a profound disadvantage.' He gestured to the towel. 'Would you like to come inside whilst I get dressed?'

'I don't think so,' Lucy said pointedly. 'You say you're the gardener but you could be anyone.'

Finn acknowledged that with an inclination of the head. 'Fair enough. Give me a moment, then, and I'll put some clothes on so we can talk out here. You could call your sister, though,' he added. 'She'll vouch for me.'

He disappeared inside leaving Lucy and Geoffrey on the doorstep. The dog gave a little yip and took a few steps into the hall as though trying to invite her to follow him inside. Lucy smiled at him, but the smile faded as she took out her phone.

Cleo had told her that the cottage was free and yet here was Finn Macintyre not only in residence but saying that Cleo would vouch for him. And Verity, whom Lucy had spoken to the week before, had also neglected to mention that there was a lodger at Gunpowder Cottage. She wondered what the hell was going on. She paused on the verge of pressing Cleo's number. Her sister *had* mentioned a big garden project taking place at the cottage, which was why it hadn't been let for the summer as usual. Presumably this Finn Macintyre had some role in that. He certainly wasn't being employed for his charm.

With a sharp, vicious stab at the contacts list she called Cleo.

'Hi!' Her sister answered at the first ring. There was music playing in the background, Taylor Swift, Lucy thought, although her taste in music had always run more to the classical side. Chalk and cheese, she and Cleo, though they could not have been closer as sisters and friends. Even now, when Lucy was reeling from the sudden changes in her life and Cleo was trying to organise her, she felt an overwhelming affection for her little sister.

'Are you at the cottage?' Cleo had muted the music now. 'How was the journey? How are you feeling?' There was a thud that Lucy identified as the sound of a pile of books falling. She could visualise her sister in her flat above the bookshop she ran in the small market town of Highworth, a few miles away. Cleo had wanted Lucy to stay with her when she came out of hospital but there was no room.

Books, stray animals, Cleo's artwork and her girlfriend Sam filled all her living space.

'I'm fine,' Lucy lied. 'And yes, I'm at Gunpowder Cottage, but Goldilocks is already here.'

'What?' Cleo's fairy tales were more contemporary than hers. 'Who?'

'Finn Macintyre,' Lucy said. 'He says he's the gardener. He's Scottish. Abrupt. Apparently, he's staying here?'

'Oh!' Cleo sounded suddenly excited. 'Finn! Yes, of course. I met him a few weeks ago. He's the garden historian who's leading the archaeological excavation on the site, but I thought he was staying in the barn conversion, not in the house.'

Lucy tried mentally to sort out these various pieces of information but her brain felt too foggy and slow. The only thing that really mattered to her at this juncture was where she could find a bed and how quickly she could fall into it. Her entire body ached and all she wanted was to curl up and sleep. Detailed questions could wait.

'Is there a dog?' Cleo, her mind as butterfly-light as ever, was going down a path of her own. 'A Labrador called Geoffrey?'

'He's right here,' Lucy said, as Geoffrey wandered back to her and sat down with a heavy sigh right on her foot.

'Isn't he adorable?' Cleo said. 'You'll love having a dog around, Lucy. You always said you wished you could have one.'

'Yes,' Lucy said, struggling slightly. 'Geoffrey is lovely, but Cleo, this wasn't what we agreed. I thought the cottage was empty. If this Finn person is here, I can't stay.'

'Like I said, Finn and Geoffrey are living in the barn,' Cleo said. 'Are you sure you haven't made a mistake?'

'There's no mistake,' Lucy said. 'A semi-naked man opened the door of Gunpowder Cottage to me. He is clearly in residence. As is his dog, lovely or otherwise.'

She turned to see that Finn had reappeared, fully clothed in a crumpled white shirt, jeans and boots. Geoffrey was greeting him as though he'd been away for months.

'Is that Cleo?' he asked.

'Yes,' Lucy said. 'She's trying to vouch for you but she's not very articulate.' She ignored Cleo's shriek of protest. 'The only thing she's said so far that makes sense is that you're supposed to be staying in the barn conversion, not in the cottage.'

Finn's mouth turned down at the corners and he looked as grumpy and intimidating as when he had first opened the door. 'Yeah,' he said. He rubbed the back of his neck, looked at Geoffrey and sighed. 'She's right, we should be at the barn. Look—' he made a slight conciliatory gesture, 'why don't you come in and I'll explain?'

Lucy shook her head. She felt drained. The post-viral exhaustion was like that; it came on suddenly and left her numb and shaking with tiredness. All she wanted was to be alone to sleep until she felt a bit better.

'We'll sort it out,' she said to Cleo. 'I'll see you tomorrow.'

'Okay, sweetie.' Cleo sounded concerned. 'You know where I am if you need me. Call me and I'll come over and fetch you back here.'

'Thanks, Cleo,' Lucy said. 'Love you.'

She turned to Finn. 'We can talk tomorrow. I'm sorry if

14

I sound abrupt, but if you're not living in the barn conversion, I presume it's free? I'm happy to stay there instead.'

'Of course.' Finn was watching her. She could feel his gaze on her, too observant for comfort. He'd seen how deep her tiredness went. It made her feel vulnerable to a near-stranger and she didn't like it. 'Are you sure?' he added. 'Geoffrey and I can go down there and kip for the night, and move our stuff in the morning. The only reason I moved up here was—'

Lucy cut him off with a quick gesture. She was feeling a bit dizzy. 'Sorry, can this wait? I'm almost literally dead on my feet. Verity told me the barn's fabulous. I'm sure I'll love it.' At that moment she was prepared to lie down on a park bench, she was so tired.

Finn reached for her case. 'Then let me take this around for you,' he said.

Lucy gripped the handle tightly. 'I can manage, thank you. And I know the way to the barn.'

Once again, she had the feeling that Finn saw and understood far more than she wanted him to do. They held each other's gaze for a moment and then he nodded. 'The key to the barn is in the safe. I'll drop by and see you tomorrow.'

The door of Gunpowder Cottage closed, leaving Lucy in the shadowed garden. Twilight had crept closer during the time they had been talking and it was now a place of secrets and mysteries. She shouldered her violin case and dragged the suitcase back down the path to the gate, going out onto the road again and almost immediately turning left along an unmade narrow track that curled downhill around the edge of the cottage garden. On her right was a paddock;

a curious donkey stuck its head over the gate and viewed her with an intelligent gaze as she rumbled past.

At the bottom of the small hill stood Gunpowder Barn. The jumble of derelict farm buildings that Lucy remembered from her childhood had been swept away with the largest one converted into a holiday home. It was the perfect combination of traditional and modern, comprising huge glass windows, exposed beams and original stonework. Where Gunpowder Cottage wrapped you about with an intimate sense of time past, the barn was an elegant fusion of the past and present that looked mainly modern. And yet... Was that not a whisper of something else, something much older, in the breeze that stirred the leaves of the gnarled trees in the orchard? Lucy thought she heard the echo of a voice calling and the patter of footsteps. A shadow slipped from the corner of the path and melted into darkness. But it was only a cat, stopping to wash its paws and view Lucy with its impenetrable gaze.

She found the key safe on the wall by the garden gate, opened the cover and realised that she'd forgotten to ask Finn for the combination. Damn, she really didn't want to have to walk all the way up to the cottage again and disturb him. If he was a gardener, he'd probably been hard at work since first light and wouldn't welcome another interruption to his evening.

She turned on the torch on her phone and squinted at the keypad. She'd try the obvious first: 1605, the year of the Gunpowder Plot. Verity had always been convinced that there was a link between the name of the cottage and the

Plot, although she hadn't been able to discover anything definite to confirm it. But the name had been one of the reasons Verity had bought the house, saying that she felt an affinity with the plotters as a result of her own career in explosives engineering. This had always struck Lucy as funny, though when she pointed out that terrorism rather than engineering had been the prime concern of Robert Catesby, Guy Fawkes and the rest of them, Verity had got a bit huffy with her.

There was a pleasing click as the compartment opened and a shiny silver key fell into Lucy's hand. She opened the door, hoicked the suitcase over the threshold and turned on the lights, flooding the barn so brightly that she blinked. Everything outside immediately melted into blackness. Inside, though, it was spectacular, an entirely open space with a kitchen, dining area and sitting room downstairs framed by a two-storey double-arched window. An open-tread wooden staircase led upwards to a balcony landing and through an open bedroom door, Lucy glimpsed a modern four-poster bed hung with opulent draperies.

She stood for a moment staring at the space until a moth bumbled past her ear, reminding her to close the door. It shut with the softest of clicks, leaving her with the oddest sensation of being trapped in a goldfish bowl. There was silence. She was entirely alone.

She'd lived alone before. She preferred it because she had always been so single-mindedly focussed on her music career, which seemed to leave no time to invest in anything else important. It wasn't the quiet that had sent the trickle of ice down her spine, though. It was the sudden knowledge that this silence was the future: never again would she live in the enchanted world of the orchestra. There would be no pre-performance excitement, no alchemy as the music came together, no swoop of elation when the last note had faded away. Instead, there would be silence and she had to find another way to fill it. She looked down at the violin case. She didn't really know why she had brought the instrument with her except that she had not been able to cut herself off from the past so completely. Not yet. She felt horribly lonely and afraid.

'*In the midst of winter, I found there was within me an invincible summer…*' She repeated the quote over in her mind; it had helped her not to give in to despair when the grief for her lost career had swamped her. She would be strong and she would find a way. Even so, the fact that it was high summer and everything was glowing and golden when inside she felt nothing but cold made her feel cut off from reality, depressed and alone.

The bright lights flickered and for a second it seemed to Lucy that the shiny modern surroundings of the barn shimmered and disappeared, leaving the old sarsen and chalk walls bare and the cobbled floor dusted with hay. Then she blinked and the white walls and chrome fittings came into focus again. She felt light-headed and dizzy but told herself it was just tiredness. She wasn't hallucinating. Both the anxiety and the vertigo were just products of a long and emotional day.

Despite it being July, the barn felt cold, perhaps because it had very thick stone walls and had stood empty for a while. Lucy grabbed the visitor handbook and flicked through to the page that dealt with turning on the heating. Doing something practical was a lifeline, and what she needed now was a hot bath and a good night's sleep. Everything would seem more positive in the morning. Cleo would be coming over, she would start to orientate herself by walking into the village, and the sun would shine again.

With that thought she rang Cleo back to let her know she was staying at the barn and not the cottage but the call went to Cleo's voicemail so she left a message to tell her sister where to find her and say that everything was fine. Then, before she even got as far as the hot bath that she had promised herself, she crawled into the bed and fell asleep almost instantly.

She dreamed that night. It wasn't like the dreams she'd been having every night in hospital, the ones where she discovered to her horror that she was running around naked, or that she was about to sit an exam on a subject about which she knew nothing. She'd woken from those in a cold sweat and with her heart pounding, only to feel the familiar weight of anxiety swamp her when she remembered what had happened to her.

Tonight's dream was very different. She fell into it almost as soon as she closed her eyes. It surrounded her. Yet even as it felt utterly real to her, she knew that she was in a very different time and a very different place. A vicious chill wrapped about her, biting into her bones and setting her shivering. Snow spiralled past, blinding her for a moment. She felt disoriented and nauseous. Then her vision cleared, the sun came out, and yet she still felt cold and cut off in some way from all reality.

She was standing on the top of a small hill, a mound

with a spiral flight of steps cut into the side like the perfect curve of a cockleshell. The view was magnificent, a grand garden of terraces, ponds and orchards spread out in front of her, but she scarcely noticed it because she was aware only of her body and how odd and alien it felt. Her feet were damp and looking down she saw that they were encased in shoes made of some tapestry-type material that felt stiff and uncomfortable. They peeped from beneath the hem of a long dress made of blue velvet that was embroidered with silver knots and trimmed with pearls. Silver slashes in the sleeves matched the silver underskirt that fluttered in the breeze. The gown felt like a carapace and deeply unnatural as though she had not only put on someone else's clothes by accident but their personality at the same time.

The same breeze that ruffled the gown was tangling her hair with the intricate headdress she wore, knotting it and pulling tight. Fair hair, she noticed, as she tried to free the long strands, golden as the ripening corn. Strange, when her hair had always been chestnut brown, cut short for convenience.

Voices carried to her on the morning air. *'Robbie! Wait for me!'*

A man, woman and child were walking through the neatly planted orchard that clothed the hillside away to her left. The child was barely more than a baby in a stiff, formal gown, waddling on tiny but sturdy legs, grasping after flowers, blades of grass and anything else that caught his attention. It was the woman who had called out to him; she walked beside him in the plain gown and white cap of an old-fashioned nanny, laughing as she bent towards him, encouraging him on, waiting to catch him if he tumbled over.

The man walked a little way apart, dark head bent as though deep in thought. Something about the droop of his shoulders and his abstracted air suggested grief, as did the rich black velvet of his attire. Like her, he was wearing strangely antiquated clothes, doublet and hose, she knew they were called; she had played in sufficient operas to know the historical fashions.

At one point the man looked up, directly at Lucy, and she felt an odd lift of excitement, her heart beating a little faster, as though she knew him. She raised a hand instinctively to wave to him, yet he looked through her and past her, and continued on his way as though she were not there...

She wanted to call out to him: 'Robert! I'm here! It's Catherine...' But no words came to her and he passed by, leaving her with the same ache in her heart she had felt earlier, bereft and alone.

Lucy woke abruptly, pulled from the dream by an unfamiliar sound, the call of a tawny owl so close by that it felt as though it was in the room with her. The name Catherine was echoing through her mind but then the owl called again and she shifted from the dream to the present reality, and the fact that she was sprawled across the big double bed at Gunpowder Barn. A thin moon was shining through the skylight directly onto her face. Apart from the owl, quiet now, the night was silent.

Briefly she thought about getting up and pulling the

blind across the window, maybe even taking the bath she should have taken earlier when she arrived. But she still felt tired and the bed was so comfortable. It was only a moment before she was asleep again.

CHAPTER 2

Anne Catesby

Ashby St Legers, Northamptonshire, November 1592

'We need to speak about Robert.'

I opened the door of William's study without knocking and saw him scramble to cover whatever it was he had been poring over at his desk. I suspected it was the household accounts; my husband knew that I tallied every last penny correctly, yet he always had to check my calculations. In more than twenty years of marriage he had never found a mistake yet that would not stop him. I ignored the furtive gesture and pinned on a smile.

'William?' I pressed.

William took off his glasses and pinched the bridge of his nose. His screwed-up eyes and furrowed brow spoke of displeasure at the interruption but he knew that I was right, as I generally am. We needed to do something about Robert, our only son, before it was too late and he ruined his life with his careless folly.

'Where is the boy now?' William asked.

'He has gone riding.' I looked towards the mullioned

windows where snow brushed against the diamond panes. I shivered. No wonder the room was so cold. William had forgotten to re-light the fire. And this was no weather for being outdoors but that would not deter Robert who would gallop through a snow drift for pleasure if the mood took him.

I swallowed my disapproval that William referred to our son as a boy when he was a man of nineteen years now. That was one of the reasons Robert got away with so much; people indulged him and made excuses for him. Except for me; I did not. Perhaps that was why he much preferred his father to me and always had done.

'It seems that he has no shame over being expelled from university,' I said. 'On the contrary, he boasts that he was named as a ringleader of the riot.'

William polished his glasses furiously on the edge of his jacket, smearing grease over them all the more. 'It was merely a scuffle,' he said mildly. 'A riot is too bold a word. The townsfolk and students of Oxford have been fighting for centuries.'

'You make it sound like a valued tradition,' I snapped. 'Robert led a rampage that smashed up shops and stalls. He destroyed innocent people's livelihoods and incited violence and injury. He has been expelled in disgrace and yet you speak of it as though it were no more than high spirits.'

'Rusticated,' William corrected me. 'Robert has only been rusticated for a while, not sent down permanently. And he hurt no one, Anne. Not physically. As for the damage, we have already paid restitution for it.'

I threw up my hands in exasperation. 'We cannot afford

to be paying Robert's way out of trouble,' I said, 'and you know it. Already our household costs are pared to the bone. Must we all starve so that our son can run amok?' I stopped, for the tears of frustration and anger closed my throat momentarily. Time and again we had been fined for our adherence to the old Catholic religion because Queen Elizabeth was intent on making us pay for our stubbornness. The harsh penalties would never make us recant our loyalty to the true faith, but they placed a heavy burden of debt on the Catesby family. And now here was Robert, fecklessly adding to our financial woes. I felt a sudden uprush of misery at his thoughtlessness. How had he grown from such a sweet boy into such a selfish and wild young man?

'*You have spoiled him…*' The words of accusation bubbled on my tongue but I managed to bite them back. In truth William *had* indulged Robert far too much but we had lost our first son when he was only five months old – could I really blame a father for doting on the son who had survived?

'I will speak to Robert,' William said, sighing. He detested any form of argument or confrontation, particularly with his son, so I knew how much this offer cost him.

'Thank you,' I said grudgingly. Then, more warmly: 'Thank you, William. He will listen to you.' I put my arms around him and rubbed my cheek against his unshaven face. After a moment I felt the tension go out of his body and heard a rumble of laughter in his chest. 'Nan,' he said, 'let me go. Someone may come in…' But he spoke mildly for there was still affection between us after all these years, and instead of freeing him, I pressed closer, turning my face into

25

his neck. He smelled familiar, of fusty parchments and smoke from the dead fire. William was a creature of the indoors, at home in the parlour and the hall. In contrast, our son was a changeling, unlike either of us, with his height, his dazzling dark good looks and charm, and his impetuous nature.

'I wish…' I started to say, but then I stopped because it was disloyal of me to want one of the others to have survived infancy instead of mercurial Robert. With so many children in the grave I should be on my knees thanking God that one son at least had survived. I shuddered, ashamed of my treacherous thoughts, and William felt it and patted my back awkwardly.

'What is it, Nan?' he said. 'What is the matter? You are in a strange mood this morning.'

'I do not know what ails me,' I said slowly. 'It is simply that I fear for Robert sometimes. He can be so rash and reckless. I worry it will lead him into great trouble.'

William released me and I saw my own concerns reflected in his eyes for a moment before he dropped his gaze to the pile of papers before him. 'I have promised to speak with him and I shall,' he said, stiffly, as though by sharing my fears I had criticised him in some way. The moment of intimacy between us turned cold. 'You may safely leave the matter with me,' he said.

When I did not reply, William sighed in his turn and shuffled the papers on his desk again. One wafted down to the floor. Before he snatched it up I saw it was a tailor's bill for Robert for some exorbitant amount. I had wondered where he had found the funds to purchase the new tawny velvet jacket that made him look so very dashing.

'More expense!' I said, not even pretending not to have seen the invoice.

William ran an exasperated hand through his hair. It was a sandy brown, still thick and tinged with silver at his temples. He was a handsome man in his own way although not as showy as Robert. In terms of temperament they were so far apart, the one careless and gregarious, the other considered and quiet. It was interesting that Robert respected his father's thoughtfulness, perhaps admiring in him qualities he did not himself possess. Though if he could recognise virtue, I could not understand why he was unable to adopt it.

'Must you be so hard on our son, Nan?' he said, finally driven to be as blunt as I. 'You always have been and I have never understood why.'

Once again, I thought guiltily of the other boys, of our firstborn, young William, lying so still and cold in his winding sheet, his face composed as though not even death could rob him of his sweet nature. So many hopes had rested on that tiny boy. I remembered the small oak coffin that for all its sturdiness looked too fragile to protect my beloved son, and I felt my heart crack again and the grief spill over, flooding through me. Twenty years of hurt, and yet the pain was still as sharp as the cut of a blade when it slipped past my defences. Why had William died and Robert survived? I knew the answer to that, secretly. It was hidden away in the same place I locked the shame and the guilt of Robert's conception. Robert was strong; he had the ability to fight.

'I… He…' I knew that William's criticism was just. It was not Robert's fault that he had thrived where his older brother had not, and even less was he to blame for his begetting. 'Robert is too wayward,' I said evasively. 'He indulges in women, and drink and now violence…'

'He is a young man,' William said with a tolerance that infuriated me. 'A handsome boy who likes carousing. Let him be.' There was a glint in his eyes as though he was remembering a time when he, for all his quietness, had been of a similar inclination, and I saw that this was an argument I could never win with my husband; very likely he envied Robert his young man's freedom.

Another shiver caught me by surprise, enough to make me repeat my fears. 'It is only that he scares me,' I said. 'There is something about Robert… When he is possessed of an idea or a cause, it can rule him beyond all sense. It becomes a fixation in him and he puts all of his passion into it.'

William did not contradict me this time. He too had seen both the way Robert could attach himself to a cause and inspire others to follow him. People loved Robert; his cousins, my sister's boys, had followed his lead blindly since childhood despite the fact that they were all older and should know better than he. They were not the only ones. Frequently such devotion led to trouble.

'It is a pity,' I added, unable to keep all sharpness out of my voice, 'that Robert does not attach himself to the tenets of his faith as readily as he does to more worldly interests such as womanising. If he were to embrace chastity, humility and poverty—'

'Then he might as well become a monk,' William said, bursting out laughing. 'You ask too much of him, Nan.

But I do agree that he can be reckless and that a steadying influence would not come amiss.'

This was indeed a change of heart. I waited, managing to hold my breath.

'Perhaps we should look for a bride for Robert,' his father said. 'After all, by his age we were already wed.'

I sat down on the wooden settle that stood at a right angle to William's desk. The room was not designed for visitors to sit in comfort, deliberately so, as William enjoyed his solitude and tried to dissuade anyone from disturbing him. I ignored the hardness of the polished bench seat and drew myself up straight.

'It might serve,' I said cautiously. I did not want to appear too eager in case it had the reverse effect on William and made him shy away from the idea. 'I wonder...' I traced a pattern in the bright wood of the armrest, 'whether if he had a family, and an estate to run, he might find in that an outlet for his energies...'

William looked cautious. Now that I had introduced an idea with financial implications, the tone of the discussion had changed. Any grant of property to Robert would have a bearing on our own financial welfare and with the frequency of the recusancy fines we could not really afford a drop in income.

'I am not certain that Robert would be equal to the responsibility of managing an estate as yet,' William said. I noted, however, that he did not dismiss the idea out of hand, which encouraged me. And he had been the one to suggest we marry Robert off in the first place.

I leaned forward. 'But he might become so,' I said.

'Responsibility would help Robert mature and—' I played my trump card, 'I do believe that if he falls in love with his wife, he will be utterly devoted to her. There is something in his nature, for good or ill, that attaches to whatever he loves and holds to it passionately. It could be the making of him. But we would need to give him a manor of his own. There he may settle and his family can grow.'

William stared at me for a long time. I could not tell what he was thinking. His expression was opaque. He and I had never experienced the sort of love I was speaking of, a passionate attachment that eclipsed all else. I had seen others share such feelings and it was a sadness to me that we did not, but I accepted that most marriages were made not in heaven but by calculating parents. William and I were more fortunate than many – we had mutual affection and respect. For Robert, though, I suspected marriage could be different. Unlike William, he did not have a cool, calculating mind. He was all fire and desire. If we found the right girl for him and he believed it was his choice, he might attach himself to her with unwavering devotion.

'Thomas Leigh has a daughter who might be suitable,' William said, after a moment. 'His eldest child, Catherine. You will have seen her at Stratford, perhaps? She attended the mummers' play last Christmas with her family.'

I looked at him suspiciously. It was starting to sound as though William had already spoken to Sir Thomas about an alliance although he had not mentioned it to me before. I wondered what else he might be up to.

The suggestion of one of the Leigh family surprised me, however. Not only were they a Protestant family but they were of merchant stock only a generation back. I was not so high in my opinion of our own status, but William was mightily proud of his ancestors' long lineage as gentlemen and courtiers. The Catesbys might have fallen on hard times of late, adhering stubbornly to our faith and paying dearly for it, but we were still old gentry. Sir Thomas Leigh was an upstart. He was, however, a very rich upstart and William was a pragmatist, so perhaps that was how they had affixed upon this mutually pleasing arrangement.

'I do not recall seeing Mistress Leigh,' I said.

'You would have remembered had you done so.' William sounded almost dreamy. 'She is as fair as an angel, tall and of beauteous countenance and with a sweet nature to boot.' He cleared his throat. 'Her dowry is sizable and she is a year younger than Robert.'

Catherine Leigh sounded almost too good to be true.

'You have clearly given the matter more consideration than I had realised,' I said dryly. 'Have you already negotiated a contract with Sir Thomas?'

William had the grace to look a little embarrassed. 'Certainly not, my dear. I would make no such momentous decision on our son's future without consulting you. Sir Thomas and I discussed the betrothal only as a possibility, and in passing.' He paused. 'But I do believe they might make a good match.'

'I will need to meet Miss Leigh first,' I said, 'before I give any match my blessing.' I stood up. 'I shall call on the family,' I added decisively. 'I would invite them here but I have no desire for Robert to meet this angel before I approve her. If I like what I find, you may speak again to

Sir Thomas and they can join us for the celebration of the twelve days this year.'

William's smile was dry. 'It may not be so simple,' he said. 'The girl's mother is a Spencer, of Althorp, and she may not see Robert as a good match. You may meet your match in her, my dear.'

It took more than a Spencer pedigree to subdue me. I suspected that Lady Leigh and I might well be cut from a similar cloth and once we came to an understanding, all would be well. My most difficult task would not be to get Robert to fall in love with Catherine Leigh but to persuade her mother that the match was a worthy one for her daughter. William was probably right that she would correctly consider Robert to be the disreputable son of an impoverished recusant, which was not the splendid catch a mother might want for her well-dowried eldest child.

'I shall look forward to it,' I said, getting to my feet, my mind already busy with the form of words I might employ in order to gain an invitation to Stoneleigh Abbey, and my strategy once I was there.

CHAPTER 3

Lucy

A loud hammering at the door dragged Lucy awake. She had been sleeping so deeply that she didn't want to stir, comfortable and cocooned in the big bed. The feeling of contentment fled as soon as she opened her eyes; immediately she felt the clutch of anxiety that accompanied every waking moment now, the realisation that she had been ill, that her world had been upended. She fell back on the pillows with a deep sigh.

'Lucy!' It was Cleo's voice, rising up to her from the terrace below.

Lucy pulled on a dressing gown over her pyjamas and headed down the wooden stairs, blinking as the full blast of sun blazed through the windows and dazzled her. The fresh morning air, when she opened the door, also helped to clear her head. The sky was the pure, bright blue of high summer and the day was full of the calling of birds and the scent of roses.

Cleo was on the doorstep, dressed minimally in shorts, a T-shirt and sandals. Tall and skinny, she never seemed to feel the cold whereas Lucy was always reaching for an extra jumper. Not that it was at all cold this morning. Lucy's dressing gown was already feeling as hot as a winter coat.

Cleo put down the basket she was carrying and wrapped her sister in an enormous hug. She smelled of shampoo and patchouli, a retro scent that Cleo loved and which permeated both her flat and the bookshop, and now Lucy as well.

Lucy hugged her sister back. For a moment she was terrified that she might lose control and cry. It felt odd and wrong, in some way, to accept Cleo's unconditional support when she was so used to being the strong and capable one. But Cleo had always been her polar opposite in terms of emotions as well as appearance. She was demonstrative where Lucy was reserved, easy-going where Lucy was driven. She also had no filter.

'How are you, darling?' Cleo pulled back a little and her huge lavender-coloured eyes searched Lucy's face with concern. 'You look terrible! It's almost noon, you know. Have you stopped dressing? Or even washing? I know what's happened to you is awful, but you mustn't give up. I'm here for you—' she hugged her again, 'and we'll soon sort you out.'

'Thank you,' Lucy said. 'And no, I haven't stopped dressing. Nor have I given up. It was a long day yesterday and I was tired, that's all. I only just woke up.'

'I'll put the kettle on whilst you have a shower, then,' Cleo said, wrinkling up her nose delicately.

When Lucy came back down half an hour later, the barn smelled of freshly brewed coffee and warm bread. Cleo had opened up the big double doors that led out onto the patio and had set the table with a checked cloth, crisp white napkins, cutlery and crockery. Lucy marvelled at her sister's ability to make a place feel warm and welcoming with such speed and ease. Perhaps it was because she had always lived out of suitcases when touring that her own flat had never had that same sense of homeliness about it as Cleo's did. Lucy had always liked her loft apartment; it was in Clerkenwell and it had suited her previous, peripatetic life but now all of a sudden it didn't feel right. Nowhere did, though. That was part of the problem. Without her work to ground her, Lucy had no idea where she should be or what she should be doing.

'Brunch,' Cleo said breezily. She was unloading two carrier bags into the fridge. 'I brought you some food as I didn't think you'd have had a chance to shop for yourself yet. There's a good local store in the village but this should get you started.'

'You're a darling.' Looking over her shoulder, Lucy saw that Cleo's basics included halloumi, sun-dried tomatoes, a couple of quiches, salad and fresh vegetables, and she had a moment of doubt that she would be able to assemble even the most basic of meals for herself. She was more of a ready meal and takeaway girl, more bad habits that had been engendered by travelling so much and working odd hours.

'Don't worry,' Cleo said, seeing her look of alarm, 'it's easy. I'll leave you a few instructions.' She smiled. 'Now might be a good opportunity to learn how to cook, Lucy. You've finally got the time instead of dashing from rehearsal to performance and back again.'

Her sister's tactlessness stole Lucy's breath for a moment then she reminded herself that it was simply the case that Cleo had immediately accepted what she herself had as yet been unable to process; that her old life was over. If her medical condition eased she might one day be able to play again, but never to concert standard, let alone soloist level. The endless hours of practice and the punishing work schedule would be too much. Cleo had realised that and had moved on, seeing it as a chance for Lucy to do other things after years dedicated to music. Lucy herself had not got her head around that at all. It was not an opportunity but a loss.

Her gaze slid to the violin case, propped up against the wall where she had left it the previous night. She wanted to take the violin out and discover that she could play after all, that there was no pain, that she would be able to resume her career. But this was real life, not a fairy tale. The diagnosis had been clear enough. So maybe she should start to think about other possibilities. She had to earn a living, after all. Her savings were relatively small and after this break she would need to get a job.

'Maybe I will,' she said half-heartedly. She didn't want to learn to cook, or do anything except play music, but she knew deep down that she had to, and it hurt.

Fortunately, Cleo realised not to push the point. She stuck her head in the oven, emerging rosy-faced with a tray of pastries.

'This is ready,' she said. 'It's just pumpkin and feta tarts, and some French toast. There's some whipped cream in a bowl—' she nodded towards the worktop, 'and could you bring the cafetière?'

'You're a goddess,' Lucy said, following her out through the doors with the coffee pot and the mugs.

'Domestically and in every other way,' Cleo agreed. She sat down and stretched her arms up to the sun. 'Oh, this is lovely. My first proper day off in ages. Sam's minding the shop.'

Lucy realised it was a Saturday. She'd lost track of time when she'd been in hospital, the days blurring one into another in a way that had a never-ending, nightmare quality to them, and since then she had never quite managed to get back into any sort of routine. Perhaps she could start now; although if she were to do as Cleo suggested she would be resting, taking a proper break. She realised she hadn't had a holiday for about ten years. Her time had been an endless round of work, practising and performance ever since, as a child, she had shown such prodigious talent.

She reached for the sunshade and tilted it to cast the shadow in her direction. Although she and Cleo shared a superficial resemblance, everything about Lucy was a shade paler. Her hair was chestnut to Cleo's almost-black, her eyes were pale blue to Cleo's deep lavender and her skin freckled where Cleo tanned easily. She watched with a little envy as Cleo extracted a battered straw hat from her bag and squashed it down on her unruly curls, somehow managing to look incredibly cool rather than simply untidy. That was the other difference between them. Cleo had style.

'Help yourself,' Cleo said, pushing the plate of tarts towards her. 'You're the one who needs feeding up and I've had breakfast.'

It was only when Lucy took a mouthful of the warm

pastry, and the flavours of roasted pumpkin, rosemary and salty cheese burst on her tongue, that she realised how hungry she was.

'Wow,' she said, with her mouth full. 'This is great.'

Cleo looked smug. 'Food is magic,' she said. 'You'll see. Soon you will feel *much* better.'

Lucy felt the tears sting her eyes again. Cleo had visited her in hospital, travelling up to London specially to bring her little food treats to leaven the blandness of the institutional meals. Often, she hadn't felt much like eating but Cleo had always sworn that good food was a cure-all. Good food, rest and sunshine... And suddenly, sitting here, she did feel a tiny spark of energy and hope breaking through the carapace of tiredness that had cocooned her since she first became ill.

'Isn't there the most beautiful view from here?' Cleo's voice was dreamy. 'I'd forgotten how high Gunpowder Cottage is, halfway up the side of the hill. And even down here there's the rest of the valley below and the view across to the Cotswold hills. Glorious.'

Lucy followed her sister's gaze. The pale green hills, far across the flat lands of the Vale of the White Horse, were dozing in a heat haze. Nearer at hand, a shaded path dipped down the valley beside the stream, curling out of view for a moment before reappearing further down where the land opened up into a series of overgrown ponds and gardens amidst old, tumbled walls. To the east of the barn was the field where the donkey grazed, and to the west was an orchard. And as she looked, Lucy saw the figure of a woman in a red gown slip between the apple trees. The sun was bright on her long fair hair and she was crowned with a daisy chain. She stepped lightly through the grass and there was a smile on her lips. Lucy felt the sense of contentment within her grow, and she snuggled down in the chair, closing her eyes for a moment, but when she looked up the woman had gone…

'Lucy?' Cleo was waving the coffee pot at her enquiringly. Lucy pushed her mug across with a word of thanks and Cleo poured, adding milk and stirring. 'Verity has done a beautiful job on the barn, hasn't she? I haven't seen it since it was finished. It's amazing.'

'It's incredibly luxurious but I haven't really had the chance to explore it all yet,' Lucy said. 'I fell asleep almost as soon as I'd arrived.' She felt confused that the woman in the red dress had disappeared, and that together with some lingering memory from the previous night made her shiver a little. 'The place didn't feel quite so warm and welcoming when I arrived last night,' she said, 'but that was probably just my imagination and the fact I was exhausted.'

Cleo looked at her curiously. 'What do you mean?' she asked.

'Oh, only that it was unnervingly dark and quiet, and it felt a bit…' Lucy paused, 'a bit eerie.' She finished her second tart and scooped up the pastry crumbs. 'Plus I had a weird dream. It's not surprising, I suppose. The medication plus all the stuff going on in my head is going to take a toll.'

Cleo nodded. She topped up Lucy's coffee mug. 'What happened?'

'In the dream?' Lucy pulled a face. 'First it felt as though I'd fallen into a snow globe. I was freezing cold, numb with it and totally lost. Then when I came round, I was wearing a Tudor gown and a pair of shoes that didn't fit me and I felt as though I was occupying someone else's personality.'

'That sounds to me as though everything you're going through has left you questioning who you really are,' Cleo said, applying whipped cream lavishly to her French toast and sprinkling cinnamon sugar over the top. 'You don't recognise your outer self and it feels unfamiliar.'

'You can say that again,' Lucy said. Cleo loved dream analysis, her own and everyone else's. Lucy wasn't convinced by many of her sister's interpretations but this one sounded plausible. Her whole identity was tied up with her career as a violinist and it had been thrown into confusion when she was taken ill so suddenly. Now she wasn't at all sure who she was or what she was going to do.

'There was a man, a woman and a child in the dream as well,' she said. 'It almost felt as though I knew him. It was very odd.'

'Dreaming about a stranger can symbolise how you feel about yourself,' Cleo said. 'And a child could symbolise your creative energies springing forth and giving birth to new ideas and identities.'

'Well, that would make sense of why the child was tottering along and falling over,' Lucy said. 'I'm stumbling along a bit right now.'

Cleo gave her a long, clear-eyed look. Lucy knew that her sister wanted to nag her about taking things easy and giving herself time to recover – all the things the doctor had also told her, in fact – but she didn't want to hear it. It would only upset and irritate her. A tiny part of her hadn't given up hope that she would soon be able to resume orchestral playing. The other part just didn't want to talk about it. She certainly didn't want them to quarrel. Cleo had been so kind and she meant well. Lucy knew her sister only wanted her to feel better and that was part of the problem.

All her life she'd felt as though she was in debt to her family, that she owed them all because they had made enormous sacrifices for her career. As soon as she had shown any promise, her parents had saved every penny for her to have violin lessons with the best teachers that they could find. She suspected they'd even raided Cleo's piggy bank for cash for her music lessons on more than one occasion. They'd paid for her to study in America and at the Guildhall School of Music in London. She'd tried to contribute to costs when she was old enough, of course, but between studying and playing she'd had little time for a job. And Cleo had never complained, not once, that she couldn't have ballet lessons or learn to ride, or have new clothes like her friends because every penny went to Lucy… She owed her sister a vast debt in so many ways and sometimes the guilt was crushing, especially now they had made those sacrifices for nothing.

She raised a hand to shade her eyes, rubbing away a wayward tear whilst pretending she was looking at the view again. The orchard looked deliciously cool, the gnarled fruit trees casting spiky shadows on the lush grass. At the top was a small, circular mound that looked man-made, it was so perfectly round. Lucy tilted her head slightly. It looked like the vantage point she had been standing on in her dream the previous night, with the orchard spread out below, where the man and the child had been walking among the trees...

A sharp bark interrupted them, then there was an equally brisk tap at the garden gate and a black Labrador stuck his nose around, then came bounding over to see them. He was followed rather more slowly by Finn Macintyre. This morning he was dressed in what looked like an ancient pair of shorts, hiking boots and a faded denim blue T-shirt. He wore the casual attire and the outdoor tan that came with it with utter assurance; a man who seemed completely at ease in himself and his environment. Lucy felt an unwelcome prickle of awareness and at the same time a rush of awkwardness as she remembered their meeting the previous night.

Finn's clothes might have been casual but the notebook in his hand looked completely professional and the camera he placed carefully on the table was top of the range. When the breeze ruffled the edges of the sketchpad Lucy saw drawing after drawing of plants, various garden designs and copious scribbled notes that were completely illegible.

'Finn!' Cleo sounded thrilled and as though she'd known Finn for years rather than having met him only once. She had a talent for immediately warming to people that made Lucy, less extrovert, feel a positive recluse.

'Thanks for dropping in,' Cleo said. She turned to Lucy. 'I had a chat with Finn on my way down to see you,' she said. Her mischievous smile suggested she too had heard about their first meeting. 'I thought it would be good for you to say hello formally as you're going to be neighbours.'

'I don't think Geoffrey understands formal,' Lucy said, stroking the dog's silky head where it lay on her lap, 'but it's good to meet you properly, Finn.' She tried to match Cleo's light tone. She knew it would be better to try and get along with Finn even if she wasn't intending to stay long and didn't expect to see much of him. Plus she felt a wayward sympathy for Finn's evident embarrassment and the fact that Cleo had steamrollered him into this meeting. She was used to Cleo and her impulsive ways but judging by the faint flush on Finn's high cheekbones, he was probably feeling uncomfortable.

'Coffee, Finn?' Cleo said hospitably, brandishing the pot. 'Come and join us. There's plenty.'

Finn looked awkward. 'I don't want to interrupt you—'

'You aren't,' Cleo said, throwing a smile in his direction as she headed inside. 'We're thrilled to see you, aren't we, Lucy?'

'Thrilled,' Lucy agreed, deadpan.

Finn's lips twitched into a tiny smile. He took one of the chairs, sitting back and stretching his long legs out. Lucy felt annoyed. She wasn't sure why she was reacting against him like this. It wasn't that she resented him interrupting her time with Cleo; she doubted he would stay long as Geoffrey looked keen for a walk. They had certainly had a difficult first meeting but they were both adults and could be civil to one another. She was aware, though, that she didn't want to get to know Finn. She didn't particularly want to make new friends, she realised, just to recover in quiet. More than that, she found him unsettling in some way. She remembered the way he had seen below the surface of her tiredness to the exhaustion and confusion that was beneath. It had felt way too intimate and she didn't want to reveal so much of herself.

She told herself she was being stupid. 'I've eaten all the French toast, I'm afraid,' she said.

Finn smiled and she had the uncomfortable sense that he had noticed the effort she was forcing herself to make. It made her feel even worse. Was she so transparent? But she was still tired, bone-deep weariness, and had no resources left to pretend.

'No problem,' he said. 'Geoffrey and I both had a cooked breakfast at the café, but coffee will be great.'

Cleo reappeared with another mug. 'What does Geoff's cooked breakfast consist of?' she asked.

'Sausage,' Finn said. 'Fortunately not eggs.' He accepted the coffee with a smile of thanks and turned to Lucy.

'I came to apologise, actually,' he said. 'You had a perfect right to expect the cottage to be empty last night. Geoffrey and I were supposed to be staying here at the barn.'

Geoffrey wagged his tail slightly, as though agreeing.

'The trouble is,' Finn said, looking slightly sheepish, 'Geoff won't go inside the building. He's fine out here but whenever I try to get him over the threshold, he just refuses point blank. On the day we arrived he sat by the door whining and I couldn't even tempt him inside with food. Eventually, as Gunpowder Cottage was empty, we moved in there instead.'

'You mean he literally won't set foot inside the barn?' Lucy looked at Geoffrey who looked back at her with sorrowful brown eyes. 'Why not?'

'Some animals are very susceptible to a sense of atmosphere.' Cleo passed Finn a plate of homemade biscuits. 'Perhaps there's something here that Geoffrey is aware of that we're not.'

'A ghost cat, perhaps,' Lucy said sarcastically. She loved Labradors but didn't think they were the most sensitive of animals. Geoffrey gave her a reproachful look as though he had read her thoughts.

Finn rubbed the back of his neck. 'Whatever the reason,' he said, 'it's probably best that we move back down here so that you can stay in the cottage. It's what you agreed with Verity and I appreciate you'll be more familiar with it since you stayed there as a child. Geoffrey will be fine. He will come inside sooner or later if he's hungry enough.'

'Oh, Lucy wouldn't do that to you – or to Geoffrey,' Cleo said. 'She was telling me just before you arrived how fabulous it is here!' She gave Lucy a meaningful look. 'You're fine here, aren't you, Lucy?'

'Totally,' Lucy said, sighing. She didn't particularly mind staying at the barn, which was indeed palatial, but she did mind Cleo rushing in to decide for her. 'I can't be responsible for adding to poor Geoffrey's neuroses, I suppose,' she said. 'Let's leave things as they are.'

Finn's brows snapped down. 'Are you sure? The climb up the hill is quite steep which isn't ideal for anyone recovering from illness—'

'Who told you I'd been ill?' Lucy felt a sharp stab of irritation that he knew. It felt as though her privacy had been invaded.

Both Finn and Cleo looked taken aback at her tone. 'I told Finn.' Cleo leaped into the breach. 'And I expect

Verity did as well.' She covered Lucy's hand with her own. 'We're only trying to look out for you, Luce.'

Lucy pressed her lips together and blinked hard. She wanted to pull her hand away from Cleo's, to snap at her and reject the sympathy, but she managed to control her anger. This wasn't Cleo's fault. It wasn't Finn's fault either. She was tired and miserable and needed to pull herself together and be grateful that people cared.

She stroked Geoffrey's ears for comfort and he turned his nose into the palm of her hand. 'I'm sorry,' she said gruffly. She looked at Finn, flinching in expectation of the pity she would see in his eyes. 'I appreciate your concern,' she said, 'but I'll be fine here at the barn.'

'No problem.' She thought Finn might laugh at the transparently grudging apology but his tone was brisk. 'If you change your mind, just let me know and I'll spruce the cottage up for you.'

'Thanks.' Lucy's sense of awkwardness faded a little. 'It's probably better that I'm tucked away down here. That way you won't need to worry about me getting in the way of your work on the cottage gardens. I understand you're involved in a historic excavation project?'

'That's right,' Finn said. He cleared his throat. 'Except that the garden excavation involves the whole estate and isn't simply up at Gunpowder Cottage. Did Verity mention anything about it to you?'

'No,' Lucy said, looking around the terrace with its terracotta pots overflowing with starflowers and fuchsia and nicotiana. It looked strikingly new and modern, hardly the site for some sort of archaeological survey.

'I know Verity's been researching the history of Gunpowder Cottage for ages,' she said, 'but we hadn't talked about it recently.' She felt a pang; she'd practically lost touch with her aunt in the past few years because both of them had been so busy. A few flying visits had not given them the chance for a proper catch-up and only now, with the enforced break, was Lucy realising how much she had missed her.

'Verity thinks that there's a lost Tudor-era garden hidden in the valley,' Cleo said. 'She found some references to it in an old book that gave some of the early history of the estate.' She looked smug. 'I found the book for her, actually. It was antiquarian and out of print.'

'I can see there was a walled garden further down the hill,' Lucy said, 'but I didn't think it was as old as that.'

Finn nodded. 'You're right, it isn't. Those are the remains of an old kitchen garden nursery from the Victorian period. Any Tudor detail would be beneath that. There are a few more well-hidden clues around the cottage and elsewhere in the valley if you know where to look. But I'm not surprised that no one noticed before, especially as there were no documentary clues until Charlie—' He stopped abruptly.

'Verity told me what had happened to your brother,' Cleo said with quick sympathy. 'I was very sorry to hear about it.'

'It's fine,' Finn said, although judging by his deep frown, Lucy thought that it was very far from fine. 'My brother Charlie was doing some research for Verity on this project,' he said, turning to her. 'We're both historians but he specialised in Tudor history whereas I focus on gardens and landscape.' He took a breath. 'Charlie was down here doing some work when he had a fatal car accident.'

'Oh God, how awful,' Lucy said. She felt sick, winded at the revelation. A wholly unexpected urge gripped her to reach across the table and touch Finn's hand to offer comfort. 'I'm so sorry,' she said, knowing how inadequate it sounded, feeling helpless.

Finn shrugged as though trying to shake off an unbearable weight. 'If you're staying for a few weeks you're bound to hear about it,' he said, a bit roughly. 'It was back at the end of March, so a while ago now.'

Only four months, Lucy thought, barely enough time for the reality of it to sink in, let alone for time to rub the rough edges from the grief. No wonder Finn was terse. She wondered why he had chosen to continue with the job for Verity after Charlie had died. She was surprised that he wanted to be within a hundred miles of Knightstone. But she didn't want to pry and she knew Finn wasn't going to offer any further information. His mouth was set in a tight line.

'Do you have any potential designs to show us?' Cleo asked, breaking the slightly tense silence.

'Yes, of course.' Finn reached for his sketchbook and flipped it open. 'I've drafted out a few ideas of the garden we think may have been here.'

'This is so exciting!' Cleo leaned forward to look at the drawings. 'So you're tackling the whole valley? Wow, that's ambitious. Will you be digging up Clarabelle's paddock as well?'

'Who?' Lucy was all at sea.

'The donkey, of course,' Cleo said, as though Lucy should have known its name. 'Her field is part of the original Gunpowder Cottage estate although I think Verity lets it out now.'

'We'll definitely investigate some of the features in it.' Finn shot her a smile. 'There are some interesting humps and bumps in that field. They could be walls or other structures, and we need to look at the landscape as a whole, so that will include the cottage gardens, the valley, the orchard and field, the area around the barn—'

'Wait a minute,' Lucy said. She could see her peaceful holiday suddenly invaded by mechanical diggers and people coming and going. It didn't matter that she hadn't a clue what she was going to do with herself whilst she was there. She'd started to imagine that she might relax in the sunshine and quiet but now that seemed highly unlikely. 'What you're saying is that basically the whole area is going to become one huge excavation site,' she said.

'I'm sure Finn won't get in your way, Lucy,' Cleo said quickly, hearing the challenge in her tone. 'He said they were only digging small test areas and the barn is pretty secluded anyway. Plus it's not as though they'll be interrupting you at work—' She stopped, looking stricken. 'Shit, sorry. I didn't mean to be tactless.'

Lucy shook her head to banish the prickle of tears. 'I know,' she said. It didn't help that Cleo hadn't meant to hurt her; it *did* hurt because she felt so pointless.

'Perhaps you could join the excavation,' Cleo said, brightening up. 'That would give you something to occupy yourself with whilst you work out what to do next with your life.'

'I certainly won't be doing any digging,' Lucy snapped. 'If I can't hold a violin bow, I wouldn't be able to hold a trowel.'

'Fair enough,' Cleo said, ploughing on, 'but what about the paperwork? I'm sure Finn could do with some help with admin and it would stop you sitting around fretting—'

'I'm sure Finn wants nothing of the sort,' Lucy interrupted, losing patience completely, 'and neither do I! I've no admin skills and anyway, I thought you wanted me to take a break? Stop trying to take control!'

She heard Cleo say something under her breath that sounded like *'I will when you stop feeling sorry for yourself'*. Her sister started to stack up the plates with some ostentatious clattering, and headed off inside the barn without another word.

'Sorry,' Lucy said to Finn, feeling even more awkward, if that were possible. 'I know that Cleo's just trying to help, but sometimes I feel taken over. Since you know I'm here to convalesce, you probably also know I had pneumonia and post-viral complications that mean I've had to give up my career—' She stopped. She wasn't sure what she was trying to say other than express the frustration that Cleo was nagging her to take it easy with one breath but trying to organise her into new activities with the next.

Finn met her eyes directly. 'I was sorry to hear that you had to give up your orchestral career,' he said. 'I imagine that's incredibly difficult to come to terms with.'

'I… Yes.' Lucy was taken aback and the surprise pushed her towards honesty. 'I don't think I *have* come to terms with it yet. Nowhere near.' Then: 'Did Verity tell you I played?'

'She did,' Finn said. 'She also gave me some of your recordings to listen to a while back.'

Lucy felt like the small child whose parents had rather embarrassingly boasted about her to strangers. 'Oh no,' she said. 'How awkward.'

'I like violin music,' Finn said easily. 'Mozart and gardens sort of go together, I find, with all that creativity and brilliance and yet a sort of mathematical order as well.' He looked at her. 'Like I say, I'm sorry about what happened. Life can be utter crap sometimes.'

'Yeah, well, I imagine you know that all too well.' Lucy bit her lip. She felt embarrassed. She wanted to be able to say something meaningful and empathetic about loss and grief, but barely knew where to start. Her own losses, whilst painful, were nothing compared to Finn's loss of a brother. He'd barely spoken of Charlie yet she had been able to tell how close they had been. And she at least could rebuild her life once she had had time and space to heal. Finn had to live without Charlie for ever after.

Cleo reappeared, wiping her hands on her apron. 'You're still here,' she said to Finn. She cast Lucy a less-than-friendly glance. 'I thought my sister might have scared you away by now with her bad moods.'

'We haven't finished looking at the garden designs yet,' Lucy said quickly to forestall further bickering. 'Tell us more about how you think it might have looked, Finn. It sounds fascinating.'

Finn's lips twitched, and for a second, Lucy thought he was going to call her out on her sudden interest but instead he pulled the sketchbook towards her and flicked over a few pages.

'Here's my concept of what the Tudor garden might have looked like,' he said.

Lucy saw a sketch of the valley with a manor house standing at the top of the hill, Gunpowder Barn below and the fields and paddocks unfolding around it. It looked familiar and yet altered; the contours of the landscape were the same but the features quite different.

'I wish I could draw as well as that,' Cleo said enviously. 'Look at the house! What a perfect little manor it was!'

'That's all notional, I'm afraid,' Finn said. 'We don't know exactly what it looked like back in the sixteenth century. Charlie was working on that, trying to put together an image from various different descriptions. It's difficult because there are no contemporary paintings and very few references to it.'

Lucy pointed to what looked like a canal in front of the barn buildings. 'Is that a moat? I thought they usually encircled a house?'

Finn nodded. 'It could be a moat – we're not sure yet, though we have found evidence of clay-lined ditches. We can't excavate the area at the front of the barn because there's the duck pond on the other side of the public footpath and it's fed by springs from the hillside so it would be too expensive and difficult to drain. But sometimes Tudor gardens were surrounded by a shallow moat or a canal. Water features like that would provide an opportunity to row amongst the flowers and shrubs, giving you a different view of the gardens. People kept fish in the moat as well sometimes.'

Cleo leaned closer, eyes alight, her irritation with Lucy

evidently forgotten. 'That sounds idyllic,' she said. 'So you would stroll down the hill from the manor house and have all these pleasure grounds around you? Awesome.'

'Pleasure grounds is exactly right,' Finn said, smiling. He glanced back at Lucy. 'I don't suppose that either of you know what was on this site before the barn was converted, do you?'

Lucy frowned, trying to recall what the rest of the estate had looked like when she and Cleo had visited as children. 'I think they were just farm buildings, weren't they?' she asked her sister. 'They were very tumbledown. We weren't allowed to play down here because they were derelict and it was too dangerous.'

'Verity had a couple of them demolished when the barn was converted,' Cleo agreed. 'But I don't think they were very old – Victorian, maybe, or early twentieth century at the latest. I think they were part of the kitchen gardens.'

'Maybe there was something else on the site here before they were built, then,' Finn said. 'A remnant of the earlier garden, perhaps.'

'Wouldn't the builders have uncovered some evidence when they converted the barn, though?' Lucy asked. She felt Cleo looking at her disapprovingly and added hastily, 'I mean, I'd love it to be true, but with all that demolition and rebuilding, surely something would have shown up?'

'They did find a few interesting artefacts,' Finn said. 'Enough to suggest that *something* was here but nothing diagnostic. And they didn't disturb the original foundations, so it's possible that something lies beneath the current building.' He measured the house with an expert eye. 'It's a nice flat area and a good size. There could have been some sort of building that was a part of the original garden design, maybe something important like a banqueting house.' He frowned. 'I'm not a hundred per cent sure about that, though. It might have been too grand.'

'Why is that?' Cleo asked.

'Well, this isn't a castle site like Kenilworth, for example,' Finn said. 'It's a country manor house so I would expect the garden to be relatively modest and in keeping with that.' He gave a little shrug. 'Hopefully we'll find out in time.'

Lucy was tracing the course of the stream on the map as it meandered down the valley. 'There's a lot of water channelled down the hillside, isn't there?' she said. 'When it's dry like it is at the moment you forget how fierce the stream can get, but I remember sometimes in winter when we visited it was almost in flood.'

'I think they harnessed the water supply for the Tudor gardens,' Finn said, nodding. He gestured to the picture. 'There's another pool here at the bottom of the valley. It's a marshy sort of pond today but we found evidence of lead-lined cisterns and some coloured glass and stone down there so it could even have been an early bathing pool.'

'The waters rise from the springs under the hill, don't they?' Lucy said. 'I remember Verity saying that the chalk hereabouts filters the water and it is exceptionally pure. A sort of early spa treatment.'

'Wow!' Cleo's eyes were round. 'Verity could open a wellbeing centre and make a fortune!'

Finn rubbed a hand over his jaw. 'Well, she's very keen to restore the gardens and open them to the public if we find enough evidence of what they looked like,' he said, 'but more for the historical value than anything else, I think.' He looked up, straight at Lucy. 'If you *did* want to help out at all on the project, you'd be doing me a big favour, actually. I haven't had the time to catch up with all of Charlie's written research yet because I've been flat out looking for clues on the ground. Someone needs to take a look at the old documents and notes he collected and see if there's anything useful in there.'

'Oh.' Lucy was startled at the offer, and instinctively thought to refuse. 'I don't really think I've got the right sort of qualifications to do that kind of work,' she said. 'I wouldn't know what I was looking for.'

Finn shrugged as though it was a matter of complete indifference to him. 'No problem,' he said. 'I just thought I'd ask.' He stood up. 'Thanks for the coffee,' he said to Cleo. He raised a hand to Lucy. 'I'll see you around – but not too often,' he added dryly. 'We'll make sure we don't disturb your holiday.'

He strolled back inside the barn, taking his coffee mug with him, and Cleo hopped up to follow and show him out. Geoffrey, meanwhile, went as far as the patio doors then stood looking helpless, ears flat.

'You really don't want to go inside the house, do you?' Lucy murmured. 'Poor old thing – no one's going to hurt you.'

Geoffrey's dark gaze flashed with misery. He made a whining sound.

Lucy could hear the rumble of Finn's voice as he spoke to Cleo, then the sound of the front door closing. Geoffrey, looking anxious, dashed over to the garden gate and waited while Finn came around to let him out. He shot out of the garden and away down the valley.

'He's quite something, isn't he?' Cleo came back out into the sunshine. 'So gruff but so capable.'

'Geoffrey?' Lucy deliberately misunderstood her. 'Yes, he's super-cute.' She watched as Finn and Geoffrey strolled away down the path, past the orchards and over a little wooden bridge that crossed the stream. At the bottom of the hill the land opened up again with pasture on one side and the tumbled walls of the Victorian kitchen garden on the other. Lucy saw Finn open his sketchbook and grope in his pocket for a pencil. The bright sunlight burnished his bent head as he started to draw.

Cleo sighed. She slid back into her seat, but her silence was charged with the weight of words unsaid. Birdsong swept back in to fill the silence. Lucy looked at her sister and shook her head slightly.

'Go on, then,' she said. 'Spit it out.'

'Where to start?' Cleo said, raising her brows. 'What on earth is going on between you and Finn?'

'What do you mean?' Lucy fidgeted with her hair.

'The whole Lady Chatterley and the gardener act,' Cleo said. 'You being haughty with the hired hand.'

'I don't think Lady Chatterley is quite the comparison you're looking for,' Lucy said. 'I'm sorry if I sounded a bit abrupt with him − and with you as well.' She looked at Cleo's stubborn face and sighed. 'I know you were only trying to help, Cleo, by suggesting I should join the dig. I know you don't want me to be sitting around moping.' She pulled a face. 'But give me a bit of time. I haven't got my head around the fact that I won't be playing professionally ever again. I feel like a failure, to be honest, and as though I've let you all down.'

'Oh, Lucy!' Cleo leaped up, sending her chair clanging backwards, and grabbed her sister in a tight hug. 'Why didn't you say? You haven't let anyone down! It's not your fault!'

'I know,' Lucy inhaled more patchouli as Cleo held her so close that she couldn't breathe, 'but you gave up so much so that I could be a professional musician. I want you to know that if you ever want those riding lessons or ballet classes now, I'll take a job to pay for them—'

Cleo gave a snort of laughter and let her go. 'I'm not bendy enough to do ballet anymore,' she said regretfully, 'but I appreciate the offer.'

'Well, let me know if you change your mind.' Lucy felt comforted – until she remembered how summarily she had dismissed Finn's request for help.

'Oh God, I suppose I'll have to apologise to Finn for pouring cold water on his idea of help with the research,' she said, 'but I'm not a historian. I wouldn't have known where to start.'

'I think he was looking for some help with the paper-work, not someone with a PhD in renaissance gardens,' Cleo said dryly. 'I was surprised he asked you, actually. Verity said he hadn't gone anywhere near the documentary side of things since Charlie died. Too painful for him, I imagine.'

'Yes,' Lucy felt another pang of sympathy for Finn,

'absolutely ghastly. I'm surprised he didn't quit the project altogether.'

'Verity said Finn was determined to complete it as a tribute to his brother,' Cleo said. 'Charlie was so sure they were on to something amazing, according to Verity. He hinted at a really exciting find – not just the garden but something even more historically significant that was associated with it.' She gave a little sigh. 'I guess we'll never know now what that was. But Finn's keen to see the garden reconstruction through.'

'How did the accident happen?' Lucy asked. 'Was anyone else involved?'

'Fortunately not,' Cleo said. 'No one seems to know quite why or how it happened. It was on the road to Wantage. Charlie's car came off on a straight stretch, ploughed through a hedge and down a bank. He was thrown clear and killed.'

Lucy shuddered, thinking of the long, straight stretches of tree-lined country road, dark tunnels that might tempt a driver to go too fast only to trick them with a sudden turn or adverse camber. Perhaps a pheasant had run out in front of Charlie's car, or a small animal had made a dash across and he had swerved to avoid it. A split second, and then the loss of control and the plunge into oblivion.

'I wish I'd been a bit less abrupt with Finn,' she said bleakly. 'Oh well… I'll have to apologise when I see him next.' She looked down the valley. Finn and Geoffrey had disappeared though she thought she could hear the distant sound of splashing. If Geoffrey was a typical Labrador, he'd probably be in the pool by now.

'It's no wonder he's a bit gruff, is it?' Cleo said. 'I can't see him opening up about it with anyone, somehow.'

'You don't know,' Lucy said. 'Maybe he has friends he can talk to. Or a girlfriend.'

'Well, he is hot, if you're into guys,' Cleo said. She gave Lucy the side-eye. 'Isn't he?'

'Sure,' Lucy said, not giving an inch.

'He's also kind,' Cleo said smugly. 'He left you some supplies. Come and see.' She led Lucy through the terrace doors into the barn's interior. It felt cool and dark inside, a cathedral-high space of shadows and mystery. Cleo peered inside a bag on the worktop. 'Hmm, Finn's choices are rather more practical than mine – milk, butter, bread…' She looked up. 'That was very thoughtful of him.'

'I'll thank him profusely,' Lucy promised, feeling guilty all over again at how prickly she'd been with him. If Finn had just lost his brother, he had every right to be a bit brusque and she shouldn't take out her own problems on him. 'I thought I'd have a rest and then walk into the village later and start finding my way around,' she said. She gave Cleo an impulsive hug. 'I'll be fine. You don't need to keep an eye on me all the time. I'll ring you every day and maybe we can meet up again in a few days?'

Cleo hugged her back. 'I really don't mind—' she started to say, but Lucy interrupted.

'I know, and it's lovely of you, but you came to see me in hospital plenty of times and you yourself said that this is your first day off in ages, so go and enjoy it.' She let Cleo go and smiled at her. 'You've been a rock, Cleo, and I love you for it, but you deserve a break too, not least from my bad temper.'

'You'll get over it,' Cleo said, then seeing Lucy's face, 'Oops, sorry, I'm being insensitive again, aren't I?'

'I'm sure you're right,' Lucy said, smiling. 'I'll get there in time.'

Her heart ached, though, as she watched Cleo drive off in her little Mini. She felt lonely. She wished she'd thought to hire a car; living in London she never really needed one but it would be useful for getting about here. It simply hadn't occurred to her that there wouldn't be shops, or a bus service right outside the door. It was stupid of her, when she knew Knightstone was very rural and that services like post offices and transport had been cut to villages like this, but she hadn't really been thinking clearly when she'd agreed to come to the village. Plus she knew deep down she'd secretly been hoping that it would only be for a couple of weeks, until she was better and could go back to work…

The dust motes danced in the sunshine as she slowly climbed the stairs to the bedroom. It seemed ridiculous to have a nap when she'd only been awake for a couple of hours but the heat of the day and the sudden enforced relaxation was making her feel incredibly sleepy. She lay down on the four-poster and almost immediately drifted off.

It was as though the dream had been waiting for her. She wore the same Tudor gown and the same slippers as she had before; she was seeing through Catherine's eyes again. This time she was inside a house. She stood in a long gallery, the wooden floor smooth and slightly uneven beneath her feet, the low sun cutting through the mullioned window to cast long shadows and gild the thick cobwebs that hung from the sconces. There were paler patches on the walls where paintings had been, or perhaps tapestries. Dust thicker than a blanket smothered everything. When she took a step forward, clouds of it rose and made her sneeze. She left footprints in it like snow.

There was a sense of panic tight in her chest. Down the stairs she ran, careless of safety. She knew she was looking for something, or someone. Yet she also knew that the house was empty, dead, and had been for some time. It was soundless. No one was there. Her anxiety increased. She had to find him. She had to find Robert.

At the bottom of the stairs was a narrow, stone-paved corridor. She ran to the door at the end, throwing it wide.

The view that met her gaze gave her a shock. Winter had come to the silent house, cloaking it in frost. The dead strands of the climbing rose glittered white in the cold sun, a tangled barrier almost blocking the doorway. Beyond that, the uneven stone path that ran down to the gate was thick with snow, each shard shining with a crystal beauty that was both beautiful and chilling.

Lucy turned around and realised that she was standing in the doorway of Gunpowder Cottage. The stairs were in the same place although the doorway on the right now led into a great hall rather than the cosy sitting room that she remembered and there was a passageway stretching away behind her that was partitioned with wooden panelling.

She was simultaneously aware of her own puzzlement overlaid on Catherine's confusion and distress. This time, in this dream, she felt so much closer to Catherine than she had before. She wasn't simply an observer. Their thoughts seemed to tangle and separate again. *Wait...* she wanted to tell Catherine, *let me catch my breath,* but Catherine was running again, down the corridor towards the kitchens, so different from the shiny modern one that Lucy knew, a place with a huge empty hearth and cold ashes that spun into a ghostly spiral when stirred by the breeze...

Lucy woke suddenly again, bathed in sweat. It was hot in the barn and she had managed to wrap the duvet around herself, pinioning her arms to her body and making her hotter still. She struggled to free herself and sat up. Her reflection gazed at her from the mirror directly opposite the bed, pale face with freckles scattered over her snub nose, short straight dark hair, wide mouth, wide-set pale-blue eyes, the whole familiar and unremarkable. It was also a very different face from the one she had seen reflected in the dusty prism when she had looked out of the window at Gunpowder Cottage. The face that had looked back at her then had been rounded, framed with fair hair. She had had a rosebud mouth and big blue eyes.

It had been Catherine's face.

CHAPTER 4

Anne Catesby

Ashby St Legers, Northamptonshire, Christmas 1592

'The advantages of the match are all on your son's side, of course,' Lady Leigh said, looking down her Spencer nose at me. She was a tall woman, expensively clad in red velvet that hung on her thin frame like a curtain. Her hair was a faded version of her daughter's vivid gold and her face still held a hint of beauty. It mattered not to her that she was in our house, partaking of our Yuletide hospitality. She was nevertheless going to make her feeling clear on the inferiority of a Catesby as a husband for a Leigh.

'Catherine is comely, rich and of elegant manners,' she added, with a self-congratulatory smile. 'She could easily ensnare a baron.'

'I am sure she could, madam,' I agreed with a warm smile. 'Your elder daughter is indeed a paragon. However, Robert would be a worthy match for her. He—' I had no chance to boast of Robert's imaginary virtues for I was interrupted by old Lady Leigh, Catherine's grandmother.

'What nonsense you talk, Kate!' she said, waddling up

to us and slapping her daughter-in-law's wrist with her fan. 'Have you *seen* the boy? He is handsome and charming and bold.' She gave a cackle of laughter that sounded unrepentantly lewd. 'There is not a woman in this room who would not wish to be in Catherine's shoes now, or more to the point, in her marriage bed when she weds Robert Catesby. I'll wager he knows a thing or two about how to please a maid!'

'Dame Alice!' Two vivid spots of red had appeared on Lady Leigh's cheekbones, a match for the puce of her gown. 'You speak out of turn!'

'I speak the truth!' her mother-in-law asserted. 'You know it but you are too mealy-mouthed to deal plainly.'

I hid my smile in my glass of wine. Dame Alice was right. Most of the women at our Twelfth Night feast were covertly watching Robert, and some were not so covert, eyeing him with a hungry gaze. He looked very dashing in his Christmastide finery of black velvet laced with silver, and not for the first time I wondered how I could possibly have produced such a peacock when I was a dull little brown hen myself.

'They make a handsome couple,' I said mildly, 'he is so dark and Catherine so fair.' Catherine and Robert stood a little apart in a corner of the parlour, deep in conversation. Her face was tilted up towards his and, illuminated by candlelight, she looked both serene and enraptured. As we watched, Robert took her hand and pressed a kiss to it in courtly fashion and she blushed before drawing it away. Robert smiled, the smile of a man who believed he could make the conquest, and a voice in my mind whispered: *'Don't make it too easy for him…'*

'Catherine should go down on her knees to God in thanks for sending her such a lovesome husband,' Dame Alice opined. She filled her cup of mead from the bowl and waddled off, spilling much of it on the rushes as she went.

Lady Leigh sighed. 'I must apologise for my husband's mother. The older generation can be a little… earthy… in their speech.'

I waved away her apologies, glad to have her at a disadvantage. 'It does not matter,' I said. 'Though I do think they look well together and seem taken with each other's company.'

Her poker demeanour softened slightly. 'That is true. Once Catherine sets her heart on something, she is both determined and loyal.' Her tone was dry. 'I believe she likes this proposed match very well.'

I was heartened by the mention of Catherine's determined will. Perhaps she would be able to manage Robert. She certainly knew her own value for though she was clearly flattered by the attentions of so handsome a young man, she was not fawning on him. Robert, I thought with satisfaction, would have to work for her regard.

And if Catherine was eager to wed, her mother might be more inclined to agree to the match. I sensed that beneath her chilly exterior, Lady Leigh was fond of her eldest child. I decided to sweeten the pill.

'I understand that you have concerns about Robert's behaviour and his financial situation,' I said casually. 'I do believe that a wife will steady him, and that the management of an estate will give him a good income and a focus for his attention…' I let that hang and as I had hoped, Lady Leigh's nose twitched slightly like a hunting dog's.

'Do you and Sir William have a particular manor in mind, Lady Catesby?' she enquired.

'The manor of Chastleton in Oxfordshire was part of Robert's grandmother's dowry along with Knightstone and Frankworth,' I said. I accepted a brimming glass of wine from a passing servant with a nod of thanks. 'When she died at the start of the year it was her wish that her lands should pass to Robert in time and his marriage would seem to provide the perfect opportunity.'

Lady Leigh cast a sideways glance at William, who was in the centre of a group of our kinsmen and friends, a tangle of Catholic sympathisers whom I could see might seem both exclusive and unfriendly to an outsider. It was no wonder that Lady Leigh had strict terms for this marriage.

'Your husband is a careful man in such matters,' she said, with a thin-lipped smile. 'If he agrees to such a plan that would certainly make Robert's suit more... worthy of consideration. Those are good estates and Catherine would make a fine mistress for them.'

'It was William's idea in the first place,' I lied smoothly. It was true that my mother-in-law had wished Robert to have her lands but not that William had necessarily agreed it was a good idea. I was sure, however, that I could persuade him. And Lady Leigh was right, Chastleton in particular was a rich estate whose owner could grow fat on the proceeds of the sheep who grazed there, and the other two manors, whilst smaller, were not insignificant.

Lady Leigh was also looking at William and our kinsmen. 'That leaves only the matter of faith,' she said. She turned her faded blue gaze back to me and for the first time, she seemed hesitant. 'Catherine has been baptised and raised in the Protestant religion,' she said. 'I would not wish her to feel that she should question what she believes in.'

I did not reply immediately. Matters of religion were a thorny thicket for a man – or woman – to discuss with their fellows. The past fifty years had made us wary. Wars had been waged, men of conscience killed, families such as ours split apart, imprisoned, robbed of our fortunes. Yet still we held fast. On the other side were the men of the future, rich, upcoming people like Sir Thomas and Lady Leigh whose Protestantism might well be as politically driven as it was heartfelt.

'It is true that Robert was educated at Douai,' I said, referring to the English Jesuit College in the Netherlands. 'But religion is a matter of conscience. Catherine will, of course, be free to worship as she chooses.'

'Robert left Oxford before completing his degree so he had no need to take the oath of allegiance to the Queen,' Lady Leigh said. She was forcing me to admit that Robert was a Catholic by conviction as well as family tradition and as such might expect his wife to follow his religion and particularly any children they might have.

I inclined my head to acknowledge her point. 'That is true,' I said, 'but—'

'What concerns me,' she cut in, 'is that your son could lose all the money from his rich estates with one foolish gesture or treasonous act. I will not have Catherine brought down with him. Our family can tolerate no such risk.'

'You may be easy on that,' I said. 'Robert is too worldly to sacrifice comfort and luxury for his faith.' Lady Leigh's brows shot up and I realised that I might have sounded a little cynical. I moderated my tone. 'Robert is young,' I said, 'and he is of an age to value money and advancement. He has also seen how adherence to our faith has damaged his father's situation. With estates of his own and a rich and beautiful wife he will see where his path lies. There is a fine Protestant church in Chastleton. Very likely he will attend it.'

'A church papist.' Lady Leigh's lips curled. 'Neither one thing nor another.'

'On the contrary,' I was not going to let that slur pass, 'I believe Robert will be a man as judicious about his advancement as your own husband, madam.'

There was a silence and then she laughed. 'How extraordinary that the two of you should have raised such a son,' she said, but the gleam in her eyes was friendlier now than it had been at any time before in our conversation. 'You and Sir William are both so...' I thought she was going to say dull, but she compromised with 'so steadfast, yet Robert is so dazzling and ambitious.'

'It has always been a mystery to me too.' I was back in control of myself now, and I sensed that somehow, I had won her over. We both glanced at Robert and Catherine, and saw that she was taking her leave of him, slipping out of the parlour, ethereal as a spirit in her silver gauze gown. She cast Robert one sweet, smiling glance backward, but it was a look that promised nothing. My heart eased a little. She was not as guileless as she appeared; she knew her own power. Already Robert burned for her and she was in no hurry to give him what he wanted.

Lady Leigh looked gratified too. It was she, I surmised, who had taught Catherine to value her own beauty and her worth. A rich, beautiful, *sensible* girl. I could not believe our good fortune. And at that moment another woman approached Robert, brushed past his arm with deliberate intent to attract his attention, and he barely noticed her, murmured an apology and walked away as though in a daze.

Lady Leigh and I looked at each other in mutual understanding and pleasure.

'I do believe,' she said, 'Catherine has captured his heart already.'

'I do believe,' I said, 'that you are correct.'

The mummers came then, full of good will and ale, and the evening descended into boisterous merry-making whilst outside the snow fell softly like a benediction on Robert's future.

CHAPTER 5
Lucy

August

Lucy put her book aside and lay back on the sun lounger, eyes closed, face tilted up, feeling the warmth on her skin. It was still early but the sun was hot. She wasn't sure how the first week at Gunpowder Barn had passed so quickly. Apart from calling her parents, she had barely spoken to anyone. One day had become two and then more as she sat outside on the terrace, ate the food that Cleo and Finn had left for her and read her way through the pile of paperbacks that Cleo had also thoughtfully provided. Once she had stopped her body seemed disinclined to start moving again, as though she was truly resting for the first time in months if not years. She slept a great deal and she did not dream at all. The ghosts and nightmares that had stalked her first day and night at Gunpowder Cottage had vanished and the barn felt warm and welcoming. She could see why it had a near-perfect score on TripAdvisor.

She saw Finn and Geoffrey a couple of times in the distance, heading down the valley for a walk, and sometimes she spotted Finn working on the garden excavation: digging and measuring, writing notes, taking pictures. On a couple of occasions he was accompanied by a tall, lanky youth with very dark hair who was carrying what looked like a sieve and a selection of trowels and brushes. Finn looked up and saw her watching and gave her a wave. Lucy scuttled off as though she had been caught spying on them. But Finn was true to his word; he didn't drop in and Lucy was aware of a vague sense of disappointment. A couple of times she also heard the low hum of a digger and guessed that the archaeologists had called in some heavy machinery but it was out of sight at the bottom of the valley. They had not yet started to explore Clarabelle the donkey's paddock and hadn't undertaken any more work at the front of the barn, where the duck pond lay weed-filled and placid beneath a summer sky.

She hadn't been completely alone. There had been loads of calls to deal with from her parents, relatives and friends checking up on her. Cleo called every day. There was nothing from her agent, whom she suspected would quietly let her go, or from the majority of her orchestra colleagues. Perhaps they felt awkward about the sudden dismal change in her career fortunes. Some, she thought, were probably superstitious that it might happen to them as well.

'Fair weather friends,' Cleo had said stoutly, when Lucy had told her. 'You're better off without them.' And Lucy was curious to find that she did feel freer, lighter in some ways, without the constant pressure of planning and schedules and work. It reminded her of the long-forgotten childhood summer holidays before the practising had got too intense, when the drowsy end days of July and August were for fun and adventure.

Her phone rang – Verity's number. And there was her aunt, sounding as crystal-clear as though she was in the next room. 'How are you, darling? Settling in all right?'

'I'm good,' Lucy said. 'Enjoying being lazy.' She felt a rush of pleasure. 'It's lovely to talk to you, Aunt Verity. Better than emailing. How's your schedule going?'

'Well,' Verity said succinctly, 'I'm in Kalgoorlie for a conference next week and after that I'm heading to Mount Isa before coming home. Will you still be at Knightstone in September, do you think?'

'I'm not sure,' Lucy said evasively, and Verity laughed. 'You don't want to talk about it. I get that. I can only imagine how tough this is for you. Well, I won't tell you what to do, but if you want to chat any time, leave me a message and I'll call you.'

'Thank you, Aunt Verity,' Lucy said, feeling deeply grateful that Verity understood. 'I'll do that.'

'Good.' Verity, always brisk, had seen no need to labour the point. 'I hope you've got everything you need? I couldn't believe it when you emailed to say that Finn needed to stay in the cottage because Geoffrey is too neurotic to go inside the barn.'

'Dogs can be very sensitive,' Lucy found herself defending the Labrador, 'and to be fair to Geoffrey I did experience some odd events at the barn when first I was here.' She thought that Verity, supremely practical, might dismiss this out of hand but to her surprise, her aunt picked up on it.

'What happened?' Verity asked. 'What did you experience?'

'Well, amongst other things, I thought I saw the ghost of a woman,' Lucy said, feeling foolish even as she admitted the least peculiar of her experiences. 'Though that wasn't in the barn but in the orchards. She was wearing a Tudor-style gown and her name was Catherine. And then the same woman invaded my dreams a couple of times; it was very vivid, almost like being possessed.' Unnerved by Verity's silence at the other end of the phone, she added: 'But I'm putting it all down to exhaustion and my medication rather than anything else.'

'Hmm,' Verity said, after a moment. 'It's an odd coincidence but Knightstone was once the property of Robert Catesby, and his wife was called Catherine.'

'Do you know that for sure?' Lucy felt winded and slightly scared. She'd only just managed to rationalise away the whole experience and here was Verity telling her that she might not be imagining it after all. 'I mean, I know you've always thought there was a connection between the cottage and the Gunpowder Plot, but is there any evidence?'

'It was the last thing that Charlie Macintyre discovered before he was killed,' Verity said. 'He was working on the documentary history behind the garden project and found some charters relating to the granting of the Knightstone estate to Robert Catesby in 1599 or thereabouts. The details are in the paperwork Finn has now.'

'I think Finn prefers to concentrate on the practical side of the work at the moment,' Lucy said, thinking of the way that Finn was out at all hours and in all weathers, concentrating fiercely on the project on the ground as a way, perhaps, to deal with his grief.

'Yes, that's understandable,' Verity conceded. 'He was always the hands-on one, though Charlie would muck in when needed. I did ask Finn last week whether he needed me to draft in anyone else to help on the archives but he said rather shortly that he'd got a student working with him now and that for the time being he preferred to focus on the archaeology.'

'He did ask if I'd like to help with the paperwork side of things,' Lucy admitted, 'but I wasn't keen. I didn't think he'd appreciate a rank amateur getting involved.'

Verity snorted. 'He wouldn't have asked you if he didn't mean it. Finn's very direct.'

'I'd spotted that,' Lucy said dryly.

'How is he?' Verity's tone had changed. Lucy sensed her aunt's concern but also a note of affection. She'd already acknowledged to herself that Finn had to be a good guy for Verity to employ him, especially given that he had the run of the place whilst she was abroad. But it seemed Verity more than rated Finn; she liked him as well.

'I don't really know,' Lucy admitted. 'I don't see much of him. He's obviously still very cut up over Charlie's death. That must have been a horrible time.'

'It was ghastly,' Verity said. 'I wasn't at the cottage the weekend it happened but I came down as soon as I heard. They were so close, Finn and Charlie, and they made a great team. The strange thing was that Charlie was always such a careful driver. He flatly refused to drive my car, saying he'd stick to the Land Rover. Finn said he'd had a near miss as a teen driving in Scotland; he almost killed someone, apparently. So for him to have crashed off the road seems completely incomprehensible.'

They chatted a bit more, sharing family news and talking about Verity's next consultancy which would be advising on mine reclamation projects.

'I'll be based in the UK for a while,' Verity said. 'It'll be great to be home for a change.' She rang off with a request that Lucy should tell Finn that she had checked the ground surveys from the time the barn had been converted and could confirm that there had been no obvious anomalies suggesting garden features. 'I like his idea of that flat platform being a part of the design,' she said, 'but the only thing that showed up was a sort of pit in the centre of the floor.'

'Did you open it?' Lucy asked.

'No,' Verity said. 'It was sealed up and there was no indication of anything underneath. We thought it was probably a storage pit for fruit or vegetables dating back to the Victorian kitchen garden.'

'Right,' Lucy said. 'I'll tell Finn.' She felt her heart sink a little at the thought she would need to go and speak to him. She'd deliberately kept away from the cottage, not wanting Finn to think she pitied him and was dropping around to try to cheer him up, or equally that she was needy and wanted company herself. She sighed as she realised she was overthinking things as usual. She made a mental note to go to see him later but didn't specify when 'later' would be.

After chatting to Verity she fancied a cup of tea but found that she'd run out of milk. It was time – finally – to walk into the village and stock up on her supplies at the shop. She felt an odd combination of apprehension and excitement to be venturing out after a week on her own. It made her laugh wryly. Only a week of her own company and she was already turning into a hermit.

Lucy put on her espadrilles, grabbed her bag and headed out of the door. The cool of the early morning had long gone and she went back for a sun hat and a pair of huge sunglasses. The barn, it transpired, had a number of locked storage cupboards where Verity kept everything from bin liners to antihistamines, including plenty of spare clothes and accessories.

'Help yourself to anything you like,' she'd told Lucy. 'And if you need stuff from the cottage, I'm sure Finn wouldn't mind. He might even invite you round for supper.'

'I'm good, thanks,' Lucy had said quickly, and Verity had laughed as though she had known somehow that Lucy was deliberately avoiding Finn.

The public footpath from the road by the cottage led downhill and past the front of Gunpowder Barn before heading up the other side of the valley directly into Knightstone village. It was slightly longer but much quieter than taking the road. At first it wound through a small beechwood that bordered the duck pond but then it forked right, a paved track lined with high hawthorn hedges interwoven with wild dog roses, brambles and convolvulus. Foxgloves and valerian sprouted along the ragged edge of the grass and the sweet scent of vanilla from the flowers hung faintly on the air.

As she walked, Lucy thought back over what Verity had said about Robert Catesby. Was it really a coincidence that he had lived at Gunpowder Cottage and that his wife had been called Catherine? Despite the heat of the day, Lucy felt a chill ripple of unease as she remembered her dreams. A woman called Catherine, in Tudor costume… Yet surely if the barn was haunted, someone else would have seen the ghost, and there was no suggestion that anyone had.

The sound of children's voices drew her back to the present and she saw that the fields that bordered the path were giving way to newly built houses. The scent of flowers was replaced by the more varied smells of barbecues, hot tarmac and mown grass. Another path opened out on the left, leading to a neat village green and children's playground. This was all new since Lucy had last visited Knightstone so she walked slowly over the grass to the car park, where she also found a long, white-painted building that proclaimed itself the village shop and café.

The relative darkness inside the shop after the bright sunlight outside made Lucy blink and feel slightly dizzy. By the time she focussed a young woman had come out from the back and was smiling at her. 'Hello! Would you like some homemade lemonade? It's a hot day to be out walking in the full sun.'

Lucy accepted gratefully and sat down in a shaded corner of the café where there was a breeze from the open window. The woman brought her the drink, ice cold and delicious, and served it with a frankly curious gaze. 'Are you Verity's niece Lucy?' she asked directly. 'We wondered if you really existed because no one had seen you.'

Lucy was slightly taken aback. There was something not quite friendly in her tone but she told herself she was being oversensitive. 'Hi,' she said. 'Yes, I'm Lucy Brown. I've just been taking it easy for a few days, settling in, you know? It's nice to have a rest.'

The girl nodded. 'It's nice to meet you,' she said, but her tone sounded slightly grudging. 'I'm Persis Redfern.' She looked about nineteen, tall, willowy with a wild burst of fair hair carelessly pulled back into a bun. She pulled a face. 'Persis is a stupid name, I know, but my mum read a book with a heroine called Persis when she was pregnant and,' she shrugged, 'that was that.'

It was an explanation Lucy felt she had probably given any number of times. 'It sounds classical,' she said. 'Unusual in an interesting way.'

'Thanks,' Persis said unenthusiastically. 'Everyone calls me—'

'Sis?' A man poked his head around from the shop. 'You've got customers.'

'There you go,' Persis said, shrugging again. 'Sis. I ask you. Strangers think I'm related to the entire village. Still, one of my brothers is called Gabriel after the archangel, so he didn't escape either. Can I get you anything else? A scone? Cake?'

'I'd love a chocolate croissant,' Lucy suddenly felt ravenous, 'and I must have a browse in the shop when I've drunk my lemonade.'

'Sis!'

Persis pulled a face and sped away, leaving Lucy to finish the drink and look around at the café. It was compact but airy, painted white like the outside, and decorated with

78

local art and crafts for sale. An amazing tapestry hung on the wall showing all the main features of the village: the church, the village hall, the war memorial, the row of thatched cottages... More amusingly it also featured various people's dogs, a cow called Doris, some sheep and a pond with multicoloured ducks. Gunpowder Cottage featured at the top left, and down a tapestry path into the hollow was the barn. It was completely charming.

'You should sell postcards of the tapestry,' Lucy said to Persis, when she came back with the croissant and butter. 'It's wonderful.'

'Loads of people worked on individual bits of it,' Persis said. She seemed to have recovered some good humour. 'It's a real piece of local storytelling.'

A group of hikers came in and she went over to take their order leaving Lucy to savour the croissant. 'Chocolate and butter,' Persis said with a grin, on her way back to the kitchens, 'is there a finer combination?'

Lucy ate the croissant slowly, resisted the idea of having a second one and licked the chocolate off her fingers before wandering through to the shop to browse. The deli section had some delicious looking soups, salads, bread and cheeses; she reflected that it was fortunate the weather was so warm that she didn't fancy hot food because she could live on this indefinitely. She added some cream-cheese-stuffed peppers, some speckled eggs and some locally-grown asparagus to her basket and went over to the counter where Persis was putting a chocolate Flake in a cone with a double scoop of pistachio ice cream. She handed the cone to a small child. 'There you are,' she said. 'Enjoy!'

'The food here is amazing,' Lucy said, smiling as she watched the little boy rush off with his treat, closely followed by the family dog who clearly had an eye to him dropping it.

'All homemade,' Persis said. 'You could make a hollandaise sauce,' she added approvingly, looking at the eggs and the asparagus, but Lucy shook her head.

'No,' she said. 'I really couldn't.'

Persis laughed. 'Ask Finn to show you,' she said. 'He's a good cook.'

Lucy wondered how Persis knew that and then chided herself. Maybe Finn gave regular dinners for everyone in the village or, more likely, when he and his brother had both been living and working at Gunpowder Cottage, they'd probably had friends round for meals. Finn didn't seem so sociable now, taking long walks with just Geoffrey for company, and who could blame him?

'I suppose Finn knows a lot about fruit and vegetables,' Lucy said, 'especially if you want them cooked to a historical recipe.'

Persis laughed. 'Finn knows a lot about all sorts of things,' she said. She sounded warm. 'He's amazing. When Charlie was alive, I used to hang out with them a lot.' She stopped, biting her lip. 'It was different then.'

'I can imagine,' Lucy said. 'I'm very sorry. Was Charlie a good friend of yours?'

'We were dating,' Persis said. 'Just casual.' She blinked, avoiding Lucy's eyes, putting the items through the till. 'I hadn't had the chance to get to know him well and then… Well, I guess you know what happened.'

'Yes,' Lucy said. 'It must have been awful for all of you.'

'The whole village was in shock,' Persis said. 'I mean, accidents do happen around here sometimes. The roads can be dangerous and people can drive too fast. But not Charlie! He was really steady. He was fun – don't get me wrong, but you knew he was sound.'

Lucy stowed the eggs carefully on the top of her bag and on impulse picked up a bunch of freesias and sweet peas, thinking that they would add a splash of colour to the barn as well as some gorgeous scent.

'I'm very sorry,' she said again. 'It's obviously hit Finn hard and I imagine it's been difficult for a lot of people, including you. Ghastly accidents like that are so difficult to get your head around because they feel so utterly pointless and unfair.'

'Thanks.' Persis gave her a brief glance and a smile. 'Yeah, it's been tough. But,' she stretched, 'it's summer now, I guess, and we all need to try to move on. It's a shame Finn decided to carry on with the research and the dig. It would have been better in a way if he'd just left after Charlie died.'

Lucy was startled, both by her words and the sudden fierceness of her tone. 'I heard he wanted to finish the job as a tribute to his brother,' she said carefully.

'I expect he did,' Persis said, 'but it would have been better if he'd just left it.' She slammed the till shut rather sharply, making it clear that the discussion was over.

Lucy took the hint. 'I picked up more than I'd intended,' she said, looking dubiously at the shopping bags. 'But it's no wonder when there's so much delicious food here.'

'We can deliver it all to the barn I suppose,' Persis offered.

'That's quite a lot to carry, especially with you having been ill. I'll keep the flowers in water, if you like, and bring the bags down at the end of my shift.'

It felt like an olive branch after her previous shortness and Lucy took it as such. 'That's so kind of you,' she said, wondering at the same time who had told Persis she'd been ill. No doubt it was something else that the whole village knew though she couldn't imagine either Verity or Finn gossiping about her.

'No problem,' Persis said. 'If you want to take a look at the heritage centre while you're up here,' she added, 'it's in the old schoolroom, just around the corner on Church Street. It's got the original historical map that inspired the village tapestry. I have to give it a shout-out,' she added, 'because Gabe works there but to be honest it's not much to write home about.'

'Who? Oh, your brother.' Lucy found the half-hearted recommendation amusing. She hadn't been intending to explore the village that day but thought that as she didn't have any bags to carry home she might as well take a look around. It would be interesting to see what had changed in the fifteen years since she was last in there, not that she remembered it terribly well.

Someone else came into the shop and Lucy smiled her thanks and went out into the sunshine. The shrieks of children at the playground nearby taken with the brightness of the day, the chatter of groups at the picnic tables on the green and the scent of barbecues made her feel a part of the life of the village. She'd worried that she might be lonely, sequestered down at Gunpowder Barn, but instead she felt a surprising sense of connection.

She turned right along the road into the middle of the village, over the crossroads and past the Knights of Old pub which featured a sign showing a fearsome-looking crusader wielding a broadsword. Persis' directions were decidedly inaccurate for there was no museum or heritage centre in sight, only rows of chocolate-box thatched cottages on either side of the street, built from the local white chalk, festooned with hollyhocks and delphiniums. Really, Lucy thought, could any village be as picture-perfect as Knightstone appeared? Then she saw the brown sign indicating a museum pointing right, opposite the church, and turning down the lane, the long, low outline of the former schoolhouse was revealed. It had been smartly renovated with big windows and fresh white paint, as though trying to tempt visitors inside, and as Lucy approached, a man of about her own age popped out, rake-thin, tall and slightly stooped. Lucy wondered whether he deliberately tried to minimise his height or if he spent much of his time hunched over books.

'Hello,' he said eagerly. 'Would you like to look round? Entry is free.'

He sounded slightly too keen. Lucy found it a little off-putting. This, she thought, must be Gabriel. His untidy cloud of fair hair and grey eyes reminded her sufficiently of Persis to make identification easy.

'Yes, please,' Lucy said. 'You must be Gabriel,' she added.

'I met your sister in the shop and she recommended that I take in the museum whilst I was here.'

The man's face lit up. 'Oh, great!' He stood aside to usher her through the door with rather more formality than the occasion seemed to warrant. Seeing that the interior of the heritage centre was empty, Lucy couldn't help wondering how many tourists were drawn there. No wonder Gabriel was lurking on the doorstep trying to lure people in.

The building, she discovered, was rather Tardis-like. It had appeared from the outside to be all on one level, yet now she could see a central spiral wooden stair rising to an upper floor. The long, low ground floor was lined on three sides with display cases. The fourth held the reception desk and a barrage of filing cabinets. The walls were covered with black-and-white photographs of Knightstone, some of which looked as though they dated back to the early part of the nineteenth century.

'There's lots of books and newspaper cuttings and old parish records in the files,' Gabriel said, 'but those are mostly for family history research. If you're just interested in getting a taste of local history, check out the display cases. I'm working my way through them trying to update the collection,' he waved an arm around vaguely, 'but there are lots of items and they haven't been properly catalogued or stored over the years. Unfortunately, there hasn't been an official curator before—' his tone held a professional's disdain for the amateurs who had preceded him, 'so it's taking a lot of time. Plus there's not much money, of course—' He smiled engagingly, dipping his head in the direction of a milk churn that had an opening in the top for donations.

Lucy took the hint, retrieved a five-pound note from her purse and pushed it into the churn. She heard it whisper down into the depths. Gabriel looked gratified. 'Thanks,' he said. 'I know I said it's free entry—'

'But the arts are underfunded and need supporting.' Lucy smiled at him. 'It's okay, I understand that. I'm… I used to be a musician.'

A sound from the floor above alerted her to the fact that they were not alone in the building after all.

'There's an exhibition upstairs,' Gabriel said, following her gaze. 'A local artist, Marilynne Redfern, aka my aunt.' He pointed to a flyer stuck to the wall that showed a painting of the Knights of Old pub sign above the name, MARILYNNE REDFERN, ARTIST AND SCULPTOR. Gabriel smoothed his hair. 'She's very good,' he said. 'It's not just nepotism.'

'It's good to support local creatives,' Lucy said. 'And I'm sure she is.' Gabriel, she thought, was an odd mixture of diffidence and boastfulness. 'Did Marilynne design the pub sign?' she asked. 'I saw it as I walked past. It's very striking and… erm… an unusual name.'

'Marilynne can tell you all about her artwork when you go upstairs,' Gabriel said. 'She does lots of signboards for businesses hereabouts. As for the pub name, it comes from the Order of the Knights Hospitaller. They are the Knights that the village is named after.'

'I had no idea,' Lucy said. 'I've been coming here for years but no one mentioned the Knights Hospitaller before. Who were they?'

'Well, they *weren't* the Knights Templar for a start,' Gabriel said, slightly aggressively, as though Lucy had mistaken the two. 'People always want to know about the Templars but the Hospitallers were *just* as interesting.'

'I'm sure they were,' Lucy said.

'The Hospitallers had a grange here at Knightstone,' Gabriel said. 'A monastic settlement.' His eyes gleamed with the passion of talking about what was clearly his favourite subject. 'In this case it was a farm. There was a granary, a hall and a brewhouse in the village, all on the site of what is now the pub. We've found evidence of some of the buildings but most of it lies beneath the current building.'

'Hence the "Knights of Old" name for the pub.' Lucy nodded. 'I see.'

'After the dissolution of the monasteries by Henry VIII, the monastic grange became an inn for travellers,' Gabriel said. 'The Order of the Knights Hospitaller was formally dissolved in 1540 although Henry's daughter Queen Mary did revive it for a brief while less than twenty years later.'

'Mary tried to restore Roman Catholicism in England, didn't she?' Lucy said.

'That's right.' Gabriel beamed his approval. 'The Hospitallers' land and property was restored to them although here in Knightstone it was too late. The inn had been sold into private hands and as far as we know, the Knights never came back here.' He sounded personally disappointed. 'And, of course, when Queen Elizabeth came to the throne it was all over for them anyway. Unlike her father, Elizabeth didn't suppress the order but she once again confiscated all their property and they became dormant, in England at least.'

'Fascinating,' Lucy said. She thought that Gabriel looked

set for a long history lesson but fortunately an elderly couple came in and he moved away to greet them, leaving Lucy feeling both relieved and rather trapped. There wasn't much that attracted her interest in the glass display cases and she couldn't see the original of the tapestry map that Persis had mentioned. She wondered if she could edge out of the door whilst Gabriel was distracted.

She was about to make a break for it when she spotted a painting high up on the wall in a dark corner. It seemed oddly hidden away, tucked into the shadows. Drawing closer she stood on tiptoe and squinted up at it, resisting the urge to pick up a nearby lamp and use it for illumination. Instead, she got out her phone and pressed the torch icon.

The picture was dark and dirty, looking as though it was composed of nothing other than shades of green and brown, covered in an uneven varnish. It showed a little manor house built around three sides of a courtyard, with a parterre garden showing neat box hedges. Leaning closer, Lucy peered at the curly golden writing in the left-hand corner and saw that it read: *Knightstone Manor, the property of Henry Lancing Esq.* A date of 1723 was painted below. The picture appeared to be unsigned.

The door of the heritage centre shut with a sharp snap and Lucy jumped and turned around, but there was no one there. A long, cold shiver ran down her neck. She felt as though she was being watched. It was an acutely disturbing sensation. Yet at the same time she was aware of hearing the murmur of Gabriel's voice, as he and the other visitors chatted to Marilynne upstairs. It was as though she was caught between two parallel worlds, one completely normal whilst the other was full of unseen shadows and threats…

A smothering sense of panic rose in Lucy but she fought it back, drawing in a deep breath and fixing her gaze on the display cabinet in front of her whilst she tried to calm down. She told herself that there was nothing wrong. She was tired after her walk and being out in the sun. It was natural she should feel a little off-kilter…

'Our toy collection is very special.' It was Gabriel's voice.

Lucy jumped for real as he popped up beside her. Evidently, he had left the other visitors upstairs and come to check up on her. She realised that he was referring to the items in the display case and focussed properly on it. Toys that must have belonged to earlier generations of Knightstone children were laid out under the glass: a rattle, a carved wooden soldier with the paint of his uniform almost worn away, a spinning top, hoops, playing cards, a battered doll that had quite the most evil grin she had seen and disjointed puppets on dusty strings. She couldn't for the life of her see what was so special about this rather sad collection of objects but Gabriel sounded quite smug.

'The Lancings, who owned Gunpowder Cottage before your aunt bought it, found the toys in a box in the loft and donated them to the history society, as it was then,' Gabriel said. 'Some of these items date back to the seventeenth century, if not before. That—' he pointed to the rattle, 'was probably for a Tudor baby. It's made of gold with little ivory balls inside.'

'An expensive gift for a baby,' Lucy said. 'I expect he or she probably only wanted to chew on it.' She pointed to the painting of Knightstone Manor. 'That's a picture of Gunpowder Cottage when it was a manor house, isn't it?' she said. 'I noticed that Henry Lancing was named as owning the estate.'

'The Lancings owned the manor estate from 1662 until they sold it to your aunt,' Gabriel said precisely. 'They demolished most of the old house in the mid-eighteenth century, soon after the picture was painted. Henry Lancing lost a lot of his money in bad business speculations and the house fell into dereliction as a result. A smaller cottage was far easier for the family to renovate and maintain.'

'It's interesting to see what it looked like originally,' Lucy said. 'What was it – Tudor? Medieval?'

'A bit of both probably.' Gabriel sounded slightly bored as though the history of domestic architecture was nowhere near as interesting to him as the Knights Hospitaller. 'There are very few records pertaining to the house; it was quite unremarkable as far as we know.'

'I see,' Lucy said, finding his dismissive attitude rather grating. 'And I see it was originally called Knightstone Manor.'

Gabriel laughed heartily. 'Well, Robert Catesby was hardly going to call it Gunpowder Cottage *before* the Gunpowder Plot, was he? That would rather have given the game away! Haha!'

'I had assumed it was given the name later,' Lucy said coldly, 'because of the Catesby connection.'

Gabriel nodded. 'The name was given to the place in the eighteenth century,' he said. 'There was an antiquarian who lived hereabouts who claimed to have found evidence that

Knightstone Manor had been the home of Robert Catesby, and apparently the Lancings rather liked the notorious connection, so they adopted the name. There's no proof of any of this, though. Antiquarians weren't like historians,' he added loftily. 'They embraced the local myths and folklore as fact and caused a lot of confusion as a result. You know the local hillfort called Arthur's Castle?' he continued, and when Lucy nodded, explained: 'The same antiquarian renamed that around the same time. Previously it had been called Knightstone Camp but this guy was convinced there was a link to King Arthur.' He snorted. 'As if Arthur even existed!'

'I like to think that he did in some shape or form,' Lucy said. She was starting to see that Gabriel was a terrific intellectual snob. 'I mean, not all legend and folklore is true but often it does have a kernel of fact at the core, and that's interesting, isn't it?'

'It's not *history*,' Gabriel said, 'it's storytelling.' His tone implied how little he rated such things.

'My aunt Verity told me wonderful stories when I was a child,' Lucy said. 'It was quite inspiring.'

'She's still busy telling stories now,' Gabriel said, showing a flash of the sharpness she had seen earlier in his sister Persis. 'All this talk of a Tudor garden at Gunpowder Cottage!' He swung around to point at the picture. 'You don't see any evidence of it in the painting, do you? It's nonsense!'

'You seem very vehement,' Lucy said, disliking him more and more each time he opened his mouth. 'If the house was derelict, maybe the garden had become overgrown and lost.'

'Perhaps.' Gabriel smiled with kindly condescension.

'I think it's a wild goose chase, to be honest, and I told your aunt that when she first raised the idea of an excavation. I always feel that history should be left to the *experts*.'

'Finn Macintyre *is* an expert in historical gardens, isn't he,' Lucy said, 'and wasn't his brother Charlie also a professional historian? And by the way, my understanding is that he *had* found proof of the connection to Robert Catesby.' She was starting to get genuinely annoyed now. Gabriel's insistence that he knew better than everyone else was infuriating. She suspected he was bitter because he hadn't been invited to be a part of the investigation. 'Anyway,' she said, 'as Finn has found some archaeological evidence, perhaps we should wait and see.'

Gabriel opened his mouth to respond but possibly fortunately, they were interrupted.

'Excuse me, Gabe.' A tall, grey-blonde woman of about sixty had appeared at the top of the stairs to the upper storey, waving to get their attention. She was swathed in shapeless clothes and various floating scarves, and smelled of a mixture of stale cigarette smoke and strong perfume.

'I'm so sorry but I've got a problem with my easel – could you come and help me out?' She smiled at Lucy. 'Apologies for barging in on the conversation.'

'Not at all,' Lucy said, with feeling.

'I'm Marilynne,' the woman continued, 'Marilynne Redfern. The artist.' She paused.

'How do you do?' Lucy said.

Marilynne waited, as though expecting Lucy to say that she recognised her, or had heard about her art, or something to acknowledge her importance, and when Lucy didn't, she smiled a little tightly. 'I assume you're Lucy Brown, Verity's niece?' she said. 'I do hope you'll be happy staying at Gunpowder Barn although I think it *quite* unlikely. It's not a happy place. Not at all.' And with that she whisked back out of sight, snapping, 'Gabriel, come!' over her shoulder, rather as though her nephew were a dog.

'Excuse me,' Lucy said to Gabriel. 'I must be getting back. Thanks for the history lesson.'

'Anytime you'd like to learn more, give me a shout,' Gabriel said, missing the sarcasm. 'I'm a qualified blue badge guide and I take tours and trips around the village on a regular basis.'

Lucy could think of few things that would be worse. 'That's very kind,' she said, 'but I've only a passing interest in the village's history and I won't be staying here long.' She gave him a brief smile. 'Thanks very much – don't let me keep you.'

She stepped out into the sunshine and it felt like a blessing as the warmth wrapped around her. The Redfern family, she reflected, were all rather odd in their own ways. Marilynne had a faintly sinister air about her, Persis' mood seemed to turn at any moment and Gabriel was as pompous as a stuffed museum piece. But then every family had their own idiosyncrasies and she could hardly accuse anyone else of being moody.

On impulse, rather than turning back into the village, she took the footpath that led up past the pub and to the iron gates of the churchyard. They swung open at the touch of her hand and she followed the cobbled path to the church door, turning when she was in the shade of the porch to look back down the hill onto the village roofs, all thatch and tile, clustered below. She hadn't noticed before that the church was directly above the Knights of Old pub. As Gabriel had said the pub was built on the site of the Knights' presbytery, she wondered whether the church grounds had also been linked to the monastic grange at one time. Perhaps some of the Knights had even been buried here...

The churchyard, however, looked to contain more modern burials and tombstones. She couldn't find anything older than the seventeenth century although there were some stones half-buried in the turf that looked ancient. In the porch she found a churchyard trail that helpfully explained that due to weathering, the inscriptions on all the oldest graves had been lost but there was a rather fine memorial stone from the late sixteenth century in the north-east corner that had been protected because it was beneath one of the ancient yew trees. Wandering up there, Lucy couldn't at first locate the stone because the yews grew so close together and stooped low over the ground; pushing beneath the branches she found herself in a sort of green cavern whose floor was carpeted with sharp fallen needles. The stone, so much smaller than the memorial she had been expecting, seemed to be made of the local sarsen rock, for it was a whitish-grey colour, pitted with lichen, and the incised letters were hard to pick out in the gloom. She had to run her fingers over them to be sure of the words: WHERE YOUR TREASURE IS, THERE WILL YOUR HEART BE ALSO. The name was illegible, but there was a date of 1598. Lucy wondered if it was a biblical quote. She wasn't particularly knowledgeable on such things.

She stood up, brushed the yew spines from her knees and stooped under the ancient boughs to emerge into the graveyard. A blackbird shot out of the tree overhead with a squawk of alarm. She heard voices carried to her on the breeze, footsteps on the cobbled path, but when she turned there was no one there. The wind felt winter-cold on her face and for a moment her head seemed to spin in much the same way it had when she had first walked into Gunpowder Barn. It was tiredness, she thought, making her feel first hot then cold. She needed to be careful. It was time to go home.

The same sense of someone watching her that she had felt in the museum ambushed Lucy quite suddenly as she went out of the graveyard onto the sunken path that led back to the road. She looked back over her shoulder but she was alone. The leaves on the trees that lined the track played hide and seek with light and shadow. Everything felt normal. And yet… She heard a crunch, as though the old, dead leaves of previous years that lay underfoot had been stirred by someone passing by, felt the sensation of skirts brushing past her and even thought she heard the whisper of a voice: *'I'm so glad you came…'* And she hurried down the ancient track to the road and normality.

CHAPTER 6

Anne Catesby

Stoneleigh, Warwickshire, Spring 1593

Catherine, on her wedding day, looked so beautiful I imagined even the angels would be dazzled. At the wedding breakfast before the ceremony she had eaten and drunk sparingly, unlike many of the guests, who were already cast away before the nuptials began. Now we were assembled at St Mary the Virgin in the village of Stoneleigh as Catherine and Robert married at the church door. Catherine promised to 'love, cherish and obey', giving Robert such a look of adoration that he actually blushed. Dame Alice Leigh, who was standing next to me, dug me in the ribs with her elbow.

'In my day we promised to be bonny and buxom in bed and at the board,' she whispered loudly, 'and I'll wager that is what your lad is thinking of at this moment.'

I winced at the words and the sharp point of the elbow. I was sure Dame Alice was right but she had been overheard by some of Robert's Wintour and Tresham cousins, who, already deep in their cups, found her outspokenness hilarious. The sniggers threatened to drown out the service.

I preferred to draw more spiritual comfort from the fact that the little church had stood on the village green from time immemorial and seen many changes. Although the marriage service was impeccably Protestant, which felt quite wrong to me, I knew that God was timeless and that He understood the words of faith no matter how they were expressed. I knew that this was the best thing for Robert, to carve a life for himself away from the religious trials and torments of both conscience and purse that had dogged previous generations of our family. He was now the son-in-law of the rich and influential Sir Thomas Leigh, with a beautiful wife and a bright future ahead of him. He could cast off the taint of recusancy and bask in the approval of a Protestant society.

When I stepped forward to congratulate the happy couple and to kiss Catherine's cheek, she caught my hands in hers and held them tight.

'Dear Lady Catesby,' she said, 'you have welcomed me into your family like a true daughter. I will always feel blessed to have you as a second mother.'

Pretty words; her eyes were gleaming with tears and I judged her to be sincere. Catherine, I had already learned, had a soft heart and a sentimental nature which only caused Robert to adore her more.

'My dear,' I said truthfully, 'I could not be happier for you or for my son. I wish you great joy.'

Catherine smiled demurely and slid her hand through Robert's arm, tripping off down the path in a flurry of spring blossom. Behind her walked her bridesmaid, her younger sister Anne, a very different young woman indeed, all dark eyes and bold gazes. Anne Leigh reminded me of myself in her self-possession and determination. Contrarily, I did not like her, thinking such forwardness was unbecoming at such a young age.

'Today has set Robert on a very different course to the one I might have imagined for him after his education at Douai.' A voice spoke in my ear. I turned to find my brother-in-law, Thomas Tresham, at my shoulder.

'I hope so,' I agreed pleasantly. 'We all want the best for our children, do we not, Thomas? It is a natural instinct.'

Thomas shook his head as though he were disappointed in me. This was no surprise. William and I had wanted to invite as few of our Catholic relatives as possible to the wedding but Thomas Tresham was difficult to ignore. Not only was he married to my sister Muriel, but he had grown up within my family at Coughton Court, educated alongside my brothers, after his own father had died young. Thomas was a man with a substantial reputation, a scholar and a philosopher, architect and builder. He stood out, like Robert, because he had both charm and an air of command. His ideas set fires in men's minds and because of that they would follow him to the ends of the earth; he was ardent and impassioned, especially about his Catholic faith, hence his disapproval that we had married Robert off to a Protestant wife.

Even when we had been children, I had recognised that Thomas was strong-minded, a leader. My parents, his guardians, admired him for it. He and I were very alike but what was considered a strength in a young man would never have been tolerated in a girl, of course, for we were expected to be compliant and my determined character was viewed as unfeminine. So whilst I was constantly reproved, Thomas was encouraged. It had made me resent him.

Thomas wore his Catholicism openly. Whilst William and I might take the mass in secret or even provide shelter for an itinerant priest, Thomas would go much further, dancing on the thin line between recusancy and rebellion. He saw it as a great game, I knew; he had been fined enormous amounts of money and imprisoned for his beliefs yet he deliberately seemed to want to draw attention to himself. Some of his correspondents were amongst the Queen's own courtiers and ministers, the highest in the land.

'I had such high hopes for Robert,' Thomas said, 'but clearly they run counter to yours.'

'If your hopes were to mould Robert in your image then I am glad you are disappointed,' I said. I felt angered that Thomas should judge us. 'Would you have Robert imprisoned and fined as you have been?' I demanded. 'As William has been? Or perhaps you see it as a noble end to be executed for treason like Edward Arden or our Cousin Francis?' My voice had risen; I fought back my indignation as I did not wish our conversation to draw attention. 'Times have changed, Thomas,' I said in a fierce whisper. 'We all know that Protestantism is the future. I want better than a half-life under constant suspicion for my children.'

Thomas put a soothing hand on my arm. 'You know that my only desire is for men to act according to their own conscience,' he said. 'I advocate no more than that.'

This I doubted. What Thomas really meant, I was sure, was that he wanted all men to realise that they should return to the true faith, and none more so than Robert. He was Robert's godfather as well as his uncle. Perhaps he genuinely believed that he had failed in his spiritual duty.

'Well,' I shook off his hand and dusted my sleeve, 'I can assure you that Robert is acting according to his own inclination with this marriage. Never more so.'

Robert was in fact kissing his new wife that very moment, with his Tresham cousins and various other younger members of the bridal party in keen encouragement. Someone gave a whoop and then the whole circle of them was laughing and cheering, raising a racket that was out of keeping in a churchyard yet full of such irrepressible high spirits that even Thomas smiled, albeit ruefully.

'Ah,' he said, 'the fierce passions of youth.' He looked at me, his dark gaze suddenly intent. 'Do you remember, Nan, when we were young and felt the same way?'

My heart beat a little faster. 'No,' I lied. 'I doubt I ever felt like that. I have always been of too practical a bent to be swept away by my feelings.'

Thomas smiled faintly. 'That is not how I recall it. 'Tis true you are a woman of great sense and practicality but you also possess strong feelings. In that we are very alike.'

Although this was only what I had been thinking a moment ago I did not want to discuss it with Thomas, least of all agree with him. Instead, I signalled with my eyes for Muriel to come and take her husband away but annoyingly, she was too busy flirting with William to pay attention. Muriel, a fairer, slimmer and gentler version of me had always been a favourite of his. In fact, I sometimes thought that had she not been betrothed to Thomas, William would have snapped her up in preference to me. I viewed them somewhat sourly for such a happy day, and prayed that Lady Leigh would soon deem it appropriate to lead the party back to the manor for the feast.

'Robert has a brilliant mind,' Thomas said, reverting, to my relief, to his previous topic. 'As his uncle, I have a keen interest in his education and future. I would not want him to waste his talents.'

'You need have no fears,' I said, still short. 'Robert is rich enough now to stock the finest library and thereby extend his education to his heart's content. As for his other talents, he will require them all to learn how to run his new estates, deal with his tenants and care for the family I am sure will come, and soon. Perhaps we may even see him as a Justice of the Peace one day.'

'I am sure he will become a pillar of Oxfordshire society.' There was amusement in Thomas' voice. 'He is to have the manor of Chastleton, William tells me, which is rich agricultural land.'

'It is a good estate,' I agreed. 'My mother-in-law wished him to have it, along with Knightstone and some others of her property and lands.'

I sensed Thomas stiffening a little as though something had startled him, yet when he replied, his tone was smooth. 'Knightstone as well?' he said. 'I had not realised. The late Dame Margaret had a great fondness for the place, as I recall.' He shifted. 'She was an admirable woman, was she not – pious, learned and with a great strength of faith. I found her inspiring in many ways.'

'She was a little *too* pious for me,' I said. My mother-in-law had been a dry fanatical stick of a woman, governed entirely by her religion. There had been no love, no humanity and no softness in her. I had not grieved for her. In fact, her death the previous year had been a relief in many ways for her cold shadow had been like a permanent mourning shroud over Ashby.

'I remember that you and she were close,' I said to Thomas now, 'for she was of your own heart in matters of religion. And I believe your grandfather took you to Knightstone as a child, did he not?' I stopped, for I had uncovered in my mind a long-buried but vivid childhood memory of my parents arguing fiercely, my father's voice a hushed angry whisper:

'*Anne, we cannot permit Sir Thomas to take the boy to Knightstone, least of all induct him into the Order of the Hospitallers! You know that that is treason!*' And my mother's reply:

'*You cannot forbid it, Robert. Sir Thomas has the right to pass on the prior's mantle to his grandson if he so chooses. The treasure must be kept safe for when the order rises again.*'

Strange words for a child to hear, and at the time I had been more concerned at the discord between my parents than the mysterious images they conjured. I had forgotten the conversation in the intervening years, but now the mention of Knightstone had brought it back to the surface of my mind. I remembered that there had been an odd atmosphere in the house for several days after that quarrel and that when Thomas returned my mother had seemed quietly pleased with whatever had passed whilst my father was loud and boisterous as though to persuade us by his false humour that there was nothing amiss at all.

That shadow, like so many other treasonous ones, had passed over us and vanished but looking at Thomas now I wondered what had happened on that fateful visit to Knightstone Manor. Thomas must have been about fifteen years of age at that time and his grandfather had died a few short months later. Old Sir Thomas, I knew, had been the last Grand Prior of the Order of the Knights Hospitallers of St John of Jerusalem during Queen Mary's reign. By 1559, the year when he had visited Knightstone, the order had had all of its properties and possessions confiscated by the new queen but whispers had abounded that some of its treasures had escaped her grasp and been taken to a place of safety…

'What are you thinking, Nan?' Thomas asked me, and I realised that I had been staring at him whilst I went through all those old memories in my mind.

'Why, nothing of importance,' I said lightly. 'I must go and prise your wife away from my husband, for Lady Leigh looks to us to return to the abbey for the feast.'

He nodded in acceptance of his dismissal. 'Of course,' he said. He touched my arm. 'I am glad Robert is to have Knightstone,' he said softly. 'He will be a splendid custodian of its treasure.'

There it was again, the word 'treasure', in uncanny echo of my thoughts. I looked into his eyes. He was smiling, guileless. Perhaps I was reading too much into his words with my half-memories of the Knights Hospitaller and their riches, but I thought not. I was sure that Thomas meant to unsettle me, as he had done all our lives.

As I walked away from him, I felt his gaze follow me and though I did not turn, I knew he was watching me.

'Come, husband,' I said, inserting myself between William and my sister Muriel, who were still chattering like magpies in the shadow of the church porch, 'it is time to toast the future happiness of our son.'

We followed the bridal party under the lych gate, across the springy grass of the village green and through the gates of the manor. The sun shone and I slipped my hand through William's arm and tried to feel content. Yet there was a cloud in my sky. I thought of Thomas talking about the other roads Robert might have taken, of his brilliance and his power to inspire men to a cause. A sensation close to fear tiptoed down my spine then. I knew in my heart of hearts that Thomas was pleased that Robert was to have Knightstone for reasons other than that it was a good estate. Something was hidden at Knightstone Manor and Thomas was glad that Robert would be its guardian.

I knew I should not interfere. Whatever secrets Knightstone held were best left undisturbed. But I vowed that should Thomas make any move to try to draw Robert into his web of secrecy and treason, then he would have to reckon with me first. Today marked a new beginning for Robert, a bright new dawn. I had been protecting my son all my life; I would not stop now.

CHAPTER 7

Lucy

It was late afternoon but still very hot so Lucy took the easiest route back home from the church, along the Portway, the road that led eastward out of the village. It had originally been made by the Romans, Verity had told her years ago, who had been annoyed that they couldn't build one of their absolutely straight roads along the base of the Berkshire Downs but had had to mirror the curve of the land. Verity, Lucy thought, had always made history intriguing rather than the dry topic it could seem when it wasn't brought to life. No matter what professionals like Gabriel thought, she'd rather have her aunt's stories any day.

The road was quiet and there was a path snaking along the grass verge beneath some shady ash trees. It was only a quarter-mile from the centre of Knightstone to the lane to Gunpowder Cottage, and when she reached it, Lucy turned back to look at the village with its jumble of new tiled roofs and old thatch, timbered cottages and modern brick. The square-set tower of the church peeked above the trees. The smooth line of the hills rose behind it against a sky dotted with tiny puffs of clouds. The scene looked reassuringly rooted in the landscape, as the village must have done for millennia.

There was something about Knightstone, Lucy thought, that made her think of time ticking by in a way that was different and more noticeable than when she was in London. There she had been busy, always hurrying from concert to practice or from her flat to the rehearsal room, and yet she was more conscious now of time passing and the weight of history than she had ever been before. London, after all, was a city based on layer after layer of history, yet it was only here that she felt she could actually reach out and touch the past...

Smiling slightly at the fanciful nature of her thoughts, Lucy turned down the lane to Gunpowder Cottage. Now that she had seen the eighteenth-century map she could visualise much more easily how it had been a part of a bigger manor house set about a courtyard, and how over time parts of that house would have been demolished to leave the core of the cottage that was there today.

The sun beat down through the dancing leaves, dazzling her. Lucy felt hot and a little bit dizzy again. She was going to have to be so careful until she was better, which was infuriating.

She could hear voices from the garden of Gunpowder Cottage and on impulse turned aside from the path down to the barn, thinking she should take the opportunity finally to thank Finn for all the food he had left for her on her first day as well as pass on Verity's message about the pit that the builders had found beneath the barn conversion.

She paused with her hand on the cottage gate, almost changing her mind when she saw that Finn, who was sitting in a striped deckchair, a beer in his hand, was deep in conversation with a couple of people and looked as though he wouldn't want to be interrupted. One of his companions was the young man of about nineteen or twenty whom she'd seen before, working on the dig, and the other was Persis. Presumably she had popped down with Lucy's delivery and dropped in for a drink as well; she looked rather at home curled up on the swing seat.

Geoffrey was chasing shadows and snuffling after scents in the flowerbeds, but he looked up, saw Lucy and gave a delighted yip, rushing across the garden to stick his nose through the gate. Finn looked across and smiled.

'Hi, Lucy,' he said. 'How are you doing?'

'Oh…' Lucy felt hot and bothered, more by the smile than the heat now. 'I'm fine, thanks. I just popped by to say thank you for the food you left me last weekend. It was really nice of you.'

'No problem.' Finn had come to join Geoffrey at the gate. 'How have you been getting on at the barn?'

'It's been lovely,' Lucy said. 'I haven't done much, just reading and sitting around. I've seen you and Geoffrey working hard, though—' She stopped, thinking that sounded as though she'd been spying on them, but Finn just laughed.

'Yeah,' he said, 'there's a lot to do now we've started expanding on the test pits. There's only Johnny and me working on it full time, although we do have a few other experts we can call on if needed.' He glanced over his shoulder as the young man who'd been sitting on the terrace, hearing his name, came over to join them. 'Johnny...' he said, 'this is Lucy Brown, Verity's niece. She's staying at the barn. Lucy, Johnny Robsart.'

'Hi, Lucy!' Johnny Robsart stuck out a hand to shake hers formally. He glanced briefly over her shoulder, as though his attention had been distracted by someone else standing there, an odd gesture that had Lucy looking behind her, but when she turned back Johnny was smiling at her and she wondered if she had imagined it.

'Hi, Johnny,' she said. 'Finn tells me you've been roped into the garden excavation. Are you an archaeologist?'

Johnny laughed. He was almost as tall as Finn and almost as good-looking though in a completely different way. Johnny was wiry and spare, where Finn was broad, and so dark that his eyes and hair were both almost black. He was also instantly recognisable from recent press reports and photographs of the marriage of Lizzie Kingdom, a former celebrity TV presenter and singer, which had been splashed across the papers and magazines. Lizzie, Lucy seemed to remember, had married Johnny's older brother and Johnny had been the best man.

'I'm only a student,' Johnny said, 'here to do the hard labour. I'm in my second year at uni and I was looking for a placement during the year so when this came up in the autumn, I jumped at the chance.'

'Johnny even blew out the opportunity to be in Umbria digging up Etruscan ruins this summer,' Finn said, 'so he could see the project through here.'

'Umbria's overrated,' Johnny said, grinning. 'This prom- ises to be much more exciting now that we've done so much of the preparation. Imagine what we might find – pleasure grounds, spiral mounds, viewing platforms, even a maze, perhaps...'

'Steady on,' Finn said, grinning. 'You're building a lot on a few footings and some bits and pieces of rubble.'

'Don't play it down,' Lucy said. 'You seemed keen enough when you showed Cleo and me all those sketches of what it might have looked like.' She saw the quizzical look Finn gave her and hurried on, feeling slightly self-conscious. 'It is odd, though, isn't it, that the garden doesn't show up on the old painting of the village? The one from the early eighteenth century.'

'You've been to the heritage centre, then.' Finn glanced over at Persis who wasn't showing any inclination to come and join them. She'd waved at Lucy when she'd first arrived but then gone back to swinging slowly backwards and forwards with her eyes closed. She looked like a cat lapping up the sunshine, Lucy thought.

'I have,' she said. 'Persis' brother Gabriel doesn't seem convinced about the garden. He told me there wasn't any documentary evidence to support it.'

'That's rubbish,' Johnny said. 'Charlie found plenty of references; it's just a matter of decoding them and piecing it all together.'

He glanced at Finn as though he was uncertain whether he should have mentioned Charlie or not, and Lucy wondered how Finn felt always hearing that silence after his brother's name, the weight and space of emptiness because Charlie was dead and no one knew quite what to say to him.

'The painting isn't exactly an accurate representation

of the village,' Finn said, ignoring any awkwardness, 'and perhaps the garden wasn't here for very long which might explain why it doesn't show up on any maps and was quickly forgotten. But yeah, Gabriel isn't our greatest fan, that's for sure.'

'I think he's more interested in the pre-Tudor history of the village, isn't he,' Lucy said, 'the Knights Hospitaller?'

Finn and Johnny exchanged a look that she couldn't quite interpret. 'There's such a mythology around the Knights,' Finn said. 'But again very little record of what, if anything, they did here.' He shook his head. 'Sorry, I should have asked if you'd like to come in and join us, Lucy. Can I get you a drink?'

'You need to try the local craft beer,' Johnny said, 'but only if you don't have any plans for the rest of the day. It's seriously strong.'

'Thanks, but I'm fine,' Lucy said, smiling. Persis was giving off the sort of vibe that suggested she wouldn't welcome an addition to the party and Lucy remembered the shopping that was probably sitting in the sun and the sweet pea bouquet that would be wilting by now.

'I need to get back to sort out the shopping Persis has brought me,' she said. 'I went a bit mad in the deli with so much great stuff to choose from.' She smiled at Johnny: 'I hope you enjoy the dig. I'll look forward to seeing what you find. Oh—' she paused, remembering Verity's request, 'I almost forgot – Finn, Verity asked me to let you know that when the barns were converted, they did a survey of the site and found some sort of pit beneath the buildings. It was sealed so they didn't see what, if anything, was inside, but as there were no results showing on the survey they assumed it was empty. The surveyor thought it was probably storage for produce from the Victorian kitchen gardens.'

Finn had been listening carefully and now he frowned. 'That's interesting,' he said. 'I'll ask Verity if I can see the original survey. I still think there may be some relics of the Tudor garden under the barn.'

'That would be amazing,' Lucy said, 'though it's a shame there's no access to the pit to help date it and see if there are any clues.'

'I'll come down and take a look anyway,' Finn said. 'If that would be okay? Once I've seen the plans and worked out where the hatch is under the current building, I can take some measurements and maybe use ground radar. We'll see. Anyway, thanks for letting me know.'

'No problem,' Lucy said.

'Actually, I wonder whether I could come down shortly,' Finn said suddenly, 'and pick up a book Verity says is on the shelves there? It's *The History and Antiquities of the Village of Knightstone* by Edmund Sharpe. Charlie had been working on it and there was a note in his files to check out something he referred to as "the black-and-white photos". I don't know what he meant but I didn't want to miss anything.'

'I haven't seen the book,' Lucy said, 'but there are all sorts of local history and natural history books down there. You're welcome to come and look for it.'

'Gabe says Edmund Sharpe has no historical credibility,' Persis drawled. Finally, she had uncurled herself from the swing seat and sauntered over to join them. 'He included folklore and myths and ghost stories in his books as though they were true. Personally, I think they might well be.'

Lucy realised that Edmund Sharpe must be the author Gabriel Redfern had mentioned to her earlier, the antiquarian who had claimed to have discovered the connection that Robert Catesby had to Gunpowder Cottage. She was more interested, however, in the look that Finn and Johnny exchanged. Clearly this was a conversation neither of them wanted to get into. Persis, however, seemed unaware of their reluctance.

'I believe in ghosts, and so does Geoffrey,' she said. She bent down to stroke Geoffrey's silky ears as she spoke. 'He sees things that other people can't. He knows there's something weird going on at the barn or why wouldn't he go in there?'

Out of the corner of her eye, Lucy saw Finn make a sharp movement. 'I don't think Geoffrey's eccentricities are the result of supernatural causes, Persis,' he said. 'Dogs develop all sorts of reactions to things for different reasons.' He gave Lucy an apologetic smile. 'We don't want to drive you away, Lucy.'

'Thanks,' Lucy said, thinking of her weird dreams and the insistent sense that there were, in fact, other presences around at the barn. 'I'm sure that, like Geoffrey, any weird experiences I have here will be the result of my own neurosis rather than anything supernatural.'

'Whatever.' Persis was looking at Johnny; it was fairly obvious that his was the attention she wanted. 'What do you think, Johnny?' she asked, looking at him slyly from out of the corner of her eye. 'You're supposed to be in touch with your paranormal side, aren't you?'

Lucy wondered what on earth she meant, but it was clear Johnny knew because he gave her a less-than-friendly look before deliberately turning away.

'I think several hundred reviewers can't be wrong,' he said. 'Gunpowder Barn has a 4.5 approval rating on the holiday rental site and no one mentions ghosts, as far as I know.'

Persis didn't seem fazed by his abruptness. 'I'm sure you're right,' she said, 'but even so there's a spooky atmosphere in Knightstone and Edmund Sharpe tuned in on that with his local legends. Wasn't he the one who believed in the myth that Odin and his ravens haunt the Roman road—' She broke off as Finn crushed the can of lager he was holding in his hand with a sharp crack. Lucy saw the whiteness of his knuckles clenched around the metal. He turned away without another word and Persis, after a half-scared, half-defiant glance at Johnny, shot out of the cottage gate and disappeared down the path.

'Phew!' Johnny released his breath sharply. He grinned ruefully. 'What a troublemaker that girl is. I could almost believe she deliberately wanted to wind us all up.' He glanced over his shoulder to where Finn was walking up the path to the house, face set, the can crumpled in his hand. Lucy followed his troubled gaze.

'What was all that stuff about Odin and ravens?' she asked.

'When Finn's brother was killed on the Wantage road,' Johnny said, 'the Roman road as it's called around here, some of the locals started trotting out the old legends about how the road is haunted and how Odin and his ravens appear out of the mists to force unwary motorists to their deaths.'

'Shit,' Lucy said. 'No wonder Finn's so angry. What a stupid thing for Persis to say.'

Johnny nodded. 'I'd better give Finn a bit of time to cool down,' he said. 'I think I'll go and take a swim.'

'And I'll go and take a look for that book,' Lucy said, 'but I won't give it to Finn yet.'

'Best not,' Johnny agreed. He raised a hand. 'It was great to meet you, Lucy. I'll see you around.'

He loped off towards the house and Lucy took the path in the opposite direction to the way that Persis had gone, down past Clarabelle's paddock to the barn. All other sounds were lost in the noise of rushing water that tumbled down the stream into the duck pond and Lucy relaxed a little. She'd found Persis friendly enough in the café, so her sly attempts to cause trouble had come as a surprise. Lucy wondered whether Persis had raised the issue of hauntings to scare her away – perhaps she had transferred her affections from Charlie to Finn, and saw Lucy as a threat – but then it was odd that she had been so thoughtless to hurt Finn with references to the place his brother had died. And what on earth had the loaded comments about Johnny 'being in touch with his paranormal side' meant? After a moment Lucy shrugged the thoughts away. It was too beautiful a day to feel haunted even if Persis' comments about the barn had struck a nerve.

Her shopping bags were waiting for her outside the

door. Persis had put them in the shade and wrapped the flowers in damp kitchen roll, which made Lucy feel slightly kinder towards her, but not much. She let herself into the barn and carried the bags inside. The first thing she saw was another bouquet sitting neatly on the worktop. Unlike the freesias and sweet peas, this one was very far from fresh. Composed of rotting flowers and dead grasses, it looked as though it had been taken from the compost heap at a cemetery.

Lucy recoiled at the smell of dying vegetation. It was gross, and someone had put it there deliberately; someone who had a key to the building or knew where a spare was kept. She felt shocked and repulsed, as though she was being stalked. Evidently someone didn't want her there and was making the point in a horrible way. The memory of Persis saying that Finn should have left Knightstone after Charlie had died rushed back to her, along with Gabriel's hostility to Verity's archaeological project. Perhaps there were others who felt the same way in the village, people who didn't like to see the old buildings and grounds disturbed?

With an exclamation of disgust, Lucy took the dead stalks outside and thrust them into the bin, slamming the lid down on them.

'Lucy?'

She spun round at the sound of Finn's voice. She hadn't seen him coming down the hill and now felt rather foolish for her violence to the compost bin.

'Hi,' she said, wiping her palms self-consciously down her jeans. 'Sorry, I didn't realise you were coming down now to collect the book or I would have waited for you.'

Finn looked at the drab, slimy strands of greenery that lay limply over the side of the bin. The smell of rotting vegetation hung in the air. 'What on earth was that?' he asked.

'Oh…' Lucy wasn't sure whether she wanted to explain to him or not. It felt too complicated. 'Someone left me a rather unpleasant welcome gift.'

Finn's brows snapped down. He opened the bin and peered at the wilting bouquet. 'What, someone left *that* on your doorstep?'

'It was inside the house,' Lucy admitted. 'I was thinking I should change the locks. It's okay when I'm inside because there's a bolt, but if someone has a key – or if they know where to find a spare—'

'Bloody hell!' Finn looked furious and intimidating. 'You should report it to the police!'

'I thought of that,' Lucy said, 'but I wondered whether it was just a bit of malice – you know, local people who don't like there being tourists staying here, or perhaps don't like the idea of the garden excavation?'

Finn fell into step with her as she walked back to the door. 'Maybe,' he said. 'I know there was initially some resentment about the barn being let, but quite a few properties around here are holiday lets and it doesn't cause any problems.' He rubbed the back of his neck. 'As for the dig, I know a few people thought I should have given up after Charlie died…' He lapsed into silence.

'Including Persis,' Lucy said. She opened the door and gestured to him to come in.

'Yeah, well, Persis was dating Charlie,' Finn said, 'so

it's understandable that she was very upset, even though it was only a casual thing from Charlie's perspective.' He grimaced. 'She's a bit of a lost soul, is Persis, to be honest. Her parents died when she was young which is how she and Gabriel ended up living with their aunt. I think she was more hooked on Charlie than he was on her and so I try to be nice to her when she comes round like she did this afternoon, but she makes it difficult to like her sometimes.'

'She certainly seemed set on stirring things up,' Lucy said. She took a glass vase off the kitchen shelf, half filled it with water and arranged the sweet peas in it. Their gentle scent filled the air. 'I need to put my shopping away,' she added, 'but please do look around for the book you mentioned. I think most of them are on the shelf over by the sofa with the visitors' book and all the leaflets on the local attractions.'

'Thanks,' Finn said. He wandered away towards the other end of the room and Lucy started to put the food away in the fridge and the cupboards. Even though her back was turned to him, she was very aware of Finn being in the room; his presence seemed to fill the space.

'Here it is,' Finn said after a moment and she turned to see he was holding in his hand a battered-looking hardback with a red leather cover and gold lettering on the spine. He flicked through it. 'Hmm, I hope I can find whatever it was that Charlie thought was useful in here. I mean, although I hate to admit it, Gabriel is right that Edmund Sharpe's writing isn't a reliable historical record. Charlie wouldn't have been using it as a primary source. Besides, he referred to photos, which is odd in an antiquarian book.'

'What a shame he didn't make it clearer,' Lucy said. 'Following his notes must be like trying to piece a puzzle together.'

Finn laughed. 'Charlie was the least-organised note-taker in the world,' he said, 'and he would have been the first to admit it. His files are in a hell of a mess. On the day he died, he rang me—' he swallowed hard and his voice was gruffer when he resumed, 'and said that he had something really exciting to tell me later, but he hadn't written down what it was, so I'll probably never know.' He ran a hand through his hair. 'Anyway, we'll piece it all together in the end one way or another.'

He turned the pages of the book absently and some loose sheets of paper tumbled out of what looked like a pocket at the back. Lucy bent to pick them up.

'Perhaps this is what he wanted you to see,' Lucy said. She unfolded the sheets and spread them on the worktop. 'They look like old newspaper cuttings. The date is just after the Second World War.'

Finn came across to look over her shoulder. He smelled of fresh air and something citrussy and clean. '*The view over the Ridgeway*,' he read aloud. '*Local flying hero James Abbott turns his hand to aerial photography.*'

The pages were in black and white, a white that had faded to an odd sort of sepia brown over the years whilst the print had turned grey. The pictures were smudgy with age but Lucy recognised the Uffington White Horse and the pudding basin roundness of Dragon Hill below it. All the pictures had been taken from the air; one had the wing of a plane in the foreground. She peered more closely.

There was a view of the railway line cutting across the vale, a miniature steam train puffing along. And next to it…

'That's Knightstone,' Lucy said, pointing. 'Look, there's Gunpowder Cottage and the valley and Clarabelle's field.'

'It says that James Abbot was an RAF pilot who was active in aerial reconnaissance during the war,' Finn said, scanning the columns of faded print rapidly, 'and that he's now working for the government, mapping post-war Britain from the air. *We are not permitted to print the more secret locations featured in James' work*, the article says, rather coyly, *but are happy to share some of the most picturesque scenes of our local landscape.*'

'I rather think he has shared something secret,' Lucy said. She peered closer at the image, pointing. 'Look there.'

Finn screwed up his eyes. 'Your sight must be very good. I can't see anything. The picture's too fuzzy.'

'Hang on a minute.' Lucy remembered seeing a magnifying glass in one Verity's boxes of miscellanea. She went into the utility room to fetch it and handed it to him. 'I spend so much time peering at musical scores,' she said. 'Or I used to do. I can spot small details on a page.'

Finn was looking through the glass. 'I see what you mean now. There's a shadow showing up on the paddock, isn't there, like a crop mark.' He looked at her. 'Sorry, I'm using jargon. A crop mark can show where a buried archaeological feature might be.'

'I know,' Lucy said, smiling. 'I've seen *Time Team*, although I will admit that's about the extent of my knowledge.' She pointed to the picture.

'There's another one on the grass by the barn,' she said,

'although that one is even fainter. Maybe if you could get hold of the original pictures, they might be a bit clearer. There might even be more of them. But it does hint at something beneath the ground, doesn't it?'

'It must have been a very dry summer that year.' Finn put the magnifying glass down and straightened. 'Fascinating. Well, I won't get my hopes up that it's garden-related but I will try and find the newspaper archive. We did check aerial photos from Historic England at the start of the project but maybe these are in a private collection.' He smiled at Lucy suddenly, a smile that was all the more stunning for being so unexpected. 'Thanks for spotting that, Lucy. I really appreciate it.'

'Oh, no problem.' Lucy felt flustered. 'Glad I could help. Let me know if you discover anything, won't you?'

'I certainly will.' Finn picked up the book and stowed the cuttings carefully back inside. Then he frowned. 'Think about calling the police over the break-in, won't you? And have you got the number of a locksmith? If not there's one on the board up at the cottage.'

'I'll find one and get straight on to it,' Lucy promised. The reminder of the dead bouquet cast a shadow over her pleasure in finding the cuttings for Finn. Suddenly she didn't want him to go, and judging by the way he lingered in the doorway, he felt the same.

'Here…' Finn took a card out of his pocket and handed it to her. 'My number's on there. Give me a ring if anything strange happens, anything at all, and Johnny, Geoff and I will be straight down to help out if you need us.'

'Thank you.' Lucy took the card, grateful both that Finn

had offered but also that he'd made light of it. She was used to coping on her own – Cleo would probably say she wasn't great at asking for help – but Gunpowder Barn was quite isolated and it was good to know she wasn't totally alone there.

Finn went out and she bolted the door after him, then immediately felt trapped and a bit lonely, which made her cross with herself. The big iron skeleton clock on the wall told her that it was a quarter to five; briefly she wondered what to do with the rest of the day. Being in the position of having time on her hands still felt odd. Seeing her violin case propped in the corner she felt a rush of apprehension mingled with longing. It was so long since she had played. Suddenly there was such a hunger in her for her old routines, the practise, the performance, the camaraderie of the orchestra.

She opened the case and took out the bow, tightening it a little. Then she picked up her violin. The old velvet lining of the case felt worn and comforting against her fingers but at the same time she felt butterflies in her stomach. She raised the violin, straightening her neck and relaxing her shoulders, balancing on both feet and making sure she was standing erect. She'd start with something easy to warm up; Beethoven's 'Minuet in G'.

The familiar notes came smoothly and easily, like old friends. Relief, sweet and heady, raced through her as the melody caught her and she started to feel the music possess her just as it always did. From Beethoven, she moved straight into Saint-Saëns' 'Introduction and Rondo Capriccioso'.

The arpeggios cascaded through the still air of the barn filling it with sound and life. And then it happened, without warning. An agonising twinge of pain shot through Lucy's right hand, cramping her fingers on the bow so that it spun away across the room and landed with a clatter against the window.

For a moment she stood frozen with shock and pain, and then she lowered the violin very carefully to place it gently on the table, rather as though she was laying it to rest. The excitement and the pleasure had gone. She had allowed herself to hope, to believe that she was getting better, that the pain had gone and she would be able to play again, and soon. Her spirits had soared with the music and then had come crashing down.

She felt numb and despairing. It was never going to happen. She had known that all along really. It was simply that for a moment she had allowed those secret hopes to resurface. Now she faced the fact that even if the pain did fade in time, she would never have the confidence in herself to stand up in a concert hall and play, knowing that at any moment, out of the blue, the cramp could paralyse her. She would be stalked by it, waiting for it, dreading it.

The despair in her deepened, as stark and hopeless as an empty void. And then a feeling grabbed her, a sensation so terrifying that for a moment she felt as though she was going to be enveloped by it and swallowed alive. It wrapped her about like a cold, dank, smothering blanket of wretchedness and she thought she would not be able to breathe. It was as though her own anguish had connected with someone else's and amplified into a huge and terrible force. A chill seemed to invade every crack and cranny of the barn as sudden as a plunge into icy water. Lucy felt a bone-deep cold; she would not have been surprised to see frost creeping over the surfaces and laying a white rime over the windows.

The sensation grew and swelled like a storm cloud, reaching out to embrace her. Lucy stumbled backward and came up against the wall, smooth against her hot palms. Now it seemed the whole barn was filled with this terrible sense of grief and loss. She wasn't sure how she could escape it. Her heart was racing. It felt only a step away, and then it would engulf her, suffocate her…

With her right hand she reached out and her fingers brushed the door handle. She grabbed it like a lifeline, turned it awkwardly and realised in horror that nothing had happened. The door remained firmly closed.

The bolt.

She groped for it, pulled it back, and almost fell sideways out of the door and into the courtyard. Immediately she felt the fresh air cut through the oppressive sensation that had threatened to stifle her. Her head cleared and she felt awake and alive again. She put her hands on her knees and drew in several deep breaths.

What the hell was that?

She didn't know whether it had come from within herself – a reaction to the shock and pain of playing the violin – or whether it was something else entirely, but whatever it was, it had terrified her.

She straightened up. The air was cooling a little as evening crept closer, the sun dropping towards the horizon again. In her paddock next door, Clarabelle the donkey munched her way through a pile of hay and Lucy could see some hikers coming down the path from the village. It was all so normal yet she felt as though time was disjointed, as though she had taken a misstep in the dark.

The door of the barn was ajar and she hesitated before pushing it wider. She really didn't want to go back inside. A different sort of fear swelled in her, the fear that she was losing herself in some way, losing her mind, or at least losing what seemed to be her tenuous grip on reality. That in itself was so frightening that it stole her breath.

Squaring her shoulders she pushed the door wide and walked inside, poised to flee the moment anything weird happened. But there was nothing; nothing but the tick of the clock on the wall, and the sun pouring in at the high windows, and the rich scent of the sweet peas and freesias filling the air.

CHAPTER 8

Anne Catesby

Ashby St Ledgers, April 1595

> *My very dear Lady Catesby,* Catherine wrote from
> Oxfordshire, in her careful, rounded hand, *I do hope
> that both you and Sir William are in good health. I thank
> you very much for the conserve of orange that you sent me as
> a cure for my recent ague. I slept for a number of days and
> am much recovered now.*

I smiled, remembering the Seville orange jelly that I had
sent to Catherine when I had heard she was ailing. The
oranges, expensive but deliciously fragrant, were mixed
with sugar and sack wine, enough to make anyone sleep for
any number of days. I had been concerned for her; she had
been frail since she had taken ill with a fever a few months
ago and had yet to properly recover her strength. I knew
that she was anxious for a child and had been for some time
but I dreaded that she might conceive before she was strong
enough to go through pregnancy. I kept my fears to myself,
though, knowing they were more to do with my experience

of losing my firstborn, little William, than anything else. Childbirth was, in my opinion, far more dangerous than any of the activities boasted of by men, the wars and duels and tournaments that they thought proved their worth. We women knew the truth of it. And once that little scrap of new life entered the world, we wanted to guard it with our lives and protect it against all ill. That that was not always possible was the hardest lesson of all.

We had visited Robert and Catherine at Chastleton House three months after they had wed. The invitation had surprised me, for I had thought that once Robert was free of our oversight, he would be in no hurry to see us again. Catherine, however, had excellent manners and had clearly pushed him into inviting us and the visit went smoothly. William had impressed upon me the need to admire everything and criticise nothing; this was not so difficult in the end, for Robert was in an expansive mood, doting on his wife and proud of his position as master of the house. With wealth and good standing, a cellar full of wine and a deer park full of game, he seemed very content. The estate was well-maintained since William had had in place an excellent tenant during the later years of his widowed mother's ownership and Robert had not yet had long enough to undo all the good work. But as William said, this sort of observation was exactly why Robert and I always ended at daggers drawn.

'You forget,' my husband said, 'that you were the one who believed that marrying Catherine would be a steadying influence on Robert. At least allow him the chance to prove you correct.'

I sighed now, remembering, for I knew that William was right. I was often too quick and too harsh to judge, but equally I knew that Robert had recently written to his father, asking for money. Some things did not change and I shuddered to imagine that he might have run through Catherine's dowry within a year of their marriage.

We would be so glad if you would join us next month for the May Day celebrations,' Catherine's letter continued. *'We shall be at the manor at Knightstone, which is my favourite of all places, so small and charming and altogether beautiful. Did I mention in my last letter that I am creating a winter garden there, with terraces, and pretty little arbours and ponds? Robert's godfather is advising me, for he plans a marvellous design himself at Lyveden...*

I had no idea what a winter garden was but I put the letter down, disquiet stirring within me. It was evident from Catherine's words that Thomas Tresham was welcomed in Robert's home more frequently than we were. Perhaps he did not even require the formal invitation that I had to wait for. I thought of the letter I had received from Catherine after her name day celebrations, mentioning the glorious embroidered taffeta that Sir Thomas had sent her from London as a gift. Jealousy tasted bitter in my mouth as it always did when I recognised the closeness that existed between Robert and his uncle, a connection I could never achieve. And now Thomas was inveigling himself into Catherine's good graces as well.

I already knew about Thomas' grand plans at his own manors in Northamptonshire. At Rushden, his main seat, he was building a folly of surpassing grandeur. He had told us that its triangular nature reflected the Holy Trinity but I thought that all the allegories and puns incorporated within its walls were really intended to reflect his own cleverness. At Lyveden he spoke of creating a lodge and moated garden; all this when he had vast debts from his determined recusancy and would only incur more. I pitied his boys, Francis and Lewis, inheriting nothing but empty coffers and grand designs, and his daughters scrabbling for dowries amongst the brick dust.

I hoped that his advice to Catherine and Robert on improving their estate would not similarly bankrupt them though I feared it might. And why would Catherine wish to develop the garden at the smaller estate of Knightstone rather than at Chastleton where they would be living for most of the time and entertaining their guests? Thomas' previous connection to Knightstone, the link to the Knights Hospitallers and their treasure, troubled me. Could he have another reason for visiting there so often, and was he involving Robert in whatever he planned? My imagination raced away with possibilities.

I mentioned the matter to William later, behind the privacy of our bed curtains. He had had a long day presiding over the monthly manor court followed by a fine meal of roasted pork in onion gravy, so I judged he would be in an expansive mood. When I told him we had been invited to Knightstone for the May Day rites he was delighted.

'I believe that Thomas may be there as well,' I ventured. 'It seems he spends a great deal of time in company with Robert and Catherine…'

William was too drunk and content to pick up the tone in my voice or perhaps he simply chose to ignore it.

'Excellent,' he said. 'I need to discuss with Thomas a matter that arose at the Lent assizes last week. It will be good to see him.' He rolled over and the bed creaked beneath his weight.

I sighed sharply. 'I do wonder—' I tried again, 'why Catherine prefers Knightstone to Chastleton, when the latter is so much more modern and comfortable?'

'Perhaps she sees it as a place she can put her own stamp upon,' William said, yawning. I could see that he was supremely uninterested. 'There have been few improvements there over the past fifty years, whereas Chastleton has always been in good repair. A woman likes to put her mark on her own household, does she not?'

'As much as a man likes to think that he has the running of his,' I muttered, but he was already asleep and snoring.

I lay awake for a while thinking of Catherine's winter garden with its pretty little arbours, ponds and terraces. It sounded delightful and entirely appropriate for a gentle-woman newly established in her country manor and set on improving her home and her status in local society. Indeed, I already knew that Catherine had a refined taste and an elegant style that would reflect well on Robert. So why, I wondered, did the idea of the garden disturb me so? Was it simply because she had mentioned that Thomas was involved and I knew that he had a long and treasonous history at Knightstone? If he were using Catherine and Robert to further his own plans of Catholic restoration, or to hide the remnants of the Knights' treasures, that could bring them into grave danger from the Queen's spies... I was accustomed to keeping quiet about all manner of illegal matters, such as the holding of secret masses and the hiding of Catholic priests, but I was not prepared to allow Thomas to endanger Robert and Catherine's future.

I told myself that I was being fanciful, that Thomas had no hidden motives and Robert and Catherine were safe in their new life, but I tossed and turned that night and when I did fall asleep, I dreamed of Thomas. He was holding in his hand the golden chalice of the Order of the Knights Hospitaller. He raised it to me in mocking toast.

'*You cannot stop me, Nan,*' he said. '*I will take the treasure and use it for the glory of the true religion and Robert will stand by me.*' And I awoke in the grey morning light, my hands clutching the sheets tight, as the cockerel began to crow.

'And here,' Catherine said, 'is where I intend to create a loggia.'

'I see,' I said. I did not, in truth, see a great deal. I had only the vaguest idea that a loggia was something Italianate and grand. Besides, I was not good at picturing things when they were only in my imagination.

Catherine laughed. 'It is a covered colonnade, Lady Catesby,' she explained without condescension. 'It has a roof and one side is open to the view whilst the other protects from the elements. I plan to entwine it in roses – musk rose and the white rose and the old velvet rose.'

We were standing on the terrace to the north of Knightstone Manor. The day was inclement for late April with low, scudding clouds and a sharp breeze with an edge of rain. Catherine had insisted that we venture out so that she could explain her garden design to me and so, wrapped tightly in cloaks and shawls, we stood on the edge of the hill, looking out over the vale below. A number of labourers were hard at work levelling and planting a knot garden around us, sweating in the cold air and making the ground underfoot rather gritty and muddy. I held my skirts high and wished I had worn pattens over my shoes to protect the leather.

'A covered colonnade is an excellent idea,' I said, 'for the wind blows hard from the high downs.' It was hardly Italy, but I admired Catherine's determination to create something beautiful. To me this landscape was quite bare and lonely; a garden would soften that sense of isolation though I still did not understand why Catherine preferred Knightstone to Chastleton, which was to my mind a gentler, sunnier place.

'I find the ponds and woodland here entirely delightful,' Catherine gave a little sigh, 'like a sylvan setting from Mr Shakespeare's work. The springs rise in the woods here and the stream runs down to a lake—' She pointed down a shallow valley where, at the bottom, I could just make out a gleam of water. 'We shall have a summerhouse there. And two small spiral mounts here and here...' She gestured towards an old orchard that climbed away across the opposite hillside.

'And you have what looks like an outdoor chessboard below,' I said. The field at the bottom of the hill was mown close in squares except for where turf banks created a curious design of an eight-pointed star in the centre of the grass.

Catherine laughed merrily. 'Why, Lady Catesby, that is

a moated labyrinth! How clever is that? It was Sir Thomas Tresham's idea — he also suggested the loggia and some of the other features.' Her tone held the same element of hero worship that I heard from Robert when Thomas was mentioned. 'Is Sir Thomas not the most fascinating gentleman? So learned and well-travelled! Robert is very fortunate to have him as his uncle and godfather.'

I stared at the eight-pointed star emblazoned in the grass below. I had seen that pattern before. 'Did Sir Thomas suggest the design for the labyrinth?' I asked.

Catherine nodded eagerly. 'It is an octagram, Lady Catesby. The eight points of the star represent the eight forms of prosperity, which are patience, health, knowledge, wealth and… umm…' She had forgotten the remaining four. Then her face brightened. 'They are all qualities to be dearly sought and valued, or so Sir Thomas tells me.'

'And, of course, the number eight also represents hope and new beginnings in the holy Bible,' I said. 'How Sir Thomas adores showing off his cleverness through allegory.' But in truth I was thinking of the Knights Hospitaller of St John and the eight-pointed cross that they had adopted to denote their aspirations: to live in truth, have faith, repent their sins, give proof of humility, love justice, be merciful, be sincere and wholehearted, and to endure persecution. Those, Thomas proclaimed to be the guiding principles of his life, just as they had been for his grandfather, the Grand Prior of the Order before him. And now here they were emblazoned on Catherine's garden design for all to see.

I suspected that despite the ruling of the Queen that the Order of the Hospitallers should be suppressed, it was flourishing here at Knightstone and not so secretly either. Perhaps the last of the Knights' treasures were here also. It would be typical of Thomas' arrogance to hide it in plain sight amidst his clever designs and allegories, daring someone to read the clues to it.

'You referred to it as a winter garden in your letter,' I said to Catherine. 'I have never heard of such a thing; is that another of Sir Thomas' fancies?'

She shook her head. 'It is my own idea,' she said, 'for I love the native plants of winter, the snowdrops with their delicate purity, and the red berry of the holly and the bright yellow aconite. I have it in mind to make the garden as bright and joyful in the winter as I can.'

'That is a delightful idea,' I said.

A shade of sorrow came into her face. 'The garden was begun in winter and it felt to me as though even in those bare and barren days it brought hope of fresh new life for the future.' She rested her hand a little self-consciously on her stomach, and I smiled at her.

'Spring is here now,' I said. 'The seasons turn and so do our fortunes. I am sure it will not be long before you conceive and then your winter garden may become a summer one.'

However, as we made our way back into the warmth of the house, it was not of a future grandchild that I was thinking, but of Thomas' involvement in the lives of my son and daughter-in-law. And sure enough, when it came to dinner, there he was. I heard his voice, his easy laughter ringing out in the gallery as he chatted to William. That in itself annoyed me; the fact that William liked him, that he could not see, as I could, that Thomas was devious and used people. How many men had been taken in by his charm and believed in the generosity of his spirit? And yet I knew that was unfair; Thomas *was* generous, a complex man who could be both kindly and yet provocative in the same person.

As for why I disliked him so much, I knew the reason for that and it made me dislike myself equally as much. Thomas was connected to my past in a way I would rather forget but his constant presence made that impossible. He saw me now and his eyes lit with a smile that was private to me. I refused to return it.

'Thomas,' I said. 'Here you are again.'

'Whereas I believe this is your first visit to Knightstone Manor,' he said smoothly. He took my hand. The smile in his eyes deepened as I snatched it back. 'How do you find the place?' he asked. 'It is quite delightful, is it not?'

I was aware of Catherine hovering near us, unwilling to interrupt our conversation but desperate for approval. In truth I found the house dark, poky and old-fashioned, but then, so was Ashby because we had had no money to spend improving it as a result of endless fines and Robert's extravagance.

'The garden promises to be remarkable,' I said truthfully. 'Catherine—' I drew her into the conversation as I had no desire to keep Thomas all to myself, 'tells me that it is a winter garden, conceived in the darkness of the year but born to give hope.'

Catherine blushed prettily, all the more so as Robert chose that moment to come up and give her a swift kiss on the cheek. He was looking particularly handsome that evening in dark red velvet and pristine white lace.

'How very biblical you make my ideas sound,' Thomas

murmured in my ear as Robert slid an arm about his wife's waist and steered her over to chat with William in the window alcove.

'Surely that was what you intended,' I said, 'with your allegories and octagram design? Really, Thomas,' I could not keep the exasperation from my tone, 'did you have to flaunt the Hospitallers' symbol here? I do not doubt that the Queen's spies keep all of us under their eye; what will they make of such a blatant provocation?'

'They will fine me more money and think me a misguided fool,' Thomas said cheerfully, 'as they do already.'

'It is not *you* who will be fined,' I said, 'but Robert and Catherine. How dare you involve them into your games? I promised Catherine's mother that she should be free of Catholic taint in this marriage and now you are deliberately drawing her into danger.'

Thomas shook his head. 'Oh, Nan,' he said, 'it is but a design, a pretty little pattern on the grass. I showed it to Catherine and she liked it. That is all. In your haste to condemn me you read too much into this.'

I glared at him. 'Don't lie to me, Thomas! I know how your mind works. You have created a shrine to the Knights Hospitaller. Very likely their treasure is hidden somewhere at Knightstone too. You think that because you wear your colours so plainly and make no secret of your faith, the Queen's men are lulled into thinking you are harmless. Well, I know differently. I know you are dangerous.'

'You misjudge me, Nan.' Thomas' smile had gone, his light manner changed. He half-turned, to block the others' view of our discussion. 'I would never raise a rebellion or wield a sword. I have no desire to lead others into danger. All I wish is for the freedom to worship as I choose. As for the treasure, my grandfather laid on me the sacred charge of conserving it until the order is free to worship again. And that is what I have done.'

'Is that an admission?' I demanded. 'You have concealed it here, hiding your treason behind Catherine's impeccably Protestant skirts?' I threw out a hand in despair. 'Can you not *see*, Thomas, that by involving yourself in Robert and Catherine's lives you are drawing them into danger? If you care for them as much as you claim, you would leave them alone. As for the garden – keep your biblical imagery for Rushden and Lyveden, but do not flaunt it here.'

We had been conversing in low tones that hid the fierceness of our exchange. Nevertheless, I jumped when William's shadow fell across me.

'What secrets are you two hatching?' he said jovially, and I must have blushed like a guilty matron caught making an assignation. Fortunately, William was completely impervious to such matters. 'Dinner is ready,' he said, offering me his arm. 'Robert knows he should be the one to escort you to the table but he cannot seem to tear himself away from his beautiful wife so I offer myself instead.'

'Dear William,' I said, sliding my hand through his arm, 'you are a more than adequate substitute,' and my heart ached that Robert and I did not have the easy affection he had with his father, and that he would not seek out my company for the sheer pleasure of it. I watched him as he and Catherine strolled into dinner ahead of us. He was such a handsome young man, so quicksilver and expressive.

I vowed that it was not too late to make amends and that I would talk to Robert after dinner and try to bridge the gaps between us. As for the Knights' treasure, I would try to forget that Thomas had admitted that it was concealed somewhere at Knightstone. Thomas knew I would not give him away and as long as he kept his pledge to hold it safe and secret, I would not interfere.

The wine and good food helped me to keep both resolutions. Catherine glowed as our hostess; Robert was merry, Thomas smoothly entertaining. By common consent we kept away from any topic that might spark discord.

The following day, May Day, dawned bright and fair after the chill of April. There was a procession from the manor into the village, led by the jack-in-the-green, with the foresters carrying the tree that had been chosen to be the maypole. On the lawn in front of the inn were the mummers and the morris men, with plays and dance and music and ribaldry. The sun shone and we laughed and feasted. Catherine washed her face in the dew of the May morning and wore green to mimic the fecundity of the earth and to bring good luck in conception. Robert seemed to find this amusing. He swept her up in his arms and kissed her heartily in front of everyone and when they slipped away hand in hand, an approving roar went up from the villagers for their young squire and his wife.

And that is how I always like to remember Catherine, on that bright May morning enveloped with hope and happiness and the sun on her golden hair as she outshone the May Queen.

CHAPTER 9
Lucy

Lucy ate one of the village shop's chickpea salads for her supper, taking it out onto the terrace so that she could enjoy the last of the day's warmth. Although both the house and the valley were peaceful now, she wasn't inclined to stay indoors. The weirdness of feeling herself taken over by that intense sense of desolation had shaken her badly. Thinking it over, it felt as though the sensation had come on as soon as she had been filled with grief for her lost music career. It had felt as though her despair and loss had connected to someone else's; to something far larger and more powerful. It had been a mirror for the feeling she had experienced when she had dreamed of being Catherine, lost in the maze of the deserted manor in winter, seeking something or someone…

She gave a convulsive shiver. She was starting to think that there was more to these experiences than simply her imagination. The only possibilities she could think of were that she was having some sort of belated reaction to her medication – she had been on it for three months now without major side effects but she supposed it could have triggered something – or that she was going mad, or that there was something supernatural happening at Gunpowder Barn. She decided to discount the idea of madness; she had been ill and she was tired and sometimes emotional, but there was a difference between that and insanity. Perhaps she should ask Cleo for a second opinion, although a doctor would be the best person to ask in the likelihood that she had developed a reaction to her medication. Perhaps she should go back to London to consult her GP.

She was surprised at the sadness that tugged at her when she had that thought. It was almost as though someone had whispered to her: *'Don't leave me...'* There was a sense of autumn melancholy and longing in the warm air.

Lucy got up and took her empty plate inside, stacking it in the dishwasher. Oddly she didn't feel unhappy or threatened at the barn despite the sometimes frightening experiences she was having. Her instinct told her that whatever or who-ever was here, they meant her no harm. Rather, she sensed a kindred spirit, someone else who was lost or uncertain. Catherine? She decided she needed to find out more about Catherine Catesby.

Deciding to call Cleo and talk it through with her the next day, she slipped her shoes back on, grabbed a jumper and a rug, put some apples, bread and cheese in her back-pack, pulled the door closed and set off down the path that bordered the stream. It was cool beneath the shade of the trees though the insects still buzzed in the evening sunlight. The water was low, no more than a quicksilver flash beneath the overhanging bank, for summer had been dry for several weeks now. It was humid, however, the air heavy, and Lucy remembered the weather bulletin promising thunderstorms by the end of the week.

She hadn't explored so far down the valley before. It wasn't quiet; a colony of rooks set up a cacophony of noise in the tall trees up by the cottage, their raucous cries undercut by the sweeter tones of the woodland birds. A helicopter passed low overhead. Lucy could hear voices carrying to her from the road and the sound of Clarabelle braying in her paddock. And yet there was something peaceful and timeless about the little hidden valley. It made her wonder about the lost Tudor garden, and how many feet had passed along the path she was standing on now.

As the ground levelled out at the bottom of the hill, the stream ran into a small lake, more of a pond, really, given that the dry weather had left the irises and reeds around the edge stranded as the waters receded. There was a grassy patch beneath a big oak tree where Lucy spread her blanket out. She kicked off her espadrilles and let her toes sink into the cool grass. This was a perfect spot. There was even a little beach where she could see a sparkle of golden grains and rainbow colours amongst the sand. Perhaps this was where Finn had said they had found evidence of a bathing place. She waded a little way out into the lake and let the cool spring waters lap the bottom of her capris.

'Hi.' Lucy hadn't heard Finn approach and only realised that he was there when Geoffrey splashed into the water beside her, sending a rainbow of droplets cascading through the air from his madly wagging tail. She patted him, which only led to more overexcited wagging, and walked back to the shore of the pool, sitting down on the blanket.

'Hi,' she said, as economically as Finn. There was something about the peace of the place that encouraged a spirit of quietness, however it didn't seem to have touched Geoffrey. They watched him cavorting across the pool with absolute joy and abandon, splashing through the shallows, pirouetting with excitement.

'He's such a water dog,' Finn said. 'Apologies if he soaked you.'

'It's fine,' Lucy said.

'May I?' Finn gestured to the space beside her.

'Be my guest,' Lucy said. 'I suspect this spot is more yours than mine anyway. I only discovered it today. I hadn't walked down the valley before.'

Finn eased himself down onto the dry grass beside her. He was silent. It was restful. A bee hummed through the purple and yellow wildflowers; Lucy remembered scabious and harebell and vetch from the times that Verity had taken her for walks as a child. It was odd what children remembered, she thought. She'd not needed to name a wildflower in the twenty years since. Those were yellow iris and water mint around the edge of the pool – she could smell the scent, and when Geoffrey plopped himself down next to her, panting and wet, he smelled minty too.

'Geoffrey!' Lucy said reproachfully, but Geoffrey just pressed his warm wet body closer to her leg, his eyes begging for some of the cheese he could smell in the bag, and Lucy felt unexpected happiness bubble up in her and she laughed.

'You're shameless,' she told him, breaking off a small piece and holding it out to him. 'You're welcome to some food as well,' she added, to Finn.

'Thanks.' Finn reached out and took a chunk of the baguette, covering it liberally with butter and cheese. Lucy thought she heard Geoffrey give a little moan of covetousness.

'I see you've put one of the test pits over on the far side of the pool,' Lucy said, nodding towards the spot where a one-metre-square hole had been dug out and carefully covered over. 'Was this the site of the summerhouse you mentioned the other day?'

Finn paused before replying. There was something very measured about everything he did, Lucy thought. She wondered whether he ever openly displayed emotion or spoke impetuously. Then she remembered the way he had crumpled the can in his hand when Persis had spoken of the Odin legend. There had been plenty of anger and passion there. Tonight, however, his mood seemed a little easier, as though he had shed some of the unhappiness that had previously clung to him.

'I used to think that the lake was the culmination of the whole design,' Finn said slowly. 'I imagined that the garden started up at the cottage – or manor house, as it was then – encompassed the valley, and finished here with the bathing pool and the summerhouse. But now I realise I got it wrong and that the focus of the design was in the centre.'

'Oh?' Lucy was intrigued.

Finn leaned over on one elbow, drawing with a fingertip in the sand that bordered the pool. 'If you imagine the manor house here...' he drew a little square, 'we know from the old maps that it faced south and had a main entrance on the front, just like today. But behind the house, facing north, was a terrace with ornamental planting, and probably obelisks and statues, and an arbour or two. Most of that is under the garage and courtyard now, but there's a remnant of it left.'

'The arbour is still there,' Lucy said, 'or at least it was when I was a child. It had a seat made out of turf and was covered in honeysuckle, which I loved. I'd never seen anything like it before and I used to play hide and seek in it with Cleo.'

Finn smiled. 'Children have probably been doing that for centuries,' he said. 'We dug a test pit near that spot and found a layer of gravel at the right strata to suggest late-sixteenth-century pathways. Some of the plants in the wild part of the back garden are old herbs and cultivars as well – they are probably the descendants of the original formal gardens.'

'They had herbs in a formal garden?' Lucy asked.

'It was a great way to provide fresh herbs for the household and scent the air at the same time,' Finn said. 'Plus some herbs and vegetables have very colourful flowers. They probably mixed them with gillyflowers – pinks and wallflowers and stocks to us.'

'How lovely,' Lucy said. She drew her knees up to her chin. 'It would be amazing to be able to recreate that.'

Finn nodded. 'I'm looking forward to it. The older designs fascinate me and it's great to have the chance to explore a knot garden.'

'How did you get interested in historic gardens in the first place?' Lucy asked.

'I studied landscape archaeology at uni,' Finn said,

brushing the baguette crumbs from his trousers, 'and one of my first projects was working on an excavation of a seventeenth-century garden at a country house that was destroyed during the Civil Wars. That gave me a taste for combining archaeology with unravelling the history behind the sites, which really interested me. I also worked on some urban community garden digs, which was great, finding evidence of the lives of people who hadn't grown up in a castle. I went on to do a Diploma in Garden History at the Royal Botanic Gardens in Edinburgh...' He rubbed his chin. 'That made my Mum laugh – the trouble she'd had getting me to help on our allotment as a kid! But I love being in the open air and doing practical work as well as poring over old maps and books, so it suits me well.'

'So you're definitely someone who could recognise a knot garden when you see one,' Lucy said, smiling, 'and I know you and Johnny have tentatively identified other features leading down the valley, but now I'm down here at the pool it's even more intriguing.' She shielded her eyes against the sparkle of the sun on the water. 'Are those the pieces of coloured glass and stone you mentioned that I can see at the edge of the pond?'

'Some of them.' Finn nodded. 'They are scattered around. The pattern's interesting, as though there has been some disturbance to them.' He stretched. 'We've got much more work to do down here so although the test pit has identified some elements, including cisterns and stone carvings, there's a load more to check out. I'm trying to prioritise where we dig; next it will be Clarabelle's field, to see whether those lines we saw on the photos earlier are garden features.'

'That was very exciting,' Lucy said. She looked at the sunlight slanting through the trees in shades of green and gold. 'There's so much hidden here, isn't there? You wouldn't even know it was originally a designed landscape, other than the orchards, I suppose. Are they original?'

'We think that they're descended from the original Tudor orchards,' Finn said. 'There are some beautiful plum, walnut and cherry trees in the valley as well as apple trees on that slope of the hill that faces the barn.'

'And there's a spiral-shaped mound at the top,' Lucy said, 'with an amazing view.' She saw Finn's thunderstruck expression and realised her mistake. 'Sorry,' she said, 'I imagined that bit, didn't I?' She felt the colour sting her cheeks. 'I dreamed it, actually. Ignore me. I forgot it was just a dream.'

'What do you mean, you dreamed it?' Finn had drawn a spiral mound shaped like a seashell in the sandy earth, exactly as Lucy had experienced it in one of her dreams and in exactly the right place.

'Oh, on the first night I was here I had a weird dream,' Lucy said reluctantly. 'It felt like winter; I was freezing cold. Anyway, I was standing on top of a little hill with a view of the orchards. The path went up it in a spiral, like a helter-skelter. That's why I called it a spiral mound.' She reached for another piece of bread and cheese to cover her embarrassment, and Geoffrey shifted hopefully beside her.

'Well,' Finn said, after a moment, 'your dreams are unnervingly accurate. We discovered the footings of an ornamental mound above the orchard and I think it was another Tudor feature. Spiral mounts were very popular

– they were used as viewing platforms, to look out across the garden.' He was watching her keenly and Lucy felt awkward, making a fuss of Geoffrey to avoid meeting his gaze. 'There's a matching one across the other side of the valley, behind the barn in Clarabelle's paddock. We didn't know it was there before as it was used as a village rubbish dump for a while and a lot of it had been dug out by the farmer. But the design is symmetrical.' Out of the corner of her eye, Lucy could see he was still watching her and his frown had deepened. 'That is weird,' he repeated. 'You really didn't know? You hadn't read it somewhere?'

'I don't think so.' Lucy finally looked at him. 'I suppose there's a chance Verity might have mentioned it to me when I was a child, but...'

'But Verity didn't know herself,' Finn said. 'I only told her recently that we suspected the mounds were there.'

Lucy thought about telling him about the other components of her dreams and decided against it. One dream like that could be considered a coincidence; if she talked about seeing the old manor house and being inside Catherine's mind, or mentioned the terrifying sense of possession she'd experienced earlier, Finn would not unnaturally assume she had some major issues. She wanted to talk to Cleo first and see what she thought about the scary things that kept recurring at Gunpowder Barn.

'If there are two spiral viewing mounds,' she said, 'it does suggest that there was some sort of feature between them where the barn is now, doesn't it? After all, when you're on the top you'd want to be viewing something.'

'Yeah,' Finn said, 'which is why I now think that the

moated feature where the barn is now was the centre of the whole site.' He paused. 'I don't suppose you saw what it was in your dream, did you? Any clues?'

Lucy looked at him suspiciously but he was deadpan and she wasn't sure whether he was making fun of her or not. 'I'm afraid I wasn't taking notes,' she said, 'but if the dream recurs, I'll be sure to check.'

'Awesome,' Finn said. He gave her a small smile. 'I'm not laughing at you,' he added. 'I've known people have those sorts of eldritch dreams before.'

'Eldritch?' The word caught Lucy's attention. 'What's that?'

'My Scots grandmother used to say it,' Finn said. 'It means fey or eerie.'

Lucy shivered. She reached for her shoes and the fleece jumper she had brought with her. The shadows were getting longer and the air was cooling by slow degrees. As soon as she had the fleece on, Geoffrey snuggled closer to her.

'Cute,' Finn said, looking at them. 'Are you cold?' he added. 'I've got a blanket in my backpack.'

'I'm fine, thanks,' Lucy said. 'Were you planning on staying out late?' She noticed that he also had a lantern and a thermos flask and various other supplies in the open rucksack.

'I sometimes camp out here overnight when the weather's warm enough,' Finn said. 'It's very peaceful. A swim, if there's enough water, a campfire and some hot chocolate looking at the stars.'

'Lovely,' Lucy said. 'Not the swimming at this time of night, but the other parts. Don't let me stop you if you want to go in,' she added, 'I'm sure Geoff would be up for another splash around.'

'I'm all right, thanks,' Finn said. He glanced sideways at her. 'Though maybe you'd like to join me another time on a hot day? The water is amazing.'

'That does sound nice,' Lucy admitted, 'and when it's as hot as it's been today...' She thought about swimming in the pool and lazing around in the sunshine with Finn. It felt rather more appealing than perhaps it should. Then she reminded herself that she needed to relax. She didn't need to second-guess everything, least of all whether her new, tenuous friendship with Finn would develop into anything else.

'I'm sorry I turned down the chance to help you out with the project when you asked me on the first day,' she said impulsively. 'That was really ungracious of me. If I can help, I will.'

Finn's smile made her feel warm inside. 'That's kind of you,' he said, 'and please don't apologise. I know you've got a lot on your mind at the moment and I wasn't exactly welcoming when you arrived.' He paused and she saw him swallow. 'It was Charlie's birthday that day,' he said, a little gruffly. 'It hit me pretty hard.'

'Oh God, I'm so sorry.' Lucy reached out and put her hand over his. 'No wonder you were like a bear with a sore head.'

'I worked so hard that day, trying to blot it out,' Finn admitted, 'and then I followed up with too much whisky. Not my finest hour.' He turned his hand over, still holding hers, and rubbed his thumb across her palm. 'It kind of helps that you know what it's like to lose something precious, you know. As though I don't need to explain. You understand.'

Lucy was startled. 'It's not the same, though,' she said. 'I mean, in my case, no one died...'

'Your future was changed in an instant,' Finn said. 'Just like mine. However, I don't want to depress you.' He released her hand and sat up. 'I'd be glad of any help you can give us, to be honest. But if you're looking for a proper job there are other opportunities in the village, especially in summer. You could try the shop, or the museum...'

'No thanks.' Lucy just managed to repress a shudder. 'I didn't really hit it off with Gabriel,' she admitted, when Finn looked amused, 'and I don't think Persis would thank me for treading on her toes at the shop either.'

'I can see your point.' Finn lay back, hands behind his head. 'Gabriel is a first-rate prick.'

Lucy burst out laughing. 'I didn't say that!'

'You meant it, though.' Finn gave her a lazy smile. 'And you're in good company. The whole village thinks so. He's done himself no favours setting himself up as the expert on everything.' He turned his head to look at her. 'What sort of work do you want to do? What are you good at?'

'Nothing much really.' Lucy plucked a blade of grass and shredded it. 'I've never done anything except play music. It's been my entire life. But I can try to learn new skills, I suppose.'

'Don't be so hard on yourself,' Finn said. 'If you're good at music then you're creative, you can handle pressure, you can plan and work with other people, and you're good at performing. There's loads of transferable skills right there.'

'I'll get you to write my CV when I apply for full-time jobs,' Lucy joked to cover how ridiculously touched she felt by his championing her. 'I'm only looking to fill a few weeks anyway, just to cover the summer. That way I can spend some time with Cleo and not go scuttling straight back to London like a frightened rabbit—' She broke off but not before Finn had picked her up on this. She was learning that he really did pay attention.

'Why would you be frightened?' he said, eyebrows raised.

'Oh, just that being on my own at the barn spooks me sometimes,' Lucy said, deliberately vague. 'But like I say, it's just for a few weeks. If there isn't any work going, that doesn't matter.'

'Mortimer Hall, the stately home up the road, is always looking for part-time volunteers to meet and greet visitors,' Finn said thoughtfully. 'I saw an advert in the shop just the other day – you welcome people, sell tickets and postcards, that sort of thing. It's nice, because there's people coming and going all the time – as long as you can handle the grumbles over car parking and the lack of a tea shop as well. I've got the phone number of the Visitor Services manager somewhere. I could dig it out for you.'

'Thanks.' Lucy lay back with a sigh. 'We used to go for picnics in the grounds of Mortimer Hall when we visited Verity back in the day,' she said. 'It's nowhere near as old as Gunpowder Cottage, is it? I thought it was an ugly sort of house and didn't like it much when I was a kid, but the grounds were lovely.'

'That should get you the job,' Finn said approvingly. 'Perfect interview answer.'

Lucy giggled. Beside her, Geoffrey snored in his sleep, twitching as he chased dream rabbits. Lucy felt light and happy. Being with Finn felt very easy.

Overhead the sky was fading to violet and deep blue and the first of the stars was coming out. The splash of the ducks on the water sounded loud in the quiet and somewhere in the tangle of trees, a tawny owl called, a shrill 'kee-wick' that sounded fierce. Lucy smothered a yawn.

'Did you manage to get hold of a locksmith?' Finn asked.

'Yes, thanks,' Lucy said. 'An emergency one came out from Swindon within the hour. I plan to get another set of keys cut when I go into Highworth to see Cleo, hopefully tomorrow,' she added. 'I imagine the letting agents will want one.'

Finn propped his head in the crook of his arm so that he could look at her. 'We keep a spare in the safe at the cottage in case of emergencies,' he said, 'so if you could get two extras, that would be great, thanks – assuming you don't mind us having one.'

'That sounds like a very good idea,' Lucy said.

Finn was frowning. 'I did wonder whether that was how someone had got a copy,' he said, after a moment. His voice was more hesitant than Lucy had heard it before and she rolled over to look at him properly.

'What do you mean?'

'You know I said that Persis and Charlie had a bit of a thing going at the start of the year,' Finn said. 'They were quite close for a while and I know Charlie talked to her about the garden project, but I don't think... I can't imagine he'd have given her the keys to the barn...' His voice tailed away as though he wasn't sure.

'Do you think they might have met there?' Lucy said carefully. 'Or that Persis maybe knew the code to the key safe?'

Finn shook his head. 'The code is restricted for security reasons,' he said, answering the second part of Lucy's question first, 'plus the barn was let almost solidly through the whole of the spring. There were only a couple of weeks when it was free.' He shifted uncomfortably. 'I wouldn't have thought Charlie would be so irresponsible as to use it when it was empty but...' his mouth tightened, 'I can't discount the possibility. I mean, I was up at the cottage, and although I wouldn't have minded him bringing someone back, he might have preferred more privacy...'

'Were you and Charlie close?' Lucy asked, reading between the lines that Charlie Macintyre might well have been a bit intimidated by his big brother. 'I know you were the elder,' she said. 'Was it just the two of you?'

'No, I've another brother and sister,' Finn said, relaxing onto his back again. The gathering shadows sculpted the line of his jaw and the stubble there, and Lucy could see the silhouette of his eyelashes against cheek. It made her feel slightly breathless.

'The others are all younger than me,' Finn was saying, 'and I guess I can be protective of them all. Charlie was the youngest and he was only twenty-two, just out of college, when he came here.' He cleared his throat. 'We all grew up on an island. There weren't that many other kids around so it was lucky we got on with each other, but the flipside of that is that we are all pretty tight, so when something bad happens…' Again, he let the sentence hang.

'It's a shame you all had to pay such a heavy price for that happy childhood,' Lucy said. 'Which island did you grow up on?'

'It's called Coll,' Finn said. 'One of the Hebrides.' He slanted her a look. 'Have you ever been to Scotland?'

'Only once,' Lucy said. 'I didn't have too many holidays. I was usually too busy practising and studying the violin. But I do remember one Duke of Edinburgh Awards trip to the Cairngorms. It rained and there were midges and we all moaned like teenage girls do when they are being particularly annoying.'

Finn laughed. 'Maybe you just didn't see the country at its best.' His voice softened, his Scots accent suddenly more pronounced. Lucy found it ridiculously seductive. 'It's a beautiful place, Scotland,' Finn said. 'And Coll is the most beautiful part of it, with white sand beaches like the tropics and clear night skies full of stars and the wind blowing the scent of the sea and the heather to you. We all ran wild as children and it was grand.'

Lucy felt a pang of envy for that sort of carefree childhood. Hers had been almost submerged under the weight of expectation and the need not to let her parents and Cleo down when they had sacrificed so much for her music.

'It sounds idyllic,' she said. 'Have you ever wanted to go back there to live?'

'One day, maybe,' Finn said. 'My parents still live on Coll. I went back after…' He paused. 'Well, Charlie is buried there.'

This time he was the one who took her hand, interlocking his fingers with hers, warm and strong. It felt very natural. Lucy stared at the sky, imagining the endlessness of that last journey home, the long, lonely hours accompanying his brother's coffin.

Geoffrey stirred with a little sleepy bark and they jumped apart as though caught in the middle of a guilty act before bursting out laughing.

'I'd forgotten he was there,' Lucy said, 'despite the snoring.'

'Geoffrey is a very effective chaperone,' Finn said. He reached for the backpack and took out the blanket and the thermos. 'Would you like some hot chocolate? I've got a spare cup.'

'That sounds wonderful,' Lucy said, 'if you have enough to share.'

They drank the hot chocolate in silence looking at the emerging stars and the tracery of dark branches against the velvet sky.

'I'm going to collect some twigs to make a fire,' Finn said, getting up. Geoffrey was on his feet in an instant. 'I won't be long. Don't feel you need to go,' he added, as Lucy started to gather her things together, 'unless you want to.'

His long shadow and Geoffrey's shorter one melted into the darkness, leaving Lucy alone at the edge of the lake. A thin moon was rising, its light reflected on the rippling surface. Lucy realised that she hadn't brought a torch, although she supposed she could use the light on her phone to find her way back up the path to the barn. She hadn't intended to stay out so late, but she had enjoyed it. Finn might want a bit of peace and quiet on his own now, beside the fire, though. Clearly, he was still grieving deeply for his brother and she didn't want to overstay her welcome.

She got to her feet and dusted her capris down. Suddenly the darkness seemed to press closer; her head spun, disorientating her completely. She felt an icy chill seize her, just as it had before, and the summer night was replaced by a blizzard of snow. Then light flared, orange and gold, like fireworks across her eyes. Turning, she saw a landscape that was quite different, a lake, wide and flat, a sullen grey against the black sky. On the edge of it was a dainty little summerhouse of brick and wood. The slender structure was shaking as fire licked up the side of it, the wood cracking and creaking as the flames took hold. There was smoke in the air, and cinders swirling up on a fierce spiral.

'Lucy!'

Finn's voice. He burst out of the darkness. She could hear Geoffrey barking, then feel the thump of his tail against her leg as Finn grabbed her, pulling her close.

'What's happened?' Now she could feel the beat of his heart. Her cheek was pressed against his jacket as his arms closed about her. It felt good. 'You called out,' Finn said. 'Are you all right?'

'Did I?' Lucy said. She felt confused. 'Sorry, I didn't realise. I...' Her voice trailed away. In her mind's eye she could see the summerhouse on fire and the flames shooting to the sky. And yet there was nothing there now, no fire and no building. The little pool was calm and the night was clear.

Was she losing her mind?

Geoffrey sniffed the air with a dog's inquisitiveness and she thought she caught the drift of smoke over the water.

'Sorry,' she said, pulling herself together. 'I heard a sound that startled me – it must have been a badger or something. I didn't know I'd shouted out.'

Finn released her. 'No worries,' he said, 'as long as you're all right.' He looked at Geoffrey. 'Geoff thought there was something wrong too. He raced back down the path to find you as though his tail was on fire.'

Lucy wondered whether Geoff, with his supernatural sensitivities, had seen the same thing that she had. He was looking at her with his limpid dark eyes, almost as though he *knew*. And Finn, she thought, was looking decidedly shifty, as though he thought he might have overreacted and was wondering if she had noticed. Well, she wouldn't read anything into it, nice as it had been to hug him.

'I appreciate the concern,' she said lightly. 'I've had a really nice evening but I'll leave the two of you to it now.' She reached up to kiss Finn's cheek. 'Thank you, Finn.'

He smiled. The combination of the smile and the scent of fresh air and cologne on his skin made her feel slightly dizzy all over again but for a completely different reason.

'You're welcome.' He looked at her. 'I don't suppose you have a torch?'

'I have one on my phone,' Lucy said, with dignity. 'I'm not a complete townie.'

'Fair enough.' Finn was laughing at her, and for a moment she wanted to confide in him, about the dreams, about the vision of the fire, to ask his advice and share how she was feeling. Then her natural reticence pulled her back.

She snapped on the torch. 'Goodnight,' she said.

★

The light from the beam was small but very bright and illuminated each step she took. She didn't look back and she didn't look around, concentrating on getting back to the barn and refusing for the time being to think about the snow, and the fire down by the lake and the summerhouse burning. If she had hallucinated it, imagined the entire thing, then she really did need medical help. Except that there was definitely a strong smell of smoke about her clothes and in her hair, and she was certain that the scene had been as real in that moment as the ripple of the stream was now in the quiet moonlight.

She reached the edge of the terrace and the patio light came on, flooding the valley in a white glare. A cat, surely the same one Lucy had seen on the first night but not since, slid around the corner of the building with a flick of its tail.

Lucy hesitated at the door, trying to gauge the atmosphere, instinctively waiting to see if she sensed any malevolence in the air, but all was still. In fact, there was a feeling of serenity that wrapped about her and made her smile. It was weird but at least it was nice-weird for a change. She turned the key and went inside, calling Cleo's number as she did, as though her sister's presence on the other end of the phone was some sort of magic charm to ward off any ghosts lurking inside.

'Hi!' Cleo, the night owl, answered straight away. 'What's up?'

'Nothing.' Lucy had decided that she didn't actually want to confide in Cleo over the phone as it would be almost impossible to explain things easily. 'I just wondered whether you'd be around tomorrow if I came over for a few hours? Sorry it's such late notice.'

'That would be lovely,' Cleo said warmly. Lucy heard voices in the background and then Cleo added: 'Sam says why not come for dinner? It's ages since she's seen you. And we could meet up for coffee in the morning if you like, as Sam and Dean are doing the first shift in the shop tomorrow.'

'I would like that, thanks,' Lucy said, 'if you're sure it's convenient? I... There's something I'd like to chat about.'

'Oh?' Cleo sounded curious.

'It can wait until tomorrow, though,' Lucy said. 'See you soon.'

She put the phone down and the silence flowed back through the house. It was very peaceful. Nothing ambushed her out of the darkness. She checked that the door was bolted as well as locked and, yawning, went up the stairs and took a shower, falling into bed with a sigh of pleasure, allowing sleep to take her. It felt as though she was almost waiting for the dream to come, waiting for Catherine. Her heart felt light; she was happy.

Catherine was happy too. As soon as Lucy slid into the dream, she knew it. Catherine was excited and joyful and so in love it felt as though she was about to burst. Lucy experienced her happiness as a huge bubble trapped in her chest, so huge it was almost painful.

Catherine was standing on the terrace at Gunpowder

Hall. Lucy stood beside her. Behind them she could see the knot garden and the back of the house, so much grander and larger than the current cottage.

'*So many blessings,*' Lucy heard Catherine whisper, and she saw her hand rest on the curve of her belly and knew that Catherine was expecting a child.

'Catherine,' she said. Was she the ghost in Catherine's world rather than the other way around? She did not know. Catherine turned her head as though she had heard Lucy's voice, but she looked through her. Then Lucy realised that there was someone else coming, a man striding across the terrace towards them. Robert Catesby. She knew it was him because she sensed Catherine's reaction to seeing him, the pleasure and excitement in her. She could hear the crunch of gravel beneath his boots, saw the breeze tousle his dark hair and catch the edge of his cloak. He was smiling and he caught Catherine in his arms and swung her around.

'*You are well, beloved?*' He kissed her, and Catherine put a hand on the nape of his neck to draw him closer.

'*I am very well,*' she whispered against his lips and he smiled and kissed her again.

Lucy was so close to them that Catesby's cloak brushed against her and she smelled the scent of his skin mixed with leather and horses. She was filled with the blissful sense of love that was emanating from Catherine, so heady it almost swept her away. And then she was tumbling over through the darkness and it was Finn she was dreaming about, holding her close and kissing her, and she woke up with a start alone in her bedroom, feeling disappointed and bereft.

CHAPTER 10

Anne Catesby

Knightstone Manor, December 1597

William and I paid another visit to our son and daughter-in-law after their second child was born. He was a boy, called Robert after his father, a brother for two-year-old William already in the nursery. My husband had been pleased with the compliment of his first grandson being named for him and it felt appropriate: the eldest son of the eldest son who would one day inherit the Catesby dignity, name and estates. I pushed from my mind the memory of another child called William, my own firstborn, dead before his first birthday, but I said prayers for his namesake.

I hope for a daughter next, Catherine wrote, *though I know I must not be greedy. We have been so blessed. Little Robbie is strong and sturdy, and as dark and handsome as his father. He is only nine months old yet already pulls himself up to stand and is determined to grasp after anything he wants…*

That I could well believe. He sounded just like his father. But I was relieved that the baby was not as frail as William, who was prone to coughs and chills, and that he had inherited Robert's tenacity. God willing, that would see him past all the illnesses and dangers of childhood.

William and I set off to Berkshire in good spirits and made a quick journey of it. The roads were dry and not too dusty, for winter had been mild so far that year, and the carriage comfortable enough to feel only every second jolt rather than each individual one. Knightstone Manor had been much improved in the two years since we had last been there; it was extravagantly and tastefully furnished, and Catherine's garden was entirely delightful, a series of pools, waterfalls, terraces and woodland dells that even out of season had a serene beauty, with arches of entwined holly and ivy, and carpets of snowdrops beneath the trees. I could not help but wonder at the cost of all this magnificence but kept quiet on the subject.

'I see you have achieved your grand design of a winter garden,' I said to Catherine, as we embraced. 'It looks glorious.'

Catherine was gratified. 'Winter can be a joyful season,' she murmured. 'I wished to celebrate that.'

We duly admired our grandson William first since he was the elder and as fair as little Robert was dark, and then cooed over baby Robbie, who was indeed a delightful child, bright and curious, full of promise, and the image of his father.

And into this happy gathering came the serpent in Eden, my sister Muriel.

Robert had mentioned casually at dinner the previous

night that he had invited Sir Thomas to visit the following day. William forestalled my reaction by appearing delighted with the news and in the light of his approval I could scarcely have complained, though of course I sulked quietly to think of my brother-in-law pushing in once again where I did not want him. And when his carriage arrived at the door it was Muriel who descended first, looking around and declaring herself delighted finally to see the house and garden that Thomas had spoken so highly of.

'And of course,' Muriel said, grasping Catherine's hands and kissing her warmly, 'my most pressing need is to admire our latest great-nephew.'

'Of course!' Catherine was all sunny smiles, concealing any irritation at having to deal with unexpected guests. Once again, I reflected that either she was a mistress of dissimulation or the sweetest-natured girl ever born. I was not sure which but I suspected the latter. There was no artifice in her. Muriel, on the other hand, could never lay claim to a sweet nature. I knew why she was here. She had told me in her letters that she resented Thomas' frequent trips to see Robert at Chastleton, his advice on the library and the development of the gardens, all the visits and the plans that excluded her. This time, she had evidently insisted on accompanying him. Her annoyance at Thomas' role in Robert's life was one of the few things that she and I had in common, though for different reasons.

The baggage was unloaded, refreshments provided, the guests washed the travel stains from their persons and, somewhat predictably, Robert bore Sir Thomas away to the library. Meanwhile little Robbie was brought from the nursery to be admired. He had been asleep and was still drowsy as the nurse placed him in my sister's arms.

'He is a handsome little fellow,' Muriel said, 'with a strong grip.' Robbie was holding a carved wooden soldier that we had given to him as a teething present.

The baby opened his eyes then and smiled at her, a bright, benign smile that tugged at the strings of my heart. 'Oh!' Muriel's tone changed. 'But he has odd eyes!' She sounded shrill, accusing. 'One green, one blue. How singular.'

I saw Catherine turn pink. 'There is nothing wrong with Robbie or his eyes,' she said, and it was the first time I had ever heard her sound ruffled. I knew then that the servants had been talking; repeating silly superstitions about changeling children and witchcraft, simply because Robbie was different.

'My dear,' I said, ignoring Muriel and addressing Catherine directly, 'no one believes any of the stories that fools tell about children with different-coloured eyes!' I gave Muriel a vicious look. 'Besides, we all know that babies' eye colour is forever changing and a babe with blue eyes at birth may develop brown ones as they grow. It is nothing to be alarmed about.'

The tension in Catherine's frame relaxed a little and she gave me a grateful smile although I could see she was still trembling on the verge of tears. As a new mother, her emotions were in flux and she was understandably upset at any perceived criticism of her child. I felt infuriated that Muriel could not see that – could not remember how vulnerable one could feel after the birth of a baby – and that she had caused this distress with her thoughtless comment.

Muriel, however, became more tense even as I tried to smooth things over.

'You misunderstand me,' she said tightly. Her sharp gaze pinned Catherine to her seat. 'Those are Tresham eyes. *Only* the Treshams have one green eye and one blue. It is a family trait down the generations.'

I felt a sharp blow below my breastbone as though all the air had been sucked out of me. I knew exactly what Muriel was intimating. Jealous of her husband's visits to Robert and Catherine's home, she was stirring up trouble in the most malicious of ways.

Before she could make her insinuations any clearer, however, William, unexpectedly, came to Catherine's aid.

'I do not think the Tresham family can lay claim to being the only ones to inherit this particular eye colour,' he said blandly. 'Rare as it may be, I have heard of other cases.'

'Have you?' Muriel sounded shrewish. 'Have you ever seen anyone who has it, other than in my husband's family? I think not!'

William looked confused at her vehemence. He, unlike me, had not caught the specific nature of her accusation. And then she made it clear:

'Both my husband and my sons have been frequent visitors to this house, have they not?'

Catherine burst into noisy tears. In that moment the door opened and Thomas came in, followed by Robert, looking buoyant and happy, a smile on his lips, bringing with him the scent of cold winter air. The smile died as he took in Catherine's weeping and his gaze turned to me, as though suspecting me of upsetting her, before he hurried across to her side, knelt down and took her hand in his.

'Sweeting—' He folded her close. 'What can have distressed you so?'

Catherine's reply, smothered by his doublet, was fortunately unintelligible.

'It is a misunderstanding only,' I said swiftly, stepping hard on Muriel's foot when she opened her mouth to contradict me. 'Your aunt spoke out of turn and I counsel her now—' I pressed harder, 'to think very carefully before she says *another word*.'

Robert and Thomas both looked baffled. Muriel glared furiously at me, then, with an angry flounce, thrust the baby at his mother and darted from the room. I followed her. She was positively running now, down the screen passage, her footsteps slapping angrily on the flagstones, and out into the knot garden.

'What the *devil* do you think you are at?' I cornered her at the end of the terrace, amidst the winter thyme and sorrel, too angry to even think of discretion or notice the sudden cold. 'What *possible* reason could you have for such patently false and hurtful accusations against Catherine?'

'They are not false!' I saw the depths of her misery and hatred reflected in her eyes and it shook me to the core. When she had written of her resentment at Thomas' visits to Knightstone, I had not suspected how deep it had cut.

'That girl is a hussy,' she said, 'a flirt, always smiling on my husband – and my sons for that matter – smiles and more for *all* the gentlemen!' Her mouth twisted. 'Those eyes! Whatever you or William say, I know the babe is a Tresham. He is the image of Thomas.'

'You speak utter nonsense,' I said. 'He is the image of Robert! And Catherine smiles because she is happy and kind, or she was until you poured your bile on her. How could you speak in such a way to such a gentle girl?' I was shaking with fury. 'How could you accuse her of such a crime, though whether it is sleeping with your husband or your sons – or both – I am not clear, though either way it is madness!' I flung out a hand. 'Can you not see that Catherine and Robert are devoted to one another? She has been the saving of him, and if you have ruined that through your spite, very likely I will kill you myself!'

Muriel's gaze fell for the first time. 'Then why does Thomas come here?' she muttered. 'Month after month, never to Chastleton, always to Knightstone, which is *her* favourite house? And the garden – her treasure garden, he calls it – speaking of it holding the greatest treasure of all?' She looked spiteful and mulish.

'Because it does!' I shouted. 'How can you know your husband so well and yet not know him at all? When we were children, Thomas' grandfather brought the Knights' Hospitallers treasure here for safekeeping. Very likely it is concealed somewhere in the garden, beneath Thomas' conceited design! He comes here to ensure it is safe until the time the order rises again – whenever that may be. It is his sacred trust.'

'He told you this?' Her eyes were wide, her jaw slack with shock.

'Of course not,' I said. At last I remembered to moderate

my voice. 'I overheard our parents speak of the treasure when we were children,' I said. 'And the rest – the garden – well, have you seen the emblem on the grass of the labyrinth? Thomas is not subtle. He thumbs his nose at the Queen's spies.'

Muriel swallowed hard. Her pretty, faded pink complexion was blotchy with tears and anger. 'It still does not explain Robbie's eye colour,' she said stubbornly.

I sighed tiredly. 'Oh, Muriel,' I said. 'I am sure that what William says is true and it is not such a rare thing. And even if it were, the Tresham and the Catesby families have intermarried for generations. It is far more likely that it is some long-forgotten inheritance from an alliance in the past than that Catherine should have played Robert false! That idea is patently absurd and you should apologise to them both.'

Muriel hesitated as though she were about to say more but then she caught sight of William hurrying along the terrace towards us, thought better of it and, muttering something under her breath, spun away in the other direction.

'Thomas is looking for her,' William said, when he reached me. 'He will prevent her from doing any more harm.'

'Thank God,' I said. 'And Catherine?'

'She is in a storm of weeping.' William was frowning. 'We must pray she does not take ill. Robert is with her, trying to calm her.'

'He does not blame her?' Fear clutched at me for I knew how unpredictable and difficult men could be if something touched their honour. 'He does not think there is any substance in Muriel's accusations?'

'Not the least in the world,' William reassured me.

'Thank God.' I released my breath.

'Can Muriel be mad?' William asked, troubled. 'Indeed, what could have prompted her to make such a claim about the child?'

'Nothing but jealousy and a twisted imagination,' I said. 'She resents the time Thomas spends here and thought that Catherine was the reason.' Once again I felt a pang, for had I not resented Thomas' closeness with Robert too? I was little better than her. I had wanted to break their bond, but unlike Muriel I was not prepared to break everything else in the process.

William was frowning. He looked at me sideways. 'I do not suppose… Could there be any truth in it?'

'No,' I said sharply. 'You have no reason to doubt your daughter-in-law and yet the moment some deranged person makes a wild accusation you are prepared to countenance it? Shame on you, William! Your son has better judgement than you do. He knows that Catherine is good and true.'

William looked ashamed and muttered an apology. I nodded curtly to acknowledge it but I still felt angry, for if this terrible row became common knowledge there would be trouble. Servants would talk. More than one person, for the sake of gossip and spite, would note Thomas' visits to Knightstone and check the dates and count the days and months against Robbie's birth, and all of it based on nothing. Vile rumour always crept forth like the stench of a sewer.

'I am sorry,' my husband said again, 'but it is true that

the Treshams do have such striking green and blue eyes. Francis has them.'

'And Thomas does not,' I pointed out. 'It is nothing but coincidence.'

'His father had them too,' William said, frowning.

I shrugged impatiently. 'Thomas is coming,' I said. 'For pity's sake, make none of your foolish observations in front of him.'

Thomas' face was grey and drawn, his usual confidence lacking. 'I am taking Muriel home,' he said. 'She told me what happened. I do not wish to put Robert in the difficult position of having to ask us to leave.'

'Better that you had not brought her here at all,' I said bitterly.

'I did not know,' Thomas said. He was looking shaken. 'I did not know how she felt or what she was thinking. I did not know she objected to my visits here, least of all that she imagined they were for Catherine's sake. I thought...' He met my eyes and I read his mind:

I thought that you were the one who wanted me gone from Knightstone...

'You should have confided in her the real reason you visit here,' I said. 'Instead of making obscure and foolish references to treasure gardens.'

Thomas' face fell. William simply looked puzzled, glancing from his face to my stony one.

'It is too late to travel,' he said, looking at the sky. 'You will have to bide the night at least, Thomas.'

'There is an inn in the village where we may stay,'

Thomas said, 'and be on our way at first light.' He looked at me and then back at my husband. He squared his shoulders.

'William,' he said, 'I wonder whether I might have a word in private with Nan? About her sister?'

'There is nothing that you cannot say before my husband,' I said, but William obligingly, was already nodding.

'Of course.' He touched Thomas' shoulder. 'I am sorry.'

Thomas nodded his acknowledgement.

'I am too cold to stand around out here any longer without a cloak,' I said. 'You must excuse me, Thomas—'

'It will take but a minute,' Thomas countered. 'Please, Nan.'

He waited until William was out of earshot. My heart started to race as I wondered what he might say. I knew I had spoken harshly to Muriel but she had deserved it. Would Thomas defend her and berate me for my words? Should I apologise first and take the wind from his sails?

'Nan,' Thomas said, and waited. I looked up at him. 'Is there any possibility,' he said, 'that Robert could be our son?'

I waited to feel a sense of shock but it did not come. It did not come because in my heart I had already considered this possibility and pushed it violently away. There was a possibility. Robert could be Thomas' son rather than William's. The truth was that I had never known, not for sure.

'No,' I said. 'There is no chance of it. I was already pregnant when we…' I stopped. I did not wish to think of it, let alone speak of it. I shuddered at my betrayal of William, the betrayal I had hidden so deep but been unable to wipe out and forget.

Thomas nodded. 'So you always said. Yet it was nine months almost to the day until Robert was born.'

'He was late,' I said. 'A ten-month baby.'

'It might explain little Robbie's eye colour,' Thomas said, 'if he were my grandson.' His voice was very gentle.

I wanted to explode with the same righteous anger with which I had attacked Muriel but I could not. The fury had gone and I felt nothing but tiredness. 'Oh Thomas,' I said, 'do not tell me that you also think it impossible for anyone other than a Tresham to have blue and green eyes? That is foolishness.'

'I did not say that,' Thomas said. 'But Francis has different-coloured eyes, as did my father and his uncle before him. It is well known in the male line and may skip a generation.' He was watching me, waiting.

'And Robert is the image of William's father, so everyone tells me.' I threw down the gauntlet.

Thomas shrugged, straightened. 'I merely thought that if this question of Robbie's parentage was to prove a… difficulty… between Robert and Catherine… If he were to believe there might be some truth in what Muriel had suggested—'

'Why would he countenance it for a moment?' I interrupted him. 'Surely you have given him no cause to do so?'

'Of course not,' Thomas soothed. 'The idea is ridiculous. I esteem Catherine greatly but no more than that. Yet you must admit that it is a curious situation and Robert may have questions… If he did, I wondered whether you might explain matters to him, in order to ensure there was no ill feeling between Robert and his wife?'

I snapped a spray of thyme between my fingers and crushed the leaves. The heady scent filled my nostrils.

'Yes,' I said, 'that sounds like an excellent idea, Thomas. I will tell my son that his wife is true to him and his son is definitely his child even if he does have Tresham blood in his veins. I will tell him that I know this because *I* was the one who was unfaithful to his father, with you, and that he is your son, not William's. You know how much Robert loves William? Can you imagine how he would feel? Do you have any other good ideas to suggest?'

Thomas smiled ruefully. 'Ah, dear Nan, always so astringent. It is one of the things I have always loved about you—'

'You never loved me!' I was infuriated. 'You wanted me, and I wanted you, and that is why it happened and that is all there is to it.'

Thomas caught my hand. 'You know that is not true, Nan. It was always you I loved, right from the start, from the time we were children—'

'Right up until the moment you chose to marry Muriel instead of me,' I said.

'You are right to reproach me,' Thomas said. 'I was a fool. When we were young I thought I loved you as a friend. Too late I came to see that a pretty face and docile manner was no substitute for wits sharper than my own and a spirit so fierce and brave.'

'Such fine words,' I said, but I let my hand rest in his for a moment longer than I should have done, remembering the heat of our affair, a dazzling excitement that had lit up a cold and barren winter for me after baby William had died and my husband had withdrawn from me in grief.

A common enough story, of another man willing to offer me comfort in my loneliness and misery, but I knew that in some ways Thomas was right; we had always been drawn to one another and I had certainly loved him from the time I was old enough to understand what love was. Now, though, I had other loyalties.

'It is far better now, twenty years later, to leave Robert a Catesby,' I said, 'and let him believe that his aunt is sick and her ravings are the product of a disordered mind.'

I heard Thomas sigh. 'Very well,' he said.

'Thank you,' I said. 'It might help,' I added bitterly, 'if you stayed away from Knightstone. Muriel cannot understand your closeness to Robert and resents it.'

Thomas scratched his chin. 'You resent it too, do you not?'

'Robert already has a father,' I said, not answering his question directly. 'He does not need you.'

'But I need him,' Thomas said, startling me. 'Do you not see, Nan? Robert is everything my sons with Muriel are not. He and I are so alike – he has that questing spirit, that confidence, that ability to inspire and attract. And you are wrong – he loves William as a father, as indeed he should, but that does not mean that he and I cannot forge a different sort of relationship. I am his godfather, after all. I can guide and inspire him too.'

I wanted to deny that Robert was like Thomas because to agree would be to tacitly admit he was Robert's father. And when I did not immediately answer, Thomas continued:

'I think that you resent me because you and Robert cannot find a way to be close. You never have been and now he does not need you, and you are jealous of those who do have a place in his life.'

The truth of his words hurt like an arrow's strike. It took me a moment to catch my breath.

'And I think, Thomas, that you have a particular way of saying the most hurtful things deliberately to make people suffer,' I said. 'I have observed that cruelty in you many times.' He took a breath to speak, but I went on: 'Yet for all that you congratulate yourself on your perspicacity, I know something that you do not. A true parent puts their child before all else. It does not matter if that child rejects or rebuffs them. They will not falter in their desire to protect them from harm. That is and always has been my aim for Robert, no matter whether he is close to me or not.' I met his eyes very directly. 'I do not believe that you are good for Robert. Yes, you and he have the same questing spirit. Yours had led you into dispute with the authorities, into danger because of your religious beliefs, to imprisonment and financial ruin. I will not countenance that happening to Robert. Keep away from him.'

I left him standing on the terrace staring after me. Wrapping my arms about myself, I hurried indoors and back to fire, for though the December day was mild enough, in my heart it felt as though winter was coming.

CHAPTER 11

Lucy

'You're up early,' Johnny said.

Lucy was curled up on one of the sun loungers on the terrace with her second cup of coffee of the day when he appeared on the footpath that skirted the garden. The dew was still shining like crystal drops on the grass and in the shade the air was cool, but the sun was already up and promised another hot day.

'I woke up at dawn,' Lucy admitted. 'There's an owl that sits on the roof and calls very loudly, and last night there was something barking away down the valley; it didn't sound like a dog, but a fox perhaps?'

'Or a deer?' Johnny suggested. 'They bark in the night sometimes.'

'And people think the country is peaceful!' Lucy said.

Johnny laughed. 'For a moment I thought you were going to say you'd been up all night,' he said. 'I thought you might be another one who enjoys impromptu camping. Finn often spends nights down at the lake in the summer.'

'I met him and Geoffrey down there last night when

I went for a walk.' Lucy waved her mug at him. 'Would you like a coffee?'

'I've just had one, thanks.' Johnny sat down on the wall that encircled the terrace, clearly happy to have a chat if not a coffee. 'I wouldn't have had you pegged as an outdoors type,' he said, 'more a sybarite like me.'

'I like luxury as much as the next person,' Lucy admitted, 'but it was such a beautiful night that I can see why you might choose to be outside.' She stretched. 'At least I got a decent night's sleep last night, which makes a change—' She stopped.

'Bad dreams?' Johnny sounded sympathetic and unsurprised. 'It can happen when you've been ill, can't it? Everything gets disrupted.'

'I guess so.' Lucy was surprised by his perspicacity but as a naturally private person she hesitated to confide in him. 'I remember you saying you were staying at Gunpowder Cottage whilst the dig is on,' she said. 'Have you got the blue bedroom, the one with the window seat? That's where I stayed when I came to visit Verity as a child.'

'That's the one,' Johnny said. 'Beams so low I keep hitting my head on them, and that amazing panelling... It must have been such an exciting place to visit when you were a kid – a place full of hidden corners and spooky old passageways. Your imagination could run wild.'

'It was lovely,' Lucy said. 'It felt like a house full of possibilities. I don't remember feeling it was haunted. Not then.'

'But now you do?' Johnny looked curious.

Lucy hesitated but was saved from answering by the arrival of Finn and Geoffrey, coming up the path from the lake. Not that it was much of a reprieve; the sight of Finn looking rumpled and unshaven only served to remind her of the previous night's dream and she felt herself turning hot. Fortunately, Geoffrey bounded over the wall and offered his usual effusive greeting which went a long way to restoring her sense of normality. It was almost impossible to indulge in erotic imaginings when a large Labrador was begging for attention. Then she noticed that Finn was averting his gaze from her pyjamas, respectable as they were, which made her want to laugh.

'Good morning,' she said. 'I hope you both slept well.'

'Geoffrey isn't the most peaceful bedfellow,' Finn said. 'He scratches and snores a lot.' He rubbed his chin where the stubble showed. 'I need a shower and a shave. Usually, I sleep well down by the lake but last night I had a nightmare that the woods were on fire. There was some sort of building down by the lake that was burning down.'

Lucy stared at him. That sounded exactly like her vision the night before.

'How strange,' she managed to say.

'I could have understood it better if it had been a flood,' Johnny said. 'That would have been Geoffrey coming back from a dip in the lake and shaking water all over you. Would you like some breakfast?' He included Lucy in the invitation. 'I'm making bacon and eggs before we start work.'

'You've actually got a day off today, remember?' Finn said. 'We're going to Burford for lunch with Lizzie and Arthur.'

'I'll save the bacon and eggs for tomorrow, then,' Johnny said. He smiled at Lucy. 'The invitation still stands.'

'Thanks,' Lucy said. 'I'd like that. I was hoping to borrow the car today,' she added, 'but it sounds as though you'll be using it.'

'Where did you want to go?' Finn asked. 'We can always give you a lift.'

'I'm meeting up with Cleo in Highworth,' Lucy said, 'but I don't want to put you out. I can get a taxi.'

'It's no problem,' Finn said. 'Highworth is on our way. Does half past ten suit you?'

'That will be great, thanks,' Lucy said.

'Okay, we'll see you up at the cottage.' Finn tilted his head towards Geoffrey in a wordless command and the dog, sensitive to his master's every move, raced off to join him.

'Succinct as ever.' Johnny was grinning as he stood up and stretched. 'I sometimes wonder how Finn has so much dating success. It can't be for his conversation.'

'I suppose the gruff, outdoorsy type does appeal to some women – and men too,' Lucy said, trying not to feel too put out at the thought of Finn's romantic conquests.

Johnny laughed and wandered off in the direction of the cottage whilst Lucy stood, picked up her empty coffee mug and went inside. Two doses of caffeine had left her feeling wide awake and a bit strung up, which wasn't ideal. She made some sourdough toast and ate it with a lavish helping of butter and strawberry jam, checking her tablet at the same time for train times from Swindon to London. She felt conflicted. She didn't really want to go back to London yet, particularly as it was high summer and the city would be full of noise and heat and tourists, but if she needed to see her GP urgently she'd have to head back. It really depended on how she felt after she'd talked to Cleo, and whether her sister thought she was suffering medically induced delusions or if she agreed with Lucy's own assessment that she was haunted in some way. Either way it felt more than a little weird.

As she ate her breakfast she thought about the previous night. First there had been the vision of the woods on fire, so sudden, vivid and terrifying. That Finn had had a similar vision in his dream was even more strange. Then there had been her latest dream about Catherine. It had left her feeling slightly like a voyeur in Catherine and Robert's relationship. There had been so much heat and passion between them but also such a strong sense of love, the type of love that hinted at pure delight in each other's company and the idea that together they were stronger than apart. Though perhaps she was just imagining that. This whole thing about being in someone else's head was new to her. Lucy shifted a little uncomfortably. What she did know was that their closeness had made her think about Finn and in her mind she and Catherine and Robert and Finn were getting confused. She was almost certain she had fallen asleep imagining that she was wrapped in Finn's arms as she had been earlier in the evening.

She finished the toast and licked the butter from her fingers. It felt as though there was some sort of emotional bond between herself and Catherine. When she was lonely or unhappy she had connected to Catherine's anguish and dreamed that Catherine was lost and lonely too. Last night she had felt happy and the barn had felt warm and welcoming too. It was the same now – it was full of light and looked ravishingly beautiful with its sleek wooden floors and white walls. It also looked far too modern to harbour some sort of centuries-old ghost so perhaps she was the one who harboured the ghost and Catherine would follow her back to London or wherever she went…

The black cat was now sitting on the patio by the pink tall-stemmed anemones, washing its white paws with studied concentration. Lucy could see Johnny out at the front of the barn, carrying a ruler and some string, presumably getting ready to measure out a test pit for the next stage of the dig. He and Finn must be planning to get a couple of hours of work in before they went out.

Lucy read for a bit, had a long soak in the frankly sumptuous wooden bath that Verity had had installed upstairs, chose her clothes with care – a belted green-and-cream floral poplin dress and her favourite sandals – and put on a dusting of blusher and a bit of lipstick. By then it was almost ten fifteen so she walked slowly up to Gunpowder Cottage, admiring the Queen Anne's lace and the poppies entangled on the grassy banks at the side of the path. The morning felt hot now, the early dew banished by the blaze of the sun.

She found Finn, Johnny and Geoffrey in the courtyard where Geoffrey was reluctantly being buckled into a dog harness and secured in the notional back seat of a sleek, fast convertible that already had the top down.

'This is not a practical car,' Lucy said. 'Are you sure there's room for us all?'

Finn laughed. 'I don't know your aunt as well as you

do,' he said, 'but from what I've heard it's in character for her to have a sports car.'

'This is Verity's?' Lucy blinked. 'I had no idea.'

Finn finished fastening a disgruntled Geoffrey in, and straightened up. 'I'm sure we'll all fit. I do have a Land Rover to transport all my gear but I thought this would be more comfortable today.'

'I don't know where you got that idea from.' Johnny was looking critically at the minuscule space next to Geoffrey. 'I doubt I can fit my legs in there, never mind the rest of me.'

'I'll go in the back—' Lucy started to say, but Johnny had already folded himself into the space in contradiction of his words.

'Does Geoffrey like the wind in his ears?' Lucy asked as she got into the passenger seat. She whipped a scarf out of her bag – she didn't want to arrive looking completely dishevelled. Unlike Cleo, it wasn't a look she could carry off.

'He seems to enjoy it,' Finn said, sliding in beside her. Immediately the car felt a lot smaller. Lucy was glad that the top was down; it would be almost unbearably intimate to be so close to Finn otherwise. She was ridiculously aware of him, which felt even less appropriate with both Johnny and Geoffrey breathing down her neck like dual chaperones.

'You're right, of course,' she said, stroking the soft-as-butter leather seat. 'This is vintage Verity. She's very cool.'

'She must have been a great auntie to have as a kid,' Finn said.

'She was.' Lucy smiled reminiscently. 'She spoke to me and Cleo as though we were adults right from the start. She was such a role model too, a real high achiever. I think

I got my drive and ambition from her…' She stopped. She still had drive and ambition but she didn't know what she was aiming for anymore. Soon she was going to have to decide. Her small savings were only going to last a short while longer.

'Everyone got their seatbelts on?' Finn glanced at her and Lucy felt a lurch in her stomach as she realised he must be thinking of Charlie, thrown clear from his car in the accident. Was it like this for Finn every time he got in a car? Did he always think about his brother? It made her heart ache to think that Finn might blame Charlie for his accident. She could imagine how angry she would be with Cleo in that situation because she loved her and couldn't bear to be without her.

'Geoff's just checking mine for me.' Johnny's voice came from behind them and Finn's expression lightened a little, though his gaze didn't waver from the road, and his hands on the wheel were very steady. They pulled out of the drive and turned right onto the road into the village, past the shop where Lucy caught a flash of Persis' bright hair and pale face turning to watch them pass. Finn took a right turn at the crossroads and headed down the hill past the chocolate-box thatched cottages and the duck pond.

Lucy turned her head to look at the passing scenery. They were crossing the flat lands of the Vale of the White Horse. Craning her neck she could see the horse's stylised outline against the deep green of the hills to the east. The road took them through another village and then they were dipping down past a farm and over a narrow bridge across a little river. Real horses drowsed in the fields on the right and the shadows of the trees that lined the road whipped overhead.

'What a beautiful place,' she said. 'It's been so long since I visited Verity. I'd forgotten how lovely it is here.'

'Have you always lived in London?' Finn asked.

'We grew up in Manchester,' Lucy said. 'I moved to London to study. So I have only ever lived in cities, really. I used to think the countryside wasn't for me, but that's mostly because it didn't suit my lifestyle. Now I don't know. I'm free to live and work where I want – once I decide what I want to do.'

Finn shifted slightly. 'That reminds me, I rang up to see if there were any current vacancies at Mortimer Hall this morning but they're fully staffed for once. Sorry.'

'That's okay,' Lucy said. 'As you pointed out last night, I probably wasn't right for them, anyway.'

Finn smiled. 'Well, you would certainly have had to rewrite your welcome speech,' he said. 'Dissing the place to visitors probably wouldn't have been the best move.'

'Are you looking for a job?' Johnny leaned forward.

'I'm looking for something temporary for a few weeks or so whilst I try and decide what to do with my future,' Lucy said. 'I'm sure something will turn up. Though I doubt Cleo will give me a job in the bookshop,' she added. 'I'd get distracted reading the stock.'

'Essential for the job, I would've thought,' Johnny said, grinning.

Lucy fell silent again, thinking that she needed to make a decision today about whether she would head home to London because that would disrupt any job-seeking anyway.

She realised she didn't want to go. Gunpowder Barn might be haunted – *she* might be haunted – but she still felt a very strong pull to the place.

'We can drop some of Charlie's notes around later if you want to help out deciphering them,' Finn offered. 'Can't offer to pay you, though, I'm afraid—'

'Except with a cooked breakfast tomorrow,' Johnny finished. 'And regular tea and cake.'

Geoffrey's ears pricked up and he looked hopeful. Finn, seeing his face in the rear-view mirror, laughed. 'Not for dogs,' he said, 'although there may be a spare sausage.'

They passed a golf club and the country road started to be bordered with houses. 'We're just coming into Highworth now,' Finn said. 'Where are you meeting Cleo?'

'In the market square,' Lucy said. 'Gosh, there are a lot of new buildings here. I haven't been to see Cleo for a good few years and the town was smaller then.' She pointed to a shop halfway down the high street. 'That's Cleo's bookshop. It's very like Cleo herself – stylish, eclectic and very cool.'

Finn smiled. 'It's nice that you're so supportive of each other,' he said. 'I can see you're very close. I've been in the shop a few times, actually, though I don't think Cleo was there. There was a very helpful bookseller who ordered some obscure sixteenth-century treatise on herbal planting for me.'

'That would be Sam, Cleo's girlfriend,' Lucy said. 'They run the place together. She's really into antiquarian books and history.'

Finn turned into the market square and stopped by

a smart-looking café with pavement tables shaded by poppy-red umbrellas. Cleo was sitting beneath one of them looking chic and fresh in a white T-shirt with a matching white scarf wrapped around her unruly black hair. She looked up and waved.

'Thanks so much.' Lucy hopped quickly out of the car and pulled the seat forward so that Johnny could extract himself and take her place in the front. Geoffrey stretched out expansively into the space. 'Have a great day,' she said. 'Have fun, Geoffrey!'

Geoffrey yawned widely and Johnny gave her a wave as Finn pulled out into the traffic.

'Hey,' Cleo said. 'How are you? And was that Johnny Robsart in the car with you and Finn?'

'Fine, thank you, and yes,' Lucy said. She followed Cleo back to the table where her sister had already ordered a cappuccino and an almond croissant. Around them the umbrellas fluttered in the breeze and people were eating brunch. A waiter came over and she ordered apple juice and a plate of pancakes with maple syrup and blueberries. The toast had been at least two hours ago.

'Good,' Cleo said approvingly. 'It's good to see you've got an appetite. It was nice of Finn to give you a lift,' she added. 'What's he doing today?'

'He and Johnny are having lunch with friends at Burford,' Lucy said, 'and yes, it was nice of him to drop me off on the way.'

'By friends you mean Lizzie Kingdom and Arthur Robsart, I expect.' Cleo's celebrity radar was well-attuned. 'They live in Burford and I read somewhere that Lizzie and

Finn had worked together on a couple of charity garden projects. I think Finn might even be godfather to her baby son.'

'I really wouldn't know,' Lucy said. 'Finn's not the type to talk about his celebrity mates,' she added pointedly. 'All I know is that Johnny's helping him with the excavation at the cottage. He's an archaeology student and he's very sweet.'

Cleo looked excited. 'Maybe Lizzie will come over too,' she said. 'Let me know if she does and I'll drop by to visit you.'

'About that...' Lucy said. She paused whilst the waiter delivered her pancakes and another coffee for Cleo. 'There's a chance I might go back to London.'

'What? Already?' Cleo put down her coffee cup with a jolt. 'But you've only been here for ten days! We talked about this and I thought you agreed to give it a bit of time. You were doing absolutely fine when we spoke a couple of days ago,' she added. 'In fact, you said you were enjoying lying in the sun and reading!' She narrowed her eyes on her sister. 'What is this really about, because I know there's something going on.'

'You have special powers,' Lucy said, smiling. She fiddled with her spoon, avoiding Cleo's eyes. Now that she'd reached the moment of confiding in her sister she felt a bit nervous. Would Cleo think she was barking mad, seeing things that weren't there? It all felt so outlandish and strange that she wasn't quite sure how to explain.

'I have been enjoying myself,' she agreed, 'but there's something about the barn, an atmosphere that's very odd. I've had some weird experiences.'

Cleo's eyebrows shot up. 'What do you mean? Is it too quiet? Because I know that can freak people out when they're used to living in a city.'

'It's not just that,' Lucy said. 'There's something there, something seriously disturbing.' She took a breath. 'I feel really stupid talking about this, but you remember I told you I'd had a strange dream on the first night I was there, about a Tudor woman called Catherine... Well, I've dreamed about her several times, not recurring dreams, but she always features in them. And they are so intense, it's as though I'm in her head, in her emotions even! I find it really disturbing.' She waved a hand to stop Cleo when she would have interrupted. She wanted to get it all out first.

'That's not the only thing, either,' she said. 'Yesterday afternoon, it felt as though there was someone else there in the barn with me, some sort of presence.' She met Cleo's eyes. 'It scared me, to be honest. It felt so real and dangerous.' She rubbed her forehead. 'So I went out for a walk, and whilst I was down the valley I had a sort of hallucination that I could see the woods on fire. It only lasted a few minutes, but again it was so real that it was terrifying. I feel haunted.' She swallowed hard and finished unhappily: 'And the worst thing is that I'm not sure whether there really is some sort of supernatural presence in the barn, or whether I'm losing my mind.'

'God, how frightening for you.' Cleo leaned across the table and touched her hand. 'I'm so sorry, Lucy.'

Lucy felt like hugging her for the simple acceptance. 'Thank you,' she said.

'I don't think it's likely that you're losing your mind as

such,' Cleo continued, spooning cappuccino foam out of her cup. 'I know you've been through a lot but you haven't shown any signs of it affecting you mentally through delusions or hallucinations, or at least not until this experience that you had yesterday.' She frowned. 'Why would it only start now, when you've been ill for several months?' She took a mouthful of coffee. 'Are you sure it isn't simply a series of random things that have scared you? I mean, nightmares can be pretty frightening, and that might put you off-kilter sufficiently to feel that there was some sort of malign presence in the barn.'

Lucy was shaking her head. 'I'd really like to think you're right,' she said, 'but I know there's more to it. I mean, yesterday, when I felt the "presence" of someone, I think I triggered it myself. I tried to play the violin and it was going so well that I was madly happy and then the pain came back and I felt devastated, you know, and it was at that moment I felt as though I'd connected with someone else's pain as well...' She turned her palms up. 'Does that make any sense at all? It feels as though there's some sort of pattern here.'

Cleo nodded slowly. 'And the hallucination about the fire? What happened there?'

'I'd met Finn down by the lake,' Lucy said, then seeing Cleo's smile: 'Don't look so smug, it wasn't planned, and we were just chatting! Anyway, he went off to fetch some kindling to make a campfire and when I turned around there was a building I hadn't noticed before on the other side of the lake and it was going up in flames. Then a second later, Finn was back and he hadn't seen anything and I realised I'd imagined it all, or hallucinated or something… I suppose him mentioning a campfire might have put the idea in my head, but then to think that I was watching a burning building?' She shook her head. 'You've got to admit it's strange. And the dreams aren't normal either.' She shivered convulsively. 'You've no idea, Cleo, how creepy it is to be looking out from behind someone's eyes and sharing their thoughts and feelings whilst knowing you are trapped there…'

'It sounds as though it could be some sort of astral projection.' Cleo was frowning. 'Your soul or spirit entering another body.'

'Whatever it is,' Lucy said, 'I find it very weird.'

'Less supernaturally, you're right that it could be the effects of your illness,' Cleo said. 'You're exhausted and you've had a lot to deal with. That sort of stress can come out in some strange ways, but—' she hesitated, 'I don't know. That explanation doesn't feel right to me. Having said that, I'm not a doctor.'

'It could also be a side effect of my medication,' Lucy said, 'but I don't think it is.' She looked down at her plate and started to eat the pancakes before they went cold. At least she hadn't lost her appetite yet. 'I've been on the same tablets for weeks now and they've never made me hallucinate before,' she said. 'But that's why I thought I'd go back to London anyway. I can see my GP and get checked out.'

'And if she tells you there are no side effects and that you're not hallucinating, what then?' Cleo asked.

Lucy looked up at the bright blue sky above the roofline. Two pigeons were sitting side by side on a telephone line and cooing peacefully. 'We're back to the idea that there's a supernatural phenomenon going on,' she said, shrugging, 'but perhaps I will have left it behind at Gunpowder Barn.'

'There are always more questions than answers,' Cleo said thoughtfully. 'That's a Johnny Nash quote, by the way.'

'I thought it was Shakespeare,' Lucy said.

'No, that's "*there are more things in heaven and earth, Horatio, than are dreamt of in your philosophy*".' Cleo finished her coffee and put the cup down with a contented sigh. 'Which is also true.' She tilted her head to one side. 'Aren't you curious to know what's going on, whether the barn really is haunted, whether *you* are? Did your arrival at the barn disturb some supernatural force in some way? What is it trying to tell you?'

'Whoa!' Lucy held up her fork. 'That's way too many questions.' She sighed. 'I don't know. I mean, I'm conflicted. Verity told me that Charlie Macintyre had found proof of the connection between the house and Robert Catesby, and that Catesby's wife was called Catherine. Potentially she could be the ghost, and a part of me wants to find out more about her and a part of me wants – literally – to let sleeping ghosts lie.'

'Well, she isn't exactly sleeping.' Cleo leaned forward eagerly. 'She's wide awake and trying to tell you something, Luce! I'm disappointed in you,' she added, when Lucy didn't say anything. 'Have you no curiosity? If it was me I'd be itching to find out more about Catherine Catesby.'

'I already know plenty,' Lucy said, thinking of the dreams. 'I know she adores Robert and that they had a child called Robbie, and that there was a beautiful garden at the manor when they lived there. I saw a spiral mound in the very first dream I had, and Finn tells me that there were probably two of them in the Tudor gardens. I've also dreamed about the manor after it fell into disrepair, which Gabriel, the guy in the heritage centre, told me had happened. So I think something terrible must have occurred...' She shuddered as though the shadow of Catherine's despair had brushed over her again. 'Something bad happened to Catherine and to the house and garden,' she said. 'I feel it and perhaps that's why I'm reluctant to know more.'

'It should be easy to find out if your hunch is true.' Cleo reached for her phone and started to tap the screen. There was a moment whilst the clatter and chat of conversation moved on around them but to Lucy it felt as though the world was oddly quiet. Then her sister looked up. 'Robert Catesby was married to a woman called Catherine Leigh,' Cleo said. 'They had two children called William and Robert. Both William and Catherine died in the late sixteenth century, as did Robert Catesby's father. It's thought that perhaps the grief from so many losses drove Robert to embrace a more radical religious faith, leading eventually to the Gunpowder Plot.'

'Poor Robert,' Lucy said. 'How horribly sad.' She shook her head. 'Wow, that's... sort of unreal. And sort of comforting in a way,' she added, surprised to discover she felt like that. 'I mean, it's reassuring to discover that I haven't imagined the whole thing.'

Cleo had continued reading but now she put her phone gently back on the table. 'Does it make a difference to how you feel, though? I mean, what will you do now?'

Lucy was silent for a moment. 'I don't know,' she eventually admitted. 'A part of me wants to know more about why Catherine seems to be bound in some way to Gunpowder Barn – and to me. But it's still weird, isn't it? I mean, I don't want to experience astral projection, or whatever it was you mentioned. That stuff is deeply peculiar and it's not really my scene.'

'Why not sleep on it,' Cleo suggested. She smiled. 'Assuming that Catherine doesn't interrupt your dreams, of course. And in the meantime, we could find out more about her.' She checked her watch. 'I must get back to the accounts but you take as long as you like.' She stood up, stacking the crockery on a tray to take back into the café. 'You're welcome to spend the afternoon in the shop with me, or look around the town. Or you could go over to visit Chastleton House. That was Robert Catesby's house up near Stow-on-the-Wold. You might learn more there about Catherine. I'll lend you the Mini if you'd like to go.'

'Would you?' It was such a beautiful day that the idea of driving out into the countryside appealed to Lucy. 'That's very kind.'

'No problem.' Cleo rummaged in her bag and took out the keys, tossing them to her sister. 'It's parked in the alley behind the shop. Sam and I will see you later for dinner – have a good time!'

Lucy ordered a coffee and sat for a little while longer, thinking about everything. The idea of visiting Chastleton had taken root in her mind now and she felt quite excited about it. She also knew that she didn't want to read any more about

Catherine before she went, but preferred simply to go to the house and see what she might find. It was the reverse of what she had expected to feel when she set out to talk to Cleo that morning. Instead of running away from the ghosts of the past she felt a sense of urgency to embrace the story and find out what had happened to Catherine and how that impacted on the present.

As she sat there, watching the shoppers mingling on the pavements, she was certain that for a second she caught sight of the figure of Catherine herself, in the red gown she had been wearing in the orchard, with the sun on her hair, beckoning her on.

'*Find me,*' Catherine seemed to be saying. '*Help me. Tell my story.*'

CHAPTER 12

Anne Catesby

Ashby St Ledgers, Northamptonshire, 1598

The summer of the year 1598 was so hot it was hard to bear. There was a drought, the earth turned yellow and brown, the leaves wilted on the trees and not a breath of cool breeze could bring relief nor did a drop of rain water the parched ground. The air suffocated like a blanket. Sickness bloated the land as though the heat encouraged it to flourish. William took to his bed, complaining of sweats and fever, and a pain in the chest. I mixed for him the bitter aromatic juice of horehound, sweetened it with honey and milk and prayed hard for his recovery. For a short while it seemed he did pick up a little, but on the seventh day the fever took hold with an even tighter grip and by the time the clock struck midday, he was dead. We had been wed for five and twenty years.

I missed him, my steady, thoughtful and companionable spouse. His loss left an enormous space in my life for I had loved him very dearly. Yet my faith – our shared faith – did give me comfort, for I knew that death was not the end and that William would surely have eternal life. Masses were said for his soul and I lit candles in his memory and thought of him and little William together at last.

I sent Byram, our steward, to Chastleton to tell Robert. William had, I knew, left a lifetime's interest in Ashby Manor to me so there would be no change in that respect, but in every other way things were different now. Robert was the head of the family and, I was sure, would be certain to demand some of Ashby's income for himself. I had no wish to quarrel with him. I wished we could both mourn together for we had both loved William; we had that much in common, at least. But Robert, when he came, was distant and formal, austere in his mourning black and his manner as cold as the grave itself.

'My condolences on your loss, madam,' he said. We stood next to one another at the graveside but we were many miles apart, so small a family, yet unable to come together. It felt as though without William to bind us, we were drifting away from each other more than we had ever done. I remember the heat of that day and how inappropriate it felt when I was so chilled inside.

Robert did not linger at Ashby, being anxious to return to Chastleton where his son William was ailing once more. Catherine had not accompanied him for this reason but she had sent the kindest letter, expressing all the sentiments that Robert could not bring himself to say.

My dearest Lady Catesby, dearest mother, she wrote, *my heart aches for you. I long to give you comfort at this terrible time. Know that I have you in my thoughts and prayers and that we shall meet again one day soon in happier times.*

But there were to be no happier times that year, for no sooner had Robert returned to Oxfordshire than word came of the loss of little William, his and Catherine's son. When I heard, I fell to my knees and the tears came as they had not for my husband. They were tears for a promise of the future that would be unfulfilled and a hope that was dashed.

I sent Byram to Chastleton again for news, wanting to go to them but not wanting to intrude at such a painful time, but when he returned it was with a face more bleak than the coldest winter.

'It was an illness like the sweating sickness of old, with shivers and giddiness, aching limbs and exhaustion,' he reported, the lines deep on his face and the dust of the journey still on him. 'They said the poor mite was screaming in pain. He took ill one morning and by the same night he was dead. So fast, milady. Struck down and gone. They buried him quickly to avoid contagion.'

'Thank God that his suffering was short,' I said, my heart wrenched to think of the child going through such a horrible experience. Worldly suffering was harsh and cruel even if he was with the angels now. Then I saw that there was worse to tell.

'Mistress Catesby is ailing too,' Byram said. 'They say she will die of a broken heart.'

I thought of Catherine, so gentle, so ill-equipped to deal with the harshness of fate. Would her love for Robert and little Robbie help her through this terrible time?

'Prepare the carriage,' I said. 'I am going to Oxfordshire.' I did not know whether Robert would be willing to accept my support, given the coldness between us, but I could not simply send a stiff note of condolence at such a terrible time.

Byram hastened away to the stables and I threw some items haphazardly into a box to take with me. It was already late in the morning of a dry, grey September day and I knew darkness would probably fall before we reached Chastleton but we would press on as quickly as we dared. The journey seemed interminable, mile after mile of ruts and dust, whilst I was gripped by a sense of dread that would not ease. Nothing, not my prayers nor the beauty of the passing landscape, could soothe my soul.

It was past eight in the evening when we rolled beneath the archway into the stable yard, the horses were exhausted and so were we. A frightened-looking boy came running to take the horses but I caught his arm as he reached for the bridles. Already I had noticed that the house had a shuttered air to it and that only one torch burned in the sconce on the wall.

'Mr Catesby,' I said, urgently. 'Is he here?'

'No, ma'am.' He recognised me and sketched a bow. 'There's no one here but the steward and I.' I saw his Adam's apple bob as he swallowed hard. 'Mr Catesby is at Knightstone, ma'am. You may not have heard – we sent a messenger but maybe you passed him on the road? Mistress Catesby died today. Fearfully quick it was, and the master is in a terrible way—'

'Saddle me a horse,' I said. I looked at Byram. 'Two horses.'

'Madam—' Byram would never hesitate to tell me if he

thought I was doing something foolish. 'Surely we should wait until tomorrow?'

'I fear for Robert and for the child,' I said. 'We will ride to Knightstone now. The night is clear; we can find our way.'

'If we journey by night, I will need a harquebus,' Byram said grimly. He patted his sword as though to check it was still there. 'This is madness, milady. You have been travelling all day and are fit to drop.'

'If you wish me to go alone,' I said, 'I'll take the gun and be on my way.'

Byram's mouth turned down at the corners. 'Very amusing, milady.'

As it transpired, we had no trouble on the road. We crossed the River Thames at Lechlade in company with a party of late-night travellers who were anxious to reach the town of Highworth by midnight. We hired fresh horses at the inn there and then the road was clear ahead of us. Outside the town we dipped down to cross a small stream overhung with willows and when we gained the ridge on the other side we could see clear across the vale to the hills beyond. All was dark, but for the moon, sailing bright and three-quarters full above us on the shreds of cloud. A few miles further on and I saw light pricking the darkness, orange red against the blackness of the night.

'Fire,' Byram called to me, and we spurred our horses forward, forgetting our own tiredness. The flames blossomed as we grew closer to Knightstone and for one terrible, heart-stopping moment I was afraid that the house might be alight. However, as we turned into the drive, scattering gravel from the horse's hooves in our haste, the dark bulk of the house crouched ahead of us, lit from behind with a backdrop of flame. We reined in, for the horses were scared of the smoke and the noise.

'Dear God,' I whispered, 'Catherine's beautiful garden is on fire.'

It seemed that the whole wood was ablaze. From our vantage point up on the terrace where only a few short years ago, Catherine had shown me her plans and planting schemes, we could see it all – the little summerhouse by the lake sagging and crumbling to cinders as the fire took it, the palisades and colonnades of tender plants like streaming torches of flame. Grasses burned, trees burned, arbours and arches caught alight. It was like a scene from hell. And all about us was the gunshot crack of snapping wood and the crackle of burning.

'Holy Mother of God,' Byram said blankly, though whether in prayer or blasphemy I could not tell.

'I am going to find Robert.' I dismounted and handed my reins to him. 'Take the horses to the stables if it is safe,' I said. 'And then I have a task for you.'

'Madam?' Byram wrenched his gaze from the fire raging below and stared at me.

'I need you to go down to the centre of the labyrinth,' I said. I pointed to the chequerboard turf lawn that was the centrepiece of the garden. It lay at the quiet centre of the chaos, a square of darkness surrounded by flame. I thought of the symbol of the Knights Hospitallers on the grass and of the secret Thomas had all but admitted that the garden concealed. The obvious place to look for the Knights' treasure would be beneath their emblem, in the very heart of the garden, just as the resting place of the order's treasure had once been in the heart of their church.

'In the centre of the labyrinth you will find an obelisk,' I said. 'There may be a trapdoor in the base, though it will probably be concealed. Beneath it I think you will find a small chamber built out of the rock. I want you to bring me whatever it is that you find inside.'

'And what might that be?' Byram asked, head cocked like an inquisitive spaniel. I could see the orange flicker of the fire reflected in his eyes.

'I do not know,' I said truthfully. 'I do not know whether you will find a hiding place, or indeed whether anything is concealed there or not. I am only guessing. But if there is, it must be saved from the flames for it is a holy trust.'

Byram nodded. Like the rest of us he was well-versed in secrecy and sacred pledges.

'Oh, and Byram—' I laid a hand on his arm, 'try not to be seen.'

He grinned. 'Anything else, ma'am?'

'Yes,' I said. 'Do not set yourself on fire in the process.'

He asked no further questions but took the horses and made for the stables whilst I walked softly through the loggia towards the house. Here on the terrace none of the garden had been damaged. The last of the late roses still bloomed, their night scent entangled in the air along with the heavy smoke. The knot garden with its neat box hedges and gillyflowers was quiet. For a moment I paused to draw breath and try to still my racing heart. I wondered whether

I was wrong to try to find the treasure and to remove it from its hiding place. Was I really doing this to keep it safe and honour Thomas' pledge to his grandfather and the knights? Or did I have a less honourable motive, a need to prove to Thomas I was as clever as he, to take the treasure from beneath his nose and to keep it safe from both his designs and Robert's ambitions?

I shrugged the questions away. There would be time later to think about the treasure; for now my urgent need was to find my son and my grandson.

There were no lights in the house. Where were the servants, I wondered, where were the villagers? I raised my hand and knocked. Silence. But no – I heard a step. The door opened and Robert stood in the aperture, a candle in his hand. He looked almost unrecognisable, eyes wild with grief, his hair and coat singed and smelling of smoke, his hand shaking so that the candle flame wavered madly, sending shadows spinning across the walls.

'Robert...' I said, but before I could continue a small child flew like an arrow across the floor, burrowing into my skirts, gripping my legs as though his life depended on it, which perhaps it did.

I knelt down and gathered him into my arms. 'Robbie,' I said. I stroked his hair and felt him shaking. 'I am here. You are safe.' I wanted to do the same to my son yet I could not tell him that all would be well for unlike a child he would know I lied and that nothing could ever be the same again. I picked Robbie up and held him in my arms, feeling the solid warmth of his little body against me and the hot burn of his tears through my gown.

And then Robert turned to me and his eyes were full of grief and pain.

'I killed her,' he said. 'I killed Catherine. It was my fault.'

CHAPTER 13

Lucy

Lucy enjoyed the drive up to Chastleton. Once she had crossed the river at the old bridge in Lechlade the towns and villages started to show their Cotswold character and golden stone. It was a softer look than the chalk and sarsen of Knightstone as though the countryside around here was less remote and more friendly. The bright sun conspired to make everything glow – houses and fields all lit as though by warm candlelight. And when she parked the Mini in the car park and crossed the road to walk down to the house, the first sight of it took her breath away.

She bought a timed ticket, which left her an hour to kill before she could go in so she wandered over to the church which was close by. Here there was more about the Catesby family – Lucy discovered that they had owned Chastleton for a number of generations and that Robert had inherited it from his grandmother. Both his sons had been baptised there.

Just before the allocated time, she walked back over to the house which – she discovered when she had bought a guidebook – had been built in 1607 by Walter Jones on the site of Robert Catesby's previous house. Nothing of the original remained, although there was a nod to the Gunpowder plotters in an engraved fire screen in the drawing room. Lucy tried to see if she could sense anything of Catherine's presence in the house but there was nothing. Perhaps all connections to her had been swept away when the previous manor had been demolished. Or perhaps Catherine had preferred Knightstone, where her presence was so very strong.

Lucy bought some gifts in the shop and then popped her head around the door of the second-hand bookshop. A sign was propped behind the till stating that someone would be back soon but until then, visitors could pay for any items in the shop. As she so often did in Cleo's bookshop, Lucy marvelled at the eclectic mix on the shelves, from bestselling fiction to fifty-year-old cookery books, sporting biographies to obscure history. And that was when she saw the book, on a pile beside the till: *The Gunpowder Plot and Life of Robert Catesby, also an Account of Chastleton House.* There was a date of 1909 on the spine.

She reached out to pick it up and a voice barked: 'You can't take that!'

Lucy jumped a mile. She hadn't heard the shop assistant returning and spun around, the book still in her hand, to see a small but determined-looking woman standing hands on hips, blocking the doorway.

'I'm sorry,' Lucy said, feeling absurdly as though she had been accused of shoplifting. 'I thought it might be for sale—'

'It's *behind* the till,' the woman said. 'It's put aside because it's *not* for sale.'

'I see.' Lucy put the book down gently on the pile. 'That's a shame,' she said. 'I'm trying to find out more about Robert Catesby. I'm from Knightstone, you see, Catesby's other estate near here, and we're researching the property he owned there for a restoration project—'

'Well, why didn't you say that?' The woman strode across to the table. 'You were supposed to come and pick the book up months ago! We were about to send it back to the library – that's why it's on that pile.' She shook her head. 'When you didn't return her calls the curator assumed you weren't interested in it any longer. She was only saying this morning it was a pity because your research might have thrown some light on Robert Catesby's time here at Chastleton as well.' She stopped, seeing Lucy's expression. 'What's the matter? You *are* Charlie Macintyre, aren't you?'

'I… Er, no.' She thought quickly. 'I'm afraid Charlie isn't working on the project anymore,' she said. 'Perhaps that's why this fell through the cracks. I'm very sorry.'

'Oh I see,' the woman said. 'Well, you're here now. Here's the book.' She handed it to Lucy like a sacred text. 'I'll just give Hazel, the curator, a ring to let her know.' Her gaze forbade Lucy from leaving the shop whilst she was speaking so Lucy tucked the book into her bag and moved away discreetly from the desk. A moment later, the woman covered the receiver and barked at her: 'Hazel would like to speak to you. Can you meet her in the café?'

Lucy checked her watch. There was plenty of time before she was due back for dinner with Cleo and Sam, and this could be an opportunity to discover what else Charlie and Hazel might have discussed. 'That would be fine,' she said.

Five minutes later she was joined by the curator, a dark, smiley woman who offered to buy Lucy a cup of coffee and a frangipane tart.

'I'm sorry about Moira,' she said. Lucy assumed she meant the woman in the shop. 'I hope she didn't give you the third degree? She can be a bit officious.' She took a bite of cake. 'What happened to Charlie Macintyre?' she asked. 'He was the person I've dealt with previously on the Knightstone project.'

'There's been a few changes,' Lucy said carefully. 'I'm Lucy Brown. I'm afraid Charlie was killed in a car crash earlier in the year.'

Hazel stopped chewing. 'Oh my God, how awful! I had no idea. I was away the day that he visited Chastleton so I never met him, only spoke to him on the phone, but he sounded like a really nice chap.'

'I think he was,' Lucy said. 'I never met him either – I only got involved in the project about ten days ago – but everyone speaks very highly of him. He was so young as well.'

'And so enthusiastic,' Hazel said. 'He was so into this project! He told me that he was doing the background research and his brother – Finn, isn't it? – was doing the specific garden research and overseeing the excavation. He said they were certain that there was a Tudor garden at Knightstone dating from the era that Robert Catesby owned the property.' She shook her head. 'I thought that would be amazing if they could uncover it. The period when Robert

Catesby was here at Chastleton isn't well recorded and of course his house is lost now, so anything new we could learn would be fascinating.'

Lucy took the book out of her bag and laid it on the table. 'Did Charlie contact you about the book specifically or did he get in touch about Robert Catesby more generally?'

'Both really,' Hazel said. 'We had a chat about the Catesby family and he said he'd tracked the book down to the National Trust collection here. I said we could lend it to him and he seemed very excited at the prospect.'

'Did he tell you why?' Lucy asked.

Hazel shook her head regretfully. 'He only said that he'd discovered some sort of Catesby connection to the Knights Hospitaller and that he hoped there would be more about it in the book.' She looked at Lucy. 'Does that make any sense to you?'

'I only know that the Knights Hospitaller had a monastic grange at Knightstone,' Lucy said, 'but I thought that was way before the Tudor period. I'm not a historian,' she added, 'I'm only helping out.'

'What happened to Charlie's assistant?' Hazel asked. 'Doesn't she know what the connection might be?'

'Who?' Lucy said blankly.

Hazel looked confused. 'Sorry, have I got the wrong end of the stick? Apparently, when he came here there was a girl with him, a student, one of my colleagues thought, young-ish, tall, blonde… She introduced herself as his research assistant.' She stopped, looking slightly embarrassed. 'Sorry,' she said again, 'I must have misunderstood.'

Persis, Lucy thought. She must have come to Chastleton

with Charlie. Perhaps she had wanted to be a part of the project, to pass herself off as his assistant rather than his girlfriend. Or perhaps Charlie *had* given her a role in helping with the research, in which case it was odd she'd never mentioned it to Finn...

'I know who you mean,' Lucy said. 'She was Charlie's girlfriend.'

'Oh.' Hazel's brow cleared. 'Yes, Kirsty did say that they seemed close. Well—' she drained her cup, 'is there anything you wanted to ask at this stage? You're very welcome to call me anytime, of course.' She passed Lucy a card.

'There's just one thing,' Lucy said. 'I saw that both Robert Catesby's children were baptised here and I know his wife died in 1598. Was she buried in the church? I couldn't find a gravestone.'

'No,' Hazel said. 'Catherine Catesby died at Knightstone but was buried in her family chapel at Stoneleigh, I think. There was a memorial at Knightstone that was later moved, or lost, I forget which.' She nodded at the book. 'There could be something in there about it.'

'Thanks so much for your time,' Lucy said. 'I really appreciate it. And the book,' she added. 'I'll get back to you with any questions and let you know as and when we uncover the Tudor gardens.'

'And I'll get in touch with you if I come across anything that might be useful,' Hazel promised. 'Good luck!'

As she walked back to the car park, passing an art exhibition in the old barn on the way, Lucy reflected that she might not have discovered anything to do with Catherine Catesby at Chastleton but she had the book and she had found out a little bit about what Charlie had been researching just before he died. The suggestion of a link between Robert Catesby and the Knights Hospitaller was intriguing. They needed to find out more about that, although perhaps not from Gabriel, as he hadn't been particularly supportive of the garden project.

She slid into the car and put her bag down next to her. Then she shrank back against the seat instinctively as Persis hurried past. She was searching the pockets of her jacket for change for the ticket machine and didn't notice her but Lucy, looking over in the direction she had come from, saw Gabriel himself leaning against the bonnet of a silver estate car.

He saw her and raised a hand in greeting, sauntering over. Cursing under her breath, Lucy lowered the window.

'Hi!' Gabriel was smiling widely, perhaps a little too widely. There was an anxious expression in his eyes and a false note of bonhomie in his voice. 'Fancy seeing you! What are you doing here?'

His stance, leaning on the roof of the car and bending down to peer inside, seemed rather aggressive to Lucy. Resisting the urge simply to drive off, she leaned away from the window, silently offering thanks that she had put the book in her bag.

'Oh, I'm just taking a look around,' she said. 'I'm visiting my sister Cleo in Highworth and she recommended a visit here. It's beautiful, isn't it? What about you?'

It didn't seem to have occurred to Gabriel that he might also have to account for himself. He gaped like a fish for a moment and then Persis popped up next to him. She also seemed a little tense.

'Hi, Lucy!' she said. 'What a coincidence seeing you here!'

'Isn't it,' Lucy agreed blandly.

'We've come to see the exhibition,' Persis went on, 'haven't we, Gabe?' Her gaze darted to him. 'Aunt Marilynne has some of her work on show.' She turned back to Lucy. 'Perhaps you saw it?'

'I saw there was an exhibition, but I didn't go in,' Lucy said. 'I wanted to get back to my sister's for tea. Maybe next time.'

'Great!' Persis' smile broadened, becoming more natural. Lucy sensed Gabriel relax slightly.

'Have you got the parking ticket?' he asked Persis, as though the conversation with Lucy no longer interested him. 'We gotta go.'

'Sorry,' Persis mouthed at Lucy as her brother dragged her away.

'It was totally weird,' Lucy said to Cleo and Sam later, as they sat on their tiny balcony looking out over the rooftops and eating a delicious chicken salad that Sam had put together. 'It was as though they were glad – relieved, even – that I hadn't been to see the exhibition. And then there's the whole issue of Persis pretending to be Charlie Macintyre's assistant rather than his girlfriend. What was that about? And why didn't she tell Finn she'd been with Charlie to Chastleton? I'm sure he didn't know about Charlie's trip there or he would have been to collect the book.'

'You could always ask Persis to explain herself,' Cleo said. 'There could be a perfectly natural explanation. Maybe she wanted to big herself up in front of the staff at Chastleton rather than admit she was just along for the ride? And perhaps she didn't tell Finn because she just forgot.'

'On the other hand...' Sam took a drink of the chilled ginger beer Lucy had bought in the Chastleton shop as a thank you present, 'if people don't mention something it's usually because they don't want you to know.' She smiled at Lucy. 'You can tell I used to be in the police, can't you.'

'You have such a suspicious mind,' Cleo grumbled, nevertheless casting her girlfriend an adoring glance. 'The trouble is, you're usually right.'

'Of course I am.' Sam looked smug. 'I know human nature. My bet is that Persis didn't want anyone to know she'd been to Chastleton with Charlie, or what was discussed whilst they were there. And if she and Gabriel didn't want you to see the exhibition, Lucy, then there must be something in it they don't want you to know about.'

'Wow.' Lucy stared at her. 'Do you really think so?'

Sam shrugged, reaching over to pass Lucy the salad bowl for a second helping. 'I'm only guessing. Time may tell whether or not I'm right. Which reminds me, whilst poor Cleo was slaving over the accounts today I had a bit of time to research Catherine Catesby. There isn't much about her, is there?'

Lucy looked suspiciously at her sister. 'Did you tell Sam that Catherine is haunting me?'

'Hmm... Maybe.' Cleo avoided her gaze. 'You know we tell each other everything.'

'I'm open-minded about these things,' Sam said with a smile. 'If you think you're haunted, Lucy, I'm not going to tell you otherwise. But I can tell you that there's pitifully little information available on Catherine Catesby. She's yet another woman from history who appears to have left very little footprint.'

'No wonder she wants to be heard, then,' Cleo said. 'Fed up with centuries of being ignored.'

'What I did find, though,' Sam continued, 'are reports of her ghost, which is why I'm open-minded about your experience. Apparently, Catherine has been seen before.'

'Oh!' Lucy said. She realised she was feeling slightly taken aback.

'I hope you don't feel too disappointed not to be the only one to see her,' Cleo said acutely.

'No.' Lucy swallowed her feelings. If Catherine had really reached out for help before, it was all the more important to try to connect with her. 'What happened?'

'It's in here.' Sam passed her a slim volume.

'*Legends and Folklore of Berkshire*,' Lucy read, glancing at the lurid cover of a shrieking spectre that looked straight from Halloween central casting. 'Not your usual stock, surely?'

'Don't judge a book by its cover,' Sam said. 'I've stuck the bookmark in the place – see what you think.'

Lucy opened up the book at the page indicated and set the bookmark to one side. *'A curious tale of haunting and lost treasure comes from the village of Knightstone near Lambourn,'* she read. *'On a very hot summer in a year soon after the war—'* She checked the publication date of the book, which was

1953. 'That's the Second World War, presumably – *a woman reported meeting a lady dressed in old-fashioned clothes who was crying amongst the trees of the orchard above the valley. When she enquired kindly as to the cause of her grief the woman said she was mourning her lost treasure and was riven with guilt and misery that she could never find it or return it to where it belonged. She said that her name was Catherine and her husband was master of the manor of Knightstone, and then with much weeping and wailing she vanished through the trees, never to be seen again...'* She put the book down. 'Crikey. That's rather melodramatic.'

'Read on,' Sam said.

'Further to the sad case,' Lucy read, *'that same summer, strange marks and shadows were observed in the fields nearby and the local populace armed themselves with spades and shovels in an attempt to find Lady Catherine's lost treasure. But though they dug for days they found nothing but a few gold coins. One labourer, Isaac Redfern, swore never to give up the hunt.'*

Lucy put the book down quietly on the table. 'Well,' Cleo said, after a moment, 'that sounds like your standard ghost-stroke-lost-treasure story, doesn't it? It's a third-hand report of something that I would have said was totally made up if it wasn't for the fact that you had met Catherine yourself.'

'I haven't *met* her,' Lucy said. 'I haven't had a conversation with her like the woman did in this story. It's more that I *am* her, or that I can see into her mind.' She gave a little shiver. 'I wonder who she was, the lady who enquired kindly as to what was wrong with Catherine?'

'Whoever she was,' Cleo said, 'she's surely dead by now. This must have been about 1946 or so.'

'That's another thing,' Lucy said. She was remembering

the newspaper cutting Finn had found in the book. 'Those strange marks and shadows that were seen on the ground were picked up on aerial photography. It must have been the same year. Finn was interested in them because he thought they might be evidence of the lost garden. It's going to be a bit disappointing if he finds they were all ruined by locals digging for treasure.'

'He'll probably be interested to hear the story anyway,' Cleo said.

'I'll tell him tomorrow,' Lucy said. She picked the book up again. 'May I borrow this?' she asked Sam.

'Of course.' Sam started to stack the empty plates. 'Were you thinking of trying to trace the origins of the story?'

'I might,' Lucy said cautiously, 'but there's something else that caught my eye as well. It may be a coincidence, but Persis and Gabriel's surname is Redfern, just like the labourer who allegedly swore to keep searching for the treasure until it was found.'

CHAPTER 14

Anne Catesby

Knightstone Manor, September 1598

'I killed them,' Robert repeated. 'It was my fault.'

A consignment of materials had arrived from London a week before, he told me. He had ordered the gift when he had last visited. There were fine silks and velvets for the dressmaker to make two new gowns for Catherine as well as toys for both the children. Catherine had unpacked the parcel herself, exclaiming over the richness and bright colours of the cloth whilst Will and Robbie had played with the wooden soldiers. But within only a couple of days, Will had a cough and a fever and then Catherine too swiftly succumbed and now both were dead.

'There was an evil that came in my gift to her,' Robert told me as he slumped in the nursery chair whilst Robbie, exhausted, slept burrowed in my lap. 'I do not know how or why it came, but it stole them both from me. It was my fault.'

There was a fire in the grate and the house was once more candlelit for I had sent Byram to the village to call back the servants. Once they knew that I was there and in charge, they crept back, still fearful, still crossing themselves against evil, as the garden smouldered about us.

'Robert.' I was both exasperated and desperately sorry for him. 'It was none of your doing. You know that sickness creeps in and strikes unseen. Blame the London tailor if you must blame someone, for he sent you tainted goods, but do not, I beg you, hold yourself to account.'

I could tell that he did not hear me. He was far away, dazed by grief, lost in the labyrinth of his mind. 'Sir Thomas told me that I had turned away from the true path,' he muttered. 'Perhaps God has taken my angel from me to turn me back to the right path, for now she is gone I have nothing of value left.'

I looked pointedly at his surviving son, asleep beside me. 'That is nonsense,' I said. 'You have another child and he is strong and well. Besides, Thomas should mind his own business.' The glimpse that Robert had given me of a rift between him and his godfather surprised me, but perhaps it was not too serious. Thomas was a man who enjoyed debate for its own sake and I could not imagine for a moment him condoning the idea that Catherine had been taken from Robert as some sort of punishment. It felt more to me that Robert was punishing himself.

'It is true that I was content to be a church papist whilst Catherine lived,' Robert said. 'I did nothing to further our Catholic cause.' He did not look up from the wine that he was swirling in his glass. He had already had far too much of it but I was not going to forbid him more. This was the first time in years that he had spoken to me; perhaps his father's ghost stood at my shoulder, reminding me to stay quiet and calm.

'You are in grief,' I said. 'It is natural that you should feel this way for you loved Catherine so dearly, as she loved you. But you have not failed our cause, Robert, or your God. It cannot always be a fight; sometimes we must be content to bide a little and wait for our time to come around again.'

I might as well not have spoken. I could see it even as the words fell from my mouth. Catherine had been Robert's guiding star. She had steadied him and now he was adrift. Perhaps if his father had been alive now matters might have been different. Robert would have turned to William and listened to him. Or perhaps it would have made no difference at all. Certainly, I could not reach him.

'How did the garden come to be on fire?' I asked him when some moments had passed and I realised that he was not going to respond to what I had said. 'It was so beautiful, Robert – a beautiful memorial to her! What happened?'

Once again I saw the unbearable pain in his eyes. 'I could not look upon it,' he said simply. 'It would always remind me of her. She was lost in the most sudden and painful of ways; it was right that the garden should be cut back also at the height of its beauty.'

'You destroyed it?' I stared at him in shock. 'You set it on fire?'

Again, he did not reply.

I swallowed the tears that blocked my throat. 'You were angry to have lost her,' I said. 'You needed to vent that anger on something or someone.'

He shrugged as though it did not matter. 'I think I shall

always be angry now,' he said. 'Whatever the case, I shall never come to Knightstone again.' He put down his empty glass. 'I am for London,' he said. 'There is nothing here for me now.' He stood up as though preparing to go in that instant.

'But Catherine is not even buried yet!' I cried, putting out a hand to him. 'And what of your son – what of Robbie? He will need you more than ever now he has lost his mother!'

Robert looked down on the sleeping baby and his expression did soften a little. 'I cannot give the boy what he needs,' he said. 'You must have him, Mother – take him to Ashby and care for him there.' He looked at me, and all the softness had fled. My heart shrank a little to see his expression. 'You always wanted a son you could mould as you wished,' he said bitterly. 'Now at last you have one.'

'That is unfair, Robert.' I was still calm though my heart pounded at the unkindness of his words. 'What I wanted was always for you to be safe, and happy, as you were with Catherine.'

He inclined his head in acknowledgement. 'And now that time has gone,' he said. He turned towards the door.

'Wait,' I called, and he paused. 'You will come and visit Robbie at Ashby, I hope,' I said. 'And me as well?'

Robert smiled then. 'I will come,' he said, 'but for now I have work to do. I am for London.'

I wanted to beg him to stay, to rest a little, to let me care for him, but I knew he would not allow it. If there was any solace to be found, Robert would find it in action, not in the places where he had been so briefly happy. I wondered whether he might seek out Thomas at Lyveden to talk to him of his grief, but I knew better than to ask that and better than to resent it. If Thomas could help Robert put his shattered soul back together then I could only be grateful and happy for it. As for the action he planned to take, I refused to worry about that now that I had my grandson to care for.

When the door had closed behind Robert I pressed a kiss on the hair of his sleeping son. 'I will care for you,' I vowed. 'I will talk to you about your mother, and love you as much as she did, and honour her memory.' And he turned closer to me in his sleep and grasped my hand in his smaller one and in that second, he lodged so tight in my heart I knew I would go through hell and high water to protect him for ever.

Later, when Robert had left for London and I had set the servants once more about their duties and the house was calm and quiet again, I sent for Byram. Dawn was breaking, a streak of pewter across the autumn sky. The steward, clearly embarrassed by his earlier desertion of his post, told me that he had sent out a messenger to Sir Thomas Leigh to notify him of his daughter's death, and that a man had gone to Lyveden as well to tell Sir Thomas Tresham on Robert's orders. The village carpenter, he added, would prepare a coffin that day for Mistress Catherine and the women were waiting to dress her body and prepare her shroud with herbs and flowers. I knew that this miserable task would also fall to me to oversee in Robert's absence and as Catherine had no other female relatives in the house. It was important to perform the appropriate rites before too much time had passed. But I wondered whether Catherine would have wished to be buried at Knightstone, which I knew she had loved, or whether her father would deem it more appropriate for her to return to Stoneleigh. There was so much to do of grief and mourning and I had so recently done the same for my own husband. I felt weary and grief-stricken deep into my bones.

'The people in the village are saying that Mr Catesby has lost his mind,' Byram reported when, having laboured to put out the last embers of the fire and sluiced himself down with water from the well, he finally joined me in the parlour. Robbie was sitting by the fireside playing with a hoop and ball, seemingly engrossed in his game. 'They say he must be bewitched by grief to desert his son and his home and ride off in the middle of the night.'

'They may well be right,' I said.

Byram nodded towards Robbie, enraptured with his toys.

'He comes home with us?'

I nodded. 'Robert decreed it,' I said. 'Robbie is to make his home with us at Ashby. I doubt the Leighs will object.'

Byram looked grimly pleased. 'We'll see him right,' he said.

I nodded. 'We shall.' I stood up, stiff and aching, and crossed to the window. Never had a day seemed to arrive with such grey and weighty dullness. It felt as though all the sadness in the world was piled up in those bleak clouds. 'I see that all the fires are out,' I said.

'By divine providence.' Byram gave me a twisted smile. 'It rained.'

I nodded. I could hear the dripping of raindrops from

the roof onto the terrace and smell the cloying scent of wet burned wood in the air.

'And the other matter from last night,' I said. 'How did you fare with that?'

'I found the chamber beneath the obelisk in the garden,' Byram said. He shook his head. 'It was empty. Whatever you expected, madam, it was not there.'

I sat down rather abruptly. I had not anticipated this. 'There was a chamber, as I had predicted?'

'Aye, madam,' he measured the room with his eyes, 'about half the width and almost the height of this space, so of considerable size. Six steps down and a trapdoor over, like you said. It is lined in stone and is as secure a storage spot as one might wish, and untouched by the fire, but as I said – empty. I nearly put my back out climbing down into it, and all for nothing.' He cocked his head. 'May I ask what it was that you thought I might discover there?'

'I thought you might find the treasure of the Knights Hospitaller,' I said. 'Golden chalices, jewelled crosses, illuminated manuscripts, holy robes, devotional relics…'

Byram's eyes bulged. 'Holy Mary!' he said. Then: 'And what a pity I did not find it.' He nodded towards little Robbie. 'A few pieces of gold and some jewels would give the youngster the best start in life. He deserves it.'

'He does,' I agreed, for I knew the road ahead of us now was going to be a bleak one. Robert would bleed Ashby dry of any income and Robbie and I would pay the price. I wished suddenly, fiercely, for some of that gold coin Byram imagined, but even as I did, I knew it would never serve.

'Even had we found it we could not have kept it,' I said

reluctantly. 'The Knights' treasure is a sacred trust. Nothing but ill fortune would come to anyone who took it for ill purposes. Remember, *whoever hastens to be rich will not go unpunished*,' I quoted to him from the Bible.

'There is nothing wrong in providing for the child,' Byram said stoutly. 'The good Lord would understand.'

'It is immaterial,' I said, 'since the treasure was not there. By providence again, we have been spared the temptation.'

Byram looked pained. 'Your faith must be a great comfort to you, madam,' he said, 'and I admire your upright spirit, but it will not keep us all warm and fed. Ashby falls about our ears and now we have another mouth to feed. And young lads always eat like horses.'

'We will find a way,' I said. I looked out at the drenched remnants of the garden. Amongst the twisted, charred and burned ruins, only the labyrinth and the water remained, though the pretty little obelisk that had marked the centre of the maze was nothing more than cinders and ashes. I thought of the sealed vault lined with stone, carefully constructed, hidden and secure. It must have served some purpose, yet it had been empty.

I rubbed my tired eyes. Perhaps someone had been ahead of us, I thought. The fire had caused chaos and under cover of that, a thief could have slipped in and no one would have noticed.

'Where there is treasure, Byram,' I said, 'there are always thieves.'

His mouth turned down at the corners. 'Is that also from the Bible, madam? Proper miserable book it can be.'

'No,' I said, 'those were my own thoughts. I must speak

with Sir Thomas Tresham,' I added. 'But for now there is only one treasure that concerns me.' I picked Robbie up and he nestled into my arms, smiling, a wooden toy clutched in one hand whilst with the other he reached inquisitively for the lace at my throat. Already he was so familiar to me, his shape, his scent, that my heart unfurled with love every time I saw him. He was the skein of light that ran through the darkness of those days. And though my bones protested that I was too old now to have the care of a young child, no power on earth or in heaven could have taken him from me.

'He is hungry again,' I said prosaically, 'just as you predicted.' I blinked back the fierce tears that flooded my eyes. 'Let us go and find something to eat.'

CHAPTER 15

Lucy

'I feel as though I missed something at Chastleton,' Lucy said to Cleo, as they drove back from Highworth to Knightstone through the twilight landscape.

'What do you mean?' Cleo took her gaze from the road to look at her briefly. 'I thought you were pleased to have got hold of the book about Robert Catesby and have that chat with the curator about Charlie?'

'Oh, I was,' Lucy said. 'No, I mean that I feel as though I missed something that *Catherine* was trying to tell me. When you first suggested the visit, I felt her presence so strongly. It felt as though she wanted me to go there. But then when I got to the house, it was as though she'd vanished completely. I couldn't connect to her at all. After days of being haunted by her it was strange to go to a place where she had lived and yet feel nothing.'

Cleo was silent for a moment. 'You do realise,' she said, 'that you've gone from talking about Catherine as though she was a hallucination you wanted to escape to a real person who is trying to communicate with you?' She gave Lucy another quick glance. 'How did that happen?'

'I'm not sure,' Lucy admitted. 'It obviously helped to talk it through with you today—' she shot her sister a smile, 'and I think that when I was reassured that I'm not imagining things, I started to feel less threatened and more curious. I'm sure Catherine connected with me in the first place because of our shared sense of loss, but…' she hesitated, 'well, there has to be more to it than that, doesn't there?'

'Not necessarily,' Cleo said. 'Hauntings can be very specific – I mean, they can be specific to a place, person or time. So you might sense Catherine's presence at Knightstone but not anywhere else, or it might be a particular time of day, or whatever.'

'I suppose so,' Lucy said, sighing. 'It's just an instinct I have, though, that Catherine wants to tell me something or that she needs my help. And before I went to Chastleton, I thought…' She stopped. 'Well, like I said, I felt strongly that she wanted me to go there for some reason. But when I did, there was nothing.' She shrugged. 'So maybe I've got it all wrong.'

'Maybe you'll find the answer in the book about Robert Catesby,' Cleo said.

'Maybe,' Lucy agreed. It felt as though the book was burning a hole in her bag. She'd wanted to dive straight into it as soon as she'd got back to Cleo and Sam's but although she'd known they wouldn't have minded, there was so much other news to catch up on and she hadn't wanted to seem rude. Now, though, she couldn't wait to get back to Gunpowder Barn and do some bedtime reading.

'I'll give the book to Finn tomorrow and tell him what I found out at Chastleton,' she said now. 'Maybe he'll be able to work out what it was that Charlie wanted it for.'

There was silence for a few moments whilst the dark countryside swept past. They were following the same route as in the morning; Lucy recognised the dip down to the little stream and the low bridge, the field where the horses were sleeping, silver in the moonlight. The road was empty.

'Poor Robert Catesby,' Cleo said suddenly. 'No wonder he felt like going round blowing things up. Did you know he lost his father and his son and his wife all in one year? It's more than one person should have to bear.'

Lucy gave a splutter of laughter. 'That's an original excuse for terrorism, Cleo. But, yes, it does feel as though all that bereavement must have destabilised him. I do find it interesting that up until that year he'd been content to be… What was it they called it – a church papist?'

'Yeah,' Cleo said. 'Someone who either pretended to be happy conforming to the Protestant religion or was genuinely content to attend Protestant church even though they were a Roman Catholic.'

'And then after Catherine died, Catesby became a fanatic,' Lucy said.

'He got involved in the Essex Rebellion, and funded Jesuit priests, and was in touch with King Philip of Spain to ask for money to support the Catholic faith in England,' Cleo said. 'Sam and I did a project on the Gunpowder Plot with the local school a few years ago,' she added. 'I read Antonia Fraser's book about it at the time.'

Had Robert Catesby always been drawn to the cause

by his spiritual beliefs, Lucy wondered, or had the balance of his mind been tipped by loss and grief to embrace a cause that was all-consuming, something that could fill the void? If Catherine had lived, would it have been different? Whatever the case, Robert had ended up as one of the most notorious men in English history.

'You didn't mind me inviting myself to stay, did you?' Cleo asked, as they turned down the lane to the barn. 'I want to keep an eye on you whilst all this weird stuff is going on.'

'I thought it was because you were hoping Lizzie Kingdom might drop in to visit Finn,' Lucy said dryly. 'No, of course I don't mind. It's sweet of you, and thank you for the lift as well.'

There were lights on in Gunpowder Cottage but the barn was in darkness and the valley below was shrouded in shadow. 'It's strange to imagine all of this as part of some elaborate garden,' Cleo said as she pulled her travelling bag out of the back of the car. 'I wonder what on earth happened to destroy every last vestige of it?'

'It was a long time ago,' Lucy said. 'Gardens disappear. Houses do too, don't they? Layer upon layer of history...' She shivered suddenly in the warm air. Now that she was back here Catherine seemed to be with her again; the air almost crackled with her presence, though not in a menacing way. Lucy looked at Cleo to see if she could feel it too but her sister seemed supremely unaware of any atmosphere. Lucy opened the door and snapped on the lights. The room burst in brightness, looking entirely normal.

'I'd almost be excited to be here,' Cleo was already

upstairs, twirling around on the galleried landing, 'if it wasn't for the fact that you've convinced me the place is haunted and I'm expecting the ghost of Catherine Catesby to pop out of the bathroom at any moment. It really is a fabulous place. Am I in here?' She took her bag into the spare bedroom. 'Do you want me to leave my door open,' she called, over her shoulder, 'in case you get spooked in the night?'

'No, you're all right.' Lucy felt unexpectedly light-hearted. It would be a determined ghost indeed who could withstand Cleo's presence, she thought. She yawned widely. Reading through the book she'd brought back from Chastleton would have to wait until the morning. She was exhausted.

'I'm going to call Sam and let her know we're here and then turn in,' Cleo said. 'It's been a long day. Shout if you need me, though.' The door of the spare room closed behind her.

Lucy took a shower, got into bed and turned out the light. The house was quiet, the softness of the bed enveloped her. She could feel herself relax and start to drift into sleep.

Then she heard screaming, followed by the slamming of the front door.

'What the hell?' She was wide awake in two seconds flat, leaping from the bed, rushing out onto the landing. All the lights were blazing; it was so bright she couldn't see. She barrelled into Cleo who was running up the stairs, and grabbed her and held on.

'Sorry, sorry…' Cleo was panting.

'What happened? Are you all right?' Lucy blinked and focussed on her sister. Cleo, she noted, was still fully dressed. She wondered what time it was. She'd been on the edge of sleep but had no idea how much time had passed.

'Someone was lurking out in the yard.' Cleo was shaking, clinging tight to Lucy. 'I needed my phone charger and realised I'd left it in the car so I nipped out to get it and as I was coming back, someone came around the corner of the house and walked straight into me. I screamed and they ran away. Ugh, that was scary.'

Lucy hugged her back tightly. 'You're not hurt, though?' she questioned urgently. 'They didn't touch you?'

Cleo shook her head. She loosened her death grip slightly. 'No. I'm just shocked. It was as though they popped up out of nowhere. Plus it was dark and I wasn't expecting it.' Her voice strengthened. 'Sorry I screamed. It was a sort of reflex action.'

'And a good one,' Lucy approved. 'You obviously scared them off.'

Cleo finally stood back, smoothing down her shirt, rubbing her arms as though she was cold. Lucy grabbed a rug from the chair on the landing and wrapped it about her sister like a jacket. 'Look,' she said, 'let's go down and get a hot chocolate or something. And I probably should make sure no one is still hanging around out there.'

Cleo had regained her composure. 'If you set foot outside that door, I'm coming with you,' she threatened, 'and I'm taking a baseball bat with me.'

'We don't have one,' Lucy said, 'but I'll have the police on speed dial. If needs be.'

They went down the stairs together. The skeleton clock on the wall said that it was twenty to one. They'd got back at eleven thirty so Lucy realised she couldn't have been asleep for long. She threw on all the switches, flooding the barn with light, plus the patio at the back and the courtyard, which was now lit up like a showground. She opened the blinds and scanned the cobbled space, jumping when she saw something moving in the shadows. But it was only the black cat, slinking away into the darkness.

'Shame I didn't think of doing that before I went outside,' Cleo said, 'but I didn't want to wake you.'

'I hope it wasn't Finn you bumped into,' Lucy said. 'He and Geoffrey sometimes spend the night down by the lake. Although I'm sure he wouldn't have run away when he saw you.'

'It definitely wasn't him,' Cleo said, 'not unless he's started chain-smoking since I last met him. Whoever it was, they were about six foot two and stank of cigarettes and camphor.'

'I'm not even sure what that smells like,' Lucy said. She pulled the long blinds closed again and immediately felt safer and less vulnerable.

'Mothballs,' Cleo said. 'Mustiness. Old spaces like second-hand bookshops—'

'And museums,' Lucy said. She remembered Gabriel leaning against the wall of the village museum, smoking. A coincidence? Perhaps not.

'I'm just going to check outside,' she said. 'Can you stick the kettle on whilst I take a look?' She grabbed the huge torch that was part of the emergency equipment for power cuts.

'Well, at least if you can't hit him with a baseball bat, you'll be able to blind him with the light.' Cleo was back to her usual self. She took the kettle over to the sink and pulled some sachets of hot chocolate out from the cupboard. 'Though I'm sure he's long gone by now.'

Lucy opened the door. The night was hot, the moon hidden behind clouds now and the air so still she could hear the trickle of the stream, the bark of a distant fox and the call of some unidentified night bird. The hairs rose on the back of her neck, though she was not sure why. Was it her imagination or something else that seemed to provide the figure of a woman, as insubstantial as shadow, yet nevertheless standing by the gate that led down the valley...

'Anything?'

Cleo popped up beside her, a saucepan brandished in one hand, making Lucy jump.

'Nothing at all,' Lucy said, sweeping the torch around the courtyard one last time.

'What's that?' Cleo darted forward. The light had caught the edge of something silver lying half-hidden between the cobbles. 'It's a key,' she said. She picked it up, bringing it over to Lucy. 'Looks like a door key.'

'Let's go back inside,' Lucy said. She could still feel the primitive sense of wariness that breathed unease along her skin. They went in, slamming the door shut and bolting it behind them. The normality of the room, lamplit and warm, was soothing but Lucy was grateful for the heat of the hot chocolate, rich and strong, and laced her fingers around the mug.

'I don't mind admitting,' she said, 'that this place gives me the creeps sometimes.'

'That was no ghost tonight, though,' Cleo said. She prodded the key, which was lying on the worktop. 'Do you recognise this?'

'Yes,' Lucy said. 'It's from the old set of keys for the barn. I had the locks changed after the incident when someone left me a dead bouquet – remember I told you about that on the phone? I had a couple of spare sets cut today when I was in Highworth.'

'Oh, yeah.' Cleo's nose wrinkled in disgust. 'You thought the security of the barn might have been compromised. Well, it looks as though you were right.' She took a sip of her drink. 'Now that I think about it, I'm almost certain I heard the sound of something dropping onto the cobbles when I cannoned into whoever it was earlier. It was a sort of clink, like metal on stone. But everything happened in a rush and I didn't really register it. Too busy screaming.'

'It looks as though your intruder might have intended to break in,' Lucy said thoughtfully. 'But thankfully you scared them off.'

'You're very calm about it!' Cleo said accusingly. 'Hell, Lucy, someone leaves you a bouquet of dead flowers and then they try to break into the barn, but you're sitting here drinking chocolate?'

'Well, they couldn't have got in anyway since I'd had the locks changed,' Lucy pointed out, 'but I will report it first thing in the morning.' She tightened her grip on the stripy mug and inhaled the rich scent of chocolate. She was nowhere near as calm as she was pretending; the thought of someone trying to get into the house when they were asleep made her feel quite sick and inclined to sit up for the rest of the night with all the lights on.

'Finn thought Persis might have somehow got hold of a key,' she said. 'He suspected that she and Charlie might have met up here occasionally. I guess we're going to have to confront her about that now.'

'Or the police are,' Cleo agreed. 'I'm sure that wasn't Persis tonight, but it might have been her brother. I don't know – I haven't met him. Is he six foot two?'

'About that, I suppose,' Lucy said. 'Plus he is a smoker. Though why he would want to break in is a bit of a mystery.'

'Yeah,' Cleo agreed. 'Despite the bouquet, I can't imagine either of them would want to *kill* you. I mean, why would they?'

'Thanks for putting that idea into my head,' Lucy said dryly. 'I hadn't thought anyone might want to do me actual bodily harm. Even when I saw the dead flowers it felt like a rather clumsy way of scaring me off rather than anything else.'

'I'm sure you're right,' Cleo said, not sounding quite sure enough to Lucy's mind.

'Gabriel's always been pretty hostile about the garden restoration, for some reason,' Lucy said. 'So that fits. Plus Hazel mentioned that there was some connection between the Knights Hospitaller and the Catesbys, and the Knights have always been Gabriel's obsession…' She yawned, rubbing her eyes. 'Does any of this add up? I'm so tired I can't work it out.'

'It does add up if Gabriel was after the book on Robert

Catesby,' Cleo said. 'That would totally make sense since he and Persis saw you at Chastleton today and might have thought that you'd gone there to pick it up on Finn's behalf. Gabriel might have waited until he thought you'd gone to bed and then come looking for it. He had the key Persis had got from Charlie – he didn't know you'd changed the locks. And then I startled him when he was about to sneak in, so he ran away.'

'It's all pure speculation.' Lucy took her mug and Cleo's over to the dishwasher and stashed them away. 'Are you feeling okay now?' she added, seeing Cleo yawning widely. 'Do you think you'll be able to sleep?'

Cleo nodded. 'I'm sure I will, barring any visits from the local ghosts.'

Lucy double-checked that the door was bolted and the two of them made their way back upstairs.

'Goodnight,' Cleo said, smothering another yawn.

Lucy, in contrast, felt annoyingly wide awake. She checked the time and decided to call Verity.

'Lucy!' Her aunt answered immediately, sounding thrilled to hear from her. 'How are you? Isn't it the middle of the night in England?'

'It's pretty late,' Lucy said with a smile. 'Cleo's here and we've been talking so I'm a bit wired. I thought it would be nice to chat before I went to bed, if that's convenient with you.'

'Sure,' Verity said. 'I've got fifteen minutes before my next meeting. Tell me what you've been up to.'

'Well, I went to Chastleton House today,' Lucy said.

'Ah, the Catesby connection!' Verity said. 'Isn't it gorgeous? Although of course the present house was built after Robert Catesby sold it.'

'I'm fascinated by Catherine Catesby's story,' Lucy said. 'I've been learning a lot about her since I got here. I was going to ask you…' She hesitated. 'You know I mentioned a little while ago that I thought I'd seen Catherine's ghost? You didn't say anything at the time but I wondered whether *you* had ever had any supernatural experiences at Gunpowder Cottage or the barn?'

There was a brief pause, then Verity sighed. 'As you've asked me directly,' she said, 'I'm not going to lie. The only reason I didn't tell you when you mentioned it before was because I hoped the whole thing would settle down and you wouldn't have anything supernatural to contend with. That was why I wanted you in the cottage, not the barn; God knows, you need a restful break, not to be ghost hunting.'

'So you already knew about Catherine,' Lucy said.

Verity sighed again. 'Until a year or two ago,' she said, 'I had no idea. There *was* one instance of haunting that I'd heard of—' her voice changed, 'but I'll come back to that. I never saw or heard anything paranormal myself despite the age of Gunpowder Cottage and the number of years I'd lived there, but the barn was a different story…' She took a breath. 'Before we opened it to the public I spent a few nights down there. I'd just lost a big contract, made a really bad judgement call and lost the respect of a company I'd worked with for years. I felt pretty lousy, to be honest. I almost threw in the towel on my whole career.'

'I'm sorry,' Lucy said, astonished. Verity had always

seemed so confident, so together. It was hard to imagine her aunt losing her self-belief.

'That was one of the reasons I wanted to give you somewhere you could go to have a bit of breathing space after you were ill,' Verity said. 'I know it can be tough when life knocks you. Anyway, I was moping around, feeling angry with myself and upset as well. I started to imagine that I could hear a woman crying sometimes at night and then occasionally I thought I could see her as well, wandering through the orchard. It was all rather disconcerting.'

'Did you ever speak to her?' Lucy asked. 'Interact in any way?'

'No,' Verity said, 'and once I'd started to feel better it felt as though I kind of lost my connection to her. But that reminds me of the earlier case I referred to. Apparently, there was a quite well-known story from after the war where a woman actually *met* the ghost of Catherine in the orchards and held a conversation with her.'

'I read about that today,' Lucy said. 'She identified herself as Catherine Catesby and was crying over her lost treasure.'

'That's the one,' Verity said. 'Extraordinary.' Her tone changed. 'I need to go in a minute, but I'm kind of concerned that you're seeing this ghost repeatedly, Lucy. Is it freaking you out?'

'No,' Lucy said. 'I'm okay. I'm curious, really. I think Catherine needs our help in some way but I haven't figured it out yet.'

'All right,' Verity said. 'Look, I'll give you a ring again tomorrow when we can have longer to talk. Hell, when I offered you a holiday I really didn't expect—' She broke off. 'It feels like she attaches herself to grief in some way, doesn't she? Catherine, I mean.'

'Yes,' Lucy said. 'I think so. It's a pity the only other mention of it was so long ago,' she added. 'I would have loved to talk to whoever it was who met Catherine.'

'Well,' Verity said, 'you can. Her name's Maud Enright and she lives in the village. She's about ninety-seven but as far as I know, she's still going strong. You'll find her in Cooper's Piece, two doors down from the Redferns.'

CHAPTER 16

Anne Catesby

Knightstone Manor, Autumn 1598

On hearing that Robert had deserted Knightstone, Sir Thomas and Lady Leigh decreed that their daughter should be taken back to Stoneleigh and buried there in the family vault. A cart came from Warwickshire, draped in black silk with the Leigh and Catesby arms entwined, and the sad little cortege, escorted by her father's retainers, took Catherine home. None of us had been invited to Stoneleigh for Catherine's funeral. It felt very much as though the Leigh family had closed ranks, its connection to the ill-fated Catesbys at an end. Nevertheless, I tried to maintain good relations for the sake of little Robbie. He had Leigh grandparents and I did not want them to forget it, not least because they would be able to pay something towards his education when the time came, if they chose to do so.

I will erect a memorial to Catherine at the church in Knightstone, I wrote to Sir Thomas and Lady Leigh.

It is fitting that she should be commemorated here in a place she loved, albeit for such a short time.

I chose a block of local sarsen stone and asked the mason to carve Catherine's name, the date and a Bible verse on it: *Where your treasure is, there will your heart be also.*

'Very fitting, my lady,' Byram said, as we stood under the dripping yews of the churchyard on a grey autumnal day, the rain and my tears mingling, 'though I might have expected you to have had your fill of treasure.' There were a scattering of servants and villagers present but no one else. This was not a funeral, after all, only a commemoration, and Robert himself had declined to return home for it. He had ordered that the manor be closed once we had finished our sad observances, so I had sent all of little Robbie's possessions to Ashby and the rest to Chastleton. Catherine's personal belongings I had returned to her father along with her body. She had left no will but as Robert seemed utterly adrift from her and from their former home, I thought it the most fitting thing to do.

The villagers began to drift away to their hearths and homes, no doubt needing the warmth of a fire and perhaps some ale after their soaking in the churchyard. I turned to see Thomas standing a little apart, by the line of old sarsen stones that marked the edge of the graveyard. He raised a hand and came forward to greet me. He was dressed all in black; it made him look older, drained of colour, tired.

'My condolences to you,' he said, bowing over my gloved hand.

'And to you,' I said. 'You cared for Catherine too.'

He nodded. 'We have lost a bright light and a noble lady,' he said. 'I am sorry it took me so long to come to Knightstone. I have been unwell, too sick to travel until now.'

'I am sorry,' I said. That accounted for his pallor, I supposed, a combination of grief and illness.

'I need to speak with you, Anne,' Thomas said abruptly. He looked at Byram. 'In private.'

'You may speak freely here,' I said. 'I have no secrets from Byram.'

'I doubt that very much.' Some of Thomas' former sardonic manner had returned. 'Shall we walk back to the manor together? Put frankly, I need to speak with you about the treasure.'

I thought I heard Byram make a choking noise, but when I looked at him his face was impassive. 'I will wait for you to send for me when you are ready, madam,' he said, and set off down the path towards the village, I suspected to join the other mourners in the alehouse.

I sighed but slipped my hand through Thomas' proffered arm, and we walked the other way, out onto the hollow way path that ran behind the church and down to the track to Knightstone. The trees made an arch over our heads, their leaves turning from green to gold, ready to fall in autumn's chill breeze.

'The seasons will keep turning,' Thomas said. 'There is some comfort in that.'

'We are in a season of loss,' I agreed. 'For now, winter is coming.' I huddled deeper within my cloak. 'I must believe that spring will also come again.'

As we drew closer to the manor, the scent of smoke still seemed to hang on the air, a mournful echo of autumn and a reminder of Robert's fierce destruction.

'You said you wished to speak of the treasure,' I reminded him. 'I wondered why you had not come to Knightstone sooner to secure it, especially after the fire, but if you have been ill I can see that would have been impossible.'

A faint smile touched Thomas' lips. 'I was not concerned about it,' he said. 'I knew it was safe.' He glanced at me. 'Did you go looking for it, Nan?'

'I did,' I said. 'Or rather, I sent Byram to find it.'

'Why would you do that?' Thomas had stopped walking and turned to look at me. 'Did you have an urge to see it for yourself, Nan? So much gold, such precious objects, articles of faith? Did you wish to keep it yourself? Set yourself up as its protector – or even take some of it for your own use?'

'No,' I said. I felt hurt and angry that he would impute evil motives to me, even as a voice in the back of my mind whispered that it was good I had been spared that precise temptation. 'You said it was a sacred trust, Thomas,' I said. 'However I feel about the way in which you goad the authorities with your religious provocations, however I worry that you may lead Robert astray or bring trouble upon him, I would never betray a holy vow. I sought only to keep it safe from the fire.'

Thomas nodded, his face breaking into a sweet smile that reminded me irresistibly of how handsome he had been when he was young.

'And where did you seek it?' he asked.

'In the vault beneath the obelisk in the centre of the

garden,' I said. 'I imagined that it was the heart of the whole plan, the labyrinth that leads one by twists and turns to find God – or treasure – at the centre.'

'It was clever of you to work that out,' Thomas said.

'Not really,' I said, tartly. 'You made it rather obvious, with your symbolism and your numerology. So obvious, now that I think about it, that it was too good to be true.'

Thomas laughed. 'Byram found nothing,' he said.

'The vault was empty,' I concurred. 'I think it has always been.' I looked at him. 'There is no treasure at Knightstone, is there, Thomas? Very likely there never has been. The vault is a decoy, built to mislead the Queen's spies, like the double-blind priest's hole at Coughton, where we grew up.'

'You remember that?' Thomas said. 'It was a cunning device.'

'It was built to lay a false trail,' I said. 'Just like the rumours of treasure here that you have so carefully perpetrated.' I gave him a rueful smile. 'Now, finally, I see that Catherine's garden was simply that – a beautiful tribute to whatever each of us values. For Catherine it was somewhere wild and magical, a private space to enjoy with Robert and her children. For you it was a symbol of your faith. But it was never a hiding place.'

We had reached the top of the valley where a path wended its way down towards Catherine's pleasure gardens and in the light of so much stark death and devastation we both fell silent. The ash of the trellises and palisades mingled with the charred remains of the dead trees. The path was strewn with broken branches. Only the stream, bright and pure, ran over the chalk stone with the same clarity as before.

The winter of devastation had come to Catherine's garden. I heard Thomas sigh.

'I am sorry,' I said impulsively to Thomas. 'I know the garden was as special to you as it was to Catherine. She made it so beautiful, whatever the season. To see it destroyed must break your heart.'

'*Sic transit gloria mundi*,' Thomas said with a wry smile. 'Thus passes earthly glory.'

By common consent we chose not to walk down through the ruined gardens but took the road to the house, passing through the grand gateway and along the oak avenue to the parterre.

'Perhaps Robert will sell,' I said, looking out over the ruined terraces. 'Someone else may cherish the house and restore the garden as Catherine would have wished.'

But Thomas shook his head. 'I will buy the house from Robert,' he said, 'but I shall never restore the garden.'

I had an unsettling vision of how the gardens might look after a few years of neglect, the labyrinth grown over, the paths lost and the pretty little waterways choked with weed. It took very little time for nature to reclaim its own. It seemed a shame but I could understand why Thomas felt he could not rebuild what was lost, and also why he would want to keep possession of Knightstone Manor.

I started to walk down the path towards the lake one last time, picking my way carefully over fallen branches and the burned skeletons of bushes. Here and there a flower had escaped the inferno – gillyflowers drooped hopelessly, a splash of pink in the barren earth. Crisp rose petals crunched underfoot. My heart was heavy and I wanted to cry for the devastation Robert had wrought and the misery that had prompted him to do it. I doubted that it had made him feel any better. In fact, I could imagine that the grief was all the sharper when he thought of how he had destroyed something so beautiful that his wife had created.

'*Wait a while,*' I wanted to counsel him, '*do not run heedlessly into action in order to drown out your sorrows.*' But he had not wanted to stay and listen to my advice and he had rejected my comfort.

By the time Thomas and I reached the edge of the lake, the hem of my gown was filthy with mud and charred earth. I'd seen the summerhouse burning on the night Catherine had died and now there was very little of it left and what there was, smelled strongly of water weed and dead wood. Thomas bent down to pick up a handful of the sand that bordered the lake and when he opened his clenched palm I saw a glint of bright colours amongst the grains. For a moment I caught my breath, thinking them to be jewels. Then I realised they were broken pieces of tile, shattered by the heat of the fire. I remembered the paintings and murals that had adorned the pavilion and felt heavy-hearted. Catherine had made it so beautiful. She had told me once it was her favourite place to dine with Robert, the two of them, in the midst of the garden. She had had such plans…

Thomas opened his fingers and the grains fell to the ground in a shower of red and blue, and vanished.

'Robbie and I leave for Ashby later today,' I said. 'We will leave you in peace to conduct your purchase of the manor with Robert, but I hope you will come to visit us before too long.'

Thomas raised his brows. 'What,' he said, 'do you have no homilies for me about how I shall be leading Robert astray by putting money into his pocket for him to spend on feckless enterprises?'

I shook my head. 'Robert will go his own way,' I said. 'He told me so.' I met Thomas' dark eyes. It was hard to admit the truth to him and to myself but I felt I had to be honest, here amongst the ruins of our hopes and dreams. 'I am sorry,' I said. 'It was always guilt that prompted me to speak as I did. I could not forgive myself for betraying William with you. I sought to drive it from my mind by trying to keep Robert away from you and I hated you both, I think, for the resemblances I perceived between you because it meant that I could never forget what had happened.'

I could feel the warmth of Thomas' hand on mine through my glove and it comforted me. After a moment he said: 'You are cold. Let me take you back to the house.'

'In a moment,' I said. 'Pray satisfy my curiosity on one thing before we return.'

Thomas waited. The pale sun, pushing out from behind the clouds at last, shone on the silver threads in his dark hair and reflected in his eyes.

'What happened to the Knights' treasure?' I said.

Thomas smiled. There was an edge of sadness to it. 'Oh, Anne,' he said, 'there is none. King Henry took the old treasure, all but for a few relics left at Clerkenwell that had no monetary value for him. There was no time in the brief period that my grandfather was Prior to rebuild the Knights' fortunes. All that is left is a holy name and a legend.'

CHAPTER 17

Lucy

'You look terrible,' Lucy said to Finn. She hadn't intended to be quite so blunt, but seeing him looking so tired and unkempt, the words had just come out. 'Bad night?'

'You might say so.' Finn's intense hazel gaze fixed on her for a moment before he opened the door of Gunpowder Cottage a little wider. 'Would you both like to come in? Johnny's making bacon sandwiches.'

He'd texted her the previous evening to ask how her day had been and to remind her that the invitation to breakfast that Johnny had issued the day before still stood. Lucy had replied that Cleo was staying with her and Finn had replied promptly to invite her too. So here they were. It was particularly convenient since there was quite a list of stuff Lucy wanted to talk to him about.

'A hangover, is it?' Cleo chirped. She was looking very fresh and bright-eyed despite the disturbances of the previous night. Cleo, Lucy had often thought, could emerge from a hurricane without a hair out of place.

'No.' Finn glanced over his shoulder as they followed him

down the corridor to the kitchen. 'Nothing so exciting. One of the farmers texted me at about two in the morning to say that someone had wrecked the excavation work down at the summerhouse. They only spotted it because whoever it was left the field gate open and some of their cows wandered out onto the road. Fortunately, they were seen and rounded up before anyone was hurt and that was when Bill saw the damage to the dig and texted me. I went down there first thing to see what had happened. It's completely trashed – trench edges caved in and holes dug in the bottom of the excavation.'

'Bastards.' Johnny was buttering rolls and reached for two more when he saw them. 'Sorry—' he said to Cleo, wiping his palms down his apron, 'that's not much of a greeting, is it? You must be Cleo. I'm Johnny Robsart.' He picked up the knife again. 'But honestly, who would do such a thing? They've totally destroyed everything we've worked for over the past three days.'

'I'm so sorry,' Lucy said. 'Do you think it was done by detectorists looking for finds?'

'More likely just vandals.' Finn looked grim. 'The same people who've been so hostile to the dig from the start, perhaps.'

Lucy shot Cleo a look. Given the odd things that had happened at the barn the previous night she wondered if there could be any link between the vandalism and the person Cleo had crashed into.

'Coffee?' Finn paused with the cafetière in his hand. 'Or would you prefer juice?'

'Juice, thanks,' Lucy said. She frowned. 'Had you

discovered anything important at the summerhouse site? I mean, I know it's all important, but did they destroy anything valuable?'

'No,' Finn said. 'There wasn't much of the structure there, though there was enough to confirm it was built on a foundation of Tudor bricks. Luckily Johnny did a sketch of it a couple of days ago. The only really interesting thing was that there was evidence of burning. We thought the building might have been destroyed in a flood but it turned out that the whole structure appeared to have burned down.'

'Burning?' Lucy remembered the vision she had seen that night in the wood; the trees aflame and the little house by the lake splintering into dust and ashes.

Johnny, who had been adding crispy bacon to the rolls, looked at her. 'Are you all right?'

'Yes,' Lucy said. 'It's just...' She shook her head. She wasn't ready to talk about all her dreams and experiences just yet. 'It seems an odd thing to have happened,' she said.

'Yes,' Finn agreed, 'and not long after it was built, either. The layers of earth on top of it suggest it can only have been standing for a year or two.'

'Some sort of accident, then?' Cleo asked. 'Back in Tudor times?'

'Something like that, perhaps,' Finn said. 'Or maybe it was deliberate. Buildings often burned down in the days of open fires and candles, but you wouldn't really expect it there, with a water source available to douse the fire.' He filled their glasses with orange juice and passed them over at the same time as Johnny brought the sandwiches over.

'Bliss,' Cleo said, sitting down at the pine table and grabbing one.

'Presumably you've reported the damage to the police?' Lucy said, and Finn nodded.

'They'll be busy today, then,' Cleo said. 'Reports coming in on all sides. Knightstone is a hotbed of crime.'

'Oh?' Johnny cocked his head. 'What else has been going on?'

'Someone tried to break into the barn,' Cleo said before Lucy could answer. 'We think it was Gabriel.'

Johnny, unaccustomed to Cleo's directness, almost spat out his coffee. 'What? Gabriel Redfern? Are you sure? He's hardly the criminal type, is he?'

'Cleo!' Lucy said reproachfully. 'You make it all so melodramatic.'

'Well, it was pretty exciting stuff.' Cleo licked butter from her fingers.

'What happened?' Finn, leaning his elbows on the table, directed the question at Lucy as Cleo was once more attacking the bacon roll.

'Cleo went out to get her phone charger from the car in the middle of the night and someone barrelled into her coming up from the valley,' Lucy said. 'She screamed and they ran off, but they dropped a key in the courtyard – the key to the barn, as it turns out. Or rather, the old key, since I've had the locks changed.'

'Hell.' Johnny looked shocked. He turned to Cleo. 'Were you okay?'

'Yes, thanks,' Cleo said cheerfully. 'Just terrified.'

Finn's frown was heavy. 'So we were right, then, Lucy,'

he said. 'Whoever left you that disgusting bunch of dead flowers *did* have a key.'

'Well, presumably it's the same person,' Lucy said, sighing. 'Cleo's given a description to the police.'

'Six foot two and smells of cigarette smoke,' Cleo said, finishing off the sandwich and washing it down with the rest of the juice. 'Thank you,' she added, 'that was awesome.'

'Very restorative,' Lucy agreed, with a smile.

'So is that why you think it was Gabriel?' Johnny swung back on his chair. 'Because of his height and the smell of smoke?' He glanced across at Finn. 'You do know that could fit any number of people, right? Even Finn when he's been down by the bonfire.'

'It's a different sort of smoke,' Finn said mildly, 'but yeah, Johnny's right. I don't think you can blame Gabriel unless you've got some other evidence.'

Cleo nudged her sister. 'Lucy?' she prompted.

Lucy sighed again. 'I know you and I had it all worked out last night,' she said to Cleo, 'but Finn's right that we can't accuse anyone without proof and we don't have any.'

'What about the book?' Cleo's eyebrows shot up. 'And your conversation with the curator at Chastleton about Charlie's research, and Persis pretending to be his assistant—'

'Wait a minute—' Finn held up a hand. 'You've lost me.'

'Me too,' Johnny said.

'This is what you get with Cleo,' Lucy said, sending her sister an affectionate glance. 'She never starts a story at the beginning. Even when she reads a book she'll plunge in at chapter three before she goes back to the start.'

'It's true, I'm afraid,' Cleo admitted.

Briefly Lucy told them about her visit to Chastleton, the book about Robert Catesby, and how that had led to the conversation with Hazel about Charlie's research.

'I haven't had the opportunity to read much of the book yet,' she said to Finn, who was sitting back in his chair, his long legs stretched out in front of him as he listened. 'I only dipped into it in a few spare moments. I'm not sure which parts are relevant to Knightstone but hopefully I'll find out when I get the chance to take a proper look.' A thought occurred to her. 'Or perhaps you'd like to read it instead? You might have a better chance of spotting what had caught Charlie's interest.'

Finn shook his head. 'No, you're all right. I've got a lot of work to do today, so if you have time to read it that would be great.' He frowned. 'I'm not sure what this has to do with Persis, though – or Gabriel, for that matter.'

'Neither do I,' Lucy admitted, 'except that Persis went to Chastleton with Charlie, apparently, and was passing herself off as his research assistant. I'm assuming she didn't tell you about their trip?' she added to Finn.

Finn shook his head. 'No, but maybe...' He shrugged. 'I dunno. It is a bit odd but maybe she just forgot.'

'Well, that's Persis,' Johnny said. 'She is a bit erratic, and as for the assistant thing, she was probably just bigging herself up.'

'My theory is that Gabriel was after the same book Charlie wanted, and was breaking in last night to try and find it,' Cleo said. 'Lucy saw him and Persis at Chastleton yesterday, acting weirdly, like there was something there that they didn't want her to discover. Isn't that right, Luce?'

'Put like that, it all sounds rather vague and circumstantial,' Lucy admitted, seeing the scepticism on Johnny's and Finn's faces. 'All we know for sure is that someone had the old key to the barn and that you surprised them out in the yard last night, Cleo. Hopefully the police will track them down.'

'It could have been the same person who trashed the archaeology site,' Finn said thoughtfully, 'if the timings fit. Maybe they were coming up from the valley when they bumped into Cleo. The most important thing—' he looked at Lucy, 'is that the barn is secure and that you're okay until this is all sorted out. Do you want to move up here with us? There's plenty of space, even with Johnny and Geoffrey and me.'

Geoffrey chose that minute to dash into the kitchen, looking supremely upset, Lucy thought, that no one had saved him any of the bacon. 'I'd love to move in with Geoffrey,' she said, stroking his head, 'but I'll be fine, thanks. The barn is very secure, there are new locks and the police are on the case.'

'Well, we'll be around keeping an eye on things,' Finn said, and seeing the determined jut of his jaw, Lucy decided not to argue.

'Thanks for the bacon roll, Johnny,' she said, getting up from the table. 'It was delicious. Come on, Cleo—' she turned to her sister, 'you've got a shop to open and I've got a couple of books to read.'

'I'll go down and get started on the trench at the barn,' Johnny said. He looked from Lucy to Finn. 'Do you want to come and take a look at the work we're doing before you go back, Cleo? Have you got time?'

'Sure,' Cleo said warmly, 'I'd love that, thanks.'

Finn put a hand on Lucy's arm as she went to follow them out. 'Are you free later?' he asked. 'It would be good to have a chat – just the two of us. If you've had the chance to read that book about Robert Catesby by then, we could discuss anything that might be relevant to the dig.'

'Of course,' Lucy said, trying not to feel too disappointed that this sounded strictly business. 'Do you want to text when you're ready?'

'Thanks,' Finn said. He frowned. 'I need to secure the summerhouse site and then we have to cover all the remaining excavations before the rain starts. There's quite a fierce storm coming, according to the forecasts. I'm not sure when I'll be free.'

'No problem,' Lucy said. 'Are you heading out now?'

They followed Cleo and Johnny down to the barn. Geoffrey was sniffing the air as though he could sense a change coming in the weather.

'This is so interesting, Lucy!' Cleo knelt down by the trench Johnny had cut at the side of the duck pond. 'Do you see these bundles of twigs? Johnny thinks they were edging sticks – when they cut a moat ditch they would embed these in the bank to stabilise and protect it. How cool is that? The barn had a moat around it!'

'Well, the barn wasn't there in Tudor times,' Johnny said, 'and we don't know for certain yet what was, but we've found both clay-lined canals and these ditches on the site so a moat or canal is a strong possibility.'

'Just like at Lyveden New Bield, Lucy!' Cleo's eyes lit up. 'Do you remember visiting there with Aunt Verity? We were on some sort of Gunpowder Plot–themed tour at the time.'

'Lyveden belonged to Sir Thomas Tresham, didn't it?' Lucy dredged her memory. 'Hazel, the curator at Chastleton, said that one of the Treshams was Catesby's cousin and was implicated in the Gunpowder Plot.'

'Francis,' Finn said. 'He was Sir Thomas' son.' He paused. 'But Lyveden wasn't started until the early seventeenth century, whereas this garden has an earlier dating. I wonder...' He raked a hand through his hair. 'It's plausible that this could be a precursor of the Lyveden design, I suppose, Thomas Tresham might have seen it – or even had a hand in designing it, perhaps.'

'That would be incredible!' Johnny was looking over-excited. 'Wow! If we could prove that—'

'If you could prove that, even Finn would get excited,' Lucy said mischievously.

'You'll be able to tell when I am,' Finn said dryly, looking her straight in the eye.

Lucy blushed, but fortunately Finn had already turned away again. 'At Lyveden the moat encircles a labyrinth,' he said slowly. He looked at the barn, measuring the dimensions with his gaze. 'It's certainly flat enough to have been a maze site,' he said. 'I assumed there was some sort of building there, but perhaps not. Johnny,' he threw him a look, 'let's measure this up properly and then I'll check out the details of the Lyveden garden and see what else we can discover.'

'I could do that if you like,' Lucy said, surprising herself. 'As I'm reading the Robert Catesby book today, I could do both. Just point me in the right direction. That is, if you'd like my help.'

Finn's smile warmed her. 'That would be great, thank you,' he said, 'especially as I need to get all the tarpaulins in place before this afternoon.' He looked at the sky, which was turning a hard brassy blue. Not a breath of wind stirred the air. It felt hot and ominous. 'There's a book about Lyveden New Bield up at the cottage as well,' he said. 'Pop up and get it later if you'd like to. The key code is 1598.'

'I'd better be going,' Cleo said regretfully. 'I wish I could stay and help.' She hugged Lucy. 'I'll just get my bag. Oh, and for God's sake be careful, okay? Lock all the doors and the windows, and check in with me every hour—'

'Cleo,' Lucy said, 'I'm on holiday, not in prison.' She relented, seeing Cleo's stubborn, anxious face. 'Of course I'll be careful, but I'm not going to overreact. Besides, Geoff will be on guard.'

After Cleo had gone and Johnny and Finn had disappeared down the valley, Lucy opened up the terrace doors and sat outside, a notepad on the table in front of her, alongside the biography of Robert Catesby. She also wanted to note down the details of her conversation with Hazel before she forgot it, just in case there was anything relevant in that as well. The sun felt violently hot and it was sweltering even beneath the shade of the umbrella; she found it hard to concentrate as she read through the pages on Catesby's birth and early life in Northamptonshire.

She thought of the lake with its golden grains of sand and cool waters. It was almost unbearably tempting to go down there for a paddle but as Johnny and Finn would be working she didn't want to get in the way. Instead, she decided to take a break and go and fetch the book about Lyveden New Bield. Perhaps she could find somewhere cool to curl up with it for a change of reading. Finn had asked her to make a note of anything to do with Thomas Tresham's connections to the Catesby family and anything about the design of his Northamptonshire garden that struck her as having any connection to Knightstone. She thought that would keep her busy for a while.

She locked the barn carefully and walked back up to the cottage, keeping in the shade of the tall poplars that sheltered the path. In her field, Clarabelle the donkey was also standing in the shadow of a large oak tree, swishing her tail and ears to keep the flies away. It was so humid now that Lucy was exhausted by the time she reached the top of the slope and the cottage, which she found infuriating. For a while she'd been able to forget about her illness but now, as she paused to cool down and draw breath, the sense of dissatisfaction rushed in to fill her; she hated this weakness and the panic it brought with it, the fear of what she could do with her life now, the sense of hopelessness.

Pushing all the negative thoughts to the back of her mind, she got the key out of the box and went into Gunpowder Cottage. The house felt unnaturally still but perhaps that was because all of her senses were on alert, expecting... what? Ghosts? Intruders? Both? Shaking her head she made her way along the corridor to Verity's study, which Finn had commandeered for the duration of the dig. The book about Lyveden New Bield and the Tresham family was on the shelf where he had told her to look. It was fortunate he had given her instructions on where to find it because the rest of the room was incredibly untidy with maps, drawings, notes and papers scattered all over the place. Lucy was surprised; she would have had Finn down as a tidy person but then, she thought, maybe she didn't know him as well as she felt she did.

Coming out of the back door she almost walked into Marilynne Redfern who appeared to be wrestling bales of straw from one of the outhouses into the back of the estate car Lucy had seen Gabriel and Persis in at Chastleton. Dressed in green wellingtons, a tweed skirt Lucy thought would surely be too hot on a summer day and a padded gilet, Marilynne looked somewhat put out to see her.

'Oh, it's you,' she said ungraciously. Her gaze dropped to the book under Lucy's arm. 'What are you reading?'

'Oh…' Lucy felt a strong urge not to tell her. 'Just some family history. What are you doing here?'

Marilynne's lips pinched together. 'I store hay for the donkey here,' she said. She turned away, thrusting the final bale viciously into the back of the car. 'I wanted to buy this house when it came up for sale,' she said, 'but your aunt gazumped me. She offered thousands over the asking price and pushed me out.'

'That was over twenty years ago,' Lucy said, wondering if she was expected to apologise for this historical injustice. Marilynne's aggrieved attitude suggested she certainly hadn't moved on. 'I thought you said this was an unhappy place,' she added, remembering Marilynne's comments to her at the heritage centre. 'Why would you want to live here if you don't like it?'

Marilynne slammed the boot of the car and stalked

around to the driver's door. 'It's only unhappy for some,' she said pointedly. She closed the door and drove off in a scatter of gravel, almost flattening Johnny who was just coming in the gate, weighed down with all his excavation gear.

'Blimey,' he said, 'who was that?'

'That was Marilynne,' Lucy said. 'Persis and Gabriel's aunt. Apparently, she keeps hay for Clarabelle in the out-house here.'

'Oh yeah, I remember Finn saying something about that,' Johnny said vaguely. 'He—' He stopped abruptly, staring across the terrace. Following his gaze, Lucy saw a woman in a long red gown pass through the rose arbour and disappear from view.

'Catherine,' she said. She looked at Johnny. 'You saw her too.'

Johnny rubbed one earth-stained hand over his hair, making it stand on end. 'I see her every time I see you,' he said.

'I'm sorry I never mentioned it before,' Johnny said, as though he was referring to something as mundane as the bus timetable, rather than a ghost. He added leaf tea to the pot and poured boiling water over it. 'No,' his voice changed, 'actually, I'm not sorry. You can't go around spooking people without good reason and I try really hard not to be *too* weird in my day-to-day life.'

They were in the kitchen at Gunpowder Cottage, back at the pine table where they'd had breakfast earlier. Johnny grabbed two mugs from the cupboard and Lucy took the milk out of the fridge.

'Persis made some comment about your paranormal abilities the day we first met,' she said, remembering. 'What did she mean? Whatever it was, you didn't seem too pleased about it.'

'I wasn't,' Johnny said. He stirred the teapot. 'I'd rather not talk about it, to be honest. I've got a bit of a reputation for being...' he hesitated, 'well, let's just say that I see things that most people don't. I can tune into the past and see it as though I'm actually there...' He shifted uncomfortably. 'A few years ago, when my sister Amelia had just died and before Lizzie and Arthur got together, I got in over my head. There was some stuff in the press about me communing with ghosts – stupid stuff, but it was newsworthy because Amelia was a supermodel married to a pop star and Lizzie...' He spread his hands in a gesture of resignation.

'I remember,' Lucy said, thinking back to the lurid headlines that had greeted the death of Amelia Dudley. She put a hand on Johnny's arm. 'I'm very sorry. Losing someone important to you is horrible.'

'Yeah,' Johnny said. 'Thank you. I still miss her so much. I think that's why Finn doesn't mind me being around him, actually. I understand how crap it is to be bereaved and I don't pretend, or try to make him talk if he doesn't want to or whatever... Anyway...' He scrubbed a hand through his hair again. 'I promised Arthur I'd never got involved with any sort of paranormal experience again after Amelia's death, so when Catherine's ghost appeared – not that I knew her name until recently – I was a bit annoyed.'

Lucy smiled. 'That's the most original reaction I've

heard to someone seeing a ghost,' she said, 'but I know what you mean.'

Johnny grinned back. 'Yeah, well... I'd given my word and then this dead person popped up and was trying to tell me something... So I'm afraid I ignored her.'

Lucy poured the tea for them both. 'So you saw her *before* I came here?' she said. 'That's interesting.'

'I had dreams about her,' Johnny said. Lucy thought he was blushing. 'That's why I was asking you whether you'd ever seen ghosts when you stayed in that room as a child... But when you arrived I stopped dreaming, which was a relief. I realised she'd attached herself to you because every time I saw you, she was around. I guess you didn't see her, though?'

'Not always,' Lucy said. 'The day we met, when you sort of looked over my shoulder as though there was someone else there...'

'Yes,' Johnny said. 'She was standing right next to you.' He looked shamefaced. 'I've been seeing these things since I was a child but it still feels odd to talk about it, you know? I'm sure people think I'm crazy.'

'I'm hardly in a position to criticise,' Lucy said. 'Nothing like this has ever happened to me before. I thought I was losing my mind when I first started experiencing it.'

'I think Catherine attached herself to you because you were grieving,' Johnny said carefully. 'Maybe you guessed that? It's the emotion that's significant. When Finn told me about what had happened to your career, I realised that must be the link. I think she's grieving for something too.'

'Losing her child, perhaps,' Lucy said. 'Catherine Catesby

and her son died within days of each other. Maybe she never had time to process the grief or even realise what had happened. But if that's so,' she added, 'what is she trying to tell us? Because it feels to me that as time's gone on it's more than just a random haunting…'

'Do you think so?' Johnny looked intrigued. 'Hmm, I don't know the answer to that.'

'Also,' Lucy said, 'if grief is the conduit through which Catherine connects with people, why didn't she choose Finn? He would seem the most obvious candidate.'

'The most obvious candidate for what?' They hadn't heard Finn come in and both of them jumped. Johnny, who'd been topping up his mug with tea, spilled it on the table and swore.

'How can someone as large as you move so quietly, Finn?' he grumbled.

'It's one of my many skills,' Finn said. He didn't take his eyes off Lucy. 'The most obvious candidate for what?' he repeated.

Lucy glanced at Johnny. Geoffrey, picking up the sudden tension in the room, pressed close to her leg in apparent reassurance.

'It's okay,' Johnny said, mopping up the tea, 'Finn knows all about my history with the supernatural. He's practically family.'

Lucy relaxed a little. 'Okay,' she said. 'So does he know about Catherine as well?'

'Sure,' Johnny said. 'I told him I'd seen her ghost as soon as weird things started to happen here.'

Lucy rolled her eyes. 'So Finn knows,' she said, 'and

you've seen her and Geoffrey probably has as well,' she said. 'I bet that's why he doesn't like the barn. And then there's an elderly lady who saw her back in the 1940s who Verity says is still around. And I've been thinking I'm going mad seeing things that no one else can. How wrong I was.'

Johnny laughed. 'Sorry. And it's not that common. Not really. I can't speak for Geoffrey but Finn hasn't seen her. He's determinedly earthbound, aren't you, Finn? I don't think any ghost would dare appear to him.'

Finn, who had crossed to the sink to wash the dirt from his hands and arms, made a sort of huffing sound. He grabbed a towel to dry himself and reached for the kettle. 'Clearly it isn't given to everyone,' he said mildly. He looked at Lucy again. 'So that's how you saw the spiral mounds?' he said. 'Through one of these dreams similar to the ones Johnny had? A sort of possession? Seeing through Catherine's eyes?'

'Yes,' Lucy said. 'It seems so.' She also took a breath. 'I saw the summerhouse burning too. That night we were down in the woods. But that was more like a vision than a dream.'

Finn nodded. 'If I hadn't also had that dream I'd be thinking both of you were mad,' he said bluntly. 'But then there's my Scottish granny—'

'The eldritch one,' Lucy said.

'Right,' Finn said. 'And we did discover archaeological evidence suggesting that the summerhouse had burned down, so…'

'It gave me a bit of a shock when you told me that,' Lucy admitted.

'Yeah,' Finn said, 'I noticed.' A smile crept into his eyes.

'So I have to accept that there's more to life than we can explain, difficult as that is for me as someone who likes empirical proof of everything.' He shook his head as though the thought, and his own acceptance of it, still sat a little uncomfortably with him.

'Well, spare a thought for me,' Lucy said with feeling. 'Before this all started, the closest I'd come to a supernatural experience was Cleo trying to read my aura.'

'I spare plenty of thoughts for you,' Finn said and before Lucy could respond he strode out of the kitchen.

CHAPTER 18

Anne Catesby

Ashby St Ledgers, Northamptonshire, Spring 1600

Thomas came to visit us at Ashby in the spring of the following year. He came on a bright April day when the laundry dried on the hedges and Robbie played with his hobby horse under the tutelage of one of the grooms and his nursemaid.

'The boy flourishes here.' Thomas came over to me at the mullioned window of the parlour as I stood looking out. 'He has found a new home and, God willing, happiness.' He took my hand and pressed a kiss to it. 'You have done that for him, Nan.'

'I hope so,' I said. Even now, tears pricked my eyes when I thought of all that Robbie had lost. 'It helps, in a way, that he barely remembers his mother, hard as that may seem. I tell him about her, of course, and he has a picture of her likeness. But perhaps it's for the best.'

Thomas nodded. 'And his father?'

'Robert came to see us a month or two back.' I felt a stirring of the old resentment. My son seemed to spend much more time with his kin the Wintours and with Francis, Thomas' son, than he did at Ashby.

'He seems much preoccupied with matters of religion and politics,' Thomas murmured. His dark gaze searched my face. 'I imagine it must be causing you some concern.'

I offered him a glass of wine and gestured to him to take a seat but he chose to remain standing, close enough to me for me to be rather too aware of him. The two of us, alone, looking out at our grandson playing in the yard... There was an intimacy there, an entwining of lives that made me uncomfortable. I handed him the glass and made sure I did not touch him in the process. My nerves were already sufficiently on edge.

'If only Robert would concern himself with religion in the private rather than the public sphere I should be content enough,' I admitted. Unlike his father and I, it was not sufficient for Robert to worship quietly, to give succour and sometimes a hiding place to a Catholic priest or to fund his ministry. No, Robert had to proclaim his faith as a challenge to the authorities and demand greater rights for those of us who followed the true religion. He was drawing attention and that scared me.

'Would you like me to speak with him?' Thomas asked. 'I could counsel discretion – in the absence of his father and with an uncle's concern?'

'I should be grateful,' I said, guardedly. It went against the grain with me to ask Thomas for help but I had learned much in the past ten years; now my sole concern was for Robbie, that he should have a safe and happy upbringing and as good a start in life as I could provide. If Thomas could guide Robert towards moderation in his behaviour then I could live with that and with the fact that my son would not listen to me. I had no desire to quarrel with him any further. We preserved the most fragile of peace for Robbie's sake.

Thomas nodded. 'I will do my best.'

'Thank you,' I said. I hesitated. 'You know, of course, that Robert has accepted loans from his father-in-law, Sir Thomas Leigh, and a number of others,' I added. 'I believe he may have offered Chastleton as surety.'

'I had heard as much.' Thomas looked grave. 'It is good of Sir Thomas to offer him aid out of kinship but I might have known there would be a price attached.'

I shrugged tiredly. Chastleton had been in the Catesby family for several generations; I would be sad to see the estates that my husband had worked so hard to build up diminished, but I sensed that was how the wind was blowing.

In truth it was so much worse than I had anticipated. As the new century took its first tentative steps, the Queen was ailing and there was a sense of unrest and discontent in the land. Thomas sent me word that Robert was deeply implicated in a plot hatched by the Earl of Essex to take the Tower, the city and the court, and overthrow Sir Robert Cecil, the Queen's advisor. The messenger found me in the still room where I was stuffing linen bags with the previous year's dried lavender; to this day I still associate the smell of the herb with that sickening lurch of the heart when I opened the missive.

Had I had the chance to speak to Robert I would have asked him to cite how frequently a rebellion was successful; hot-headed men, I thought wearily, seldom seemed to learn from history and always seemed to believe that this time would be different. It never was. Essex and his co-conspirators were captured, the ringleaders executed and Robert and the rest thrown into the debtor's prison at Wood Street. He sent word to me that his fine was four thousand marks. It was a huge sum; in despair I sold the last of our silver and plate, and some of the jewels that William had given me. They were only modest and of little value but we did what we could.

Thomas came a month after the rebellion was foiled. It was March and the catkins shook on the trees in the spring gales. The wind whistled down through the gaps in the walls and windows of Ashby and I felt old and aching.

'Robert will have to speed the sale of Chastleton now to pay off the money-lenders,' Thomas said, for although he had contributed to paying Robert's fine, as had I, we had also had to turn to the usurers. He strode across the parlour to warm himself on the meagre fire. 'Walter Jones is keen to buy it and is happy to allow him to have use of the house for a little while longer, which would save him having to return to live here with you, dear Anne.' He smiled sympathetically. 'I imagine that would suit the two of you ill.'

'This is Robert's home,' I said stiffly, 'and he is always welcome here.' But inside I seethed because Robbie was growing like a strong young tree, needing new clothes and shoes all the time, eating like a gannet whilst I picked at food like a sparrow. The rest of us went cold and hungry to feed him whilst his own father sacrificed us all for his high-flown principles.

'If only Robert were safe from attaching himself to other foolish plots that can only end in disaster,' I said, twisting my hands together. 'I cannot believe he will let this rest.'

Thomas sat down opposite me. I had not offered him wine this time for we had none. 'He is passionate in wanting better treatment for his fellow believers,' he said mildly. 'The Queen's attitude is harsh; all he wishes – as do I – is freedom to worship without persecution.'

'Attempting to overthrow the government is no way to achieve that,' I said. Bitterness rose in me and burst out no matter how hard I tried to stop it. 'Surely you counselled him against the rebellion, Thomas? How are we to eat – how are we to *live*, when Robert brings upon us penalties that are so harsh? Robbie needs books and tutelage or his education will suffer. He needs toys and games, like a normal child. He needs a *father*!' The word exploded out of me.

The Queen's health worsened throughout that summer of 1601 and Robert, viewed as a leading papist by the government, was imprisoned again for the best part of the following year. With suspicion of the chief Catholic families rife one more, life was difficult for all of us, that intricate web of my relatives, the Throckmortons and Treshams and Wrights and Wintours. We wrote nothing but the most innocuous letters, one cousin to another, reporting news of children's ailments and achievements, the yield from the orchards and herb gardens, the weather in Warwickshire and Northamptonshire. The Queen's spymasters, I thought, as I sealed my most recent letter to my sister Muriel, would find nothing of interest here.

Robbie was my pride and joy, the only brightness in this dark world. He grew and thrived, requiring yet more new clothes more quickly than I could afford to pay for them, so I made them from the drapes and curtains in the house. Ashby was falling down around us but we were happy enough through that summer; I employed a tutor for my grandson and paid him by selling off the last of my jewels.

And then the Queen died and Robert was released from prison and I think we all breathed a little easier for a while, for her successor was none other than James, the son of the martyred Queen Mary of Scotland. Though he was a Protestant I think we expected him to have some tolerance of Catholics because of his mother's faith if nothing else. We hoped for moderation in the new government's treatment of us, for the right to worship freely according to our consciences, as Thomas had always wanted.

It took only a short while to disabuse us of that hope. The new king banished all Catholic priests and Jesuits and re-imposed the recusancy fines.

Thomas is in a fine fury, Muriel wrote from Rushden. *His new lodge at Lyveden lies unfinished for there is no money to live, let alone to build. I fear it may never be finished.*

I wanted to tell her that if they reined in Francis and Lewis, their feckless sons, it might help conserve some of the family fortunes, but given that the two had been led astray by their cousin Robert since they had been children, I had no leg to stand on. I bit the end of my quill and reported that Ashby's roof leaked and the chimney smoked, and that Robbie had turned eight in November last and was doing well in mathematics and less well in Latin.

When we had not seen Robert for nearly three months, I sent Byram to try to discover what he was doing. Byram reported that Robert was dividing his time between Oxfordshire and his house in Lambeth. 'He spends much time in company with your cousins Wintour and Wright, and one of the Percy brood,' Byram said. 'They drink and practise swordplay and I doubt they are up to any good.'

'Can you not discover for me what it is they plan?' I asked, but Byram shook his head. 'I have no money for bribes and am well known as your servant,' he said bluntly. 'There is a limit to how close I can get.'

It was the same message the following year.

'Robert admits more of his family and acquaintance to his close circle,' Byram said when, dry-throated and dusty from the road, he reached me from London that August. 'He plans something, madam, and soon, though I know not what.'

It would be another rebellion, I thought, or some foolish plot to get close to the King and kill him, and it would end the same way in defeat and imprisonment, fines and disgrace. I watched Robbie out on the lawn with his skittles. He had a very accurate eye. He bowled the ball and they all fell, one after another, knocking into each other until the last one tumbled. In that moment I had a vivid memory of his father doing the same, twenty-odd years before; Robert, out in the gardens with William, his excited cries reaching my ears as I watched them from an upstairs window. The recollection was so vivid I could almost hear their voices though both were lost to me now in their different ways. There was only Robbie; he was the centre of my world.

'Perhaps I should go to Lambeth,' I started to say, but Byram interrupted me with the familiarity of an old servant. 'Pardon me, madam, but for what purpose?' he asked. He sank the last of his ale and rubbed his sleeve across his mouth. 'Mr Catesby will tell you nothing, nor will any word of yours sway him from his course. You would do better to stay here and enjoy your time with Master Robbie. Far better to know nothing.'

Still I fretted. 'Perhaps, then, I should go to Rushden,' I said. 'Mayhap Thomas will be able to tell me more.'

'He is sick,' Byram said. 'I called in there on my way home.' He patted his jacket. 'I have a letter for you here from Lady Tresham—'

I took it, feeling an odd sense of premonition, as though I had been waiting for this moment in some way, as though it was the beginning of the end. And even as I reached to unfold it there was a knocking at the door, and the maid burst in to say that a messenger had come from Rushden. Sir Thomas had taken a turn for the worse and was asking to see me before he died.

CHAPTER 19

Lucy

The first thing Lucy did that afternoon was to ring the number she had found for Maud Enright, the elderly lady in Knightstone village whom Verity had mentioned as being the person who had encountered Catherine's ghost decades before. She had toyed with the idea of calling around to see her but thought it better to ring first; the errand was so strange and there were so many reasons Mrs Enright might not want to talk to her, or even be able to remember or discuss what had happened back in the 1940s.

The phone was answered by a brisk woman who identified herself as Janet, Mrs Enright's daughter. Lucy explained tentatively that she was staying at Gunpowder Barn and was doing some research in support of the garden project. Would Mrs Enright be prepared to talk about the article that was in a book about Knightstone history and legends, published in the 1950s? She heard a brief, muffled conversation in the background and then Janet came back. 'Mum would be glad to talk to you,' she said. 'Come for coffee tomorrow morning if you're free.'

This was more than Lucy had hoped for so she thanked Janet profusely and made an arrangement to drop by at eleven o'clock. She wasn't sure if the story was a red herring or whether it might yield anything of interest about the ghost, the treasure or the garden – or all three – but she wanted to try to find out.

She spent the rest of the afternoon scouring the book about Lyveden New Bield for comparisons with the garden at Knightstone and also making a note of anything that seemed relevant from the Robert Catesby biography. Finn and Johnny had gone over to the spiral mounds in the orchard and in Clarabelle's field to cover up the test pits before the rain started. As the day went on the hot sun vanished behind a thick bank of cloud that piled in from the west, building higher and higher like an anvil.

It was interesting to have the description and pictures of the garden at Lyveden New Bield, which the National Trust had recreated. It enabled Lucy to see what the Knightstone garden had probably looked like before it was destroyed. The Robert Catesby book was more hard-going because she didn't really know what she was looking for and didn't want to skip any passages in case they were crucial. She kept searching for a reference to the connection between Robert Catesby, Thomas Tresham and the Knights Hospitaller, but although Tresham did seem to pop up everywhere, she couldn't put her finger on whatever it was that Charlie had discovered.

On impulse, she rang the Museum of the Knights Hospitallers in London.

'I'm not quite sure what it is I'm asking,' Lucy began,

when she had been put through to one of the archivists, 'but I wondered whether there is any evidence of connection between Knightstone in Oxfordshire and the Knights Hospitaller? I mean, I know they had a monastic grange here, but I'm trying to find out what happened after the dissolution of the monasteries, in particular anything to do with Sir Thomas Tresham and… erm… the Knights' treasure.'

She felt self-conscious even mentioning the word 'treasure' but the man at the other end, Nicholas Saint, responded politely and helpfully, as though he was quite accustomed to such enquiries, which, she thought, perhaps he was. From him she learned that Sir Thomas Tresham 'the elder', the man said helpfully, had been the last Grand Prior of the Order before Queen Elizabeth I had closed it down and that there was an old story that when Queen Mary had died, Sir Thomas had taken what was left of the Knights' treasure and hidden them in the cellars under in the old priory at Knightstone, in the Hollow Hills.

'We've done a lot of research into the legend,' Nicholas said, 'and we think it's a fabrication. Even if the Knights did plan to hide the treasure away for safekeeping, there wouldn't have been much of it left at this stage. Henry VIII had already dissolved the order once and taken its land and possessions. It was only revived for a short time under Mary I before Elizabeth shut it down for good.'

'So we're not talking about huge piles of gold or that sort of thing?' Lucy said.

Nicholas laughed. 'It's highly unlikely. There might have been some coin or some religious artefacts, and indeed some were discovered hidden at the priory building here in London in the nineteenth century. However, there simply wouldn't have been the time to accumulate a vast treasure horde during Mary I's reign, nor the time to pay for it and create it either.'

'I see,' Lucy said. 'Well, that's very helpful, thank you.' She put the phone down thinking of all the legends that swirled around Knightstone, of Odin and the Knights Hospitaller and the ghost of Catherine Catesby. Folklore and legend, she thought, might have a large part of imagination in them but sometimes there was also more than a grain of truth – they were based on real people, or places, or events that had happened in history. Perhaps they became magnified but if you dug into their origins there was usually a connection to find...

She looked up Sir Thomas Tresham the elder and discovered that he had been the grandfather of the younger Sir Thomas and had clearly inculcated his grandson with his strong Catholic beliefs. Sir Thomas the younger's buildings at Rushden and Lyveden all included allegories with religious significance, often based on the number three in an echo of his name 'tres' for Tresham and the Holy Trinity. She wondered whether there had been any religious significance built into the garden at Knightstone. That might be worth talking to Finn about.

The thing that interested her the most, however, was the reference to the Hollow Hills. She wondered if this was a chalk cave somewhere near the village. She hadn't heard any mention of a place like it and surely if it had been beneath the monastic buildings – and now the pub

– someone would have known about it. She made another mental note to ask Finn.

By now Lucy's eyes were tired from poring over the books and her screen and she suddenly realised how dark the room had become. A second later, she heard the first distant rumble of thunder and the patter of raindrops on the glass roof of the barn. She hurried to close the French windows. A hot wind was gusting up the valley, shaking the leaves and sending a couple of the patio pots tumbling over. Lucy wondered whether Finn and Johnny had managed to get all their work safely covered.

It was six o'clock and she had no idea where the time had gone. Her head still full of knights and old legends, she made herself an avocado and feta salad and ate it looking out on the valley as the storm edged closer. Sitting up here on the flat ledge above the tumbling stream felt exposed at a time like this when nature was running wild and yet it seemed to be taking the storm for ever to gather its strength and burst overhead. She'd never liked storms at the best of times; there was something about the primitive power of them that made her feel vulnerable. As a child she'd seen a neighbour's house catch fire from a lightning strike and had never forgotten it. Being in a glass house at a time like this suddenly felt far too exposed, just as it had done when she and Cleo had been alone on the night the intruder had been on the loose.

She made herself a cup of tea and curled up on the sofa with a magazine, preparing to sit out the storm. It was either that or go upstairs and get under the bed covers. She didn't understand why she was feeling so jumpy but there was some sort of current in the air. Perhaps it was electricity from the storm, but it felt more like the wired feeling she had had when she'd first come to Gunpowder Barn and seen Catherine's ghost. She shuddered. How could she be cold when the night was so humid? Yet she felt shivery and afraid.

She turned on all the lights and the television in order to distract from the creeping sense of gloom. Immediately the room was filled with the sound of Beethoven's violin concerto from an orchestral concert at the Royal Albert Hall. Great, that was all she needed, a reminder of her previous life. She'd do better to watch a reality TV show or a comedy, something that didn't have any personal resonances.

The storm broke overhead at that moment, a huge flash of lightning illuminating the barn followed almost immediately by a crack of thunder so loud the entire barn seemed to shudder. The rain, previously a patter, started to beat a tattoo on the roof, getting louder and louder, drowning out the music.

Lucy reached for the remote to change channels but instead found herself transfixed suddenly, unable to look away from the screen, from the orchestra, from the life that was denied to her. She could barely hear a note now but it didn't matter; she knew every last chord, every beat, every melody. It was within her, in her blood, a part of her. A huge sadness raced through her like a tide.

She watched the sweep and glide of the violinists' bows and suddenly she knew she was going to cry, not daintily or with any self-control, but messily expelling all the feelings she had kept bottled up ever since she had come out of hospital. The emotion surrounded her, different now from the fierce rage she had felt before when her feelings had connected with Catherine's anger and frustration, and had terrified her. Now she felt a huge sense of loss, Catherine's loss as well as her own bereavement, as though her heart truly was breaking.

Even though she knew it was going to happen, the force of the sobs that wracked her took her by surprise. Then the anger rose in her as well as despair and it burned through her. She hated the unfairness of what had happened and felt Catherine's impotent grief and fury possess her alongside her own.

She grabbed her violin from its case and ran to the door. It was a shock to step outside. The storm, for all its power, had been muted inside. Now the full force of the noise hit her, the rain pounding relentlessly on the cobbled yard, soaking her within seconds. The sky split with another livid flash of lightning, illuminating the trees in the orchard shivering beneath the onslaught. The thunder rumbled around the bowl of the valley.

Lucy wasn't sure whether the water on her face was tears or rain. It didn't matter. She didn't really know what she was doing, other than that she needed to get away from the mockery of the music and she wanted to take her violin and smash it apart, venting all her misery in destroying it. Behind her the lights of the barn shone like a liner battered by a stormy sea but the yard was deep in shadow. When someone appeared out of the dark tunnel of trees that lined the path up to the cottage, she screamed.

'It's me.' Finn was shouting above the noise of the storm. She recognised him at the same moment she heard his voice. He was wearing a fisherman's sou'wester, which was actually perfect for the weather – far more so than Lucy's own soaking top and shorts, and he pushed the hood back so that the light fell on his face. It was then he saw the violin in her hand.

'What the hell are you doing?' he said. He sounded incredulous. He grabbed her arm with one hand and the violin in the other and dashed across to the barn. The slam of the door behind them sounded above the retreating thunder.

'Here—' Finn threw her the blanket from the back of the sofa. 'Wrap yourself up in this for a moment.' He took a couple of the oldest, softest tea towels from the drawer and wrapped them around the violin, placing it gently on the table.

'I came down to see if you were all right,' Finn was saying, snapping off the TV. 'I texted but got no answer. Anyway, the question seems superfluous.' He stared at her from beneath his brows in the way she used to find intimidating. 'Clearly anyone who takes a Stradivarius out in a thunderstorm is very far from all right,' he said.

Lucy gave a gurgle of laughter. 'It isn't a Stradivarius, it's a Mendini.'

'Whatever.' Finn gave a dismissive shrug. 'It's disrespectful to treat a beautiful instrument like that. Are you hysterical?'

'Very likely,' Lucy said. 'Thank you for wrapping him up, Finn. If I put him in the airing cupboard, I'm sure he'll be fine.'

Finn was glaring. 'It's not funny.'

'You're absolutely right,' Lucy said. She clutched the blanket to her, trying to find some equilibrium. What the hell had happened to her? The explosion of emotion had been so fierce, so strange, and as before, tangled up in some way with Catherine and her feelings. And now here was Finn looking fierce and worried and she felt an odd sense of protectiveness towards him as well as a disconcerting flash of lust.

She put a hand up to touch his wet face. 'Thank you,' she said again, softly. She placed both hands on the nape of his neck and drew his head down so that she could kiss him. After a moment's hesitation, he kissed her back and then everything else fell away – the misery she'd felt at the unfairness of fate, her anxiety about the future, the visions and strange experiences, all lost in the heat of the moment.

'I have a bit of an issue taking advantage of a woman who's so clearly upset,' Finn said, when they finally broke apart. He was breathing hard and put her from him with deliberate gentleness. 'You need to get into some dry clothes, Lucy, then we should talk.'

'Sorry,' Lucy said, suddenly feeling acutely self-conscious. 'I seem to be doing everything the wrong way round…'

'Hey, no worries,' Finn said. He smiled at her. 'I'll put some coffee on while you get changed.'

The sky was lightening shade by grey shade as Lucy went upstairs, the storm slowly passing away to the east. The noise of the rain was fading too and other sounds were coming back in; the drip of water from the gutters onto the stone of the yard, the faintest cheep of birds in the hedge, the distant sound of a car on the road splashing through the puddles. Lucy noticed that the atmosphere, previously as tight as a violin string, had eased.

Peering in the mirror in her bedroom she was horrified by what she saw – eyes puffy with crying, cheeks bright red, her hair a rats' nest and her clothes soaked. No wonder Finn had backed away. Whatever had possessed her to kiss him? For a musician, she had an appalling sense of timing.

She stripped off her shorts and top, towelled herself down and dressed in jeans and a T-shirt. Pulling a comb through her hair she checked her reflection again, shuddered, and grabbed her favourite stripy jumper. That was the best she could do.

As she went downstairs, she could hear Finn moving around making the coffee, and she could smell the rich scent of it. Warm now, she felt her tension easing slightly. Explaining would be a challenge, though.

Finn had shed the sou'wester and his boots, and was looking formidably practical and businesslike in the jumper and dark trousers. When he saw her he smiled again and she felt another tumble of lust. She made an effort to drown it in the coffee he handed her, which tasted really good and strong.

'How are you doing?' Finn asked.

'I'm good, thanks,' Lucy said. 'I'm sorry – that must all have seemed a little weird.'

'You think?' Finn cocked a brow. 'I am starting to expect the unexpected around you.'

Lucy sat down on the sofa and tucked her feet under her. 'Yeah, it seems to come with this place.' She shook her head. 'I was a bit on edge because of the storm, and then I turned on the TV and realised there was a concert on and I should have switched it off, but somehow I couldn't...' She stopped, feeling an echo of the previous, fierce emotion.

'Tough for you to listen to?' Finn had come to sit beside her. 'I'm sorry.'

'I think I needed to cry, to be honest,' Lucy said. 'I've been feeling a bit better these last few days but I was aware that I'd never really mourned the loss of my career properly. I've bottled things up. Then this evening when I heard the music, all the grief seemed to flood out. It was so intense, wrapped up with everything that's been going on here and my visions of Catherine...' She rubbed her eyes. 'It was kind of you to come down to check up on me,' she added, 'and thank you for saving Guido.'

'Who?' Finn said. His expression cleared. 'Oh, you mean the violin? He has a name?' He laughed. 'Of course he does.'

'All musical instruments should have a name,' Lucy said.

'You know,' Finn said, 'when I first met you I thought you were very serious but I know better now. And anyone who calls their violin Guido must have a sense of humour. Is he named for Guy Fawkes, as we seem to be on a Gunpowder Plot theme around here?'

'No.' Lucy said. 'I called him after the pizza restaurant around the corner from my flat.'

They looked at each other. Finn, Lucy realised, would not make the first move. She felt her whole body heat up. She was so out of practice at all this.

'About earlier,' she said awkwardly. 'I think I was the

one taking advantage, not you.' The colour stung her face. 'I'm sorry.'

'I can reassure you that I don't feel remotely exploited,' Finn said gravely but the smile still lurked in his eyes. He put down his coffee mug. 'I just wanted to be certain that you knew what you were doing and that you were happy about it.'

Lucy's throat felt dry. 'I did and I was,' she said. 'But there's something I wanted to ask first.'

Finn laughed. 'Go ahead. Is it, "Are you in a relationship?"'

'Are you?' Lucy asked.

'No,' Finn said. He sat back. 'My last relationship broke up after Charlie died. It wasn't Kara's fault – I kind of withdrew into myself and wouldn't talk to her. Plus we'd not known each other very long. There wasn't much foundation to see us through.'

'I'm sorry,' Lucy said. 'As if things weren't difficult enough for you.'

Finn shrugged. 'It was a bad time.' The smile lit his eyes again. 'Things may be improving now, though.' He looked at her. 'What about you?'

'Me? Oh…' Lucy shrugged. 'I lived with a cellist for a while. We were in different orchestras and never saw each other because our schedules hardly ever matched. He was more of a flatmate than a boyfriend actually and when we realised that… Well, we knew it was time to call it a day.'

The rain was increasing in intensity again, another storm rolling in from the west. 'I hope Geoffrey is okay,' Lucy said, as a fork of lightning lit the sky overhead. 'Dogs hate thunderstorms, don't they?'

'He'll be curled up on Johnny's bed and blissfully happy,' Finn said.

'Johnny's not likely to send out a search party for you, is he?' Lucy asked.

'No,' Finn said. He laughed. 'He's a perceptive kid. He knows I'm hooked on you.'

Just like that he'd taken Lucy's breath away again. 'Does he?' She put her mug down, splashing the coffee rather haphazardly onto the table. 'I mean, I didn't really know you were—' She stopped at the look Finn gave her.

'I think you did,' Finn said.

'Maybe,' Lucy admitted. 'I mean, I hoped that it was… erm… a mutual thing.'

'Glad to hear it,' Finn said. 'So now we've sorted that out—' He dipped his head and brushed his lips against hers. 'Okay?' he asked.

'Very,' Lucy managed, and he pulled her closer and slid a hand into her hair, angling her head so that he could kiss her more deeply. It felt so good; she'd forgotten how good it could be to be held. It was a shock as well as a draught of pure pleasure. She closed her eyes and breathed in the scent of his skin and felt all the heap of troubles melt away.

'Will you stay?' she asked when they drew apart a few inches. 'If,' she added, 'you think you'd like to experience my visions and dreams first hand.'

She felt Finn smile against her mouth. 'I'd like that very much,' he said.

CHAPTER 20

Anne Catesby

Rushden, Northamptonshire, October 1605

Thomas' bedchamber smelled of urine and sickness and was shrouded in darkness. I wanted to throw the window wide and allow the early autumn sunshine in but I doubted even that would banish the spectre of death that lurked in the bed hangings, waiting. Thomas looked gaunt, his body wasted, his skin the colour of old parchment. It was a shock to see him so, the vital spark that had driven him all but extinguished. I felt a pang of misery. So much loss and grief. Where did it end?

'Come sit by me, Anne,' Thomas said, gesturing weakly to the little wooden stool beside the bed. I did not care for it; not only was it low and hard, there was no backrest to support my aching bones. Instead, I asked a servant to draw up the heavy armchair, and saw Thomas smile at all the scraping and puffing my order entailed.

'I married the wrong sister,' he said, a little dreamily. 'Ah, what a partnership we would have made, Anne!'

Muriel, naturally enough, looked furious to hear this.

'Do not regard him,' I said. 'He has the fever and speaks nonsense. Can you imagine Thomas and I wed? We would have fought likes cats in a sack.'

Muriel smiled but it did not reach her eyes. 'I will leave the two of you to whisper sweet nothings,' she said spitefully, sweeping from the room in an indignant rustle of silk.

'I meant it,' Thomas said, when the door had closed behind his wife and the servant. 'Ah, Anne, you are a woman of such strength and principle. Together we could have taken on the world!'

'I move a chair and you hail me as Joan of Arc?' I said. 'As usual you have everything the wrong way around, Thomas. You would not have tolerated opposition in your own household for a moment. No wife could have suited you better than Muriel. She is biddable and relies on your judgement whereas I would have challenged you every step of the way. It would have been exhausting.'

Thomas gave me a ghost of a smile. 'Perhaps you are right. She will fare badly when I am gone, I fear.'

That was typical Thomas, I thought, with a mixture of exasperation and indulgence. He was dying and still it flattered him to think of his wife lost without him to guide her. I could have told him then that the entire family was doomed without him – his elder son Francis was hot-headed and unreliable, the younger one Lewis was a wastrel, and Muriel was without a single independent thought. The girls, though… I had some hopes for them. Surely there was one of my nieces who had inherited some of Thomas' stubborn will and would use it to good purpose? He had made or planned grand marriages for them all as part of his desire to live and to die a great man. I hoped it had been worth it.

'Now that I am dying,' Thomas said, appearing to read my mind, 'I wish to beg a favour from you, Nan.' He coughed and in a moment of softness I held the cup of water to his lips but he did not take it. Instead, his hand closed around my wrist, spilling the water on the bedclothes. His grip was hard.

'I want you to take the last of the treasure and hide it at Knightstone,' he said.

I drew back. 'You told me there was no treasure!' I said. 'You said the Queen had taken it all but for the few pieces left at Clerkenwell.'

Thomas' lips twisted. He let me go and fell back on the bed. 'I told you the truth,' he said.

'Then—' I was at a loss. 'What can you mean?'

Thomas moved his head slightly. 'Go to the chest,' he said. 'At the very bottom is a cloth wrapped in linen. Bring it to me.'

I disliked taking orders but he could hardly fetch the thing himself. I went over to the chest, moved the heavy iron candelabrum from the top and lifted the lid. It was full of linens and smelled of cedar and lavender, my least favourite herb. Rifling through the piles of cloth I finally touched the bottom and found the small packet he had indicated. The linen was so old and worn that it was soft as gossamer against my fingers and when I drew it out into the light I saw it was tied with ribbon again so old and frayed that it had lost all colour.

'Bring it here,' Thomas said. 'Untie it.'

I did so, laying the parcel on the bed and gently releasing the knot that had held the linen closed for so long. The covering fell back. Beneath it I saw the shimmer of silk, pure black, with the eight-pointed star of the Knights Hospitaller emblazon upon it. I touched it lightly with the tip of one finger.

'The mantle of the Grand Prior of the Knights Hospitaller,' I said, but my words were no more than a whisper.

'A sacred trust,' Thomas agreed.

'Which you cannot give to me,' I objected. 'Just as your grandfather passed it to you, so you must pass it to the one who is to come after you.'

A tear slid from the corner of Thomas' eye. For some reason that moved me more than anything else I had seen in that room; this mercurial and dazzling man defeated at the last.

'I wanted it to be Robert,' he whispered, 'but it would not serve.'

'No,' I agreed. 'That would never have worked.'

Thomas' gaze sought mine. 'All I ever wanted,' he said, 'was that men should have the freedom to worship as they wished. I employed my fortune and my pen in that service and I suffered for it, but that was my choice. But Robert—' he moistened his lips, 'he has taken up the sword I would not wield in pursuit of what he believes to be right.' His eyes closed. He lay very still.

'Yes,' I said. 'Robert has rebelled and may do so again.' Together we faced the truth of it. Our son had chosen a different path to ours. I had often blamed Thomas for filling Robert's head with high religious ideals but Thomas had never advocated violence to achieve them.

'Robert is not worthy to be the custodian of the Knights,' Thomas said. He sounded regretful. 'I wished it for him but I saw that it would not serve. There is no one.' He opened his eyes. 'Therefore, it is my wish that the order be laid to rest amongst the Hollow Hills of Knightstone, Nan. You must take the mantle and conceal it there. Promise me – do this for me.'

I released a long breath. It was a man's dying wish, Thomas' dying wish, and to him it was so important, the symbol of all he had tried to achieve in his life, the fight for religious tolerance by peaceful means. I knew that the order was finished and finally he had accepted it too.

'I will do it,' I promised, and I saw the rigidity leave his body and his breath came a little more easily. 'I will leave you to rest now,' I murmured. Muriel, I knew, would feel I had been long enough.

Quickly I rewrapped the prior's cope in its linen covering and tied the ribbons, straightening the pile in the chest and closing the lid. The mantle was weightier than I had noticed when I had taken it out and I realised that there must be a jewelled clasp or something similar to fasten it. No matter; I would not look at it again. I would seal it up safely and take it to Knightstone. I already knew the place of safety where I would put it to rest.

I paused by the bed to clasp Thomas' hand one last time. It was impossible to equate this withered man with the handsome and vibrant youth I had known in my childhood, the man who had briefly swept me off my feet when I had been so lonely and lost in the aftermath of my first son's death. All that power and passion for living was banked down now and almost extinguished. I pressed a kiss on his brow and felt my heart crack a little.

'Anne...' Thomas' lips barely moved. I had to bend close to hear. 'You should try to stop Robert, for little Robbie's sake. He has a plan. He has gunpowder.'

I stared at him in consternation. What could he mean?

'Thomas!' I shook his shoulder. He did not move; his breathing was shallow and peaceful.

'Thomas!' I raised my voice. I wanted to shake his entire body, wake him and force him to tell me what Robert planned. My hands itched to slap him. I wanted to drag him back from the gates of death if needs be but he did not stir. I could not reach him.

The door burst open; the manservant, disturbed by my shouting, had gone to fetch Muriel. Pale-faced, she tumbled into the room and rushed across to the bed. It was only then that I realised that I was on my feet and the chair was overturned.

'What is it?' She hung over Thomas, fear in her face. 'The servant said you shouted so loud! Has he had a fit? Is he dead?'

'No.' I took a deep breath and rubbed my damp palms against my skirts. 'Your pardon, sister,' I said. 'He was so quiet that for a moment I thought he had slipped away from us but he breathes still.'

She gave me a look full of mistrust. Thomas' chest rose and fell softly. He looked entirely at peace.

'I will stay with him now,' she said, and it was tantamount to an order to me to leave the room – so I went.

In the parlour, I sat by the window and looked out over the gardens in their autumn splendour. The pleasure grounds were quiet beneath the fading blue of the sky, the waters of the canal catching the falling golden leaves. The raspberries and damask roses were withering in the labyrinth; Thomas' pilgrimage through life was reaching its end. I thought then of Catherine's ambitious plans for the garden at Knightstone and the ruthless destruction of them that Robert had wrought in his grief. I felt a tear fall onto my skirts. It surprised me, for I so seldom cried, but here, stalked by death and with the shell of Thomas' new building at the top of the hill looking down on us, I was run through with despair. What use were Thomas' grand architectural designs now, when he lay dying? He had claimed they were for the glory of God and I knew that this was in part true, but they were in equal part a testament to his own glory. And now that was all but blown out like a spent candle.

I thought too of Thomas' words about Robert: *'He has taken up the sword I would not wield… He has gunpowder…'*

I had known Robert was lost after the death of his family. I could not reach him and I had been content in some ways, if not happy, to see him turn back to the church, because I had thought it might comfort him when I could not. But I had always known that Robert's way was to fight. He had proved it by joining Essex's rebellion and now it sounded as though he had other plans afoot. And Thomas was right – Robert would bring down not only himself but also his son's future. The thought of it made me feel sick with fear.

I jumped up, intending to go to my chamber and start to pack my bags at once so that I might go to London and make some desperate attempt to find my son, but then Muriel came in, her face puffy with exhaustion and her eyes red from crying. 'He is gone,' she said. 'He went as quietly as a lamb in the end. The priest was with him.' She sat down heavily on the settle, as though her limbs could no longer support her.

'What am I to do, Anne?' She addressed me, though she too had her gaze fixed on the skeleton of the house up on the hill. 'Thomas has left us with nothing but grief and debt. How am I to bear it?' And she cried again, her body heaving with sobs, the sound tearing through the silent house.

I was desperate to be gone, for Thomas' words about Robert ate away at me all the more now that he was dead, but I could not leave my sister at such a time.

'I will send for Francis,' I said, thinking that once her children were with her I could slip away. 'Is he at Hoxton? And Elizabeth and Mary too. It will comfort you to have your children with you.'

But Muriel gave no sign of having heard me. She was comfortless for she had lost not only her husband but her guiding light, the rudder that steered her world.

'Don't go!' She grabbed my hand as I made to leave the room to find the steward and give him instruction. 'Stay with me, Anne. I need you.'

'Of course,' I said, and I went to the library and wrote hasty notes to Francis Tresham and his sisters Elizabeth Parker and Mary Brudenell, and I made possets of chamomile for Anne and sat with her whilst she told me endlessly what a wonderful man Thomas had been and how she was a broken reed without him.

It took five days for Francis to arrive, riding hard, his wife and children following behind him in a carriage. His sisters and their families followed and Lyveden was suddenly full of people and voices but not even the children's presence could lift the gloom as the business of death ground onward. Meanwhile, my preoccupation was to find Robert and to that end I cornered Francis one evening after dinner.

'Have you seen your cousin Robert lately?' I asked him. 'I believe he has been in London these past few weeks? Indeed, I wondered whether he might come with you when he heard the news of his uncle, for he loved Sir Thomas so dearly.'

I sensed rather than saw his sisters Elizabeth and Mary exchange a glance that was loaded with meaning.

'I haven't seen Robert for many months,' Francis said. He had been a tall, fair and easy-going youth who had grown into a man whose edges seemed blurred by soft living. 'I am not in his confidence these days.' He sounded piqued and I knew that even though he was the elder, he had always hung on Robert's favour. Perhaps they had had a falling-out.

'Ladies,' I turned to Elizabeth and Mary, 'do you have any news of my son?'

They looked as guilty as a pair of naughty children and it reminded me of the days long past when the cousins had all egged each other on in some scrape. But this was no childish prank; this was treason.

'I know that there is mischief afoot,' I said bluntly. 'Your father told me before he died. It is imperative I speak with Robert. Where do I find him?'

A rather uncomfortable silence had fallen over the table now, not the silence of respectful grieving but a blanket of secrets and lies.

The girls looked at each other. again. 'Madam,' Mary said reluctantly, 'we do not know.'

I realised that they spoke the truth. 'Then tell me what you *do* know,' I urged. 'What would your father have meant when he said that Robert had taken up the sword he would not wield? To what use would Robert put gunpowder?'

'Father pledged himself to the restoration of the Catholic faith,' Mary said, 'but he was not prepared to carry arms for the cause.'

'He saw that as a weakness in himself,' Elizabeth put in. 'He deplored his lack of courage and wished he had Robert's boldness of spirit.'

I looked at Francis, who sank another full glass of wine and looked surly. Beneath his hero-worship of Robert, I thought, there ran a strong strand of resentment. He knew that his father had preferred Robert to him.

'Do you know,' I asked, 'what Robert is planning? Is it another insurrection?'

How many times, I thought viciously, must men fail before they realised that rebellions were seldom won? For ever, in all likelihood.

There was a long silence. Neither Elizabeth nor Mary would meet my eyes.

'When Catherine died,' I said, 'and I took on the care of little Robbie, I vowed to do everything in my power to protect him from danger. I promised Catherine's bright spirit that I would give my life for him if need be. No matter my own desire to see the true faith restored, no matter my love for my son, the safety and future happiness of my grandson became the most important thing in the world to me. So

I beseech you both—' my voice wavered and I stopped, and took a breath, 'if you know *anything* of what Robert intends, pray tell me, so that I may prevent *all* our children from suffering in the same way that past generations have suffered.'

'We do not know!' Elizabeth burst out. Her face was suffused with colour and her eyes were bright. She looked at Mary, and then at her brother slouched in his chair. 'They do not trust us,' she said finally, 'for we feel as you do, madam. Nothing is worth the risk to our homes and families that would come from a renewed attack.'

'Who are they?' I asked.

'Our cousins,' Elizabeth said. 'The Wintours and Rob Percy and the Wrights.'

The Wintours and Rob Percy and the Wrights, I thought. The men that Robert had been keeping company with all this time. Our kin, who had attended family weddings and feast days for time immemorial. We were all bound together through our faith yet now it was forcing us apart.

'You must have heard something,' I pressed, 'some whisper of treason. What use would Robert have for gunpowder?'

Once again there was silence and then Francis Tresham spoke. 'It is to kill the King,' he said.

His aim is to kill the King.

My bags were packed. In the privacy of my chamber, before I departed, I called Byram to me. 'I need you to find Robert,' I said, 'immediately. I'm told his aim is to kill the King. I would like to prevent that if it is at all possible.'

Byram blinked. 'Yes, madam,' he said. 'That would be wise.'

'So I think,' I said. 'Thank you, Byram.' I knew that I did not need to tell him to be covert and to keep his own counsel.

'What do you want me to do with him when I find him?' Byram asked.

'Kidnap him,' I said. 'Incapacitate him. Do anything you need to do, short of killing him. Lock him away until I can reach London and speak with him. I shall be there as swiftly as I can.'

'Aye, madam,' Byram said.

I put out a hand to delay him for a moment. 'Byram,' I said, 'if your aim was to kill the King and you had gunpowder, how would you achieve it?'

'I would blow him up, madam,' Byram said, bluntly. 'I would find a time and place I could be certain he would be present and then I would light the fuse.'

'The state opening of Parliament is on November fifth,' I said.

'Then I had best be gone,' Byram said, 'and pray to God that that is not the plan in Mr Catesby's mind.'

'Godspeed,' I said, 'and I too pray I may be mistaken.'

CHAPTER 21

Lucy

Maud Enright lived in a neat bungalow in a cul de sac on the edge of Knightstone with a view down the hill and across the open fields of the Vale of the White Horse. Her daughter Janet led Lucy through the house and out into a bright conservatory at the back which was full of sunshine and roses. The scent of them hung in the warm air.

'How beautiful it is here!' Lucy said as she shook hands with the white-haired old lady sitting in a high-backed chair. 'Thank you very much for agreeing to see me, Mrs Enright.'

'Call me Maud,' Maud Enright said. Her voice was clipped, cut glass. She gestured to the table on which were laid out various books and what looked like a scrapbook of cuttings from newspapers. 'Janet's helped me to find all the bits and pieces I collected on Catherine Catesby. It's been a while—' her sharp grey eyes appraised Lucy, 'since anyone was interested in them.'

Janet offered refreshments and Lucy chose lemonade with ice whilst Maud asked for tea. 'No sugar, dear!' she called after her daughter. 'She always forgets,' she added, to Lucy, with a twinkle in her eye. 'Takes three spoons of it herself and automatically adds it to mine.'

There was what was for Lucy, a slightly unnerving silence whilst Maud waited for her to broach what she was there for. She realised that she hadn't really imagined what Maud would be like or prepared herself properly for their meeting. Her encounter with Finn the previous night had put everything else from her mind in the nicest possible way. And now here she was at a bit of a loss to explain herself whilst Maud Enright looked like one of those scarily clever old ladies who had been at Bletchley Park or in the SOE, or something, and was impatient for her to begin.

'I found a reference in a book to a woman encountering the ghost of Catherine Catesby in the orchards at Gunpowder Cottage in the 1940s,' she said, slightly at random. 'It interested me because—' she paused. She'd been about to say it was because she had seen Catherine too but this wasn't about her; she wanted to hear Maud's experience without prejudice. 'Because I'm involved with the dig at Gunpowder Cottage, and we think there may be some connection between the Tudor gardens and Catherine's ghost.' Put like that it sounded odd, she realised, but Maud simply smiled.

'I see,' she said.

Janet arrived with the drinks and a plate of muffins at that moment, but when her daughter had gone out, Maud added: 'How did you know that I was the one who had seen Catherine?'

'My aunt Verity told me,' Lucy said. 'I'm not sure how she knew – is it common knowledge hereabouts?'

Maud spread her hands. 'Who knows? Most things are in a village. But as I say, no one has seemed particularly interested for many years. It was one of those things that was a flash in the pan – all very sensational at the time and then quickly forgotten.'

'What happened?' Lucy said. 'I know it was a long time ago...'

'But I remember it clearly.' Maud took a sip of her tea. Her hands were old and knotted with arthritis but still looked strong. 'It was the summer of '46 and I was twenty years old and I had lost my sweetie less than a year before. Henry. He'd been in the RAF. Shot down in the very last days of the war.'

Sweetie, Lucy thought, thinking of Finn. That sounded warm and lovely but the grief of losing him would surely have been devastating.

'I'm very sorry,' she said.

Maud's smile had an edge of sadness. 'He was my first love. Our parents thought we were too young to marry, too young even to get engaged, especially with a war on, but I knew he was for me. It was our anniversary – the anniversary of the first time we'd made love – and I went to the orchard to be alone and think about him.'

Lucy almost spat out her lemonade. She'd had very chaste ideas of Maud's romance up until that point but of course even old ladies of ninety-plus had their pasts.

'I was a little bit happy and a lot sad,' Maud said softly, and Lucy's heart ached for her. 'I sat down under one of the apple trees and had a good cry. It's very cathartic to cry when you need to – I don't hold with this "buck up and get on" philosophy. For a lost glove, perhaps, but not when someone's died. Give them the respect their loss deserves, I say. And then I saw her – Catherine. She was crying too.'

Lucy felt her heart start to speed up. Grief calls to grief, she thought. There had been Maud and Johnny and now her, and perhaps there had been others…

'Of course it wasn't the done thing to intrude on private grief in those days,' Maud said, 'but that's all nonsense too. It's common humanity to offer comfort, isn't it? So I asked her if she was all right and offered her my rather sodden handkerchief. I didn't notice to start with that she looked rather odd – the outfit, you know – but when she spoke I knew at once there was something strange about her. I thought she might be a foreigner.' She laughed. 'Little did I know how foreign she was!'

'It said in the book,' Lucy said, 'that Catherine identified herself by name and as the wife of the lord of the manor, and told you she was mourning her lost treasure and was riven with guilt and misery that she could never find it or return it to where it belonged.'

Maud tutted. 'That book!' She gestured towards the table where Lucy saw a copy of *Legends and Folklore of Berkshire* open at the pages she had read. 'It wasn't even a second-hand version of the tale,' she said. 'It was fourth hand! I tried to put them right but the editor didn't want to know. It was the same with the newspapers; they were only interested in sensationalism – and treasure.'

'Oh dear,' Lucy said. At the same time she was feeling a little bit excited. If the folklore was wrong, the right story might have something more useful to tell them.

'It's true she did say that her name was Catherine,' Maud said thoughtfully, 'but the rest was all wrong. I asked her what had upset her and she said that she had lost her most treasured possession and couldn't rest until it was found again.' She sighed. 'It was foolish of me but when I got home I confided the tale in my family and one of my brothers mentioned it later when he was down at the pub. The next thing I knew, it was all over the newspapers. Really, as though we didn't know that loose talk cost lives, after five years of war! I never told him a secret again. Would you be so kind as to refill my cup, dear?'

Lucy poured for her and Maud stirred in a little milk. 'How did you feel about encountering a ghost?' Lucy asked. 'I mean, it's not entirely normal, is it?'

'Oh, I was accustomed to oddities,' Maud said vaguely. 'I worked with Alan Turing, you know, and he believed in telepathy. And even Winston Churchill himself saw ghosts, so they say. I would never be *too* sceptical.' She tilted her head to one side. 'And what about you, my dear? Have you also seen Catherine Catesby?'

Lucy jumped. 'I don't know how you would know that,' she said, 'unless you are also telepathic.'

Maud laughed. 'Oh, I make no such claims,' she said, 'but there is something about you, Lucy, that makes me feel she might be drawn to you. A sadness, perhaps, but a kindness too.'

'That's very lovely of you,' Lucy said, feeling very touched. 'And yes, I have… encountered her a couple of times. It scared me to begin with but I'd like to help her find whatever it is she is searching for.'

'So much depends upon what it was that she treasured,' Maud said, thoughtfully. 'For me it is my health these days, as well as my family. During the war years it was our liberty above all else. It varies at different times and from person to person: wisdom, money, life and love…'

'For me it was my orchestral career more than anything else,' Lucy said, 'but I'm learning to value other things more now.' She thought of Cleo and Sam, of Verity and of Finn, of love and friendship, and smiled. 'For Catherine, though,' she said, 'I don't know. We know so little of her! She created the beautiful Tudor garden, I think, so she must have loved that, and she certainly loved Robert Catesby and her children…'

'And she lost all of those,' Maud said, 'through the sudden death of her eldest child and then her own death so soon after. Perhaps she was unprepared; there was something she treasured but it was left unfinished, hidden or discarded.'

'Her most treasured possession…' Lucy repeated. 'People – our family or friends – aren't really possessions, are they? But perhaps it was something that related to them or reminded her of them?' She put the thought to one side for a moment and looked at the other bits and pieces of memorabilia that Maud had set out for her. There was the same newspaper clipping that she had found in the book at the barn, showing the marks in the soil of Clarabelle's field. 'This was the same summer, wasn't it,' she said, 'when the aerial photos showed some strange buried structures? It said in the book that when people heard there was treasure in the fields at Knightstone they all went out digging for it.'

'Yes,' Maud said. 'So foolish! Because, of course, it was

all made up. The newspapers were looking for a story – it was the summer season, the silly season they used to call it in news terms – so they put together the story of the ghost who had lost her treasure with the strange marks in the soil, and started a rumour that led to a frenzy.'

'And all they found were a few coins, a toy or two, and an old key,' she added, with a sigh, 'which I think are all in the museum now. It was very far from treasure, but people are still convinced it's out there somewhere.'

'It sounds as though they conflated the treasure of the Knights Hospitaller with the treasure the ghost had supposedly lost,' Lucy said. 'There are old legends that the Knights' treasure is hidden here at Knightstone too.'

'People enjoy a good mystery,' Maud said comfortably. 'It adds some excitement to life, don't you think? I imagine there are plenty of people around here who still believe in it. It's that sort of place, full of myth and legend, and who's to say it isn't true?'

Who indeed? Lucy thought. She remembered something that Maud had said. 'Sorry,' she said, 'did you mention that they found a key when they were digging for treasure in 1946?'

'That's right.' Maud passed her the other newspaper cutting, from the *Wiltshire Gazette*. *'Amongst other items found by the treasure seekers,'* Lucy read, *'were part of a clay pipe, two broken glass bottles thought to be Victorian, some coins which have been sent to Oxford for dating and analysis, and a small key. No more valuable treasure was discovered but one of the villagers, Isaac Redfern, swore to continue the search. "It's hidden there," Mr Redfern said. "I knows it and I'll find it."'*

'He was Marilynne's father,' Maud said. 'The father of Persis and Gabriel's mother as well. A cantankerous old fellow.'

'I don't remember seeing a key in the museum,' Lucy said thoughtfully. 'I'll check on my way back.'

'One other thing I should tell you,' Maud said, gathering together the cuttings and books in a neat pile. 'I saw Catherine another time. It was winter and by then all interest in the story had died down.' She smiled. 'Memories can be short and people are fickle, aren't they? It was all forgotten. But as I say, it was January and a harsh winter that year. We had been cooped up indoors with the snow but on the very first day of fine weather I went for a walk.'

Lucy smiled, imagining a determined Maud wrapping herself up against the cold and ploughing through the snowdrifts to get some exercise and fresh air.

'When I reached Gunpowder Cottage the gardens looked enchanting,' Maud said. 'There were arches adorned with holly and ivy, and pine garlands and lanterns. The paths were thick with snow but the bushes were such bright splashes of color with their juniper and hawthorn and spindleberries. It was extraordinary – like a fairy tale.'

'And Catherine?' Lucy prompted.

'She was in the winter garden,' Maud said. There was a misty look in her eyes; she smiled. 'She looked beautiful – and happy. I glimpsed her for a moment only, then she was gone. And when I turned back the garden was gone too. There was nothing but snow.'

Lucy was surprised to find herself blinking back tears. 'It sounds as though the garden was very special,' she said. 'A haven in all seasons.'

She thanked Maud, was issued a warm invitation to visit any time she liked and went out into the summer sunshine, still thinking about the winter garden. She wanted to talk to Finn about it; archaeology could only tell you so much, she thought. Her admittedly limited reading on Tudor gardens had been almost exclusively about the designs and plants that would look best in summer, but perhaps Catherine had had a vision for the winter as well.

Something was also nagging at the back of her mind, something about a box without a key. She was trying to remember where she had seen or read about it. A couple of cars passed her as she crossed the road and walked along the lane to the museum. This was the oldest part of the village with the core of ancient, thatched cottages set around a little village green. A stream led to a millpond; it was postcard-perfect.

Lucy checked her watch and on impulse, rang Finn's mobile. He had gone up to London that morning to discuss creating a historically themed garden for the next Chelsea Flower Show but she thought she might catch him between meetings. He answered at once, sounding warm.

'Hi,' Lucy said, feeling ridiculously shy all of a sudden. 'How are you getting on?'

'Great,' Finn said. 'It's an exciting project. I'm sorry it had to be today, though. I miss you.'

Now she felt ridiculously happy. 'I miss you too,' she said. 'I've lots to tell you when I see you tonight.'

'I'll be quite late,' Finn said, 'but I'll text you as soon as I get back and maybe we could have supper together? If you'd like that,' he added.

'I would,' Lucy said. It felt good, she realised, to relax and see what might happen with Finn. Her life had always been so planned, each step regimented to fit with her career. This new sensation of leaving time and space for things to develop, whether it was work, interests or relationships, was exciting. And she liked him. She really liked him. He was straightforward, comfortable in his own skin. She admired that.

The museum was as sepulchrally quiet as on the first occasion she had visited. Fortunately, this time Gabriel didn't seem to be around; an older man was handing out tickets and selling souvenirs from behind the counter. The police had told her that Gabriel had an alibi for the night that Cleo had seen the intruder at the barn but even so, Lucy didn't feel comfortable around him which she acknowledged might purely have been down to guilt on her part for suspecting him.

She walked over to the case that contained the artefacts that had been found by the treasure hunters in Clarabelle's field back in the 1940s. It was as she remembered, and as it was outlined in the newspaper cutting: a couple of glass bottles described as originally containing medicinal salts, part of a seventeenth-century clay pipe, a few bits of Roman pottery, coins from the Middle Ages to the eighteenth century, and the battered toy soldier.

There was no sign of a key.

The cold blast of sensation, when it came, was exactly like the previous time. Lucy felt as though someone was watching her, felt the hairs rise on the back of her neck and the chill creep along her skin like frost. The feeling intensified, ice-cold and terrifying, and she turned and blundered out of the museum, past the poster advertising Marilynne's autumn art show, the counter assistant's face an astonished blur, and out into the street.

Once outside the feeling receded and she took deep breaths of the clear summer air. She needed to get back and think about all of this; write down all the snippets of information she'd put together from the books, the newspaper cuttings, Maud's conversation, Finn and Johnny's work, her own experiences of Catherine... And look for a pattern.

The walk back through the village and down the footpath to the barn was blissfully free of anything strange and Lucy enjoyed the sun slipping through the branches overhead, the constantly moving shadows on the path, the birdsong and ripple of the stream, and the scents of rose and honeysuckle. They had reached that time in high summer when nature ran rampant.

She met Johnny as she walked down the footpath to the barn. He was rolling up a long tape measure whilst away in Clarabelle's field, two people could be seen walking up and down with what looked like complicated pieces of machinery.

'The geophysics team is here today,' Johnny said. 'Finn's called in some extra help so we can put the history of the whole site together a bit faster. Now we know we're dealing with something so potentially exciting, he's keen to get more people involved and some more funding so that Verity isn't bearing all the cost.' His face was alight with pleasure. 'This could be really something, you know, Lucy – something nationally important.'

'Wow,' Lucy said. 'It seems impossible, doesn't it, when you look at Clarabelle's paddock and the valley... How can something so amazing be hidden under here?'

'It's great, isn't it!' Johnny was buzzing. 'The more we discover the stranger it becomes.' He put the tape measure away in the toolbox. 'Did Finn tell you?' he asked. 'It turns out that it wasn't only the summerhouse pavilion that was burned down back in Tudor times. A mate of his took some earth-drilling samples in the woods and found a layer of fire damage in the soil. Dates suggest it all happened at the same time, in around 1600 give or take a few years.'

'So the woods caught fire and burned down the whole garden,' Lucy said. 'What a dreadful thing to happen so soon after it had been planted. I wonder if it was a lightning strike? You could imagine that happening last night.'

'Yeah,' Johnny said. 'It's a strong possibility. Or it could have been the other way around, someone set fire to something – the pavilion, for example – then the whole wood caught alight. Though I can't imagine why anyone would do that. Whatever happened, it was devastating.'

'I had a look at the Lyveden New Bield book yesterday,' Lucy said. 'If this garden was the prototype for the one there, we can probably redesign it based on the plan of Lyveden plus the results from your excavations. Verity will be so excited. I wondered...' She hesitated but Johnny looked so interested she pushed on: 'There's a lot of religious imagery in the house and gardens at Lyveden, apparently. I wondered whether it might be the same here as the Catesbys were also a Catholic family. Though I'm not sure there would be any traces of it left now.'

'It's a fascinating thought,' Johnny said. 'I think the summerhouse pavilion was an octagon, and there are eight different paths in the knot garden so perhaps the imagery here is around the number eight.'

'Eight…' That tugged at Lucy's memory too and she suddenly remembered where she'd seen it. 'The eight-pointed star was the symbol of the Knights Hospitaller,' she said. 'And Thomas Tresham's grandfather was the last Grand Prior of the Order. I spoke to the Hospitallers Museum yesterday too,' she added. 'I feel sure I'm on the same track Charlie was on, somehow. There *was* a story that the Hospitaller treasure was hidden at Knightstone after the order was dissolved but it's just a legend, there's no evidence. It was supposed to be somewhere called the Hollow Hill.'

'The term "Hollow Hills" usually refers to burial chambers,' Johnny said thoughtfully. 'Old ones, I mean, like the neolithic barrow at Waylands Smithy. But it can also relate to features like chalk pits or quarries. There was quite a bit of quarrying on the Berkshire Downs.' He smiled at her. 'You're really into this, aren't you, Lucy? Have you told Finn all this stuff?'

'Not yet.' Lucy blushed, hoping Johnny wouldn't wonder what she and Finn had been doing all evening instead. 'I'm still trying to piece it all together really. Plus today I went to see Maud Enright – you know I mentioned there was someone other than us who had seen Catherine's ghost?

She had some interesting stuff to tell. But I'm going to try and sort my thoughts out – and tell Finn all about it later.'

Johnny packed up the tool kit and went off to speak to the geophysics team and Lucy went inside.

The barn felt cool and peaceful. She realised that she wasn't as tired as the last time she had done the same walk into the village and back. She was definitely getting stronger, and she felt lighter and happier inside as well. It made her smile. A text from Finn saying he'd be back at about nine o'clock made her feel even happier.

She spent the afternoon with a big notepad, listing everything that had happened since she had come to Gunpowder Barn and looking for patterns and connections. There was the lost garden and all its intriguing secrets. There was Catherine's ghostly presence. There were all-too-real human vandals and intruders, and there was a lost treasure. Or perhaps two if Catherine's and the Knights Hospitallers' treasure were two separate things. Or perhaps there was no treasure at all if both of these were mere legends. And what *was* treasure anyway? As Maud Enright had said, it could be your loved ones or your freedom or the cause you believed in…

With a start, Lucy realised that it was eight o'clock and her phone had buzzed with a text.

It's Persis, the message said. I need to talk to you urgently. Can you meet me?

Lucy felt a shiver of premonition. This was odd. She hadn't seen Persis since Chastleton and had tried to ignore the wilder speculations that either she or Gabriel were up to anything suspicious, especially after the police had exonerated him of the vandalism at the summerhouse.

Okay, she texted back reluctantly. But what is it about?

It's about Charlie's research. The message came back immediately. There's something I need to show you. Meet me at the White Hart in Hinton in fifteen minutes? Please. It's urgent.

The chills along Lucy's skin increased. I'll be there, she texted back and got a thumbs-up in reply.

Hinton was a couple of villages along the Ridgeway towards Wantage. Lucy knew she would need to borrow Verity's car, but perhaps Persis had deliberately chosen somewhere away from Knightstone so that no one would see them. She wondered if this was to do with Persis' trip to Chastleton with Charlie, or something else he had uncovered before his death. Dashing off a quick text to Finn to tell him where she was in case he arrived back whilst she was out, she took the spare set of car keys from the drawer and walked up the track.

There were no lights on at Gunpowder Cottage. Johnny must be out that evening too. Lucy eased the car out of the garage, set off down the drive and turned onto the road to Wantage. The car felt unfamiliar, lots of power under the bonnet and rather skittish, she thought, and she took it very steadily. Although they were into August now and the nights were lengthening, the daylight still lingered at this time of the evening. Only when the road dipped beneath the trees did it suddenly seem much darker. She drove through the next village, Compton, where there was a shop with a painted signboard outside that was clearly one of Marilynne's creations. A woman in a Swiss-style dirndl was carrying a wicker basket full of fresh bread and dairy items whilst a procession of children skipped along behind her. It all looked very wholesome, if rather old-fashioned. COMPTON VILLAGE STORES, it read.

Lucy wondered idly whether most of Marilynne's income came from signs and illustrations rather than the big landscapes she clearly preferred. Still, she shouldn't be snooty about it. She knew how difficult it was to make a living from a creative career. The car plunged into another of the tree tunnels along the road. It took a second for her eyes to adjust to the blackness. A bird scuttled away into the shadows with a harsh cry. This, she remembered, was the stretch of road that Charlie had been driving along when he crashed. Had he seen a bird or small animal and swerved to avoid it? Had he been peering through the twilight just as she was now? Had he been thinking, as she was, about the strange myths of the Roman road and Odin and his ravens appearing from the dark? She shivered although it wasn't cold in the car, and turned on the radio to try to ward off the sense of isolation. A car passed her in the other direction, its headlights temporarily blinding her. She was driving very carefully, aware of anxiety in the pit of her stomach and a rather horrible sense of watching Charlie's final drive unroll before her eyes. Another bend in the tree-lined road, a signpost approaching…

Someone stepped out from the side of the road directly into her path. She saw them at the last moment as they had been hidden in the shadows beneath the trees. Her eyes registered a confused impression of a tall, hooded figure in a long black cloak and the incongruous sight of what looked like a flock of ravens bursting out of the trees above like arrows. Shock and fear paralysed her for a split second and then she swung the wheel hard and felt the car bump over the edge of the grass verge and start to slide down the bank towards the field below. Everything seemed to be happening so slowly. Powerless to do anything, she waited with sick anticipation for the car to flip over.

They hit something hard. The airbag deployed and engulfed her, deflating almost as soon as it had filled, and leaving Lucy gasping for breath with the seatbelt like a vice across her chest. Her blood was pounding in her ears. Her head spun giddily. She felt sick.

Finally, she managed to steady her shaking fingers sufficiently to release the seatbelt and scramble out of the car. It was canted at a sharp angle down the bank; she half rolled, half fell down to the bottom and found herself sitting in a pile of brambles.

Incongruously her phone chose that moment to ring and she groped in her pocket for it.

'Lucy?' Finn's voice. 'I got your message. I've just got back. Is everything okay?'

'No,' Lucy said. Despite the adrenaline pumping through her, she most definitely was not okay.

'I've had an accident,' she said, remembering to add, quickly, 'I'm fine, shaken but not hurt, but I think the car's a write-off. I hit a tree and the bonnet's all crumpled...'

She heard Finn swear. 'I'm on my way,' he said. 'I'll call the police.' Then: 'Where are you?'

'I'm near Hinton,' Lucy said, 'where the road cuts through the beech avenue.'

There was a long silence whilst Finn digested her location and Lucy felt sick all over again at the horrible resonances the situation had with Charlie's death.

'Finn,' she said, 'I'm sorry—'

He cut her off curtly: 'I'll see you in ten minutes. Hold on. I'll be right there.'

He was gone. Lucy found she was shaking. It was quiet on the road and suddenly she felt desperately lonely. Surely someone would come by, she thought, but there was nothing but silence, just the owls calling, the wind in the beeches. Was that a snap of a twig she heard, or a footstep? Had the shadows moved and blurred for a moment? She thought of the cloaked figure pinned in the headlights. She knew she had not imagined it, even if only seconds before she'd been thinking of Charlie Macintyre driving on this same stretch of road...

Someone had been waiting. They had deliberately stepped out in front of her. Were they still there, watching her? How long would it take Finn to get to her? What should she tell him? She couldn't bear to think how he must be feeling after the last time...

Lights cut through the darkness and she heard a car door slam. 'Lucy?' It was Finn's voice and she felt overwhelming relief.

'I'm here,' she called. She managed to struggle up the slope onto the road where he had left the Land Rover with its hazard lights and full beam on. His arms closed about her and she felt the urgency in him, the fear in his grip.

'I'm all right,' she said, answering his unspoken question,

and his arms tightened about her and she felt his mouth pressed against her hair and heard the thud of his heart against her ear.

'Thank God,' he said, and his voice was very rough. 'I don't think I could go through that again.'

'I'm so sorry,' Lucy said. 'So sorry.' She clung to him.

'Don't be.' Finn sounded fierce. 'It's not your fault.'

'There was someone on the road.' Lucy was shivering convulsively. 'I'm sorry, Finn, I really wouldn't say it if it wasn't true. They stepped right out in front of me at the last minute. I didn't stand a chance.'

She felt his body stiffen and then he released her very gently. In the darkness she couldn't see his expression and she held her breath as she waited for his reaction.

'We need to get you into the Land Rover,' he said after a moment. 'Then we can talk.'

The thudding of Lucy's heart settled a little. She allowed him to guide her to the passenger seat and help her inside. She already felt stiff, and was scratched all over from the brambles that had cushioned her landing at the bottom of the bank, but when he wrapped a blanket about her and tucked her in, her heart almost melted at the tenderness of it. Reaction was setting in now and she wanted to cry. She sniffed hard instead and blinked back the tears.

Without a word Finn took a torch from the back of the car and snapped it on to illuminate the crash. Her stomach lurched. How had she survived that? The car was at right angles to the road and practically on its nose. Splintered branches and crushed vegetation marked its journey from the tarmac to the field below.

Finn climbed in beside her and placed the torch on the back seat. 'You were lucky,' he said. She couldn't read his tone. 'Very lucky.'

Lucy found she wanted to apologise for being alive when Charlie had died; the tears crowded her throat again. But then Finn put his arms about her again, very carefully, and drew her against him.

'Sorry,' he said, his cheek resting against hers. 'I just need a moment. To hold you. To…' His voice broke.

'I can't even imagine what this must be like for you,' Lucy said, pressing closer. She felt a rush of relief that Finn had accepted her word without question, but the issues it must raise for him were huge.

After a moment, Finn's grip eased a little. 'I always suspected there was more to Charlie's death than an accident,' he said fiercely. 'He was always so bloody *careful*.'

'Yes.' Lucy wondered whether it could, in fact, be no more than a horrible coincidence. Yet the similarity in the two cases, the same stretch of road, the fact that she could easily have been thrown from the car, all looked very suspicious. Plus she had *seen* someone, someone who had deliberately stepped out into the road. And despite the black cloak and the ravens, she didn't think it had been Odin.

Bright blue lights along the road indicated the arrival of the police.

'Oh God,' Lucy said suddenly, 'I forgot I was supposed to be meeting Persis! She'll be sitting in the pub wondering what's happened to me.'

'I saw Persis closing up the shop when I came through

the village on the way back from the motorway,' Finn inter-rupted. 'That was about five minutes before I called you. She certainly wasn't in Hinton. I thought it was weird because you mentioned in your message you were going to meet her.'

'Are you sure?' Lucy stared at him, feeling suddenly a little cold. 'I got the message quite late on in the evening; I assumed she was already there from the way it was worded. Look…' She reached for her phone and showed him.

Finn keyed in the number and called it. 'It's blocked,' he said.

There was silence whilst they looked at each other. 'Well, that's weird,' Lucy said. Her tired mind tried to grapple with the implications but came up blank. 'There must be some mistake,' she said, and saw that Finn was frowning.

'Tell the police anyway,' he counselled, 'and we can talk it through tomorrow when you're feeling a bit better.'

The police arrived then and shortly after, a pick-up truck came and took the car away. Once the police had ascertained that she didn't need to go to hospital, they agreed to call to interview her the following day and Finn was allowed to take her home. The whole thing felt like a horror film running through Lucy's mind; explanations, arrangements, insurance… She was exhausted, feeling every bruise and scratch, wanting nothing more than to sleep.

'Thank you for the lift home,' she said to Finn with a yawn. 'I'd rather not have walked.'

Finn took her hand for a second, his grip conveying that he understood everything she wasn't saying, and she closed her eyes and rested her aching head against the seat back. It seemed extraordinary to her that it was still only ten o'clock.

'Do you want to call Cleo to come over and keep you company?' Finn asked. 'Or...' He stopped. Lucy wondered what the 'or' had meant. It seemed very early in their relationship to ask him to stay but it also felt as though they had somehow by-passed several stages during the drama of the evening.

'No, it's fine,' she said. 'Cleo deserves an evening off from fussing about me. I'll ring her in the morning. Besides, she'd only make me drink very sweet tea, which is her solution for any sort of trauma. But—'

'One of us is going to need to finish a sentence,' Finn said.

'But if you don't mind staying,' Lucy said in a rush, 'I'd really appreciate that. Just to hold me,' she added quickly. 'I'd rather not be alone.'

'Sure,' Finn said, and she heard the smile in his voice. His hand covered hers again briefly. 'This is a bit strange, right?' he said. 'Sort of like a speed relationship?'

'Yes,' Lucy said, thinking how quickly they had moved in the past few weeks. 'Exactly like that.'

'I like it,' Finn said, after a moment. 'But if it's too fast for you, just say.'

'No.' Despite her aches and pains, despite the exhaustion blanketing her, Lucy felt warm inside. It felt exactly right. 'I like it too,' she said.

CHAPTER 22

Anne Catesby

London, 26 October 1605

'My Lord, out of the love I bear to some of your friends, I have a care of your preservation.'

My hand shook. A droplet of ink smeared the paper. I took a breath to steady myself and dipped the goose quill once more into the horn. 'Therefore I would advise you, as you tender your life, to devise some excuse to shift your attendance at this Parliament...'

The flame of the candle flickered in some unseen draught. I stopped. It was not too late. I could burn the letter, let fate take its course and return home to Warwickshire and to Robbie. For a moment the temptation overwhelmed me.

I stood up and moved over to the window. London at night in late October was a grim and dingy place. All the gaudiness of the day was overtaken by shadows and coldness. It was the sort of place where men begged, borrowed and stole to survive on the streets. It was the sort of place where plots were hatched and conspiracies made in smoky alehouses. I hated it.

Robert had refused to see me when I had been to his house in Clerkenwell. I stood out in the cold street, like a vagrant, like a stranger. I knew there were people inside but they would not open to me, though I stood there for over two hours, until I was tired and hungry. In the end a servant came out: Mr Catesby was occupied with business and had no desire to make his lady mother wait; he would therefore call upon me at a more convenient time. And pigs might fly.

When I got back home, Byram was waiting to see me.

'It is true, I am afraid, your ladyship,' he said. He looked grey with fatigue and fear. 'I met up with Thomas Bates, who used to serve you at Ashby. He says there is a plot afoot to blow up the King and his government at the next opening of the Parliament. They have gunpowder aplenty. They plan to put Princess Elizabeth on the throne and marry her off to a Catholic who will allow religious tolerance to flourish.'

'It is a plot so foolhardy that only Robert could have hatched it,' I said wearily. 'Thank God that Bates betrayed him to you.'

'I cannot see that there is anything you can do, madam,' Byram said, 'other than return home like the other wives and mothers, and wait to see what transpires.'

It had been the traditional role for women since time immemorial in battle or conflict or rebellion. Watch and wait, suffer and grieve. My mind ran feverishly over alternatives. It was out of the question to betray Robert directly to the King's ministers. That way the plot would be stopped but Robert would surely die. I could not do such a thing.

Yet perhaps I could give a warning, anonymously, privately, to those I loved.

So here I was. *'My Lord, out of the love I bear to some of your friends…'* A faint scent of syrup rose from the ink, catching in my throat.

My nephew by marriage, William Parker, Lord Monteagle, was one such who would perish in the Parliament along with his King if Robert's plan succeeded. I shuddered at the vision of explosion and fire, men's bodies torn apart, the indiscriminate slaughter. His wife Elizabeth and their children would be left unprotected and alone. There would be many more like them, widowed, orphaned.

'…The danger is passed as soon as you have burned this letter. And I hope God will give you the grace to make good use of it…'

I reflected that William Parker was not a clever man but he was a self-important one. He would see the threat and would send word immediately to the King's advisors, to Lord Cecil, whose mind was sharper than a whetted knife. Robert would get wind that the plot had been uncovered and would call off his plans.

I got up to put another log on the fire. I felt old and my bones ached. The damp of London autumn seeped into the chill heart of me. The firewood was damp too; it hissed and belched acrid smoke into the room. I shivered, tucking my hands into the wide sleeves of my gown to try to warm them and stop the shaking. A vivid image flashed across my mind's eye: Robert as a child in his baptismal robes, so warm, rounded and smiling, a happy boy who had grown into the charming young man who could draw all others to him. Robert, the dark star, intense and passionate. How many times had I wondered how that burning fervour of his had changed into a destructive force that threatened us all? I had lost count and I understood him no better now than I had at the beginning.

Would Robert Cecil unmask the plotters?

It was the greatest risk and I heard my late husband's voice reproach me: *'How can you place our son in such danger, Nan?'*

I knew it was dangerous. That was why I was trembling. I was also praying: *'Dear God, you know my reasons are pure. Save Robert from himself and the rest of us from his recklessness. See into my heart and know I am true...'*

The heat of the fire barely reached me at my desk. Its glow gave only an illusion of warmth. Instead of thinking of Robert I turned my mind to his son, to little Robbie. That hardened my resolve to put an end to this for good, so that the plot could be foiled and Robert would return home to Ashby and his son. I finished my prayer, begging God to ensure that Robert's plot was foiled, that lives were saved and that no one would be caught and blamed for this treason.

My quill scuttered across the paper, spreading blots. Truly there had been no need to try to disguise my writing. It was almost unrecognisable even to me.

Byram was waiting outside the door. I had already given him the instruction; to go disguised, not to approach the house but to wait and accost Lord Monteagle's man in the street. He must make clear how urgent the letter was, and how important. He was to tell no one.

Byram asked no questions. I gave him the letter and heard the door close behind him and his footsteps die away. Suddenly I was possessed by a terrible fear, as though the world hung by a thread in the dark realms of space. I groped for the chair and sat down again. I placed the quill in the glowing embers of the fire and watched it curl in on itself and die.

My hope that once Robert heard that his plot was known he would call it off was quickly dashed.

Hours after I had sent him, Byram returned to me as I sat silent and cold in my parlour.

'Did you deliver the letter?' I could not contain myself.

'Aye, milady,' Byram said. 'Lord Monteagle read it aloud at dinner to his noble guests and then took it to Sir Robert Cecil.'

I felt an enormous wash of relief. 'Then the treason will be stopped,' I said, 'and the plot will be foiled.'

Byram said nothing.

'Does Robert know?' I pressed. 'Does he know that Cecil is aware of the plot?'

'Aye, madam,' Byram said. 'I made sure that word was carried to Mr Catesby directly, just as you asked.'

I slumped back in the chair. 'Then all may yet be well,' I said. I looked at him sharply, for I could tell that there was more. 'What is it?' I questioned. 'Does he realise that I was the one who betrayed them?'

'No, madam,' Byram said. 'He thinks it was his cousin. He accused Sir Francis Tresham of writing the letter.'

I nodded. This was logical; Lord Monteagle was Francis' brother-in-law after all. He might well warn him of danger.

'There was a terrible argument,' Byram said. 'It was very violent. Sir Francis denied it, and he was so sincere he convinced the others of his honesty.'

I thought about this. It was unfortunate and it seemed Francis had sustained some hurt as well as the rupturing of family ties, but that was a small price to pay.

'No matter.' I shrugged. 'The work is done and the plot foiled, for none but a fool would persist when word was out.'

There was a long and terrible quiet. I already knew what Byram was going to say when he spoke.

'Mr Catesby vows to go ahead with the plan,' he said. 'He swears that none will stop him.'

I stared at him. I could not believe I had heard a'right, for his words seemed arrant nonsense.

'I beg your pardon,' I said. 'I thought you said...' My voice trailed away. 'How can this possibly be?' I realised that I was about to cry. The tears swelled and dropped onto my lap. I could not see for them; all I could think was that I had played my final card and lost the game, that God had forsaken me and my family, that Robert must surely be mad. The pain was so strong that I almost cried out in anguish.

'Come, madam.' Byram knew that I would not want him to see my weakness. His hand was on my arm; with gruff gentleness he raised me to my feet. 'You are overwrought and need your rest. Who knows how matters will play out? You have done your best. It is in God's hands now.'

'Yes,' I said. I looked at him. Poor dear Byram. He knew as well as I what would happen now. I straightened my back and rubbed a hand across my eyes.

'I do not believe that London agrees with me,' I said. 'I miss Robbie so very much. At first light we shall return to Northamptonshire. See to it, Byram. Take us home to Ashby.'

CHAPTER 23

Lucy

Lucy woke in Finn's arms. It was blissful if she discounted the fact that she was covered in cuts and bruises. The barn was silent and peaceful, and Lucy was possessed with such a deep sense of wellbeing that for a moment she felt scared; was she confusing her own emotions once again with Catherine's love for Robert? It was frightening that the two seemed to merge so easily. She had known Finn for such a short time and it felt as though she should, in some way, resist this feeling and yet she didn't want to.

She turned her head against his shoulder and saw that Finn was awake and watching her. Everything, from the gentleness with which he had held her and not woken her, to the way that the golden stubble shadowed his jaw, to the line of his cheek and the smile she could see lurking in his eyes as he looked at her... Everything about him made her feel quite helplessly happy inside and she didn't want to fight it.

'What are you thinking?' Finn asked.

'I was thinking I need to call my parents and tell them what's happened, and ring Verity to apologise for writing off her car,' Lucy said. 'And then there's Persis to tackle, and the insurance company and the police to talk to…'

'Romantic,' Finn said.

'I was also thinking,' Lucy said, in a rush, 'that I'm not sure whether the feelings I have for you are my own or are influenced by Catherine's for Robert. I dreamed about you, you see,' she went on, aware that she wasn't sounding particularly coherent, 'when I was first possessed by Catherine and she and Robert were together…'

'Well, that sounds exciting,' Finn said. 'But don't forget that even if you are under the influence, I'm not. So if you turn around and tell me that none of this is real I'm going to be pretty damn disappointed.'

Lucy laughed. 'If you put it like that—'

'I do,' Finn said. He kissed her gently. 'I've got to get to work, but I predict Cleo will already have texted to check up on you and to tell you to take it easy. I hope you're going to take her advice.'

'I will,' Lucy promised, 'except like I said, there's going to be a lot of admin and before I get started, I need some fresh air.'

'Well,' Finn said, checking his watch, 'Johnny's coming down soon. Do you want to walk down the valley with us? We're starting to draw up a rough design of how we think the lake complex and summerhouse would have looked when it was first built.'

'Great,' Lucy said, 'I'll have some breakfast and then head down there with you.'

★

Geoffrey greeted them both like long-lost friends, his tail circling like a helicopter blade, whilst Johnny was somewhat less effusive but still very warm in his greeting.

'Thank God you're all right,' he said to Lucy. 'What a horrible thing to happen.'

'I was pretty shaken up,' Lucy admitted, 'but there's no lasting damage other than to the car.'

'The word in the village is that you skidded to avoid someone on the road,' Johnny said. 'It's all over the Facebook discussion group.'

Lucy and Finn exchanged a look. 'How do people know that?' Lucy demanded. 'I told the police but no one else.'

'I think a witness might have come forward,' Johnny said. 'No one knows really but you know what villages are like for gossip.'

'I expect I'll get the full story from the police later,' Lucy said with a sigh. 'They're coming in three quarters of an hour.'

It was a beautiful clear day but the stream still roared down the hillside from the storm two nights before and broken branches were littered around. The valley path was muddy but passable.

'It's strange how there can be so much water for a little while and then it all disappears,' Lucy said. 'I suppose that's why it can be so dangerous to be caught in a flash flood. For a while there's so much volume and it has nowhere to go and just destroys everything in its path.'

'I'm afraid the old oak was struck by lightning,' Johnny said, indicating the tree Lucy and Finn had sat beneath on the night she had seen the fire ripping through the pavilion. The trunk was split straight down the middle and one branch was resting in the water. 'Such a pity because it was one of the trees that might conceivably have been here when the original Tudor garden was built—' He stopped, his tone changing. 'Shit, what's that?'

As Johnny froze, Finn and Lucy turned to see where he was pointing. A body that had previously been concealed behind the fallen branch was bobbing in the shallows, face down, one arm outstretched. It appeared to be wearing a long black cloak that was floating on the surface of the water. The hood had fallen back and the figure's bright fair hair was spread in an aureole about their head. All these details seemed to imprint themselves on Lucy's mind in a split second against the incongruous backdrop of the glorious blue sky and the puffy white clouds and the placid peace of the pool.

'Persis!' she said, starting forward. 'Oh my God.'

'Stay back,' Finn said sharply, 'it's too late—'

But then there were running steps on the path behind and Lucy swung around, realising that Finn hadn't been speaking to her. Persis herself shot past her, a blur of movement, pushing Lucy aside, ignoring Johnny too when he reached out to catch her arm, going down on her knees in the water beside the body, sobbing.

'Aunt Marilynne!' She reached out to touch the still figure but Finn caught her, pulling her to her feet. Immediately Persis wrenched herself from his grasp, repudiating his help and comfort. She rounded on them all and instead of the grief Lucy had expected to see on her face, it was etched with rage.

'It wasn't supposed to be like this!' Persis shouted. 'It

wasn't meant to end this way!' And she started to cry, her sobbing a raw contrast to the gentle rock of Marilynne's body in the water.

'It wasn't meant to be like this,' Persis said. Her eyes were pink from so much crying, the tip of her nose red, a tissue shredded between her restless fingers. They were all in the kitchen at Gunpowder Barn; so was Gabriel, whom Persis had called as soon as Lucy and Finn had been able to coax her away from Marilynne and up to the house. The police and ambulance service were dealing with the body and had asked them all to wait at the barn.

'All Aunt Marilynne wanted was the treasure,' Persis said miserably. 'She said it was ours, that Grandad Isaac had been on the trail of it and that it was her duty to continue the search.' She drooped in her chair. 'No one was supposed to die,' she said.

'Here.' Lucy pressed a mug of tea into her hands, sparing a thought for Cleo's advice as she added three spoonfuls of sugar to it. 'We don't know what happened yet,' she said. 'It could just have been a terrible accident.'

Persis looked at her with bruised-looking eyes. 'You don't understand,' she said. 'I'm talking about *your* accident . I'm talking about *Charlie*.'

Lucy's heart jumped. Beside her she heard Finn draw in his breath sharply.

'I don't know anything about this,' Gabriel said plaintively, though whether to exonerate himself from any blame or because he felt aggrieved, Lucy wasn't sure.

'No one tells you anything because you can't keep

a secret,' Persis snapped, rounding on him. 'Aunt M made me promise. She said you'd only blab if you knew.' She sniffed, her eyes filling with tears again, and Lucy pushed the box of tissues across the table towards her. She didn't want to comfort Persis – she felt horrified and repelled and she didn't even know the story yet, but at the same time Persis looked so lost and small it was difficult not to respond to that. And Persis was looking at Finn.

'I didn't know at the time,' she said. 'I swear it. I didn't know she meant to kill him.'

'Don't say anything else, Persis,' Gabriel said. 'You'll incriminate yourself, you'll incriminate all of us!' His jaw jutted and he turned to Finn. 'I want a lawyer.'

'Oh, go to hell, Gabe,' Persis said, turning on him. 'Charlie was a good person. Finn and Lucy are good people. I want them to know the truth. You leave if you want to, and that way you won't be implicated, but I'm going to tell them.'

Gabriel shrugged angrily and slumped back in his chair. 'Suit yourself.'

'Gabriel's right,' Finn said quietly to Persis. 'The police will want to talk to you about this. You should wait.'

Lucy reached for his hand and squeezed it. She knew how much that offer must have cost him. He wanted to know what had happened to Charlie, needed to know for the sake of closure and his own sanity. But he wasn't going to do it at the cost of Persis' future. He returned the squeeze and gave her a faint smile.

'Thanks,' Persis said, 'but I'm doing this for me as well, you know? The way Aunt M made me feel – sort of torn in my loyalties and all twisted up inside…' She straightened her shoulders. 'I'm not that person. I want to set the record straight.' She took a gulp from the mug of tea.

'Okay,' she said. 'So for years Aunt M had been searching for treasure on the basis of Grandad's stories but she'd found nothing. Then Verity—' she looked at Lucy, 'started to talk about a lost Elizabethan garden and her plans for an archaeological dig. Aunt Marilynne was furious. She'd always viewed Gunpowder Cottage as *hers*, in some odd way; she resented that Verity had bought the place from under her nose and never really got over it.'

'She always did seem rather hostile,' Lucy said, remembering the odd encounter at the museum as well as Marilynne's bitter words in the stable yard.

Persis nodded. 'She was afraid the dig would uncover the treasure – whatever it was – and she would lose her chance. But then I started seeing Charlie and—' Persis blushed, 'I thought she'd be angry with me because she always was ridiculously strict about stuff like that, but she seemed totally thrilled. It puzzled me for a while until she started to ask me to pass on all the details of Charlie's research, where the team planned to dig, what he'd found in the archives…

'Then I twigged that basically she wanted Charlie and Finn to do all the work and for me to spy on them and tell her where to find the treasure. To be honest, I was worried about her. I thought she was deluded. She believed in all sorts of mad stuff, like the Odin legend and so on. It was a bit weird and I didn't take it seriously.' She rubbed her eyes.

'Anyway, I didn't really know what to do.' She looked at Finn beseechingly. 'I liked Charlie, really liked him, and

I didn't want to do anything to spoil the dig or the work you were doing. But at the same time—' she swallowed hard, 'Aunt M had looked after us since we were kids.' She glanced at Gabriel, who was looking sulky. 'I sort of felt it wouldn't hurt to tell her what Charlie was working on, especially since I didn't really think there was anything in the treasure idea. Not really. So I passed on a few things – the newspaper cuttings that showed the marks in the fields, the fact that Charlie thought the bits and pieces in the museum might be a clue to something… That sort of thing. And then Charlie and I went to Chastleton together.'

Lucy glanced at Finn. His jaw was rigid, a muscle working in his cheek. 'You told Marilynne that Charlie had found a book there that linked Robert Catesby to the Order of the Knights Hospitaller,' he said.

Persis nodded sadly. 'After that it was a whole new obsession with her,' she said. 'She had Gabe digging around for all sorts of information on the Knights although she didn't tell him why—' She gave her brother a glance that was half-scornful, half-affectionate. 'Set Gabe off with anything like that and he'll run like clockwork, no questions asked.'

'I thought she wanted inspiration for one of her art projects,' Gabriel said, looking even more sulky.

'Aunt M wanted me to get hold of the book,' Persis said, 'but the curator hadn't been at Chastleton when we visited and they wouldn't lend it out without her agreement. Charlie was going to go back, but then I…' her voice faltered, 'I did something really stupid. I see that now.' She pushed her hair back from her face. 'He was all excited about the things he was discovering and I was happy for him and…' She looked up. 'I wanted to be a part of it. So I showed him a key that Aunt Marilynne had taken from the museum. It had been in the cabinet with the other finds from the site but she was certain it had some significance so she purloined it one day when Gabe wasn't looking.' She gulped down some more of her tea. 'When Charlie saw it, it immediately reminded him of something he'd seen at Chastleton. A box, or something. I told Aunt M later that day...'

'And that night Charlie was killed,' Finn finished softly.

'I hoped it was just a coincidence,' Persis said. 'I mean, Aunt M never said anything about what happened to me and I didn't ask, but I sort of just *knew*.' She shuddered. 'And one day, after Charlie's accident when I was crying, she just said it had been for the best. That the treasure could now be hers as had been meant all along.'

'But there *is* no treasure,' Gabriel said plaintively. 'I've been telling everyone that all along.'

'The woman who saw Catherine Catesby's ghost says there was,' Persis said, 'at least that's what Aunt M told me.'

'It doesn't really matter whether there was or not if you believe it,' Lucy said. 'And Marilynne evidently did.' She turned to Persis. 'Why didn't she simply go along to Chastleton and take the box, or whatever it was, after Charlie died?'

'She didn't know exactly what it was or where to find it,' Persis said unhappily. 'She kept badgering me about it but I couldn't remember. She was so angry with me! And the police were sniffing around and people were talking. I think she got scared and thought she'd wait awhile. But then you came back, Finn, when we all thought the project would be abandoned, and Lucy arrived and seemed to be following up on all Charlie's research. She tried to scare you off but it didn't work.'

'So that was Marilynne with the dead bouquet and the vandalism and all the other stuff,' Finn said. He fixed Persis with a stern look. 'Did you give her a key to the barn?'

Persis shook her head. 'But Charlie had given one to me a while back and it disappeared,' she admitted.

There was silence. Lucy thought of Cleo talking about the masked intruder she'd bumped into. It had never occurred to her that Marilynne was almost as tall as Gabriel and also smoked.

The police, Lucy thought, would no doubt piece it all together in time. They would trace Marilynne's movements on the day Charlie died just as they would for the previous night when she had had her accident. She wondered whether Marilynne had been in the museum that morning and had seen her looking in the display case for the key. Was that what had triggered her to decide Lucy had to be eliminated as Charlie had been? Since Marilynne herself could no longer explain what had really happened, there would be no arrest or trial but Persis and Gabriel would have to live with what their aunt had done for ever.

'When I met you both that day at Chastleton,' she said, 'had you gone to collect the book about Robert Catesby on Marilynne's behalf?'

Gabriel looked puzzled but Persis shook her head. 'No. Aunt M had sent us to look for a box that might fit the key she had,' she said. 'She was as obsessed as ever – more so I think because she thought you were getting close to the truth, Lucy. I know I was weird when we saw you,' Persis finished sadly. 'I mentioned Aunt M straight away because I was feeling guilty and thinking of her. I just wanted the whole thing to go away. Except it's not so easy, is it?' She dropped her head into her hands. 'You can't just wipe these things from your mind and pretend they never happened, can you? They really do haunt you.'

CHAPTER 24

Anne Catesby

Ashby St Legers, 5 November 1605

We went home to Ashby via Knightstone. The house that Thomas had bought from Robert after Catherine's death was shuttered and still. The garden, in those dying days of autumn, was all but lost beneath fallen leaves.

'I have a sacred trust to perform for Sir Thomas Tresham,' I told Byram, as we rested our horses at the old village inn that had once been the Knights' presbytery. 'Or rather you have. Pray, borrow a shovel from the gravedigger and join me in the churchyard.'

Byram gave me a look and went out, muttering, *'Bloody Thomas Tresham and his sacred trust'* under his breath loud enough for me to hear.

I took the mantle of the Knights Hospitaller from my saddlebags where it had resided since I had left Lyveden. It was wrapped within a leather purse now, and inside that there were several layers of linen encasing the silk mantle itself. Whether it would survive burial was another matter and one that I was prepared to leave in the hands of God.

I had promised Thomas only that I would take the symbol of the Knights Hospitallers back where it belonged and lodge it in safety. I had thought of the chalk pit beneath the garden but in the end I decided it needed to be as close to the original presbytery as possible, high on the hill beneath Catherine's memorial stone.

Byram dug out a small cavity beneath the sarsen and I slipped the package within, murmuring a prayer that it would be blessed. We shovelled the soil back as it was and the sarsen sat there immovably with its engraving:

'Where your treasure is, there will your heart be also.'

'Very good,' I said to Byram, brushing the soil from my hands. 'Now all is finished and we can go home.'

I saw Robert for the last time nine days after I left London. I had gone back home and, like all the other wives and mothers in my extended family, I sat and waited in silence and fear for news, whilst trying to pretend for Robbie's sake that nothing was wrong.

It was the evening of the fifth of November and Robbie and I had been out in the forest collecting wood for the fires. It had been a beautiful autumn day full of crisp fresh air and crunchy golden leaves. Robbie had filled his pockets with acorns and conkers and my old apron was stuffed with kindling.

By the gate into the gardens we stopped as we saw a man riding up the bridleway towards us. Robbie pressed against my skirts, his arms encircling my legs as he did when he wanted to burrow close for comfort. I put a hand on his head, feeling the soft, springy dark hair beneath my fingers.

I recognised Robert and opened my mouth to tell Robbie his father was coming to visit us. I felt strange, full of hope, fear and excitement all at the same time. My heart soared. My premonitions had been wrong. Robert had abandoned his plans after all. He was here now to tell us that all was well, he was coming home and we would all start afresh together.

Then I saw him rein in his horse fifty yards from us and I realised he had no intention of coming any closer. My hope crashed down as I understood. He was on the run. He would not approach us because now, at the end, he did not want to taint us with his treason.

He raised his hat then and saluted us. Although the evening was pressing close and I could not see clearly, I think he smiled.

I saw not the fugitive in tattered clothing, travel-stained and exhausted, but the young man on his wedding day who had been so full of vitality and love. He waved to us, almost a joyful wave, and then he turned and rode away and he did not look back. Robbie and I stood watching until he was out of sight and the sound of the horse's hooves had died away.

Behind me in the gardens a torch flared. I heard footsteps and I felt Byram touch my arm. 'They're coming, madam,' he said, and I knew that he meant the King's men. 'Remember that you have not seen Mr Catesby and you know nothing.'

'I remember,' I said. I took Robbie's hand in mine and knew that now it was my turn to fight, to fight for my grandson and his future with every weapon I had.

'I'm ready,' I said.

CHAPTER 25

Lucy

Since the accident ten days previously, Lucy had become accustomed to her sleep being broken by flashbacks. She would wake with a sickening jolt at the moment of impact between the car and the tree. Sometimes she would experience a panic attack; at others her breathing would slow and steady as the terror drained away and she recognised where she was. Either way she was then wide awake, her mind running over everything that had happened in a loop that was difficult to break. It reminded her of when she had first been diagnosed with post-viral fatigue and had had repeating nightmares. The only thing that made it better was when Finn was with her but she wasn't prepared to ask him to move in as a cure for her anxieties.

Talking helped, though. They both did a lot of that, Finn opening up to her in a way Lucy knew he hadn't after Charlie's death. They talked about Marilynne too. The police had ruled her death an accident and there was to be an inquest. It was thought she had gone back down to the summerhouse site because she was still obsessed with the idea that something was hidden there. It appeared from the evidence that she had slipped and knocked herself out, subsequently drowning in the pond. Her role in Charlie's accident and in Lucy's seemed clear but with her death any proof had been extinguished and for Persis and Gabriel's sake Lucy felt it was better that way.

Tonight, after going through the familiar loop of thoughts in her head, Lucy got up and went downstairs to make herself a drink. It was a stunningly beautiful night and on the eastern horizon she could see the constellation Orion the hunter, and a scattering of stars like diamonds studded across the gauzy line of the Milky Way. It felt peaceful. She made a cup of cocoa and took it outside onto the patio. The air was warm. The black cat was curled up on one of the sun loungers and looked affronted when Lucy joined her.

'Who do you belong to?' Lucy wondered as it got up and stalked off in a huff.

It felt like a long time since Lucy had seen or experienced Catherine's ghost because the questions and investigations around Marilynne's death had filled her mind and inevitably distracted her from everything else. She had wondered whether, with the mystery of Charlie's death unravelled, Catherine had in fact found peace. It seemed certain that there was no Knights Hospitaller treasure to be found but what of Catherine's own 'treasure'? Lucy sensed that there was something she needed to remember, a whisper that she still heard at the back of her mind, and so she had waited for Catherine to come.

'I am here. It is time.'

The hairs rose on the back of Lucy's neck and she turned her head very slowly. Catherine was standing on the edge of the terrace. The light from the barn shone on her golden hair and made the red gown glow with rich colour. There were pearls on her sleeves and looped in her hair. She was smiling and in her hand was a box, an exquisite box whose rich patina also glowed in the light and showed patterns in the wood, dark and shade. In that moment Lucy recognised the box and also where she had seen it before; then she blinked and Catherine had gone.

Car headlights cut through the dark at the top of the track and the sound of an engine stirred the silence. Someone was driving down to the barn. Lucy got up. Her head was still full of Catherine and the sight of the wooden box. She made her way through the living room and turned on all the lights in the courtyard. The open approach suggested that this was no covert night-time visitor and the orange flash of a taxi sign outside the window confirmed it. She opened the front door.

'Oh, thank goodness you're awake!' Verity was emerging from the back seat of the taxi, looking fresh as a new pin for all that she must have endured over twenty-four hours of travel. 'I didn't want to disturb you but I wanted to get back home as soon as I could. I felt—' An unusual note of uncertainty entered her voice. 'Well, I needed to be here. I did send a text when I landed,' she added, enfolding Lucy in a warm hug that reminded her irresistibly of her childhood. 'I didn't want it to be a complete surprise.'

'I've had my phone off,' Lucy said. 'It doesn't matter at all. I'm just glad you're here. It feels… right.' She hugged Verity back.

'It feels right to me too,' Verity said, beaming. Behind her the taxi driver was stolidly unloading suitcase after suitcase onto the cobbles.

'Come on in,' Lucy said. 'I've got so much to tell you.'

It was late that morning when Lucy walked up to the village heritage centre. She passed the café on the way and Persis gave her a determinedly ordinary wave through the window. Perhaps in time, Lucy thought, things would start to feel more normal but they would never be the same again. In the museum, Gabriel was listlessly moving various items around. His previous air of superiority seemed to have vanished. So had Marilynne's exhibition, replaced by a series of pictures from the primary school which were rather charming.

'Hello!' Gabriel said to Lucy, quite as though nothing untoward had ever happened. 'What can I do for you?'

'I've got a rather unusual request,' Lucy said. She unfolded a piece of paper from her bag. 'I wondered if I could borrow the key from the local artefacts cabinet? The curator at Chastleton House thinks they have a match for it and would appreciate an inter-museum loan.' She waved the paper. 'I have the authorisation here.'

Gabriel took the sheet from her. 'It's very irregular,' he said, though Lucy thought he had been soothed by the use of the phrase 'inter-museum loan'. 'We've only just put the key back on display.'

'I appreciate that,' Lucy said. After years in Marilynne's possession the key had been reunited with the other objects her father had found in 1946 that were on display. 'However, it would only be for a short time and as you can see—' she gestured to the printed email, 'they would be extremely grateful.'

Gabriel sighed and went off to fill in the paperwork, which Lucy had guessed would be extensive. It was an hour later that she finally emerged into the sunshine with the key properly wrapped in approved museum packaging and boxed up, and papers signed in triplicate. She could only be grateful that Hazel at Chastleton had arranged insurance.

Finn was waiting for her outside in the Land Rover.

'Thanks so much for dropping everything to come with me,' Lucy said, leaning in for a kiss. 'It feels important that you should be there.'

'No problem,' Finn said. 'I'm thrilled to hear Verity's back, by the way,' he added. 'It'll be great to see her and there's so much I want to discuss with her.'

'She's sleeping off some of the jet lag now,' Lucy said, 'but she mentioned coming up to the cottage to chat to you and Johnny later, if that's okay.'

Chastleton, when they reached it forty-five minutes later, was basking in the sunshine like an elegant cat. 'What a stunning house,' Finn said, staring. 'I love the way they've recreated the gardens as well.'

'It's lovely to see you again.' Hazel, the curator, was waiting at the door and shook Lucy's hand warmly. 'And to meet you, Finn.' Her smile dimmed. 'I was very sorry to hear about your brother. Such a tragic accident and a great loss. He sounded like a tremendous young man.'

'He was, thank you,' Finn said, giving her his rare, heart-shaking smile. He squeezed Lucy's hand.

Hazel gestured to them to precede her into the Chastleton library. The house was closed to the public that day; a smell of old dust and beeswax polish permeated the air and without the noise of visitors it felt shuttered and too silent, as though all the ghosts of the past four hundred years might step out of the panelling at any moment.

'It blows my mind that this house was built by a man who knew Robert Catesby,' Lucy said, looking around, 'and we're standing here now four hundred years later.'

Hazel smiled. 'I feel like that every day,' she said. 'All those layers of the past; they are almost tangible in a place like this.' She gestured to a long wooden table that was covered in documents. A small wooden box stood in the middle. It didn't look much like the box Lucy had seen Catherine holding. The wood looked dull and battered, all polish and shine lost. The edges were splintered a little with age and wear.

Hazel saw Lucy looking at it. 'I'm sorry it doesn't look like much,' she said, almost apologetically. 'It was deprioritised for restoration because we couldn't find the key and there were so many other items in need of work. But I rather liked it so I displayed it discreetly in a corner of the nursery. I'm surprised you noticed it actually,' she added. 'It's not very eye-catching.'

'That's probably why it took me ages to remember where I'd seen it,' Lucy said.

343

'And when you saw the key in the museum at Knightstone you had an instinct that it matched!' Hazel was shaking her head. 'Extraordinary!'

Lucy caught Finn's eye. She'd told him the whole story; how she felt Catherine had been trying to show her something when she'd visited Chastleton; how she'd realised the key had been missing from the museum collection and how Catherine had shown her the box the night before. She wasn't about to tell Hazel that her hunch was based on nothing more than a ghostly premonition, though.

'Given the connection between the Catesbys, Chastleton and Knightstone,' she said, 'and the dating of both the key and the box, I thought it was worth considering.'

She saw Finn smother a smile. 'Shall we try it?' he asked.

Lucy took the package with the key out of her bag and passed it over to Hazel. 'I'd rather you do this,' she said, 'if you would.'

Hazel unwrapped the key and for a moment it sat, plain and unprepossessing in the palm of her hand. 'I see what you mean,' she said. 'It is exactly the right design and age, and it does look the correct size. I wonder…' She slid it into the lock on the wooden box and tried to turn it. 'It's stiff,' she said. 'I don't want to force it. After four hundred years I suppose it's no wonder.'

Lucy, whose heart had been racing, felt a thud of disappointment. She'd been so sure that this was the box that Catherine had shown her, that she had meant to find. Were they to be thwarted at the last moment by some ancient rust? But Hazel was opening a drawer in the library table and taking out what looked like a little tube of oil. 'This should do the trick,' she said.

'Specialist WD40,' Finn murmured.

'Exactly.' Hazel beamed. This time, after some slight jiggling, the key turned. The box opened.

It was lined in black velvet and it was empty.

'Oh!' Lucy said, feeling monstrously disappointed.

Hazel's smile dimmed at her evident dismay. 'But it's wonderful! The key and the box match!'

'Yes,' Lucy said. 'But…' She was remembering Maud Enright's words: *'She said that she had lost her most treasured possession and couldn't rest until it was found again…'* Had that possession been the box – or the key – rather than what was inside?

'Do you mind if I examine it?' Finn asked Hazel. 'I'll be very careful.' He put on a pair of gloves. 'I saw something similar at Coughton Court,' he said. 'It was a box designed to keep secret correspondence in and there was a catch—' Gently he pressed the velvet base in one corner. 'There,' he finished, as the catch was released, and the base lifted up.

'Oh!' This time it was Hazel who exclaimed. Lucy couldn't speak.

In the base of the box were two miniature paintings side by side, exquisite little pictures in gold frames that were only slightly tarnished with the passing of the years. Both were of children, one slight and fair with golden curls and pensive blue eyes; the other dark, younger, chubbier in face, little more than a baby.

Lucy felt her own eyes fill with tears. 'William and Robert Catesby,' she said.

'*My most treasured possession…*' She could hear Catherine's whisper in her ears and despite the tears, felt joy burst in her heart. Both boys, safe, together, found once again…

Hazel was speaking. 'Well, I suppose it could be William and Robert Catesby,' she was saying. 'They are the right period – perhaps even the work of Isaac Oliver, for they are very fine. If the box had somehow been overlooked when Chastleton was sold to the Joneses it might easily have been put away and lost in the attics along with all the other bits and pieces down the years…' She looked up, excitement in her voice. 'Whatever the case, it's a major find. We'll call in our art specialists at once.' For a moment Lucy thought Hazel might hug her but she managed to restrain herself. 'My goodness,' she repeated, 'what a find.'

Finn slipped his hand into Lucy's. 'All right?' he asked her and she nodded at him through her tears. Those tiny, perfectly detailed pictures of the two small boys Catherine had adored… She felt all of Catherine's relief and a sense of peace.

'I feel we should call for champagne,' Hazel said, 'but a cup of tea will have to do.' She was looking at Lucy rather oddly. 'Are you all right? It's a lot to take in, isn't it?'

'It is indeed,' Lucy agreed shakily.

Whilst Hazel went to put a kettle on and presumably call her boss with the news, Lucy and Finn stood quietly looking at the portraits.

'I don't suppose we'll ever know for sure how Catherine came to lose the key,' Finn said.

Lucy shook her head. 'I think it wasn't long before she died,' she said. 'Otherwise there would have been time for her to have had a new lock made. And perhaps she didn't realise at first that it was lost. But whatever happened, she must have treasured these pictures so much, and everything that they represented.'

'Her family was her world,' Finn said, and he slipped an arm about her and drew her close.

Hazel clattered through the door with a tea tray and they stepped apart a little self-consciously but she only smiled. 'I realise this will be a bit of an anticlimax after discovering the miniatures,' she said, 'but there is something else I wanted to show you today.' She poured tea into little delicate china cups and passed the biscuit plate to Lucy.

'I hope you don't mind…' Hazel was addressing Finn, 'but after Lucy told me a bit about your project with the garden at Knightstone I started digging into the topic a bit myself.'

'We're delighted, thank you,' Finn said, giving her his rare, special smile. Lucy thought Hazel looked slightly dazzled. She knew the feeling. 'We're such a small team,' Finn added, 'and privately financed, so any extra help is very welcome.'

'Good, yes. Well…' Hazel smoothed the documents and seemed to pull herself together. 'Well, I took a look at the Tresham family papers to see what connection there was between the Knightstone garden and Sir Thomas Tresham, and I found a rather interesting record. It's in a private collection so you may not have come across it.' She selected a paper from the pile in front of her. 'It was written a few days before Sir Thomas' death and it's entitled "*an account of*

the treasures of the Knights Hospitaller of St John in the last days".
In it he writes of the mission that he and his grandfather
undertook in 1544 to Knightstone where he was initiated
into the Order of the Knights Hospitaller and given the
mantle of the Prior as a sign of office. Poor boy, he was only
fourteen – it must have weighed heavily on him, literally
and metaphorically.'

'That's fascinating.' Lucy sat forwards. 'And is there any
other mention of the Knights' treasure in the village?'

Hazel smiled. 'No. In point of fact, Sir Thomas records
that there was no treasure and that the garden that he
designed at Knightstone "*for the delight of my godson Robert
Catesby and his wife Catherine*" was in remembrance of the
order "*to honour a treasured memory*".'

'That word "treasure" again,' Finn said. 'In Sir Thomas'
case it seems it was the garden that was the treasured
object.'

'Absolutely,' Hazel said. She smiled. 'It's a slippery
word, isn't it, "treasure"? But there is one final twist that
you might like.' She selected a second sheet of paper. 'Sir
Thomas records that he has summoned his sister-in-law
Anne Catesby to Lyveden to lay upon her the sacred trust
of preserving the mantle of the Knights Prior and to take
it back to Knightstone for safekeeping. There's no record
of whether Lady Catesby did so, however. Sir Thomas
died a few days later and this was the time preceding the
Gunpowder Plot – Anne Catesby's main concern would
surely have been whatever her son was up to, and the danger
to her surviving grandson.'

'I'm not an expert on the Gunpowder Plot,' Finn said,

'but didn't Anne Catesby have to fight very hard to preserve her grandson's inheritance after Robert was attainted a traitor?'

'Yes,' Hazel said. 'Anne fought and won. Her own marriage settlement from Sir William Catesby was saved and she left it all to the younger Robert. He married Mary Percy, the daughter of another of the Gunpowder plotters.'

They finished their tea and left Hazel to start the process of authentication of the miniatures. 'It goes without saying that we'll keep in touch every step of the way,' Hazel said. 'It's going to be an exceptionally exciting time.'

'Poor Gabriel,' Lucy said as they got into the car, 'he's never going to get that key back now, is he?'

'As long as he gets a credit as the curator of the museum where it was found,' Finn said, 'I'm sure he'll be happy.'

'He'd be even happier if the mantle of the Prior of the Order of the Knights Hospitaller was found at Knightstone,' Lucy said. 'I wonder… There's one other treasure reference in the village, isn't there?' Then as Finn looked blank: 'The old memorial stone up at the church has a quotation about treasure on it.'

'I didn't know that,' Finn said. 'Let's take a look at it on the way back.'

They had lunch in Stow-on-the-Wold before driving back to Knightstone and taking the narrow road up the hill to the church.

'Hazel told me when I last visited Chastleton that whilst Catherine is buried at Stoneleigh, there's a memorial to her here,' Lucy said. 'I assumed she meant in the church but it would be amazing if it was the stone.'

They were approaching the old sarsen through the churchyard. Sun fell through the pointed leaves of the yew, shadows shifted and danced.

'I know the stone you mean now,' Finn said, striding across the neatly cut grass, 'but it doesn't have an inscription.'

'Yes it does!' Lucy said. 'I saw it! It says, "*Where your treasure is, there will your heart be also.*"' She remembered Catherine's presence that day in the graveyard, the brush of her skirt, her words: *'I'm so glad you came.'*

'There's no inscription,' Finn repeated, drawing aside the trailing branches of the yew so that she could see the sarsen beneath. 'There was once…' He ran his fingers over the rough stone. 'I can tell there was lettering here, but it's worn away.'

Lucy stared. She knew she had seen it. 'I think it would be good to ask an expert to take a look and see if they can decipher it,' she said. 'And at the same time, maybe they could look beneath. I think they might find something.'

Finn laughed. 'The mantle? Well, it looks as though the badgers have already started an excavation.' He ran a handful of chalky soil through his fingers. 'I'll ask the vicar for permission to dig.' He sighed.

'What?' Lucy asked.

'I'm just wondering,' Finn said, 'whether all my future work will be predicated on your premonitions rather than on good old-fashioned scholarship?'

'I doubt it,' Lucy said. She took his hand and drew him out from under the curtain of yew. 'I think all the premonitions are gone now, all stories told, all secrets revealed. And don't forget—' she moved into his arms, 'that you are the one creating the best memorial to Catherine Catesby. You are rebuilding her garden.'

And they kissed there in the shadow of the yew and it felt like a new beginning.

Lucy

5 November

'This looks amazing!' Cleo said. She wandered out onto the terrace at Gunpowder Cottage, glass of champagne in hand. 'A fire pit!' She laughed. 'How appropriate!'

'There are marshmallows to be roasted,' Lucy said, 'but only after we've eaten the traditional sausages and jacket potatoes. We wanted a bonfire and lights to celebrate Guy Fawkes Night but no fireworks to scare Geoffrey and no risk that we might set anything alight by accident. Not after what happened to the first Tudor garden on the site.'

Cleo shuddered. 'Finn would never forgive himself if all his work went up in flames. But the lanterns are a gorgeous touch, and much safer.' She pirouetted to take in the reconstructed loggia with multicoloured lights strung along its length, and the neat low hedges of the knot garden. 'It looks stunning, Lucy.'

'Thanks,' Lucy said. She felt incredibly proud of what Finn, Johnny and their small team were achieving with the garden reconstruction. So far they had rebuilt the terrace and the loggia and the gardens near the house. Winter, she had learned, was a good time for landscaping the valley where they would be concentrating on the spiral mounds and the pond. Verity, not surprisingly, had refused to dismantle the barn so that they could recreate a labyrinth there but she had agreed to surround it with a moat and Finn was designing a new, smaller maze that would be created in part of Clarabelle's field.

Verity had also opened up the chalk chamber below the building, just to make sure that there was nothing significant in there. It had proved much older than they had suspected, and was thought to be contemporary with the original garden rather than a Victorian farm addition. They had all pondered long and hard over why there would be an empty chalk pit in the centre of the Tudor labyrinth until Johnny had suggested that it might have been a priest's hole. 'Or a treasure hole,' he had added with a wicked grin, and everyone had groaned.

'We're aiming for a grand opening next summer.' Lucy threaded her arm through Cleo's and they walked together over to the edge of the terrace. The barn lay below, illuminated like the cottage with lanterns. 'There's loads to do but we want to coincide with the Chastleton Catesby exhibition when they unveil the miniatures.'

'Not to mention the Museum of the Hospitallers unveiling the Tudor mantle,' Cleo said. 'What a find that was!'

'I know.' Lucy smiled faintly. 'Who would have thought that in restoring Catherine's memorial stone up at the church we would have found a lost treasure that was dug up... ahem... by badgers?'

'It's extraordinary, isn't it?' Cleo said dryly, giving her arm a little squeeze. 'And Catherine's ghost?' she added softly.

'Gone in one sense,' Lucy said, 'yet present in another. I think she's at peace now that the miniatures of her boys are safe and will always be treasured. But I also think her spirit will always be found here, especially now the garden is coming back to life.' She glanced at Cleo and smiled. 'Finn and I are designing a winter garden as well,' she said. 'It was Maud who gave us the inspiration.'

'That amazing old lady from the village?' Cleo asked. 'The one who saw Catherine's ghost? She's a phenomenon, isn't she! But what do you mean by a winter garden?'

'Based on analysis of the plants and seeds,' Lucy said, 'it seems that Catherine's Tudor garden was designed to look as beautiful in the winter as it did in summer. Maud saw a vision of it once, full of evergreens and bright berries. I've done some research into native plants and come up with some suggestions for what we can use to recreate those holly arches and ivy arbours. I think it could look stunning, especially as Finn has some great ideas for structural planting that will look amazing in the frost and snow.'

'How perfect,' Cleo said. 'Catherine's vision will be recreated. I'm sure that will make her spirit glad.' She gave Lucy a sideways glance. 'And you've rediscovered your joy as well, it seems.'

'I have,' Lucy said. 'I love being project manager here and once this job is finished I think I'll probably look for something similar, though maybe for a music charity.

Who knows? But it turns out Finn was right when he said I had transferable skills.'

'I think Finn is often right,' Cleo said. 'I overheard him telling Sam just now that our bookshop is one of the best in the country. Can't argue with that.' She looked at her sister. 'Finn is great, Lucy. I'm so happy for you.'

Music and laughter drifted out from Gunpowder Cottage, indicating that the others would be joining them soon. Lucy touched Cleo's arm. 'Will you excuse me for a moment? There's something I need to do.'

'Of course.' Cleo smiled at her and wandered off towards the knot garden whilst Lucy turned back to look at the view. This was the place where she could see the whole of the garden spread out below: the lake, where they were reconstructing an octagonal pavilion, the orchard and the two spiral mounds that looked down on Gunpowder Barn. The night was crisp, cold and clear, and away on the horizon, bonfire night fireworks were already starting to light up the skies.

'I want you to be happy too, Catherine,' Lucy whispered.

She raised a hand to her lips and blew a kiss out over the valley. The sky seemed to cloud over, the stars dimming for a moment. Looking down from the terrace, Lucy saw the most perfect vision: a glorious little Tudor garden spread out below her, the labyrinth crisp with fresh snowfall, the trees hung with frost like jewels. In the middle of it a woman in a red gown and a tall, handsome man stood entwined, whilst around them two small boys tumbled through the snow and their calls and laughter reached Lucy, echoing through the darkness.

Acknowledgements

Writing can be a solitary business so I would like to thank all those readers, reviewers, librarians, friends and colleagues who buy my books, send encouragement and support, and chat to me about reading and history. I would not be able to do this without you. Thank you so much!

My family and friends have been a constant source of love, patience and generosity, especially through the recent difficult times, and I am immensely grateful to them all. A particular vote of thanks goes to Sarah Morgan for her support and encouragement and to Christina Courtenay and my blog colleagues the Word Wenches. I'd also like to thank the two Julies at Park House for helping me keep focussed!

Thank you as ever to my publishing teams at HQ and at Graydon House for their commitment during such challenging times for publishing, particularly to my editor Emily Kitchin, to Susan Swinwood and to Joe Thomas.

This book is dedicated to Angus who was for nine years

the very best animal companion a writer could have, loyal, patient, keen to chew through laptop cables and lie under my desk, preventing me from getting close enough to my keyboard to do any actual writing.

Read on for an extract from Nicola Cornick's spellbinding historical mystery, *The Last Daughter*

Prologue

Snow spattered the windows of the Old Hall, carried on the sharp north wind that spun it into fierce spirals before battering it against the diamond mullions. The wind howled down the chimney and the snow fell on the hot embers of the fire with a hiss and burned away in an instant. No one noticed. There had been a wedding at Minster Lovell that day and the hall was hot, the guests drowsy with wine and good food, the atmosphere merry. Mistletoe boughs hung from the rafters and meat congealed on the plates. The minstrel sang a soft song of love whilst the bridegroom toyed with his empty goblet and contemplated his marriage bed. Then a shout went up for games and charades, for hoodsman's blind or shove ha'penny or hide and seek.

The suggestion prompted a burst of clapping mingled with the groans of the drunkards. The room was split between those who wanted to play and those whose senses were too fuddled. The groom's uncle and the dogs were all snoring, unashamedly asleep. There were no guests on the bride's side; she was a beautiful, orphaned heiress, and no one knew where John Lovell had found her. Some whispered that she was really a harlot who had ensnared him, others that she was a witch who had used sorcery to capture his heart. John Lovell laughed at the folly of the whisperers and seemed well pleased with his good fortune. He was a baron, noble but poor; the only item of worth in the entire house was said to be the Lovell lodestar, a sacred stone that the family had held in trust since the earliest of times. All the food, the wine, the jewelled goblets they drank from and the golden platters crammed with meat had been provided by the bride as part of her dowry. Gossip about her was surely mere jealousy.

'Let's play hide and seek.' Ginevra, the bride, cast her new husband a coquettish look from beneath her dark lashes. 'I shall hide and you may come and seek me out.'

A roar went up at her words. There were whistles and catcalls. The wedding guests knew how that would end. No doubt Lord Lovell would find his bride hiding in their bed and then the game would instantly be forgotten in favour of another, more pleasurable one. A mood of faintly debauched anticipation began to seep into the room with the wine tossed back and the singing growing louder.

Ginevra stood, smiling, enjoying the attention of the crowd. For a moment she waited, poised, like a deer on the edge of flight, and then she ran, followed by the cheers and hunting calls of the wedding guests.

John Lovell stood too, flushed and a little unsteady,

barely able to restrain his pursuit until his bride had had time to hide. He listened to the patter of her slippers die away and then with a shot he was off, eager for the conquest. He tripped over furniture, searched behind curtains and clattered up the stairs. Excitement and the thrill of the chase sustained him for the first ten minutes and determination not to be bested for the next ten but after a half-hour he rolled back into the great hall, out of breath, a little sullen, his lust frustrated. All the other guests were quaffing more ale and eating more pie. They seemed surprised to see him. Quiet fell over the hall like a shroud. The drunks sobered abruptly.

'Ginevra!' John Lovell bellowed, torn between indulgence and injured pride. 'You win the game! Come out!'

There was a moment when the wind seemed to die away and the sudden hush in the house grew to become a complete and terrifying silence. It was a silence that seemed alive, reaching out from another time to steal them away.

'Ginevra!' John Lovell called again, but this time his voice shook as doubt and fear tightened its grip on him. He marched to the front door, men crowding at his shoulder, and flung it wide. Nothing but blank snow met their gaze, no footprints, no sign of life, nothing but December's cold moon shining on the empty land.

'The lodestar!' Suddenly John Lovell turned and ran back down the cross passage to the library. Here his father, a most learned man, had kept those manuscripts and documents so cherished by the monks of the early Minster church that had stood on the site centuries before. Here was the heart of Minster Lovell, the lodestar, a holy relic locked away in its gold and enamelled box. No one in living memory had seen the stone; no one had dared to look, for it was said to possess miraculous power beyond man's wildest imaginings.

The room was as still and cold as the rest of the house; colder, for it felt as though the very soul of winter had set within those walls. The ancient oaken chest, bound within iron bands, that had held the golden box safely locked within, lay open and empty. The lodestar had gone.

John Lovell slammed the lid of the chest down in fury. His shout of anguish echoed through the house and seemed to seep into the very stones.

The Lovell lodestar was lost, the bridegroom deceived, the thief bride had vanished.

CHAPTER I

Serena

Santa Barbara, California, Present Day

Serena stretched out on the sun lounger, relishing the sensation of the last heat of the day against her skin. Above her, a sky of a cloudless azure blue was starting to fade to pale violet in the west. Below her, a long way below, the white sails of the yachts clustered in the harbour. From the kitchen came the scent of garlic and herbs as Polly prepared supper and beside her on the penthouse balcony was a frosted glass of white wine whose icy coolness contrasted deliciously with the heat radiating from the tiled floor.

Polly came out with the bottle, a chef's apron over her chic black-and-white swimming costume. She smiled indulgently when she saw her niece, book discarded on the lounger beside her, sunglasses removed and face tilted up to capture the last rays of the setting sun.

'Supper will be ten minutes.' She waved the bottle. 'Would you like a top-up?'

Serena opened her eyes and smiled. 'I'll have some with

my meal, thanks.' She groped for her sandals. 'Can I help? Make a salad or something?'

'It's already done.' Polly put the bottle down on the little black steel table at Serena's side and sat in the fat, cushioned chair opposite. 'You stay here a while longer. You look so much better, hon. You look… happy.'

'Why wouldn't I be?' Serena ignored the tiny shadow that crossed her mind at Polly's words. 'This is an amazing place, Aunt Pol.'

Polly's face eased into another smile. 'Better than Bristol?'

'Better than anywhere.' Serena yawned, stretched. 'Thank you so much for inviting me.'

'You've been working hard,' Polly said. 'You deserve a break.'

'I can't remember when I last took a holiday,' Serena admitted. 'If you hadn't encouraged me…'

'Nagged you, you mean.' Polly sounded rueful. 'I know it's full-on running your own business but sometimes people function better after a rest and you do drive yourself hard.'

'That's true.' Serena stretched luxuriously again. 'You're a wise woman, Aunt Pol.'

Polly picked up her wine glass. Her gaze was fixed on the distant horizon where the sea seemed to slip into infinity.

'It's lovely to have you here,' she said. 'It reminds me of when you and Caitlin were children, and we all went to Oxfordshire for your school holidays and spent time together at Minster Lovell—' She stopped abruptly, the

6

warmth falling away from her expression. 'Sorry,' she said. 'I don't know why I said that. It's nothing like those times.'

Suddenly the sun seemed to have lost all its heat. Serena reached for her wrap, shivering.

'I do understand what you mean,' she said slowly. 'It feels… easy… like those old holidays did. There were no shadows, no ghosts looking over our shoulders.'

Polly hesitated and Serena knew what she was thinking. She never normally talked about the past or her sister, Caitlin. Her aunt was wondering why this time was different – and whether it was safe to pursue the conversation. Everyone was very careful around Serena on the subject of her twin. She had experienced so much trauma when Caitlin had disappeared eleven years before that she had suffered from dissociative amnesia. No one wanted to open up those scars again but as a result they tiptoed around the subject and Serena knew she colluded with them. She'd built a wall of silence around Caitlin that became more difficult to break down every day.

'I never think of Caitlin as a ghost,' Polly said, surprising her. 'She was too alive, too vivid. I mean—' She caught herself, glancing at Serena again. 'She probably still is. We don't know she's dead. Hell.' She took a big gulp of wine. 'I *really* don't know why I started this.'

There was a silence. Far below, there was a splash of water and the faint cries of children's voices. Far above, an aeroplane arrowed into the blue.

'I think about Caitlin every day, you know,' Serena said. She met her aunt's eyes. 'Every single day I remember her, and I wonder. I wonder if she's alive and if so, where she is and what she's doing, and why she wouldn't want to contact us, and a million other things. And then I think she must be dead because how could she leave us all like that without a word and never get in touch with us again? How – why – would she be so cruel? That's not the Caitlin we knew.' She pulled the wrap tighter about her. 'I have the same conversation with myself over and over, and I never find any answers.'

'I'm sorry, hon,' Polly said. She leaned forward and touched Serena's arm. 'I shouldn't have mentioned it. I've spoiled the moment.'

'No, you haven't.' Serena smiled at her although she could feel tears pricking her eyes. 'We should talk about Caitlin more. We did at the start.'

When her sister had first disappeared, the family had drawn together, closer than close, a bulwark against the horror of the outside world. Eleven years on, though, things had changed. The case was cold. Serena's lost memories of the night her twin had vanished had never been recovered. Her parents, diminished somehow by years of stress and loss, only spoke about the superficial – their latest bowls club successes, the dinner they had enjoyed the previous week. Serena's grandfather had slipped into dementia. Only Polly, who possessed the same bright spark and indomitable spirit that had lit Caitlin, remained the same. Serena knew that time passed and people changed. It was natural. Sometimes, though, she felt that for all the changes in her own life, a part of her was still trapped in the moment of Caitlin's disappearance, unable to recover those memories and in some ways unable to move on.

The buzzer on the oven sounded and they both jumped.

'Come on in,' Polly said, getting to her feet with what Serena could only think was relief. 'The chicken should be ready now.'

Serena picked up her glass and followed her aunt inside, blinking as her eyes adjusted to the cool darkness. Polly, originally from England as she was, had worked in real estate in California for the past twenty years and her sense of style was enviable. The penthouse had 360-degree views and exuded modernity with neutral shades, lots of wood and chrome, and bold splashes of colour in paintings and soft furnishings. When Serena had first arrived, she had been almost afraid to move in case she ruffled the pristine surface of the apartment, so different from the chaotic mix of her own flat back in Bristol. It was odd; she was so organised in her working life and yet her living space overflowed with books, magazines, clothes, stuffed toys, all sorts of bits and pieces. It was some excuse that she had so little space, using the spare room as an office and squashing everything else into her living room and bedroom but somehow there was an impermanence to it as well.

Jonah, her ex, had told her bluntly when he had left that her whole life was rootless and that it was her choice to be like that. 'You don't commit to anything,' he had said, as he had shoved the last of his shirts into his bag, already halfway out of the door and miles away mentally, 'whether it's people or places or jobs. You complain about feeling lonely but you won't let people close to you. I've tried, Serena. But you were always determined to push me away.' He'd stared at her for a moment then, his dark hair ruffled, glasses askew in the way she had once found so endearing. 'It's not me,' he said. 'It really is you.' And he was gone, to move in with his colleague Maddie, as it turned out, because Maddie was apparently so much more fun to be with and was prepared to commit to him.

His criticisms had been harsh and, Serena thought, untrue. She'd worked really hard over the past five years to make her company successful. She and her friend Ella specialised in arranging bespoke historical tours and were starting to get the business on a sound footing at last. It was true that she *had* moved around a lot in the past ten years and she had lost touch with almost all the friends she'd had from her childhood and college years, but so did a lot of people. She had had a couple of unsuccessful relationships but again, that wasn't unusual. It was only when she thought about Jonah, which she did less and less since the split, that a tiny doubt crept into her mind that on the issue of people, at least, he might have been right and that she didn't really want to commit to anyone. Losing Caitlin, the person who had once been closer to her than anyone else in the world, had inevitably taken a toll in terms of how much she was prepared to invest in a relationship. She had the self-awareness to know that and absolutely no idea how to change it.

The glass dining table was set with bright blue plates and crisp napkins. There was fragrant chicken with salad and a creamy herb dressing, chilled white wine… Serena relaxed again. She had another two weeks in California with Polly. Ella was handling the business with the help of a temp and sent her cheerful updates on how well it was all going without her. Tomorrow she and Polly were taking a trip to the Gaviota State Park and she'd also pencilled in a visit to some of the wineries and, most exciting of all, a day trip to Hearst Castle. Even though history was her job, she never, ever got tired of it.

Her phone rang. She ignored it as she took another forkful of salad.

'It's your mother,' Polly said helpfully, reading the screen upside-down.

Serena felt two sensations hot on the heels of each other: irritation and a whisper of dread. Both were instinctive and both were unfair. She knew it wasn't her mother's fault that she found her needy and felt the pressure of being an only child.

The only remaining child.

'I'll call her back later,' she said.

'It's the early hours in the UK,' Polly said. 'Maybe there's some sort of emergency?'

The chicken seemed to turn to ashes in Serena's mouth. She stared at Polly for what seemed like forever as the phone buzzed on and on. She refused to frame the thoughts that were hovering at the edge of her mind. Then the phone stopped abruptly and the silence sounded very loud indeed.

'Serena—' Polly said, but then her own phone started to ring with the same brash insistence.

'Don't answer it.' Serena's sense of dread increased.

Polly looked exasperated and ignored her.

'Hello, Jackie. You're up late tonight. Is everything all right? How's Paul?' Polly always exaggerated her British accent when speaking to her sister-in-law. Serena was never sure whether it was deliberate or not. Her aunt and her mother did not get on particularly well, although they did a good enough job of pretending that they did for the sake of family unity.

'We have nothing in common,' Polly had said once when Serena had asked her about their relationship. 'It's not even that we dislike each other, there's just nothing to build on.'

Serena thought that like everything else, the differences, the cracks in their relationship, hadn't been so obvious before Caitlin had vanished. Or perhaps she had just missed them. She had only been seventeen when she lost her twin and as far as she remembered, pretty self-absorbed. She could see that Polly, the independent, childless career-woman and her mother, the stay-at-home housewife who felt slightly defensive about it, might not have had that much in common.

There was a tide of words from the other end of the phone. Polly was frowning. 'Wait,' she said sharply. 'Slow down. I don't understand…' Then more quietly: 'Yes of course. She's here.'

She passed the phone across the table to Serena who took it without a word. She already knew what it was that she was going to hear. Superstitiously she wondered whether it had been the mention of her sister's name earlier that evening that had somehow invited Caitlin to invade her peace; invited her back into her life to banish the tenuous contentment she had found in the last couple of weeks.

'Mum?' she said.

Her mother's voice sounded crackly and broken over the vast distance:

'The police have just left,' she said. 'They've found Caitlin. They've found a *body*. Serena, you've got to come home.'

Serena's heart started to race. Her stomach knotted. How was it possible, she wondered, to have anticipated this, to have *sensed* that her mother must have devastating news, and yet still to feel so sick and hollow and unprepared? Over the past eleven years, not a day had passed when she hadn't wondered when, *if*, they would ever know the truth of what had happened to her. Yet now that she stood on the edge of discovery, she felt as though the world had dropped away beneath her feet and left her in freefall.

Her mother was still talking, the words tumbling over each other, interrupted by sobs. Serena didn't stop her, didn't really listen to the words, only the tone and the emotion. Her mind seemed to have frozen, stuck on that one thought:

'Caitlin's body has been found…'

'You still there, love?' It was her father now. He sounded exhausted, confused and old. Serena could hear her mother still crying in the background.

'We don't have many details at the moment, just that the police have identified your sister from her dental records. We don't even know where she was found. How soon can you get here?'

Serena swallowed hard, trying to focus. It seemed so difficult. All she could see in her mind's eyes was a vision of Caitlin, blonde hair flying as she ran, arms outstretched, smiling and full of life.

'I'll come straight away,' she said. 'Tonight. Tomorrow. As soon as I can get a flight.' She could see that Polly had already reached for her tablet and was searching for the next flight from Los Angeles to London. Serena's mind started to race. She would need to hire a car when she got to Heathrow to take her from London to Gloucestershire. Could she do that now, or should she wait…? She felt a desperate impatience to be on her way home but at the same time, a sliding horror that this was happening again, the police, the questions, the tantalising and terrifying gaps in her memory…

'Have you told Grandpa yet?' she said.

'No.' Her father sounded shocked that she should suggest it. There was a pause. 'We thought perhaps it would be better not to…' His voice strengthened. 'He wouldn't understand anyway, not with the dementia.'

'He might,' Serena said. There was a very hard lump in her throat. 'Someone is going to have to tell him, Dad.'

There was silence at the end of the line, strong with denial. Polly put her hand over Serena's, her gaze intent and concerned, and Serena unclenched her fingers from the tight fist they had formed. She smiled shakily at her aunt.

'Well, we can talk about that when I see you, Dad,' she said. 'I've got to go. I need to get a ticket, pack… I'll let you know when I'm arriving.' She tried, not entirely successfully, to stop her voice from wobbling. 'I love you,' she said. 'Give Mum a big hug from me. I'll see you soon.'

She pressed 'end' and cut off the sound of her mother's crying. The warmth seemed to flow back into the apartment, bringing with it the sunshine and the faint sounds

14

of the world outside but everything was different now, out of reach. In her mind she was already on her way home, back to England and the horror that was waiting.

'Shit,' Polly said. 'I'm so sorry, hon. How awful. Do you want to talk about it?'

Serena shook her head. 'I'm sorry, Aunt Pol, I can't. I don't really know how I feel yet.' She clenched her hands. 'I just want to get on and *do* something.'

'Of course.' Polly sighed. She squeezed Serena's arm and stood up. 'There's a flight leaving LAX at eleven that has some space. If we hurry—'

'Great.' Serena jumped up, abandoning the chicken salad. She had lost her appetite completely. 'I'll get my stuff together.'

Polly wrapped her in a hug. 'I wish I could come with you, hon. I want to support you.'

'You've got work,' Serena said. 'You can't just drop everything, I know that. I'll be fine. Really.'

'You'll be supporting everyone else,' Polly said, suddenly fierce. 'Your mother's in bits and Paul never was very good in a crisis.'

Serena tightened the hug for a moment before letting Polly go. She gave her aunt a watery smile. 'Dad does his best,' she said, knowing that Polly's unsentimental assessment of her brother was right. 'I'm sure he'll be a big comfort to Mum, and I'm happy to talk to Grandpa. Actually, I'd rather I tried to tell him about Caitlin than them.' She rubbed her eyes. 'I'll ring you every day, OK? That would really help.'

The worry lightened a little in Polly's eyes. 'That would be great, hon.'

As she threw her holiday clothes haphazardly into her suitcase, Serena started to feel more grounded again. It was a relief to have something practical to concentrate on. She was always able to ward off the dark, Caitlin-shaped thoughts with action. In the aftermath of her sister vanishing she had talked to everyone – to family, the police, counsellors and psychologists – and tried so hard to recover the memories of that night that she had lost through cognitive amnesia. The psychiatrists she had seen had told her that her memory could return at any time or not at all. Dissociative amnesia was completely unpredictable, and in the event, no treatment had made any difference at all. No memories had come back to her and she had ended up exhausted and emotionally battered by the endless effort at recall. Not only had it felt as though she had lost those hours, more potently it had felt as though she had completely failed her sister.

For a second, she froze, her hands still full of T-shirts and shorts, possessed by the agonising thought that she had in some way betrayed the trust that Caitlin had placed in her. She had always been the stronger one.

'You should have found me, helped me, saved me…'

She squashed the rest of her clothes into the bag and forced the zip to close. There would be questions, memories and hard truths to face up to now She was not at all sure she was ready but she had no choice.

ONE PLACE. MANY STORIES

Bold, innovative and
empowering publishing.

FOLLOW US ON:

@HQStories